THE UNEXPECTED HOLIDAY GIFT

BY
SOPHIE PEMBROKE

MILLS & BOON

First Published in Great Britain 2016
By Mills & Boon, an imprint of HarperCollins*Publishers*
1 London Bridge Street, London, SE1 9GF

ISBN: 978-0-263-92026-0

23-1016

Our polic[illegible]ble and recyclable products a[illegible] forests. The logging and manufact[illegible] legal environmental regulations of the countr[illegible]

Printed a[illegible] by CPI, B[illegible]

Sophie Pembroke has been reading and writing romance ever since she read her first Mills & Boon romance at university, so getting to write them for a living is a dream come true! Sophie lives in a little Hertfordshire market town in the UK with her scientist husband and her incredibly imaginative six-year-old daughter. She writes stories about friends, family and falling in love—usually while drinking too much tea and eating homemade cakes. She also keeps a blog at www.sophiepembroke.com.

For Auntie Barbara and Uncle Viv,
for so many perfect Christmas days!

CHAPTER ONE

CLARA TUGGED THE candy-striped ribbon just a millimetre farther out, then leaned back to admire the neatly wrapped present with beautifully tied bow. Really, it was a shame to give it away.

'Are we done?' Her business partner, Merry, added one last gift to the pile and looked hopefully at Clara. 'That was definitely the last one, right?'

'For this client, yes.' Clara grinned. 'But I'm fairly sure we've got another three Christmas lists to work through before the big day. Not to mention the five decorating projects, three last-minute requests for tickets as presents and two Christmas dinners we need to arrange.'

'And a partridge in a pear tree,' Merry grumbled. 'Whose stupid idea was this business anyway?'

'Yours,' Clara reminded her cheerfully. 'And I know you love it, really.'

Clara hadn't been sure there was a market for this sort of thing when Merry had first suggested it. Did Londoners really need another concierge and events service? Would people really pay them to organise their lives, buy their gifts, arrange special access and perks, plan their parties and family gatherings, their holidays and so on? Merry had been adamant that they would.

With your magic at making things perfect and my business knowledge, we can't fail, she'd insisted over a bottle of wine at Clara's tiny rented flat one evening.

So Perfect London had been born and, four years later, business was booming. Especially at Christmas.

'I suppose it's all right,' Merry said, the smirk she threw Clara's way showing her real feelings. 'Pays the bills, anyway.'

And then some. Clara was still amazed at just how successful they'd been. Successful enough that she'd been able to move out of that tiny flat into her own house two years ago. Successful enough that she no longer lay awake at night, panicking about how she would provide for her daughter, Ivy, alone.

Clara stared at the mountain of presents again, then turned her attention to the Christmas tree standing in their shop front office window. Gazing at the star on top, she made a wish. The same wish she'd made every year since Perfect London had taken the city by storm that first Christmas, when media mentions and word of mouth had seen them triple their income in a month and the numbers had held at that level for the following year.

Please, let things stay this good for another year?

The fact that they had so far went a long way to wiping out some of the less than wonderful Christmas memories from her childhood. Clara would even go so far as to say that, these days, Christmas was a magical time of year for her—especially with Ivy around to share it with.

'What have you and Ivy got planned for Christmas?' Merry asked.

Clara shrugged. 'Nothing much. She wants a bike, so I imagine we'll be taking that out for a ride.' She frowned just for a moment, remembering that a bike wasn't the only thing her daughter had asked Father Christmas for that year. Ivy didn't know that she'd overheard, but Clara couldn't shake the memory of her whispering to the man in the red suit at the shopping centre that what she wanted most in the world was 'to have a dad'.

At least the bike was more achievable, even if keeping it hidden was proving tricky. She could walk out and buy a bike at any number of shops in the city.

A father was rather more difficult to procure. Especially Ivy's real dad.

She shook the thought away. There were only a couple of weeks until the big day, and Clara was going to focus on the wonderful Christmas she *could* give her daughter.

'Other than that,' she went on, 'pancakes for breakfast, the usual turkey for lunch and a good Christmas movie in the afternoon.' Quiet, cosy and just the way Clara liked it.

Worlds away from the Christmases she had once expected to have, before Ivy had come along, before Perfect London. Before she had walked out on her marriage.

It was strange to think about it now. Most of the time, she could barely imagine herself still married to Jacob. But every now and then, something would happen to remind her and she'd find herself picturing the way her life might have gone. Like a parallel universe she kept getting glimpses of, all the might-have-beens she'd walked away from.

They would probably be spending Christmas in one of his many modern, bright white, soulless properties. They were barely houses, let alone homes, and they were certainly not cosy. Maybe his family would be with them this year, maybe not. There'd be expensive, generic presents, designer decorations. Maybe she'd have thrown a party, the sort she loved organising for clients these days—but it would have felt just as much like business, when all the guests would have been Jacob's business associates rather than friends.

But there was the other side of it too. They'd only managed two Christmases together, but they had both been packed with happy moments—as well as the awful ones. She had memories of waking up in Jacob's arms, the times when it had been just the two of them and a bunch of mistletoe. A walk in the snow with his arm around her waist. The heat in his eyes as he watched her get ready for another party. The way he smiled, just sometimes, as if she was everything he'd ever imagined having in the world and so much more.

Except she wasn't, and she knew that now. More than that, she knew that she was worth more than he was willing to give her—only bestowing his attention on her when it suited him, or when he could drag himself away from work. When you truly loved someone, it wasn't a chore to spend time with them and they should never have to beg you for scraps of attention. Ivy had taught her that—and so much more. She had taught her things Clara couldn't imagine she'd spent twenty-seven years not understanding but that Ivy had been born knowing.

So Clara seldom thought twice about her decision to leave—she knew it had been the right one. But still, from time to time those parallel universes would sneak up and catch her unguarded, reminding her of the good things about her marriage as well as the bad.

'What are you thinking about?' Merry asked. 'You've been staring at that tree for five solid minutes and you haven't even asked me to start on the next job. I'm beginning to worry.'

Clara shook her head and turned away from the tree. It didn't matter, anyway. Because in all those visions of that other life, there was always one person missing.

Ivy.

And Clara refused to imagine her life without her daughter.

'Nothing,' she lied. 'Just Christmas Past, I suppose.'

'I prefer Christmas Presents,' Merry joked. 'Or even Christmas Future if it means we're done working for the year.'

'Done for the year?' Clara asked incredulously. 'Have you forgotten the Harrisons' New Year's Eve Charity Gala?'

Merry rolled her eyes. 'As if I could. Who really needs that much caviar anyway?'

'Two hundred of London's richest, most famous and most influential people.' Twenty tables of ten, at ten thousand pounds a plate, with all proceeds going to the children's charity the Harrison family had set up in memory of their youngest child, who'd died ten years ago from a rare type of blood cancer.

No one else would have dared to hold such an important—and expensive—fundraiser on New Year's Eve. The one night of the year when everyone had plans and people they wanted to be with. But the Harrisons had the money, the influence, the charm and the celebrity to pull it off. Especially with Perfect London organising everything for them.

Clara had been nervous when Melody Harrison—activist, author and all-round beautiful woman—had approached her. The Harrisons were possibly the most recognisable family in London: the epitome of a perfect family. And Melody wanted *Clara* to organise the most important charity event in their calendar.

'You did such a beautiful job with the True Blue launch event,' she'd said. 'I just know Perfect London is the right fit for our little charity gala.'

'Little', Clara had found out soon enough, had been the biggest understatement of the year. Possibly of the last decade.

But they'd managed it—with plenty of outsourcing, hiring in extra staff for the event and more than a few late nights. Everything was in place as much as it could be while they finished dealing with their more usual Christmas bookings. Clara planned to take Christmas Eve, Christmas Day and Boxing Day off entirely to spend the time with Ivy. Her own perfect little family.

It was natural for Ivy to be curious about her dad, Clara knew. But she also knew, deep in her heart, that they were better off with just the two of them. They were a team. A duo. They didn't need anyone else, people who could walk out at any moment or decide they'd found something better or more important to focus on.

Right now, Ivy knew she was the most important thing in her mother's world, and Clara would never do a thing to risk ruining that.

'You're staring at the tree again,' Merry said. 'It's getting creepy. What's got you all pensive? Christmas Past… Are you thinking about your ex?'

'Sort of, I suppose.' Clara busied herself, tidying up the wrapping paper and ribbons. As much as she loved Merry, she really didn't want to talk about Jacob.

Merry, apparently, didn't get that memo. 'Do you ever regret leaving him?'

'No,' Clara said firmly. Did she feel guilty about it? Yes. Did she wonder what might have happened if she'd stayed? Sure. But regret… How could she regret the life she had now, with her daughter? 'But…I guess I'm still missing some closure, you know?'

'You know what would help with that?' Merry said. 'An actual divorce. Honestly, it's been, what, five years?'

'It's not like I haven't asked for one. Repeatedly.' But Jacob had money and, more important, better lawyers. If he wanted to stall, they knew all the possible ways to make it happen. And, for some reason, he didn't seem to want their divorce to go through.

'Yeah, but it's not like you're even asking for anything from him. Not that it wouldn't have been a help at the start.' Merry still hadn't quite got over the fact that Clara had walked out with nothing but the clothes on her back and a small bag of personal belongings. But she had wanted to leave that whole part of her life behind, and taking money from Jacob would have tied her to him.

Although, as it turned out, she'd walked away with something much more binding than money. Even if she hadn't known it then.

That was where the closure came in. It wasn't just about them—it was about Ivy too. Had she done the right thing, not going back when she'd discovered she was pregnant? At the time, she'd been so sure. Jacob had made it very, very clear that they would *not* be having a family together. And she'd wanted her baby so desperately, in a way she'd never realised she would until the moment she'd seen the word *pregnant* appear on the test.

But, every now and then, she couldn't help but wonder what might have happened if she'd told him.

'I don't know what goes on in my ex-husband's brain,' Clara said. 'I never did. If I had known, maybe we'd still be married.'

'And then you wouldn't be here with me,' Merry replied. 'And that would suck. So, let's just forget all about him.'

'Good plan,' Clara agreed, relieved. 'Besides, I need to talk to you about the decorations for the Colemans' house…'

The Christmas lights twinkled along the length of the trendy London street, illuminating coffee shops and gift boutiques with flashes of glittering brightness. Jacob Foster moved slowly through the crowds of shoppers, feeling conspicuous in his lack of shopping bags, lists and most of all haste, even in the cold winter drizzle.

It wasn't that his errand wasn't urgent. He just wasn't all that keen to jump into it. Especially since he had no idea how it was likely to go. He'd been trying to think his way through it for the whole journey there; which approach had the best chance of success, what he could say to get her to say yes. He'd still not come to a final decision.

He still wasn't completely sure he should be there at all. This might be the worst idea he'd had since he was sixteen. He'd spent five years putting distance between them, moving on and forgetting her. The last thing he needed was to let Clara in again.

But he was doing it anyway. For family. Because, despite everything that had happened between them, Clara was still family—and this job couldn't be given to anybody but family.

He turned down a small side street lined with offices and within moments he found himself standing outside a neat apple-green office with the words 'Perfect London' emblazoned above the door, and knew his thinking time was up.

He paused, his hand on the door ready to push it open, and stared for a moment through the large window. There she was. Clara.

Her dark hair hung down over her face as she leant across a colleague's desk to point at something on a computer screen. It obscured her eyes but, since that meant she couldn't see him, Jacob supposed that was for the best.

She looked well, he supposed. The cranberry-coloured wrap dress she wore clung to curves he remembered too well, and his gaze followed the length of her left arm from the shoulder down to where her hand rested on the desk. He looked closer. No ring.

Jacob took a breath, trying to quieten the large part of his brain that was screaming at him that this was a stupid idea and that he should just turn and leave now. It had been five long years; what was five more? Or ten? Or forever? He'd already been stung by failure with Clara before. Why risk that again?

But no. His plan mattered, far more than any history he and Clara shared, no matter how miserable. He'd decided he would make this thing happen, and he would. Jacob Foster kept his word and he didn't let people down. Especially not his family.

And they were all counting on him. Even if they didn't actually know about his plan just yet.

But he needed help. Clara's help, to be specific. So he couldn't turn and walk away.

He just had to make it clear that this was business, not

pleasure. He wasn't there to win her back, or remind her how good they'd been together. He was there to ask for her professional help, that was all.

He took another deep breath and steeled himself to open the door.

She'd listen, at least, he hoped. Hear him out. She had to. She was still his wife, after all.

Clara brushed the hair back from her face and peered at the screen again. 'I'm still not sure it's going to be big enough.'

Sitting at the desk beside her, Merry sighed. 'It's the biggest I've been able to find, so it might just have to do.'

'*Have to do* doesn't sound very Perfect London,' Clara admonished. 'If it's not right—'

'We keep looking,' Merry finished for her. 'I know. But can I keep looking tomorrow? Only I've got that thing tonight.'

'Thing?' Clara searched her memory for the details. Best friends and business partners were supposed to know this stuff, she was sure. 'Oh! The thing at the art gallery! Yes! Get out of here now!'

Merry pushed her chair back from the desk, obviously wasting no time. 'Thanks. Don't you need to pick Ivy up?'

Clara checked her watch. 'I've got another twenty minutes or so. She's having dinner round at Francesca's tonight, so I might as well use the time to finish things up here.'

'Okay.' Grabbing her bag and coat, Merry started layering up to face the winter chill outside. 'But don't work too late tonight, right?'

'I told you; I've got to leave in twenty minutes. I'll be out of here in no time.'

'I meant once you get home, and Ivy's in bed.' Merry leant over and gave Clara a swift kiss on the cheek. 'I mean it. Take a night off for once.'

Clara blushed, just a little. She hadn't thought her friend

knew about all the extra hours she put in during the long, dark evenings. It was just that, once Ivy was asleep, what else was there to do, really, but work? She didn't have dates or any real desire to go out and meet people, even if her childminder was available to babysit for Ivy. It made more sense to get on top of the work, so that when she did have time with her daughter at weekends she didn't have to be tied to her computer. That was all.

'I was just going to finish up the accounts,' she admitted.

'Leave it,' Merry instructed. 'I'll do it tomorrow. You can take over finding the biggest Christmas tree in existence!'

'Somehow, I think I've been played,' Clara said drily. 'Go on, get gone. You don't want to be late.'

Merry flashed her a grin and reached for the door but before she could grab the handle it opened, revealing a dark shadow of a man in the doorway. Clara stared at the shape. It was too dark to make out any particulars, certainly not a face or any recognisable features. And yet, somehow, that shadow was very, very familiar…

'I'm very sorry,' Merry said politely. 'We're just closing up, actually.'

'I only need to talk to Clara,' the man in the doorway said, and Clara's heart dropped like a stone through her body.

'Jacob.' The word was barely a whisper but Merry's head swung round to look at her anyway, her eyes wide.

'Maybe you could come back—' Merry began, already pushing the door closed, but Clara stopped her.

'No. No, it's okay.' She swallowed, wishing the lump that had taken up residence in her throat would lessen. 'Come in, Jacob. What can I do for you?'

Maybe he'd met somebody else at last and was here to

finalise the divorce. That would make sense. For a brief moment, relief lapped against the edges of her panic—until a far worse idea filled her mind.

Maybe he's found out about Ivy.

But no. That was impossible. She'd covered her tracks too well for that; even Merry believed that Ivy was the result of a one-night stand shortly after her marriage broke down. There was no one in the world except Clara herself who knew the truth about Ivy's conception.

And she had no plans to share that information.

'Want me to stay?' Merry asked as Jacob brushed past her. When he stepped into the light, it was hard to imagine that she hadn't known who he was, even for a second. He was exactly the same man she'd walked out on five Christmases ago. Same dark hair, with maybe just a hint of grey now at the temples. Same broad shoulders and even the same style of classic dark wool coat stretched across them. Same suit underneath, she was sure. Still all business, all the time.

Which made her wonder again what he was doing there, wasting time on her. Clara had no illusions about how her still-not-officially-ex-husband felt about her. He'd made it crystal-clear every single time he'd refused to sign the divorce papers, purely out of spite it seemed, sending his decision via his lawyers rather than talking to her in person. He'd made it clear how unimportant she, and what she wanted, was to him long before she'd ever left. He had never needed her before. What on earth could have made him start now?

Merry was still waiting for an answer, she realised. 'I'll be fine,' she said, shaking her head. Her friend looked unconvinced but resigned.

'I'll call you later,' she promised, and Clara nodded. 'And don't forget—you need to leave in twenty minutes.'

The seconds stretched out as the door swung slowly shut behind Merry. And then, with the noise of the street blocked out, it was just them again. Just Clara, Jacob and the sense of impending dread that filled Clara's veins.

CHAPTER TWO

SHE *DID* LOOK DIFFERENT.

Jacob hadn't been able to clock all the changes through the window, it dawned on him now. He'd thought she looked the same, but she didn't, not really. And it wasn't just that her hair was longer, or that slight extra curve to her body, or even that her wedding ring was missing.

It was just *her*.

Her shoulders straightened, just an inch, and he realised that was part of it. An air of confidence he hadn't seen in her before. When they'd been married—properly married, living together and in love, not this strange limbo he'd been perpetuating—she'd been…what, exactly? Attentive, loving…undemanding, he supposed. She had just always been there, at home, happy to organise his business dinners or fly with him across the world at a moment's notice. She'd been the perfect hostess, the perfect businessman's wife, just like his mother had been for his father for so many years.

His father, he remembered, had been delighted in Jacob's choice of wife. *'She won't let you down, that one,'* he'd said.

Until she'd walked out and left him, of course.

Perhaps he'd been underestimating Clara all along. So much for a five-minute job convincing her to help him. This was going to take work. This new Clara, he feared, would ask questions. Lots of them.

'Jacob,' she said again, impatiently. 'What can I do for you?'

'You need to leave soon, your friend said?'

Clara gave a sharp nod. 'I do. So if we could make this quick…'

Unlikely. 'Perhaps it would be better if we met up later.

For dinner, perhaps?' Somewhere he could ply her with wine, good food and charm and convince her that this was a good idea.

'Sorry, I can't do that.' There was no debate, no maybe and no other offer. Even the apology at the start didn't sound much like one. This Clara knew her own mind and she was sticking to it.

It was kind of hot, actually. Or it would have been if he didn't sense it was going to make his life considerably more difficult.

Clara sighed and perched on the edge of the desk. 'You might as well start talking, Jacob,' she said, glancing down at her watch. 'I'm leaving in…fifteen minutes, now. Whether you've said what you came here to say or not.'

What was so important, he wondered, that she still had to run out of here, even after the arrival of a husband she hadn't seen in five years? Another man? Probably.

Not that he cared, of course. All that mattered to him was her professional availability. Not her personal life.

'I want to hire you. Your firm, I mean. But specifically you.' There, he'd said it. And, judging by the look on his wife's face, he'd managed to surprise her in the process. The shock in her expression gave him a measure of control back, which he appreciated.

'Whatever for?' she asked eventually.

'My father.' The words came out tight, the way they always did when he spoke about it. The unfairness of it all. 'He's dying.'

And that was the only reason he was there. The only thing that could make him seek out his ex-in-all-but-paperwork-wife and ask for her help.

'I'm so sorry, Jacob.' Clara's eyes softened instantly, but he didn't want to see that. He looked down at his hands and kept talking instead.

'Cancer,' he said harshly, hating the very word. 'The

doctors haven't given him more than a couple of months. If he'd gone to them sooner…' He swallowed. 'Anyway. This is going to be his last Christmas. I want to make it memorable.'

'Of course you do,' Clara said, and he felt something inside him relax, just a little. He'd known that she would understand. And what he needed would require more than the sort of competence he could buy. He needed someone who would give *everything* to his project. Who would do what he needed, just like she always had before.

And, for some reason, Clara had always been very fond of his father.

'I'm planning a family Christmas up in the Highlands,' Jacob explained. 'Just like one we had one year when I was a boy.'

'I remember you all talking about it once. It sounds perfect,' Clara agreed. 'And like you've got it all in hand, so I don't really see why—'

'That's it,' Jacob interrupted her. 'That idea. That's all I have.'

'Oh.' Clara winced. 'So you want to hire Perfect London to…?'

'Do everything else. Organise it. Make it perfect.' That, she'd always been good at. She'd been the perfect businessman's wife, the perfect housewife, the perfect beauty on his arm at functions, even the perfect daughter-in-law. Up until the day she wasn't his perfect anything at all.

'But…' Clara started, and he jumped in to stop whatever objection she was conjuring up.

'I'll pay, of course. Double your normal rate.' He'd pay triple to make this happen but he'd keep that information in reserve in case he needed it later.

'Why?' Bafflement covered Clara's expression.

'Who else?' Jacob asked. 'It's what you do, isn't it? It's right there in the name of your company.' The company she'd left him to build—and which, by the looks of things, seemed to be doing well enough. He'd never even imagined, when they were married, that she'd wanted this—her own business, her own life apart from him. How could he? She'd never told him.

Well. If she was determined to go off and be happy and successful without him, the least she could do was help him out now, when he needed it.

'Perfect *London,*' Clara said, emphasising the second word. 'We mostly work locally. Very locally.'

'I imagine that most of the arrangements can be made from here,' Jacob conceded. 'Although I would need you in Scotland for the final set-up.'

'No.' Clara shook her head. 'I can't do that. I have… obligations here. I can't just leave.'

Obligations. A whole new life, he imagined. A new man…but not her husband, though. That, at least, she couldn't have. Not unless he let her.

Jacob took a breath and prepared to use his final bargaining chip.

The only thing he had left to give her.

This made no sense. None at all. Why on earth would Jacob come to her, of all people, to organise this? There must be a hundred other party planners or concierge services he could have gone to. Unless this was a punishment of some sort, Clara could not imagine why her ex-husband would want to hire her for this task.

Except…she knew his family. She knew his father, and could already picture exactly the sort of Christmas he'd want.

Maybe Jacob wasn't so crazy after all. But that didn't mean she had to say yes.

She had her own family to think about this Christmas—her and Ivy, celebrating together in gingerbread-man pyjamas and drinking hot chocolate with Merry on Christmas Eve. That was how it had been for the last four years, and the way it would be this Christmas too, thank you very much. She wasn't going to abandon her daughter to go and arrange Christmas deep in the Highlands, however much Jacob was willing to pay. Especially not with the Harrisons' gala coming up so soon afterwards.

'No,' she said again, just to make it doubly clear. 'I'm sorry. It's impossible.'

Except…a small whisper in the back of her mind told her that this could be her chance. Her one opportunity to see if he'd really changed. If Jacob Foster was ready to be a father at last. If she could risk telling him about Ivy, introduce them even, without the fear that Jacob would treat his daughter the way Clara's own father had treated her.

Even twenty years later, the memory of her father walking out of the front door, without looking back to see Clara waving him goodbye, still made her heart contract. And Jacob had been a champion at forgetting all about his wife whenever work got too absorbing, walking out and forgetting to look back until a deal was signed or a project tied up.

She wouldn't put Ivy through that, not for anything. She wanted so much more than that for her daughter. Clara might work hard but she always, *always* had time for her child and always put her first. Ivy would never be an afterthought, never slip through the cracks when something more interesting came up. Even if that meant she only ever had one parent.

But Jacob had come here to organise a family Christmas. The Jacob she'd been married to wouldn't have even *thought* of that. Could he really have changed? And could she risk finding out?

'This Christmas I'd like to have a dad, please.' Ivy's whispered words floated through her mind.

She shook her head again, uncertain.

'What if I promise you a divorce?' Jacob asked.

For a moment, it was as if the rain had stopped falling outside, as if the world had paused in its turning.

A divorce. She'd be completely free at last. No more imagining a life she no longer possessed. Her new life would truly be hers, clear and free.

It was tempting.

But then reality set in. That divorce would cut the final tie between them—the last link between Ivy and her father. How could she do that before she even told Jacob he had a daughter?

Clara bit the inside of her cheek as she acknowledged a truth she'd long held at bay. It hadn't just been Jacob holding up their divorce for five long years. If she'd wanted to push for it she could have, at any time. But she'd always known that she'd have to come clean about Ivy first…and she was terrified.

The risk was always, always there. Jacob might reject them both instantly and walk away, but she could cope with that, she hoped, as long as Ivy didn't know, didn't hurt. But what if he wanted to be involved? What if he wanted to meet her, to be a part of her life—and then ignored Ivy the same way he'd kept himself apart from Clara after they were married? What if he hurt Ivy with his distracted, even unintentional, neglect? Nothing had ever meant more to Jacob than his work—not even her. Why would Ivy be any different?

So even if he thought he wanted to be a father…could she really risk Ivy's heart that way?

No. She had to be sure. And the only way to be certain was to spend time with him, to learn who he was all over again. Then she could decide, either to divorce him freely, or to let him into Ivy's life, whichever was best for her daughter. That was all that mattered.

But to spend time with him she'd have to organise his

perfect family Christmas. Could she really do that? With all her other clients, the Harrisons' Charity Gala—and her own Christmas with Ivy? It was too much. And she was still too scared.

'I'm sorry, Jacob. Really I am.' She was; part of her heart hurt at the thought of James Foster suffering and her not being there to ease it. An even larger part, although she hated to admit it, stung at the idea of Jacob going through this without her too.

That's not my place any more. It's not my life.

She had to focus on the life she had, the one she'd built. Her new life for her and Ivy.

'I can't help you,' she said, the words final and heavy.

Jacob gave her a slow, stiff nod. 'Right. Of course.' He turned away but as he reached the door he looked back, his eyes so full of sorrow and pain that Clara could have wept. 'Please. Just think about it.'

I can't. I can't. I won't. I... She nodded. 'I'll think about it,' she promised and instantly hated herself.

This was why she'd had to leave. She could never say no to him.

I'll think about it.

One year of marriage, five years of estrangement and now she was thinking. He supposed that was something.

Jacob paused briefly on the corner of the street, rain dripping down his collar, and watched from a distance as Clara locked up the offices of Perfect London and hurried off in the opposite direction. She was a woman on a mission; she clearly had somewhere far more important to be. Things that mattered much more in her life than her ex-husband.

Well. So did he, of course.

The office was deserted by the time he'd walked back across the river to it, but the security guard on duty didn't look surprised to see him. Given how rarely Jacob made it to the London office, he wondered what that said about the legend of his work ethic.

But once he had sat at his desk he found he couldn't settle. His eyes slid away from emails, and spreadsheets seemed to merge into one on the screen. Eventually, he closed the lid of his laptop, sat back in his chair and swung it around to take in the London skyline outside the window.

Was it just seeing Clara again that was distracting him? No. She didn't have that kind of power over him any more. It was everything else in his life right now, most likely. His father's illness more than anything.

His mobile phone vibrated on the glass desk, buzzing its way across the smooth surface. Jacob grabbed it and, seeing his younger sister's name on the screen, smiled.

'Heather. Why aren't you out at some all-night rave or something? Isn't that what you students do?'

He could practically hear her rolling her eyes on the other end of the phone.

'We're having a Christmas movie night at the flat,' Heather said. 'Mulled wine, mince pies, soppy movies and lots of wrapping paper. I was halfway through wrapping my stack of presents when it occurred to me that there was still one person who hadn't got back to me about what they wanted…'

'You don't have to buy me anything,' Jacob said automatically. It wasn't as if he couldn't buy whatever he wanted when he wanted it, anyway. And, besides, Heather, more than anyone, never owed him a gift. Her continued existence was plenty for him.

'It's Christmas, Jacob.' She spoke slowly, as if to a slightly stupid dog. 'Everyone gets a present. You know the rules. So tell me what you want or I'll buy you a surprise.'

Only his sister could make a surprise gift sound like a

threat. Although, given the tie she'd bought him last year, maybe it was.

'A surprise will be lovely,' he said, anyway. 'Anything you think I'd like.'

'You're impossible.' Heather sighed. 'While I have you, when are you heading home for Christmas?'

'Actually…'

'Oh, no! Don't say you're not coming!' She groaned dramatically. 'Come on, Jacob! The office can cope for one day without you, you know. Especially since *no one else will be working*!'

Jacob blinked as an almost exact echo of Heather's words flooded his memory—except this time it was Clara speaking them, over and over. He shook his head to disperse the memory.

'That's not what I was going to say,' he said. 'In fact…I went to see Clara today.'

'Clara?' Heather asked, the surprise clear in her voice. 'Why? What on earth for?'

'I wanted to ask for her help.' He took a breath. Time to share the plan, he supposed. If Clara wouldn't help, it would all fall on him and Heather anyway. 'I was thinking about Dad. This is going to be his last Christmas, Heather, and I want it to be special.'

His sister went quiet. Jacob waited. He knew Heather was still struggling to come to terms with their father's diagnosis. He wouldn't rush her.

'So, what have you got planned?' she asked eventually.

'Do you remember that year we hired that cottage in Scotland? You can only have been about five at the time, but we had a roaring log fire, stockings hung next to it, the biggest Christmas tree you've ever seen… It was everything Christmas is meant to be.' It had also been the last Christmas before the accident. Before everything had changed in his relationship with his family.

'You mean a movie-set Christmas,' Heather joked. 'But, yeah, I remember, I think. Bits of it, anyway. You want to do that again?'

'That's the plan.'

'And what? You're going to rope Clara into coming along to pretend that you've made up and everything is just rosy, just to keep Dad happy? Because, Jacob, that's exactly the sort of stupid plan that *will* backfire when Dad defies all the doctors' expectations.'

'That's not… No.' That wasn't the plan. He had no intention of pretending anything. Except, now that Heather had said it, he was already imagining what it would be like. Clara beside him on Christmas morning, opening presents together, his dad happy and smiling, seeing his family back together again…

But no. That was *not* the plan. The last thing he needed was to get embroiled with his almost-ex-wife again. And, once Christmas was out of the way, he'd give her the divorce she wanted so desperately and make a clean break altogether.

'She runs a concierge and events company here in London now,' he explained. 'They can source anything you need, put together any party, any plan. I wanted to hire her to organise our Christmas.'

Heather sounded pitying as she said, 'Jacob. Don't you think that's just a little bit desperate? If you wanted to see your ex-wife, you could have just called her up.'

'Wife,' he corrected automatically, then wished he hadn't. 'We're still married. Technically.'

His sister sighed. 'It's been five years, Jacob. When are you going to get over her?'

'I'm over her,' he assured her. 'Very over her. Trust me. But she knows Dad and she knows the family. She could make this Christmas everything it needs to be, far better than I ever could. You probably don't remember the parties she used to throw…'

'I remember them,' Heather said. 'They were spectacular.'

'Look, she hasn't even said yes yet. And if she doesn't I'll find someone else to do it. It won't be the end of the world.' But it wouldn't be the perfect Christmas he wanted either. Somehow, he knew in his bones that only Clara could give them that. She had a talent for seeing right to the heart of people, knowing exactly what made them light up inside—and what didn't.

He wondered sometimes, late at night, what she'd seen inside him that had made her leave. And then he realised he probably already knew.

'Okay,' Heather said, still sounding dubious. 'I guess I'm in, in principle. But Jacob…be careful, yeah?'

'I'm always careful,' he joked, even though it wasn't funny. Just true.

'I'm serious. I don't want to spend my Christmas holiday watching you nurse a broken heart. Again.'

Jacob shook his head. 'It's not like that. Trust me.'

Not this time. Even if he was harbouring any residual feelings for Clara, he would bury them deep, far deeper than even she could dig out.

He wasn't going to risk his heart that way a second time. Marriage might be the one thing he'd failed at—but he would only ever fail once.

CHAPTER THREE

'WHAT DID HE WANT?' Merry asked the moment Clara picked up the phone.

Clara sighed. 'Hang on.'

Peeking around Ivy's door one last time, she assured herself that her daughter was firmly asleep and pulled the door to. Then, phone in hand, she padded down the stairs to the kitchen, poured herself a glass of wine and headed for the sofa.

'Right,' she said, once she was settled. 'Let's start with your thing at the art gallery. How was it?'

Merry laughed. 'Not a chance. Come on, your ex-husband walks into our offices right before Christmas, after five years of nothing except letters from his lawyers finding reasons to put off the divorce, and you think I'm not going to want details? Talk, woman.'

So much for diversion tactics. 'He wanted to hire Perfect London.'

There was a brief moment of shocked silence on the other end of the phone. Clara took the opportunity to snag a chocolate off the potted Christmas tree in her front window and pop it in her mouth.

'Seriously?' Merry said at last. 'Why?'

'God only knows,' Clara replied, then sighed again. 'No, I know, I suppose. He wants us to arrange a perfect last Christmas for his dad. He's sick. Very sick.'

'And he thought his ex-wife would be the best person to organise it because…?'

It wasn't as if Clara hadn't had the same thought. 'I guess because I know him. All of them, really. I know what he means when he says "a perfect Christmas for Dad". With anyone else he'd have to spell it out.'

'So nothing to do with wanting to win you back, then,' Merry said, the scepticism clear in her voice.

'No. Definitely not.' That, at least, was one thing Clara was very sure of. 'He offered me a divorce if I do it.'

'Finally!' Merry gave a little whoop of joy, which made Clara smile. Sometimes, having a good friend on side made everything so much easier. Even seeing Jacob Foster again for the first time in five years. 'Well, in that case, we have to do it.'

'You haven't heard the fine print.' Clara filled her in on the details, including the whole 'have to travel to Scotland on Christmas Eve' part. 'It's just not doable. Especially not with the Charity Gala at New Year to finalise.' Which was a shame, in a way. A project like this would be a great selling point for future clients. And a good testimonial from Foster Medical—especially alongside delivering a great event for the Harrisons—could go a long way to convincing people that Perfect London was a big-time player. It could make the next year of their business.

Merry was obviously thinking the same thing. 'There's got to be some way we can pull it off.'

'Not without disrupting Ivy's Christmas,' Clara said. 'And I won't do that. She's four, Merry. This might be the first proper Christmas she's able to remember in years to come. I want it to be perfect for her too.' Of course, it could also be an ideal opportunity to discover if Jacob was ready to hear about the existence of his daughter. The guilt had been eating her up ever since he'd left her office that evening. Watching Ivy splash about in her bath, tucking her in after her story… She couldn't help but think how Jacob had already missed four years of those things. And even if he didn't want to be part of them, she knew she owed him the chance to choose for himself.

Except that he'd already made his decision painfully clear five years ago. She had no reason to imagine that decision had changed—apart from him wanting to organise Christmas for his family. Was that enough proof? How could she be sure? Only by spending time with him. And there was the rub.

'You always want everything to be perfect,' Merry moaned. 'But I take your point. Does…does he know? About Ivy?'

A chill slithered down Clara's spine. 'I don't think so. Not that it would be any of his business, anyway. I didn't fall pregnant with her until after I left.' She hated lying. But she'd been telling this one for so long she didn't know how to stop.

If she told Jacob the truth, she'd have to tell Merry too. And Ivy, of course. And Jacob's family. She'd be turning everybody's lives upside down. Did she have the right to do that? But then, how could she not? Didn't Jacob's father deserve the chance to know his granddaughter before he died? Or would that only make it worse, having so little time with her?

What on earth was she supposed to do? When she'd left, it had all seemed so clear. But now…

'I know, I know. Your one and only one-night stand,' Merry said, still blissfully ignorant of the truth, and Clara's internal battle. 'Still, it might make a difference if you explained why you can't go to Scotland for Christmas. Maybe he'd be satisfied with me going instead, once you've done the set-up.'

'Maybe,' Clara allowed, but even as she said it she knew it wasn't true. Jacob wouldn't take second best. Not that Merry was, of course—she was every bit as brilliant at her job as Clara was at hers. That was why Perfect London worked so well. But Jacob's plan involved Clara being there, and she suspected he wouldn't give that up for anything. Even if it meant letting down a little girl at Christmas. 'I'd rather not tell him,' she said finally. 'The dates are close, I'll admit, and I don't want him using Ivy as an excuse to hold up the divorce while we get paternity tests done and so on. Not when I'm finally on the verge of getting my freedom back.' And not when the results wouldn't be in her favour.

'Only if you take on the project,' Merry pointed out. 'That was the deal, right? Organise Christmas, get divorce. Turn him down...'

'And he'll drag this out with the lawyers for another five years,' Clara finished. 'You're right. Damn him.'

She tried to sound upset at the prospect, for Merry's sake. But another five years of limbo meant another five years of not having to pluck up the courage to tell Jacob the truth. And part of her, the weakest part, couldn't deny that the idea had its appeal.

But no. If his arriving unannounced had taught her anything it was that it was time for the truth to come out, or be buried forever. No more *maybe one day.* She needed to move on properly. If Jacob still felt the same way about kids as he had when they were married, then her decision was easy. Get the divorce, move on with her life and let him live his own without worrying about a daughter that he'd never wanted.

If he'd changed his mind, however...

Clara sighed. If she'd known she was pregnant before she'd left, she would have had to tell him. But finding out afterwards... She hadn't even known how to try.

Jacob had always made it painfully clear that he didn't want a family. At least he had once they were married. During their frantic whirlwind courtship and their impulsive elopement, the future had rarely come up in conversation. And, if it had, all Clara could imagine then was them, together, just the two of them.

It wasn't until the next summer, when she'd realised she was late one month and Jacob had come home to a still-boxed pregnancy test on the kitchen table, that she'd discovered how strongly he felt about not having kids.

What the hell is that? Clara? Tell me this is a joke...

The horror on his face, the panic in his eyes… She could still see it when she closed her eyes. The way he'd suddenly decided that her oral contraceptive wasn't reliable enough and had started investigating other options. The tension in the house, so taut she'd thought she might snap, and then the pure relief, three days later, when her period finally arrived. The way he'd held her, as if they'd avoided the Apocalypse.

And the growing emptiness she'd felt inside her as it had first dawned on her that she *wanted* to be a mother.

So she'd known, staring at a positive pregnancy test alone in a hotel bathroom six months later, that it was the end for them, even if he didn't realise it. She could never go back.

He wouldn't want her if she did and she wanted the baby growing inside her more than anything. She hadn't changed her mind about that in the years since. Had he changed his?

'There's got to be a way,' Merry said thoughtfully. 'A way we can take the job, still give Ivy a wonderful Christmas—*and* pull off the New Year's gala.'

Clara sat on the other end of the phone and waited. She knew that tone. It meant Merry was on the verge of something brilliant. Something that would solve all of Clara's problems.

She'd sounded exactly like that the night they'd dreamt up Perfect London. Clara had been clutching a wine glass, staring helplessly at the baby monitor, wondering what on earth she would do next—and Merry had found the perfect solution.

Clara reached for another chocolate while she waited,

and had just shoved it into her mouth whole when Merry cried out, 'I've got it!'

Chewing and swallowing quickly, Clara said, 'Tell me.'

'We do Christmas together in Scotland too!'

For a second Clara imagined her, Ivy and Merry all joining the Fosters in their Highland castle and worried that she might be on the verge of a heart attack. That, whatever Merry might think, was possibly the worst idea that anyone had ever had. In the history of the world.

'Not with them, of course,' Merry clarified, and Clara let herself breathe again. 'We find a really luscious hotel, somewhere nearby, and book in for the duration, right? You'll be on hand to manage Project Perfect Christmas, I'll be there if you need me and to watch Ivy, and then, once things are set up at the castle, we can have our own Christmas, just the three of us.'

Clara had to admit, that did sound pretty good. It would give her the chance to get to know this new Jacob—and see if he was ready to be Ivy's father. Then, in January, once the crazily busy season was over, she could find the best moment to tell him.

It gave her palpitations just thinking about it, but in lots of ways it was the perfect plan.

'Do you think Ivy will mind having Christmas at a hotel instead of at home?'

'I don't see why,' Merry said. 'I mean, we'll have roaring log fires, mince pies by the dozen and probably even snow, that far up in the country. What more could a little girl want?'

'She has been asking about building snowmen,' Clara admitted. *And about having a father.* Maybe this could just work after all. 'But what about you? Are you sure you don't mind spending Christmas with us?'

'Are you kidding? My parents are heading down to Devon to stay with my sister and her four kids for the holidays. I was looking at either a four-hour trek followed by three days minding the brats or a microwave turkey dinner for one.'

'Why didn't you say?' Clara asked. 'We could have done something here. You know you're always welcome.'

'Ah, that was my secret plan,' Merry admitted. 'I was going to let on at the last minute and gatecrash your day. Ivy's much better company than any of my nephews and nieces anyway.'

'So Scotland could work, then.' Just saying it aloud felt weird. 'I mean, I'll need to talk to Ivy about it…' She might only be four, but Ivy had very definite 'opinions' on things like Christmas.

'But if Ivy says yes, I'm in.' Merry sounded positively cheerful at the idea. In fact, the whole plan was starting to appeal to Clara too.

As long as she could keep Jacob away from Ivy until she was ready. If he didn't want anything to do with his daughter then it was better if Ivy never knew he existed. She wouldn't let Jacob Foster abandon them.

Clara reached for one last chocolate. 'Then all I need to do is call Jacob and tell him yes.' It was funny how that was the most terrifying part of all.

Jacob awoke the next morning to his desk phone ringing right next to his head. Rubbing his itching eyes, he sat up in his chair, cursed himself for falling asleep at work *again* and answered the phone.

'Mr Foster, there's a woman here to see you.' The receptionist paused, sounding uncertain. 'She says she's your wife.'

Ah. That would explain the uncertainty. But not why Clara was visiting his offices at—he checked his watch—eight-thirty in the morning.

'Send her up,' he said. The time it would take her to

reach his office on the top floor, via two elevators and a long corridor, should give him time to make himself presentable.

'Um…she's already on her way?' Jacob wondered why she phrased it as a question as Clara barrelled through his door with a perfunctory knock.

He put down the phone and made a mental note to send all the company's receptionists for refresher training on *how to do their job.*

'Clara. This is a surprise.' He made an effort to sound professional, and not as if he'd just woken up two minutes earlier.

Except Clara knew exactly what he looked like when he'd just woken up. 'Your hair's sticking up at the back,' she said helpfully.

Smoothing it down, Jacob took in the sight of his ex-wife. Clara stood just inside the doorway, a dark red coat wrapped around her, her gloved hands tucked under her arms for added warmth. She had a grey felt hat perched on top of her glossy brown hair and her make-up was immaculate.

He knew that look. She was wearing her 'impressing people' make-up—lots of dark lipstick and she'd managed some trick or another that made her eyes look even larger than normal. He blamed the receptionist a little less for letting her through. This new confident Clara, combined with her old charm, was hard to say no to.

'You've come to a decision?' he asked, motioning her towards the comfortable sitting area at the side of the office. It was too early for guessing games. And visitors, come to that.

'Yes.' She took her hat from her head and placed it on the table by the sofas, then removed her coat to reveal another flattering form-fitting wrap dress, this one in a dark forest green. Settling onto the chocolate-brown leather sofa, she looked utterly at home. As if she belonged not just in his office but in the corporate world. He supposed she did, now.

Jacob turned away, moving towards the high-end coffee machine behind the sitting area. This conversation definitely needed coffee.

'I've spoken with my partner,' Clara said. 'We think we've found a way to work around our other commitments so we can take on your project.' She didn't sound entirely happy about the conclusion, but that wasn't his problem. Neither was this partner, whoever the unlucky man was. Jacob felt something loosen inside him, something he hadn't even realised was wound up too tight.

She was going to help him. That was all that mattered.

'That's good news,' he said, trying not to let his relief show too much. Instead, he busied himself making them both a cup of strong black coffee. 'I assume you have a standard contract with payment schedules and so on?'

'Of course,' Clara replied. 'Although, given the timescales, I rather think we're going to require full payment up front, don't you?'

'Understandable.' Paying wasn't a problem. And once she had his money, she'd have to follow through. It was far harder to pay back money than walk out on the potential of it. And heaven knew Jacob would do everything in his power to stop Clara walking out on him again.

He placed the coffee on the table in front of her, and her nose wrinkled up. 'Actually, I don't drink coffee any more.'

'Really?' She used to drink it by the bucketload, he remembered. Her favourite wedding present, in amongst far more expensive and luxury items, had been a simple filter coffee maker from Heather. 'I can offer you tea. Probably.' He frowned at the machine. Did it even make tea? 'Or ask someone else to bring some up.' Maybe he'd ask the receptionist—a small, perhaps petty act of revenge.

Especially if he insisted that she bring it via the stairs instead of the lift…

'It's fine. I don't need anything.' Jacob bit back a sharp smile at her words. Clara had made that clear five years ago when she'd refused any support after she'd left.

'So, just business then.' Jacob lifted his own coffee cup to his lips and breathed in the dark scent of it. *This* was what he needed. Not his ex-wife in his office at eight-thirty in the morning.

'Yes. Except…the usual contracts don't cover the more… personal side of this arrangement,' Clara went on delicately.

Jacob would have laughed if it weren't so miserable a topic. 'You mean the divorce.' The idea that she wanted one still rankled. What was it about him that made him want to just keep flogging this dead horse? Why couldn't he just cut her loose and get on with his life? Even his lawyer had started rolling his eyes whenever the subject came up. Jacob knew it was time to move on—past time, really. But, until the paperwork was signed, he hadn't failed at marriage. Not completely.

He rather imagined that Clara would say differently, though.

'Yes,' she said. 'The divorce. I think…I'd like to get that sorted in the New Year, if we could. I think it would be good for us both. We could move on properly.'

'Are you planning to get married again?' He regretted asking the moment the words were out of his mouth, but it was too late.

'No! I mean maybe, one day, I suppose. But not right now. Why do you ask?'

Yes, Jacob, why did you ask that? He didn't care what she did now. So why let her think he did?

He shrugged, trying to play nonchalant. 'You mentioned a partner.'

'Business partner. Merry. You met her yesterday, actually.'

The redhead at the office. Well, in that case, unless Clara had changed far more than he'd realised, there wasn't a marriage in the making. 'You're not seeing anyone then?' He wished it didn't sound as if he cared, but he couldn't not ask. He needed all the facts. He always had done.

'No. Not right now. It's hard when…' She cut herself off. 'Well, you know.'

'When your husband won't give you a divorce,' he guessed. Although why that should make a difference he wasn't sure. They'd been apart five years as it was; if she'd really wanted to move on with another guy, he couldn't imagine a lousy piece of paper would stop her. Her wedding vows hadn't kept her married to him, after all.

If she'd really, truly wanted the divorce, he doubted he could have stopped her. His lawyers were good, but some things were inevitable. He'd known all along he was only stalling, and somewhere on the way he'd even forgotten why. But Clara hadn't wanted to take anything from him, hadn't wanted to make anything difficult. Really, it should have been straightforward.

But she'd never pushed, never insisted, never kicked up a real fuss. Surely, if she'd really wanted this divorce she'd have done all that and more.

Unless she *didn't* really want it. Unless she'd been waiting for him to come after her.

Which he was doing, right now, in a way.

It didn't feel like Clara, that kind of complicated long game. And to drag it out over five years seemed a little excessive. But still, logic dictated that *something* had to be stopping her from forcing through the divorce. And he couldn't for the life of him think of anything else it might be.

But working with her on his Perfect Christmas project would give him the ideal opportunity to find out.

CHAPTER FOUR

CLARA TRIED TO BREATHE through her mouth to avoid taking in the smell of the coffee. It was ridiculous, really. She'd *loved* coffee, almost as much as she'd loved Jacob. But then she'd fallen pregnant and suddenly she couldn't stand the smell of it, let alone the taste. She'd always assumed that once the baby was born she'd get her love of coffee back again, but no. Even now, four years later, the very smell made her want to gag.

So unfair.

As if this morning wasn't bad enough already, the universe had to throw in coffee.

Ivy had woken up bright and early at six and Clara hadn't seen much point in dragging things out so, over their traditional weekday morning breakfast of toast and cereal, she'd broached the subject of Christmas.

'How would you like the idea of going somewhere snowy for Christmas? With Merry?' Merry was a definite favourite with Ivy, so that was bound to be more of a draw than most other things, Clara had decided.

'Where?' Ivy had asked in between mouthfuls.

'Scotland.' Clara had held her breath, waiting for an answer.

'What about Norman?'

'Norman?' Clara had been briefly concerned that her daughter had suddenly gained a seventy-year-old imaginary friend until Ivy clarified.

'Our Christmas tree,' she'd said. 'You said he was called Norman.'

Clara had blinked, ran back through a mental movie of

the day they'd bought the tree and finally figured it out. 'Nordmann. He's a Nordmann Fir.'

Ivy had nodded. 'Norman the Nordmann. What will happen to him while we're away?'

'We'll ask Mr Jenkins next door to come and water him, shall we? Then Norman will still be here when we get back.' Good grief, she had a Christmas tree with a name. How had this happened? 'Is that all you're worried about? Do you think Scotland might be okay for Christmas?'

Ivy's little face had scrunched up as she considered. 'Will they have pancakes there for Christmas morning?' she'd asked.

Clara had added pancakes to their list of hotel requirements, dropped Ivy at the childminder's house and headed off to talk to Jacob. There was no point putting it off, especially since she knew exactly where to find him—Foster Medical head office. He might more usually work from one of the American offices these days, but if he was in London, Clara knew he'd be at work.

But his work was going to have to wait. They only had a week and a half to put together a perfect Christmas. Two Christmases, if you counted Ivy's, and Clara did. So she'd rushed across London to the imposing skyscraper of an office, only pausing long enough to explain to the receptionist exactly who she was, and then bustled along to Jacob's office.

But now, with the scent of coffee making her queasy, and Jacob's sleep-ruffled hair looking all too familiar, Clara really wished she'd waited. Or even called instead.

'Anyway. If that's all settled…' She picked up her hat from the table.

'I wouldn't call it settled,' Jacob said and she lowered the hat again. No, of course not. That would be too easy. 'We still need to discuss the particulars.' Putting his coffee cup down, Jacob came around from the counter to sit beside her.

The leather sofa was vast—ridiculously so, for an office—and there was a more than reasonable gap between them. But, suddenly, it wasn't coffee she could smell any more. It was *him.* That familiar combination of aftershave, soap and *Jacob* that tugged at her memory and made her want to relive every moment. To imagine that this was that other life she could have been living, where they were together in London, still married, still happy.

'Particulars?' she asked, shaking her head a little to try and stop herself being so distracted by his nearness.

'Like where we want it to take place, how many people, what the menu should be, timings… Little things like that.' He was laughing at her, but Clara couldn't find it amusing. It just reminded her how much there was to do.

'I'm assuming the timings are fairly self-explanatory,' she said drily. 'Christmas Eve to Boxing Day would be my best guess—I can't imagine you wanting to take any more time off work than that, regardless of the circumstances.' Even that was two days more than he'd managed for their last Christmas together. Two and a half if she counted him sloping off to the study for an hour or two after Christmas lunch. 'Guests. I'm assuming just your parents and Heather, unless she has a partner she'd like to bring? Or you do,' she added, belatedly realising that just because her love life was a desert didn't mean his was.

'No, you're right, just the four of us.' He still looked amused, but there was less mockery in his expression. 'Go on.'

'Location. you said the Highlands, and I happen to know of a very festive, exclusive castle that would be brilliant for your celebrations.' And particularly helpful to her, since the client she'd originally booked it for had pulled out and she'd promised the owner she'd do her best to find someone else to take over the booking. If she didn't find someone, thanks to a contract mishap Perfect London would be losing the rather hefty deposit.

'Sounds ideal.'

'As for the menu—traditional Christmas turkey dinner plus appetizers, puddings, wine and liquors, cold cuts and chutneys in the fridge, then smoked salmon and scrambled eggs with croissant for breakfast. Sound about right?'

'Yes.' He blinked, looking slightly bemused. 'How did you know all that?'

'It's my job, Jacob,' Clara said, irritation rising. He might not have appreciated everything she'd done to keep his nice little business gatherings and parties ticking over, but even he had to respect that she'd built up a successful business with her skills. 'And it's not like you're asking for anything out of the ordinary.' If she was lucky and used every contact she had, she could pull this off for Jacob and manage her own wonderful Christmas with Ivy too.

'No, I suppose not. Of course, snow is obviously essential,' Jacob added.

Clara stared at him. Was the man insane? 'Snow. You want me to arrange snow?'

Jacob lifted one shoulder. Was he teasing? She never *could* tell when he was teasing her. 'Well, it is Christmas, after all. I think we can all agree that the perfect Christmas would have to be a white one.'

Clara's mouth tightened. 'I'll check the weather forecast then.' Jacob looked as if he might be trying to dream up some more outlandish requests, just to throw her off her game, so Clara hurried on.

'Which just leaves us with the presents.' This, she knew, was the real test. If Jacob truly had changed—if this perfect Christmas idea was a sign that he was ready to embrace a family and, just possibly, the daughter he didn't know he had—the presents would be the giveaway.

'Presents?' Jacob frowned, and Clara's heart fell. 'Aren't

you going to buy those? I'd have thought it would be part of the contract.'

'Usually, Perfect London would be delighted to source the perfect gift for every member of your family,' she said sweetly. 'But, under the circumstances—with less than a fortnight to go, not to mention this being your father's last Christmas—I am sure that you will want to select them yourself.' She stared at him until he seemed to get the idea that this was not a suggestion.

'But what would I buy them?' He looked so adorably flustered at the very idea that for a moment Clara forgot that she was testing him.

Then she realised this could be an even better opportunity.

'I'll tell you what,' she said, making it clear that this was a favour, just for him. 'Why don't we go shopping together and choose them?'

'That would be great.' The relief was evident in his voice.

'Right now,' Clara finished, and his eyebrows shot up.

'Now? But I'm working.'

'So am I,' she pointed out. 'By taking a client shopping.'

'Yes, but I can't just leave! There are meetings. Emails. Important decisions to be made.'

'Like whether your sister would prefer a handbag or a scarf.'

'Like the future of the company!'

Now it was Clara's turn to raise her eyebrows. 'Do you really expect that to come up in the three hours you'll be gone?'

'Three hours!' Clara waited and finally he sighed. 'No, I suppose not.'

'Then I think that your father's last Christmas might matter rather more than emails and meetings. Don't you?'

He looked torn and Clara held her breath until, finally, he said, 'Yes. It does.'

She grinned. The old Jacob would never have left work at 9:00 a.m. on a weekday to go Christmas shopping. *Ha!* He'd never left work *or* done Christmas shopping.

Maybe he really had changed after all. She could hope so. After all, Christmas *was* the season of hope and goodwill. Even towards ex-husbands.

'What about this?' Clara held up a gossamer-thin scarf in various shades of purple that Jacob suspected cost more than his entire suit. Everything else Clara had suggested had and, since his suit had been handmade especially for him, that was quite an achievement.

'For Mum?' he asked with a frown.

'No. For Heather.' Clara sighed. Jacob had a feeling she was starting to regret her insistence on taking him shopping.

'She's a student,' he pointed out. 'She wouldn't wear something like that.'

'She graduating this summer, right? So she'll have interviews, internships, all sorts of professional opportunities coming her way. A statement accessory like this can make any outfit look polished.' As always, Clara had a point. He'd almost forgotten how irritating that was.

'Maybe,' he allowed. But Clara was already walking on, probably in search of an even more expensive gift for his sister. He didn't begrudge spending the money but he was beginning to think this was some sort of game for Clara. She'd certainly never encouraged him to buy such luxurious gifts for her.

The high-end shopping district Clara had directed the taxi to was filled with tiny boutiques, all stocking a minimum of products at maximum cost. Even the Christmas decorations strung between the shops on either side of the street, high above the heads of the passing shoppers, were discreet, refined and—Jacob was willing to bet—costly.

'Is this where you usually shop for your clients?' he asked, lengthening his stride to catch up with her as she swung into another shop.

Clara shrugged. 'Sometimes. It depends on the client.'

Which told him nothing. Jacob wasn't entirely sure why he was so interested in the day-to-day details of her job, but he suspected it had something to do with never realising she wanted one. He'd thought he'd known Clara better than anyone in the world, and that she'd known him just as well. It had been a jolt to discover there were some parts of her he'd never known at all. What if this entrepreneurial side of her was just the start?

Of course, for all that he'd shared with Clara, there were some things *he'd* kept back too. He couldn't entirely blame her for that.

'This would be just right for your father.' Jacob turned to find her holding up a beautifully wrought dark leather briefcase, with silver detailing and exquisite stitching. She was right; his father would love it. Except…

'He won't be coming in to the office much longer.' It still caught him by surprise, almost daily. In some ways, he suspected he was in denial as much as Heather; he wanted to believe that if he could just make Christmas perfect then the rest would fall into place.

But he couldn't save his father's life. Even if a part of him felt he should be able to, if he just worked long enough, tried hard enough. If he was good enough.

Jacob knew he'd never been good enough, had known it long before his father fell sick.

Clara dropped the briefcase back onto the shelf. 'You're right. Come on.'

Even Jacob had to agree the next shop was spot on.

'You want something your dad can enjoy.' Clara opened her arms and gestured to the bottles of vintage wine lining the shelves. 'From what I remember, this should suit him.'

Jacob smiled, turning slowly to take in the selection. 'Yes, I think this will do nicely.'

One in-depth conversation with the proprietor later, and Jacob felt sure that he had the perfect gift for at least one member of his family, ready to be delivered directly to Clara's offices in time to be shipped up to Scotland.

'How are they all?' Clara asked as she led him into a tiny arcade off the main street. The shops inside looked even more sparse and expensive. 'Your family, I mean. The news about your dad… It must have been terrible for you all. I can't imagine.'

'It was,' Jacob said simply. 'It still is. Mum… She takes everything in her stride—you know her. But Heather's still hoping for a miracle, I think.'

Clara looked sideways at him. 'And you're not?'

'Perhaps,' he admitted. 'It's just too hard to imagine a world without him.'

Watching as she paused by a display of necklaces, Jacob remembered the first time he'd brought Clara home to meet his family—just days after their elopement. He remembered his mother's shock and forced cheer as she realised she'd been done out of the big wedding she'd always imagined for him.

But, more than anything, he remembered his father's reaction. How he'd taken him into his study and poured him a brandy in one of the last two crystal glasses handed down from James's own great-grandfather. A sign of trust that had shocked Jacob's hands into trembling, even as he'd reminded himself that he was grown up now. A married man.

'You've taken on a big responsibility, son,' James had said. 'A wife is more than a lover, more than a friend. More even than family. She is your whole world—and you are responsible for making that world perfect.'

He'd known instantly what his father was really saying. *Don't screw it up this time. Remember what happened last time we gave you any responsibility. You can't take that kind of chance again.*

And he hadn't. He'd thought that Clara—easy-going, eager to please Clara—would be safe. She was an adult, her own person, after all. Far less responsibility than a child, far harder to hurt. He'd tried to make things just right for her—with the right house, the right people, the right levels of success. But, in the end, he'd done just as his father had so obviously expected him to, that day in the study drinking brandy.

Why else would she have left?

'They must all be looking forward to this Christmas together, though?' Clara had moved on from the necklaces, Jacob realised belatedly, and he hurried to join her on the other side of the shop.

'I haven't told them yet,' he admitted, admiring the silver-and-gold charm bracelet draped across her fingers.

Clara paused, her eyebrows raised ever so slightly, in that way she always had when she was giving him a chance to realise he was making a mistake. Except he was giving his family a dream Christmas. What was the mistake in that? How had he screwed up this time?

'Don't you think you'd better check with them before we go too much further?' Clara went on, her eyebrows just a little higher.

'I want it to be a surprise,' Jacob said mulishly.

'Right. Well, if that's how you want to play it.'

'It is.'

'Fine.' Somehow, just that one word made him utterly sure that she thought he was making a mistake. Now she had him second-guessing himself. How did she do that?

She was almost as good at it as his father was.

'So, beyond the wine we've already ordered, what would James's perfect Christmas look like?' Clara asked, and suddenly Jacob felt on surer ground again.

'That's easy,' he said with a shrug. 'He always says the best Christmas we ever had was the one we spent in Scotland, just the family, spending time together.'

'How old were you?' Clara asked.

'Fifteen, I think.'

'Okay, so what did you do that Christmas?'

'Do?' Jacob frowned, trying to remember. 'I mean, there were presents and turkey and so on.'

'Yes, but beyond that,' Clara said with exaggerated patience. 'Did you play games? Charades or Monopoly or something? Did you sing carols around a piano? Did you open presents on Christmas Eve or Christmas morning? Were there cracker hats? Did you go to church? Were there stockings? Did you stay up until midnight on Christmas Eve or get an early night? Think, Jacob.'

'Cluedo,' Jacob said finally. 'That Christmas was the year we taught Heather to play Cluedo. Sort of.'

Suddenly, the memory was unbearably clear. Sitting around the wooden cottage kitchen table, Heather watching from her dad's lap, him explaining the rules as they went along. Jacob wanted to take that brief, shining moment in time and hold it close. That was what he wanted his father's last Christmas to be—a return to the way things used to be. Before the accident. Before everything had changed for ever.

Clara beamed at him. 'Wonderful! There's a shop down here somewhere that sells high-end board games—you know, gemstone chess sets and Monopoly with gold playing pieces. I think they had a Cluedo set last time I was in… Come with me!'

Jacob followed, wondering if the board would be made of solid gold, and whether his perfect Christmas might actually exhaust even his bank accounts.

Maybe then it would be good enough for his father.

CHAPTER FIVE

'I KNEW THIS WAS a bad idea,' Clara grumbled, tagging yet another email from Jacob with a 'deal with this urgently' flag. If five hours of Christmas shopping hadn't convinced her that his demands were going to require going far above and beyond the usual levels of customer service, his half hourly emails since certainly had. 'Why on earth was he sending me emails at four a.m.?'

'Because he couldn't sleep, thinking about you?' Merry suggested.

Clara pulled a face. Merry's new enthusiasm for her ex-husband wasn't encouraging either. Just because he'd sent flowers and chocolates the day after they had signed the contract. Her friend was cheaply bought, it seemed.

'More likely he was still at the office and counts emailing me about Christmas as taking a break.' She was almost certain he'd slept at his desk the night before she'd taken him shopping. It had happened often enough towards the end of their marriage that she'd begun to suspect an affair—until she'd realised he wouldn't have time in between meetings. 'Trust me, he's only thinking about what we—as a company—can do for him.' All business; that was Jacob. It always had been.

'Then why send the flowers?' Merry asked, rummaging through what was left of the box of chocolates for one she liked. 'I mean, flowers are personal.'

'Not when he had his assistant send them.' Clara dived into the chocolates too. There was no point in letting Merry have all the soft centres just because she was still mad with the man who'd sent them.

'How do you know that?' Merry asked around a mouthful of caramel.

Clara shrugged and picked out a strawberry and champagne truffle. *Divine.* 'That's just what he does,' she explained. 'Our last Christmas together, he gave me this really over-the-top diamond bracelet.'

'Damn him,' Merry said, straight-faced. 'What kind of guy gives a girl diamonds for Christmas?'

Clara glared at her. Merry knew better than most that she wasn't a diamonds sort of girl. She liked her jewellery small, discreet and preferably featuring her birthstone. And, since Merry had given her a pair of tiny garnet earrings for her birthday last year, she clearly understood that better than Jacob ever had.

'The diamonds weren't the worst part.' She could remember it so clearly, even so many years later. The weight of the heavy gold clasp and setting on her wrist, the sparkle of the stones, the awkward smile she'd tried to give. And then the moment when she'd looked back into the jewellery box it had come in. 'I found a note, sitting next to the bracelet. It was from his assistant, saying she hoped this would do for his wife's Christmas gift.'

'He had his assistant choose your Christmas present?' Merry asked, incredulous.

'Why not?' Clara asked. 'That's how he does things, after all. He's a businessman. It's all about delegating the unimportant tasks so he can get on with the ones that matter.' That bracelet had been her number one reason for forcing him to go Christmas shopping with her. His father deserved that much.

'So diamonds, in this instance, were a sign that you didn't matter.'

'I clearly didn't even matter all that much to his assistant,' Clara replied. 'If her note was anything to go by.'

Merry pushed the box of chocolates towards her and

Clara dug out another strawberry truffle. It was strange, but the image that next came to mind wasn't of that Christmas, no matter how dreadful she'd felt in that moment. It was of another Christmas, a few years after her mother's remarriage, after the twins were born. Her half-siblings would have been maybe eighteen months old to Clara's thirteen. As she'd unwrapped the one present under the tree with her name on it to find a pair of pyjamas—pink, with roses on, and two sizes too small—she'd watched as the toddlers dived into a mountain of wrapping paper, brightly coloured plastic and all-singing, all-dancing toys and tried not to feel jealous.

Of course, even that year had been better than the following one—when her father had called to say she couldn't come and stay for Christmas after all because his new girlfriend wanted it to be just the two of them. And both of those memories were trumped by the first Christmas after she'd left for university, when her mum and stepdad had taken the twins to Lapland for the festivities, leaving Clara behind.

'You're eighteen now! You don't want to come on holiday with us. You should be with your boyfriend, or your friends!'

Never mind that she hadn't had either.

Christmas, Clara mused, had always been a complete let-down—until the year she'd met Jacob on Christmas Eve, when she was twenty-one. They'd been married by Valentine's Day.

She'd thought she'd never feel unwanted again. How wrong she'd been.

Merry's voice broke through her thoughts and she realised she'd just eaten four chocolates in quick succession. 'What did he say when you asked him about the bracelet?'

'I didn't,' Clara admitted. 'I know, I know, I should have confronted him. But it was Christmas Day, his family were all there…and besides, by the time I could have got him alone to ask, he'd already gone back to work.'

'Suddenly I have a better understanding of why you left this man.' Not just once, but many times—although Clara didn't really want to go into that sort of detail with Merry. Besides, every other time she'd left, she'd gone back, so they didn't really count.

'I left the bracelet too.' Clara could still see it sitting there on the dressing table, a symbol of everything she didn't want from her marriage. 'I walked out the next day.' And almost had a breakdown when she discovered she was pregnant two weeks later.

'Is that why you left?' Merry asked. 'I mean, you've never really spoken about it. All you said was that you couldn't be married to him any more.'

'It was part of it, I suppose,' Clara said. It was hard to put into words the loneliness, the isolation and the feeling of insignificance she'd felt pressing down on her. Jacob had so many things in his life; she was just one more. But she only had him, and the big, empty white houses he owned across the world. And when she'd thought of having more… he'd shut her down completely.

It had reached the point where she couldn't even bring herself to *ask* for what she wanted because she didn't want to risk driving him further away. But that didn't stop her wanting. She remembered watching mothers with their babies in prams during the long seven days that summer when she'd thought she might be pregnant. She remembered the glow that had started to fill her, slowly lighting her up from the inside with the knowledge of what her future should be.

Until Jacob had snuffed out that light with the revulsion on his face as she'd told him she might be expecting his child. Then the realisation had come that she wasn't—and that if Jacob had his way she never would be. *'I have no space in my life for children, Clara. And no desire for them either.'*

And no space for her either, she'd realised as the months had trickled on. Desire… They'd still had that, right to the end. Even if it turned out that was *all* that they'd had.

She hadn't set out to become pregnant. She'd never trick someone into parenthood and wouldn't wish being unwanted on any child. Her own experience—a mother who'd fallen pregnant at sixteen, been forced to marry the father, then had resented both her child and her husband ever since—had ensured that she understood those consequences better than most. But when she'd realised that she *was*... That glow had returned, brighter than ever before. And she'd known that this was her chance—maybe her only chance—to have a family of her own. One where she mattered, where she belonged—and where her child could have all the love and attention that she'd missed out on.

Would Merry understand any of that? She'd try to, Clara knew. She was her best friend, after all. But if you hadn't lived it, the pain and weight that grew every day from simply not mattering… It was hard to imagine.

'Mostly, we wanted different things,' she said, gathering up her paperwork. Time to move on. 'I wanted a family—he didn't.' *Didn't* was a bit of an understatement. *Vehemently refused to even consider the idea* was closer to the truth.

'And now you have Ivy,' Merry said. 'So everything worked out in the end.'

'Yes, it did.' She wouldn't give Ivy up for all the diamond bracelets in the world. She'd hate for Ivy to suffer the sort of rejection she had suffered—the feeling of knowing you were unwanted by your own family, the very people who were supposed to love you more than anyone in the world. She knew how that burned. She never wanted Ivy to experience that.

But now she had to make a choice. Let Jacob into his

daughter's life—or cut him out forever. And the worst part was, it wasn't entirely her choice to make.

Clara sighed and picked up a stack of email printouts. It was far easier to focus on organising the perfect Christmas than to figure out how to tell her ex-husband he was a father.

'Right. These are all the latest things Jacob has requested for his Christmas retreat. Think you can start working your way through them?'

Merry looked resigned as she took the pile of paper from Clara. 'Any chance you think he might give you another diamond bracelet this year?'

Clara laughed in spite of herself. 'I doubt it. Why?'

'If he does, don't leave it this time, yeah? Some of us like a bit of sparkle in our lives.'

Jacob pressed the code into the number pad and waited for the gate to swing open before driving through and parking behind his father's big black car on the gravel driveway. Heather's pink Mini was missing but his mum's little red convertible was still there. That was okay. Heather already knew what he was planning and it was probably best to tell his parents together anyway.

It hadn't occurred to him until Clara asked what his parents thought about their Scottish Christmas that they might be anything other than thrilled. He was giving them the perfect retreat—what more could they want? But the look in Clara's eye on their shopping trip had told him he was missing something. Hence the drive to Surrey to fill them in on the plan.

He let himself in the front door without knocking, and the scent of evergreen pine and cinnamon hit him instantly. The hallway as a whole was dominated by an oversized Christmas tree, tastefully decorated in gold and red, with touches of tartan. The wide, curving staircase had garlands of greenery and red berries twirling around the banister all the way to the first floor, and bowls of dried fruits and spices sat on the console table next to the front door.

Christmas, as he remembered it at home, had always been a very traditional affair. Apart from that year when everyone had come out to California to his beach house, to celebrate with him and Clara. Clara had cooked a full English roast and they'd eaten it in the sunshine. The stockings had hung by the artisan steel-and-glass fire display, looking out of place in their red velvet glory.

It hadn't been traditional, maybe, but he'd been happy. Happy—and terrified, he realised now. Scared that it could all go wrong. That he'd screw it up.

They'd gone from meeting to marriage so fast, and never even thought to talk about what their lives together would look like. And it had never felt real, somehow. As if, from the moment he'd said 'I do' in that clichéd Vegas chapel, he'd been waiting for it to end. For Clara to realise that he wasn't enough, that she couldn't rely on him. That he was bound to hurt her, eventually.

Even his family knew better than to trust him with anything more than business. Work was easy. People were breakable.

He'd woken up the next morning to find Clara gone, a note propped up against the bracelet he'd given her the day before.

Jacob shook away the memories and called out. 'Any chance of a mince pie?'

His mum appeared from the kitchen instantly, a tartan apron wrapped over her skirt and blouse. 'Jacob! What a surprise. Why didn't you call and let us know you were coming?'

'Spur-of-the-moment decision.' He pressed a kiss to her cheek. 'Is Dad here?'

'Upstairs. Working, of course.' She rolled her eyes. 'I

thought he might slow down a bit once…well, never mind. He seems happy enough.'

'Think we can risk interrupting him? I've got something to talk to you both about.' He knew as soon as he said it that it was a mistake, but it was too late. His mother's eyes took on the sort of gleam that meant she was picturing grandchildren, and the smile she gave him made him fear for his life once he'd explained what was actually happening.

'By all means,' she said, grabbing his arm and leading him towards the stairs. 'It'll do him good to take a break, anyway. Now, let me see if I can guess…'

'It's nothing to do with a woman,' Jacob said quickly, then realised that wasn't strictly true. 'Well, not in the way you're thinking, anyway.'

'So you're saying I shouldn't buy a hat but I might want to start thinking about nursery curtains?'

'No! Definitely not that.' The very thought of it made him shudder. If people were breakable, children were a million times more so. He'd learnt that early enough. Fatherhood was one responsibility he'd proved himself incapable of, and sworn never to have. And, given how badly he'd screwed up his marriage, it just proved that was the right decision.

His mother might be disappointed now, but even she had to accept that. There was, after all, a reason why she'd never asked him to babysit Heather again. Not after the accident.

Jacob sighed as they reached the top of the stairs. There was no way out of this that wasn't going to make things worse. 'Just…wait. Let's go and find Dad. Then you'll both know soon enough.'

James Foster's office was at the far end of the hallway, its window looking out over the apple orchard behind the house. Jacob knocked on the door and waited, feeling like a sixteen-year-old boy again, in trouble because his science marks weren't quite as high as they needed to be.

In the end, of course, it had been his flair for business that had taken the family company to new heights, not his scientific talents. For him, science had become something to work around rather than to experiment in. It was safer that way.

'Come in.'

Even his dad's voice sounded tired, Jacob realised. Whatever Heather wanted to believe, there was no denying that he wasn't as healthy as he'd been even one month ago. But maybe his Christmas surprise would help. Remind his father of everything he had to live for.

Jacob pushed open the door and stepped into the study, his mother close behind him.

'Jacob!' James said, struggling to his feet. His arms felt brittle around him, Jacob thought. 'To what do we owe the pleasure?'

'Jacob has something to tell us.' His mum had already settled herself into the armchair by the window, ready to listen. 'And it has absolutely nothing to do with a woman, except that it might.'

'Sounds interesting,' his father said, sitting back down in his desk chair. 'So, do tell.'

Jacob perched on the edge of a table, pushed up against the old fireplace. 'Well, it's about Christmas, actually.'

'You're bringing someone new?' His mother clapped her hands in enthusiasm. 'Except you said not a woman.' Her eyes grew wide. 'Is it a man? Because, darling, really, we just want you to be happy. And you can adopt these days, you know—'

'I'm not bringing anyone,' Jacob said firmly. 'But I am taking you somewhere.'

'Somewhere…not here?' she asked. 'But it's Christmas.'

For a horrible moment it struck Jacob that Clara might actually have read his parents better than he had this time.

'Do you remember that year we spent Christmas in Scotland?' he asked, changing tack.

'In the cottage?' James said. 'Of course. It was possibly the best Christmas we ever had.'

Of course it had been. The last Christmas before the accident. The last time his family had been able to look at Jacob without that shadow in their eyes. The one that told him that they *loved* him, of course—they just couldn't trust him. Couldn't believe in him. Couldn't move past what had happened.

And neither could he.

This Christmas might not fix his mistakes but it was at least one more step in a long line of atonements. Maybe the last one he'd get to make to his father. He had to make it count.

Jacob forced a smile. 'Well, good. Because I wanted to give you another Christmas like that.'

'So you hired the cottage for Christmas?' James frowned. 'I thought that cottage was sold on, a few years later. Do you remember, Sheila? We tried to book again, didn't we? Let me check my files…'

'Not the same cottage.' The last thing he needed was his dad disappearing into his filing cabinet for the afternoon. 'Actually, I've found a castle, up in the Highlands. It has huge old fireplaces, four-poster beds… It'll be perfect.' Or so Clara promised him.

'A castle? Jacob, where on earth do you find a castle for Christmas?' His mother asked, astonished.

'On the Internet, I imagine,' his father said. 'Was it on eBay, Jacob? Because I've heard some stories…'

'I haven't bought the castle,' Jacob explained. 'We're just hiring it. Clara said—'

'Clara?' Mum might be woolly on some things, but she homed right in on the mention of her ex-daughter-in-law. Jacob winced. He'd half hoped to get through this without having to explain the exact logistics. 'What has Clara got to do with this plan? Are you two back together? What happened?'

'No, it's nothing like that.' How to explain? 'She runs a concierge and events company in London now, you see. I've hired her to organise us the perfect Christmas. I figured that since she already knew us…'

'And left you,' his mum pointed out. 'Jacob, really. Are you sure this isn't just an excuse to see her again? We all remember how mad you were over her. And how heartbroken you were when she left. We just don't want to see that happen to you again.'

Jacob had a horrible feeling that they were going to believe this was all a cunning ploy to win his wife back, whatever he said. Unless…unless he told them about the divorce. He took one glance at his father and dismissed the idea. He couldn't bear to lay that last disappointment, that last failure, on the old man.

'I'm sure,' he said instead. 'My heart is fine.'

'Well, I suppose it will be good for you to have some closure at last,' his mum said dubiously. 'But are you sure—'

'Apparently it's done,' his father interrupted. Jacob's mother looked at James in surprise.

'Well, I only meant—'

'And I meant it's decided. We're all having Christmas in Scotland.' Jacob couldn't quite tell if his father was pleased or disappointed by this news until he smiled, a broad grin that spread slowly across his whole face.

The tension in Jacob's shoulders relaxed slightly. This *was* a good idea after all.

'It'll be good to see Clara again too,' James said, casting a meaningful look in Jacob's direction.

Jacob wasn't at all sure that Clara planned to hang around long enough to be seen, but the moment his dad spoke the words he knew he'd try to make it so. His dad had always adored Clara; they'd had a strange connection she'd never quite managed with his mum or sister. Suddenly, Clara was just one more thing Jacob wanted to give his father for his perfect Christmas.

Even if it was only temporary. After all, Clara had never stayed past Boxing Day.

CHAPTER SIX

'HAVE WE GOT the decorations?' Clara asked, checking the list on her clipboard for the fiftieth time. They'd started their final checks at 6:00 a.m., and now it was almost seven. The early start was a pain, but necessary. Nothing could go wrong with this project.

'Ours or theirs?' Merry's head popped out from deep inside a box emblazoned with courier logos. 'I mean we have both, but which list are you ticking off right now?'

'Theirs first.' Organising two perfect Christmases at once had turned out to be rather more work than Clara had anticipated. What with Jacob's ever-increasing wish list and Ivy's last-minute announcement that, actually, she needed to send another letter to Father Christmas because she'd changed her mind about the colour of her bike, the last week had been rather more tense than Clara had hoped for.

Still, it was only two days until Christmas Day and the courier boxes were almost ready to go. Most would be sent to the Highland castle for the Fosters' Christmas, and one or two would go to the hotel down the hill from the castle where Clara, Merry and Ivy would be spending their Christmas.

Ivy was still snoozing at home with her usual childminder, who'd come over super early as a favour. Clara had them all booked on the mid-morning train, first class, and planned to be at the hotel in time for tea.

She had an hour-by-hour plan for the next seventy two hours, much to Merry's amusement. But there was plenty of setting up still to be done, and Clara wasn't taking a single chance with the project. Everything had to be sorted, seamless and—most important—all in place before Jacob and his family arrived on Christmas Eve. That way she could be back at the hotel with Ivy and Merry in time for mince pies and mulled wine by the fire, and she wouldn't have to see her ex-in-laws at all. She couldn't run the risk of any of them meeting Ivy before Clara wanted them to.

It was all going to be perfect, as long as they stuck to the plan.

The plan also had an extra secret page that Merry would never see. A page planning exactly how and where to tell Jacob about Ivy. At the moment, she was opting for January. She'd set up a meeting with him early in the New Year, ostensibly to review the Perfect Christmas Project and discuss terms for the divorce. There was no sense in doing it sooner—she was pretty sure that discovering he was a father would *not* give Jacob his ideal Christmas. And by January surely she'd know for sure how best to do it.

Merry taped closed the box of decorations and added it to the stack waiting for the courier. 'Okay. What's next?'

'Presents.' It might have taken five hours, but Clara was pretty sure they'd found just the right gifts for Jacob's family. Of course, if they had any sense they'd know instantly that Jacob hadn't chosen them by himself. But then, Clara had found in the past with clients that they believed what they wanted to believe. So the chances were that James, Sheila and Heather would all open their gifts on Christmas morning and gush at how wonderful they were to Jacob.

Quite honestly, as long as Clara wasn't there to see it, she didn't care if the whole family spontaneously began believing in Santa again when they opened them.

'Right. I've got all the gifts from Jacob to his family here, wrapped and labelled. I've got the presents that he dropped round from his mum and dad to ship up there too. And I've got Ivy's bike, plus her stocking, and a suspiciously shiny gold parcel with no tag on it…' Merry looked at Clara expectantly, gold parcel in hand. She gave it a little shake and listened carefully.

Clara rolled her eyes. 'Yes, that's yours. And no, you can't open it until Christmas Day.'

'Spoilsport.' Merry pouted.

'What about our suitcases?' Clara asked as Merry put the gold parcel back in the courier box.

'All packed and ready to go too.' Merry gave her a patient smile. 'Honestly, Clara, I know you want everything to be just perfect, but we're on top of it. In fact we've gone one better than Santa already.'

Clara frowned. 'One better than Santa?'

'We've already made our list and checked it at least *three* times! We're ready. It's time to start looking forward to Christmas instead of fretting about it.'

Clara didn't think she was going to be looking forward to anything until at least January the first—especially with the Harrisons' Charity Gala still to pull off when they got back from Scotland. She'd been working double time after Ivy was in bed all week to try and get everything organised, and to make sure she could still take Boxing Day off to spend with her girl.

'I just don't want anything to go wrong. We just need to stick to the plan…'

As she said the words, the door from the street opened and she felt her heart drop. There, standing in the doorway in his coat and bright red wool scarf, was the one person guaranteed to make her life more difficult.

'Jacob,' she said, trying to muster up a smile. It would all be so much easier if the very sight of him didn't send her mind spiralling into thoughts of what might have been, all over again. 'You're up bright and early. What can we do for you? We're pretty much ready to go here, so if you've got anything you need to add to the courier boxes, speak now.'

'No, I think you're right.' He flashed her a smile but his eyes were still serious. 'We're all ready to go.'

'Great!' Merry clapped her hands together. 'In that case, I'll get these picked up and we can go and catch our train!' Clara allowed herself just a smidgen of hope. Maybe her plan could stay intact after all.

'Actually, I came here to suggest some alternative arrangements,' Jacob said.

No. No alternative arrangements. No deviating from the plan.

Clara swallowed, her mouth suddenly dry and uncomfortable. 'Alternative arrangements?'

'Yes. It seems silly for you to go by train when I'm driving up myself. We'd get up there with much more time to spare. Why don't you come with me?'

Clara glanced across at Merry, wondering how exactly to explain without words that driving to Scotland with her ex-husband sounded like the worst idea anyone had ever had in the history of the world. From the wideness of Merry's eyes, she suspected her friend already knew that.

And she didn't even know about Ivy being Jacob's daughter.

Oh, this was just a nightmare.

Jacob watched as Clara and Merry appeared to undertake some sort of lengthy conversation without actually saying anything. He wished he was adept at translating the facial expressions and eye movements they employed but, as it was, he couldn't follow at all.

Still, he could probably guess the gist of it. Clara would be begging her friend to help her get out of driving to Scotland with him, and Merry would be asking how, exactly, she wanted her to do that.

He was still the client, after all. And the client was always satisfied when it came to Perfect London.

The idea of asking Clara to drive up with him hadn't occurred to him until he was halfway home from his parents' house the day before. Once it had, it had all seemed astonishingly simple.

His father wanted Clara there for Christmas. And, if he was honest, so did Jacob. This was a last-chance family Christmas and, whether she liked it or not, Clara was still family. She was still his wife.

But not for much longer. He was ready to let her go. But if keeping her by his side one last time made his dad feel like all was right with the world, then Jacob would make it happen.

He'd spent the last fifteen years trying to win back his father's pride and love through the family business. It was time to try something new—and marrying Clara had been one of the few decisions Jacob had made outside business that his dad had ever approved of.

Besides, Clara *owed* him. She'd walked out, left him alone on the day after Christmas with barely a word of explanation. Well, there'd been a letter, but it hadn't made any sense to him.

All he'd understood was that he'd failed. Failed as a husband, as a partner. Failed at the whole institution of marriage.

And Fosters did not fail. That one universal truth had been drilled into him from birth and even now it rang through his bones, chastising him every time he thought of Clara.

Jacob had failed once in his life—just the once that mattered—before he'd met Clara. And after that he'd vowed that it would never happen again.

This Christmas, fate had given him a chance to keep that vow. To prove to his father that he was still a success.

He just needed to convince Clara to go along with it.

Eight hours trapped in a car with him should do it, he reckoned.

'So?' he asked, breaking up the silent discussion going on before him. 'What do you think? Drive up with me? You can choose the music.' Which, given what he knew of Clara's musical taste, was quite the concession indeed.

'I can't,' she said, sounding apologetic even though he knew she wasn't. 'I've already got a seat booked on the train up with Merry, and we'll have a few last-minute items to bring up with us…'

'I'm sure she can manage that alone, can't you, Merry?' Jacob turned his best smile onto the petite redhead. Merry, flustered, turned to Clara, her hands outspread.

'I don't know,' she said. 'Can I?'

'Well, there's that…um…extra special thing that needs… transporting,' Clara said, the words coming out halting and strange.

Interesting. Given that he was paying for and had ordered everything that needed to go up to Scotland, what exactly was she trying to hide from him?

Merry knew, it seemed, and caught on instantly. 'Exactly. I mean, if you're happy for me to transport…it, then of course I will. I mean, I'm sure we'll… I'll… I'm sure it will be fine,' she finished, obviously unable to say whatever it was she actually wanted to.

Something else for Jacob to uncover during that eight-hour drive.

'Are you sure? I mean it's a big…responsibility,' Clara said, and the concern in her eyes told him that this had nothing to do with his Christmas. Which just made the whole thing even more interesting.

Merry shook her head. 'It'll be fine,' she said, belying the movement. 'Honestly. I'll just meet you up there with…it.'

'Okay. Well.' Clara turned to Jacob. 'I guess, if you insist.'

'I do,' Jacob confirmed. 'You and I have an awful lot to talk about.'

Clara actually winced at that. He almost wasn't sure he blamed her.

He was going to have a lot of fun on this drive.

'Are you ready to go now?' he asked, more to fluster her than anything else.

'Now?' Her eyes grew extra wide and she looked to Merry in panic. 'No! I mean, I have to do a few things first. And pop home. Um, can we leave a little later?'

By which point they wouldn't arrive any earlier than the train. Since his reasoning for insisting she travel with him was sketchy enough to start with, he really didn't want to put the journey off any longer than necessary.

'I'll pick you up at nine,' Jacob said. 'That gives you over an hour and a half to get everything squared away here. I'm sure, for someone with your efficiency and work ethic, that will be plenty of time.'

'I'm sure it will,' Clara said. But he was pretty sure she was talking through gritted teeth.

He'd take it, anyway.

'I'll see you then,' Jacob said, turning and leaving the office.

It was a rush but Clara managed to get home, explain to her daughter and childminder that Ivy was going to have a brilliant train adventure with Merry and meet Mummy in Scotland, apologise to Merry again for putting her in this position, explain all of Ivy's routines and travel quirks, load her friend up with games, colouring books, snacks and other entertainment for the journey, grab her case and get back to Perfect London by nine o'clock.

Which was why she was still reapplying lipstick and trying to do something with her weather-stricken hair when Jacob arrived again, looking every bit as calm and collected as he had been when he'd demanded that she travel with him.

She'd loathed him when he'd insisted. Even though she knew the problem was half hers. If she'd been able to explain about Ivy, he'd have understood and probably relented. But she couldn't—and even Merry was starting to get suspicious.

At first a one-night stand had seemed like the ideal explanation, when she had realised she was pregnant just weeks after walking out on her husband. The dates were close enough to be believable—even likely, given that Ivy had been born a full two weeks late. But still, it was a little too close for Clara's comfort.

She'd been telling the 'ill-advised one-night stand who didn't want to know when she told him she was pregnant' story for so long now, sometimes she almost believed it herself. But then Ivy would do something—look at her a certain way, tilt her head the same way Jacob did, or just open those all too familiar blue eyes wide—and she'd know without a doubt that Ivy was Jacob's daughter.

Of course, barring a miracle, she'd have to be. There hadn't been anyone else for Clara since she'd left. Or before, for that matter.

'Are you ready?' Jacob asked, eyebrows raised.

Clara pushed the lid back onto her lipstick, checked her reflection one last time, then nodded.

'Ready.'

Part of her wasn't even sure why she was bothering with make-up, just to sit in a car with Jacob for hours. But another part knew the truth. This was warpaint, a mask, camouflage. All of the above.

She needed something between her and her ex-husband. Something to stop him seeing through her and discovering the truth she'd been hiding all these years.

Truths, really. But one of those she wouldn't admit even to herself. 'Let's go,' she said, striding past him.

It was just too depressing. Who wanted to admit they were probably still in love with their husband, five years after they'd walked out on him?

CHAPTER SEVEN

OUTSIDE, PARKED ON the street in a miraculously free parking spot, was the car Clara knew instantly had to be Jacob's. Top of the range, brand-new, flashy and silver—and only two seats. 'Why would I need more?' he'd always said when she'd questioned his penchant for two-seater cars. 'There's room for me and you, isn't there?'

Jacob, she knew, would never understand the need for space; a boot to fit the shopping in, or even a pram. The joy of a tiny face beaming at you from the back seat the minute you opened the door. The space for toys and spare clothes, cloths and nappies and board books and, well, life. Everything she'd lived since she left her marriage.

And everything she'd felt was missing while she'd stayed.

Jacob opened the door for her and she slid in, trying to keep her feet together in their tall black boots, even though her skirt came down to touch her knees. It was all about appearances. Decorum and manners could mask even the most unpleasant of situations.

Wasn't that the British way, after all?

Except Jacob had clearly been living in America too long. The moment he shut the door behind him and started the engine, he dived straight into a conversation she'd been hoping to avoid.

'So, what little extra is Merry bringing to Scotland that you don't want me to know about?'

'It's nothing to do with your perfect Christmas,' Clara assured him. 'Nothing for you to worry about at all, actually.'

'And here was me hoping it might be my Christmas

present,' Jacob said lightly, but the very words made Clara go cold.

She could almost imagine it. *Happy Christmas, Jacob! Here's your four-year-old daughter! Just what you never wanted!*

No. Not happening. Not to her Ivy.

'Not a present,' Clara said shortly. 'Just something I need with me this Christmas.'

'Intriguing.'

'It's really not.'

Jacob was silent for long minutes and Clara almost allowed herself to hope that he might let the rest of the journey pass the same way. But then he spoke again.

'Were you planning to see your family this Christmas?' he asked. 'Before I made you change your plans, I mean.'

The question startled her. Her first instinct was to reply that she *was* spending Christmas with her family, except of course Jacob didn't mean Ivy. He meant her mother and stepfather, or father and his girlfriend of the week, and all the little half-siblings that had replaced her on both sides.

'No. Why would I?'

'I know things were difficult between you—' But he didn't really know, she realised belatedly. She might have hinted that they weren't close but she'd never gone into detail. Never explained what her childhood had been like. Why? Had it just never come up? After all, they'd eloped to Vegas a month and a half after meeting, and she'd left him the following Christmas. There had been no wedding invitations, no seating plans. And whenever he'd mentioned meeting her relatives she'd put him off—until he'd stopped suggesting it altogether.

She supposed she hadn't wanted him to know how unlovable her own family had found her. Not when she was still hoping he really did love and want her.

And so he'd been left with the impression that her family

relationships were 'difficult'. Understatement of the year. 'Difficult' implied differences people could move past. Problems that could be solved.

Being unwanted, unnecessary—those problems didn't have easy fixes. Once her mother had remarried and started her new family, after Clara's dad had walked out, there'd been no place in her mother's life for the accidental result of a teenage pregnancy and shotgun marriage. Clara was merely a reminder of her mistakes—to her mother, her stepdad and the whole community.

Far better to let them get on with their lives, while she made her own. The Fosters had been the closest thing Clara had had to a family in years—until Ivy came along. Now she knew exactly what family meant, and Clara wasn't accepting anything less than a perfect family for her or her daughter.

'I just wondered if things had changed. Since you left, I mean,' Jacob went on, apparently unaware of quite how much she *really* didn't want to have this conversation.

'I can't imagine any circumstances under which they would,' Clara said firmly.

'You might be surprised.' Jacob sounded strangely far away, as if speaking about something he was experiencing right then, only elsewhere.

'My family have never once surprised me.' The words came out flat—the depressing truth by which Clara had lived her life since the age of seven. Until the day she'd turned eighteen and Clara had taken matters into her own hands instead. In the eight years between her mother's remarriage and her eighteenth birthday, Clara had learned a most useful truth: never stay where you're not wanted.

'Wait until you get a phone call from them one day that changes your whole life,' Jacob told her. 'Then we'll talk.'

He was thinking of his father, Clara realised, almost too

late. The way *life* changed, never mind relationships, when days became sharply numbered.

That phone call would never come for her—just like she'd never make it. She didn't even have contact numbers for her parents any more. But that was *her* decision—made moments after Ivy was born, and Clara had known deep in her bones that this tiny scrap of a baby was all the family she would ever need. She'd vowed silently, lying in her hospital bed, that Ivy would always be loved, wanted and cared for. She didn't need grandparents who were incapable of doing that.

But that call *had* come for Jacob.

'When did you find out?' she asked. 'About your dad, I mean.'

'Six months ago. I was in New York on business when he called.'

'And you flew home?'

'Immediately.'

She smiled. That was further evidence that Jacob was beginning to realise the importance and the power of his family. The Fosters were the sort of family that stuck together through everything, because they were glued together with the sort of love that ought to come with a birth certificate…but sometimes didn't. She didn't understand how someone who'd grown up with all of that could be so against the idea of having it for their own family, their own children.

She'd been jealous of that kind of love, once. Even when they were married, she'd always felt on the outside. Now she could only imagine the kind of words they used to describe her in the Foster family.

But she'd been right to leave, Clara knew, and right to stay away. Even if she had been wanted in Jacob's world—and if she'd been sure of that she'd never have felt she had to walk away in the first place—she knew that Ivy wasn't. She wouldn't put her daughter through that, not for anything.

'Dad sent me back to the US,' Jacob went on and Clara turned to him, surprised.

'Why?'

'Because he didn't want his personal ill health to impact on the health of the business.' That was a quote from James Foster, Clara could tell, even though she hadn't seen the man in five years. Success mattered to the Fosters almost as much as family, she'd always thought.

Now she wondered if, sometimes, it might matter even more.

Still, she'd always been very fond of James Foster. A self-made millionaire who had made his fortune by inventing a medical instrument Clara didn't even truly understand the application of, James had all of Jacob's charm, good looks and determination. But it was his son who had taken the company—Foster Medical—to new heights. It was his business brain that had seen the opportunities in a shrinking market, and the path they needed to take.

And James had trusted Jacob to do just that. Not many fathers, Clara thought, would have so happily surrendered the reins of their life's work to their son. She'd always admired James for making that decision.

Of course, he'd been repaid handsomely since then—in money, prestige and the simple pleasure of watching the company he'd founded go from strength to strength. Watching his son succeed, over and over again.

'How is the *business*?' she asked, trying not to sound bitter just speaking the word. She knew for a fact that business success had mattered more than *her*.

'Booming. As is yours, by all accounts.'

That knowledge surprised her, although when she thought about it she realised it shouldn't. He was hiring her company, not just her. Of course he'd look into how well they were doing.

'Merry and I have worked very hard at building up Perfect London,' she said.

'I could tell.' Jacob glanced across at her from the driver's seat. 'I'm glad everything worked out for you.'

'Really?' Clara raised her eyebrows. 'Remember, I was married to you. I'm pretty sure there's a part of you that wishes I'd failed miserably so that you could have swept in and told me you told me so.'

'I never told you so,' Jacob said, frowning. 'I never even realised that you wanted to run your own business. If I had, I'd have helped you. Maybe we could even have worked together.'

Had she even known herself? All she knew for sure was that Jacob had never thought she wanted anything more than he could give her—and that she hadn't known *what* she wanted to do with her life.

Had they really known each other at all? Their whole relationship—from meeting to the moment she'd left—had lasted a year and two days, and it seemed that they'd never talked about the things that really mattered until it was too late. All Jacob had known was the person Clara had shown him—a person so starved for love and attention that she'd done everything she could to be what he wanted.

She'd escaped her family, found a job and a flat-share with a friend, and thought that was all she needed until she'd met Jacob in a London bar one Christmas Eve. Then, all too quickly, really, she'd found love and friendship and family and marriage and for ever...and suddenly she was twenty-one, a wife, and still had no idea what she wanted for herself beyond that.

She hadn't found herself until she'd left him, Clara realised. How sad.

Now she didn't need his approval, his attention. Not just

because she had Ivy and Merry in her life, but because she knew who she was, what she wanted—and she believed she could achieve it all. Realising how she'd changed over the past five years made her want to weep for the girl she'd been.

Turning away, Clara stared out of the window at the passing countryside and wondered what else spending twenty-four hours preparing the perfect Foster family Christmas would teach her about her marriage.

Clara hadn't thought she'd actually be capable of sleeping, not with Jacob in the car next to her, and certainly not the whole way to Scotland. But she'd figured it would at least curb the disturbing conversations if she *pretended* to be asleep, so she'd kept her head turned away, her breathing even, and hadn't even stirred when they stopped for petrol fifteen minutes later. But somehow when she next opened her eyes the scenery around her was decidedly more Highland-like in appearance.

'Sorry about the bends,' Jacob said, his eyes never moving from the road, and Clara realised what had woken her up. 'The satnav seems certain it's this way.'

The car turned another nausea-inducing curve and Clara looked up to see an imposing stone building looming ahead. Crenellations, thick grey stone, arrow slit windows… 'I think that's it!'

'Thank God. Hang on.' Jacob swung the car onto the side of the road and pulled to a stop. Pulling his phone from his pocket, he angled himself out of the car and held it up to capture the view. Clara watched him snap a few shots, then climb back into the car and start the engine again.

'I don't remember you being much of a photographer.' It was an easy subject, at least. With the castle so nearly in sight, and the realisation that she still had the rest of the day and most of tomorrow to spend in his company, at the least, Clara was very grateful for that.

Jacob shrugged. 'It's for posterity. I want Mum and Heather to have something to remember this Christmas by for the rest of their lives.'

'I'm sure they wouldn't forget,' Clara murmured. 'But the photos will be lovely.'

It struck her again what a big thing this was for Jacob to do. Not in terms of money—that was nothing to him, she was sure. No, Jacob had poured something far more valuable into this Christmas weekend. His time, his energy and his thoughts. Jacob was a busy man; Clara knew that better than most. Usually, showing up in time for Christmas lunch and staying long enough for pudding was an achievement for him. This year, not only was he giving his family a whole weekend, he had also helped with the preparation. Well, after some nudging, anyway.

He wasn't just giving his father a perfect last Christmas; he was giving his whole family memories of James that they'd treasure always.

Clara stared up at the castle and pretended the stone walls weren't a little blurry through her suddenly wet eyes.

Maybe Jacob *had* changed, after all. She knew beyond a shadow of a doubt that the man she'd walked out on would never have even thought of arranging a Christmas like this one, let alone being so involved in making it happen.

But could she trust him with her daughter's heart—when he'd already broken her own?

CHAPTER EIGHT

JACOB PULLED THE CAR to a halt just outside the imposing wooden doors of the castle and got out to take a closer look at the location of his Perfect Christmas.

'It doesn't exactly say *homely*,' he said, staring up at the forbidding grey Scottish stone.

'Nor do any of your homes.' Clara slammed the boot closed, their suitcases at her feet, and he winced at the noise.

'My homes are…' he searched for the words '…state-of-the-art.'

'They're all white.' She'd always complained about that, Jacob remembered now. But he couldn't for the life of him remember why he hadn't just told her to decorate if it bothered her that much.

Probably because white was what his interior designer had decided on—what she'd told him was current and up-market and professional. In fact, he distinctly recalled her saying, 'It screams success, darling. Says you don't need anything to stand out.'

Jacob wondered if Clara would have stayed if the walls had been yellow. Or covered in flowers.

Probably not.

'My parents' home isn't white,' he pointed out instead. 'Honeysuckle House is officially the colour of afternoon tea and Victoria sponge.' His mother went out of her way to make their house, by far the largest in their village, appear just like all the others—at least, inside the security gates. As if they didn't have eight times the money of anyone else in their already very affluent surroundings.

'So, somewhere between brown and beige, then?' Clara asked.

'I meant it's homely,' Jacob replied, taking his suitcase from her.

'It is,' Clara admitted. 'I always loved Honeysuckle House.'

'You should go and visit. Dad would love to see you.' The thought of Clara in that space again, the place where he'd grown up, made Jacob's spine tingle. As if his past and his present were mingling and he didn't know what it might mean for his future.

It was something he'd been contemplating on the drive, while she'd slept, merrily scuppering his plans to talk her into staying for Christmas Day with his family. Organising this Christmas had brought Clara back into his life and he couldn't help but think that couldn't just be the end of it. After five years of only communicating through lawyers, they were here together, being civil—friendly, even.

Maybe there wasn't any hope for their marriage, but could they manage to be friends after this? People did become friends with their exes sometimes, didn't they? And the thought of going back to a world without Clara in it… It felt strange. Unwelcoming.

Distinctly unhomely.

Clara ignored his suggestion about visiting his father and instead hefted her handbag onto her shoulder and extended the handle of her tiny suitcase to drag it along behind her. He assumed that she'd sent most of her stuff up with the courier, or poor Merry, because there was no way she had more than the bare essentials in that bag. It was another sign, as if he needed one, that she didn't plan to stay any longer than necessary.

Well, he had the whole of Christmas Eve to work on that. And perhaps her fondness for his father was his way in. After all, it had persuaded her to take on the job in the first place. What was a couple more days at this point?

The thought that he might actually end up paying his ex-wife to spend Christmas with him caused him to frown for a moment, but if that was what it took to give James Foster his dream Christmas then Jacob knew he'd swallow his pride and do it.

Clara pulled a large metal key from her pocket and opened the doors, using her shoulder to help shove them open. Jacob couldn't help but feel that fortifications didn't really scream cosy Christmas, but Clara had said this place was just right so for now he was inclined to trust her.

'Okay, so this is your grand hall,' she said, turning around in the expansive space just beyond the doors.

'There's a suit of armour.' Jacob crossed the hall to touch it. It was real metal armour. 'Are you planning on festooning it with tinsel?'

'I'm planning on putting the tree—which should be arriving this evening, incidentally—here at the bottom of the stairs. I guarantee that by the time I've finished decorating it, no one will be looking at the armour.' He turned to see where she was pointing and clocked the massive staircase that twisted its way up to the first floor. He could almost imagine his mother and Heather descending it, dressed in their Christmas finery. Another photo for the album.

'Besides,' Clara went on, 'I rather thought your father would enjoy the armour. Doesn't he have a thing about medieval military history?'

Jacob blinked. How had he forgotten that? 'Actually, yes. Okay, I'll give you the armour. Now, how about the grand tour?'

'Absolutely.' Clara nodded and, leaning her suitcase against the wall, disappeared down a passageway.

Jacob followed, wondering whether medieval castles also came with central heating.

Clara headed for the kitchen, her heart racing. Okay, so maybe she'd underestimated quite how…*castley* this place was. Still, she could already see it, decorated for Christmas, with the scent of turkey wafting out from the kitchen, presents under the tree…and a couple of glasses of something down everyone's throats. Then it would be perfect.

But first she had to convince Jacob of that.

He'd said that the original perfect Christmas had been spent in a cottage in the Highlands, so she started with the kitchen. She knew from the photos the owner had sent over that it had a large farmhouse-style kitchen table that would be ideal for breakfasts or board games or just chatting over coffee. Between that and the Aga, hopefully Jacob would start to get the sort of feel he wanted from the place.

'This is nice,' he said as he ducked through the low doorway behind her. Rows of copper pots and pans hung from the ceiling and the range cooker had been left on low, keeping the room cosy and warm.

'The owner did the whole place up a year or so ago, to hire out for corporate retreats and the like. It must have cost him a fortune to finish it to this kind of standard but…' She remembered the rates that she—well, Jacob—was paying, and why she'd been so desperate to fill the castle and not have to pay her cancellation charge. 'I guess he figures it's worth the investment.'

'He's done a good job,' Jacob admitted, running his fingers across the cascade of copper on the ceiling. 'So, what is he—some sort of displaced laird, trying to make money from the old family pile?'

'Something like that,' Clara replied. 'Do you want to see the rest?'

Jacob gave a sharp nod and Clara took off through the other door into the next part of the castle. That was another reason why she really wished she'd been able to get up here first and alone. She'd have been able to get the lie of the land, get her bearings. She had a feeling that studying the castle floor plans the night before might not totally cut it.

Still, Jacob seemed impressed by the pantry, already filled

with the food she'd ordered for the festivities. And, once they found their way back into the main part of the castle, the banqueting room, the snug, the parlour and sunroom all went down well. Whilst Jacob managed to make a cutting comment about each, Clara could tell that he was secretly impressed.

So was she. And relieved.

'I still say that nowhere in Scotland needs a sun anything,' Jacob grumbled as they made their way back through the grand hallway to the staircase.

'Ah, but imagine the views from the sunroom if the sun did actually come out,' Clara said. 'And I know you think the banqueting hall is too large—'

'It has a table that sits thirty,' Jacob interjected. 'There's going to be four of us. Five if you agree to stay. You should, you know, just to make the numbers up.'

'But it won't feel big once I've finished decorating it. Well, not so big, anyway,' Clara said. 'And I'm not staying.' He was joking, right? The last place she wanted to spend Christmas was here with her ex-in-laws.

But the look Jacob gave her told her that she was missing something. What on earth had he got planned now? He couldn't really be expecting her to stay, could he? If so, she really needed to nip that idea in the bud.

'We'll see.' Jacob started up the stairs before she could reiterate her determination to head back to the hotel for Christmas Day.

Oh, he was infuriating. Had he been this infuriating when they'd been married? Most likely; she had left him, after all. And if it hadn't been so obvious before their elopement, it was probably only because they'd spent so much of their time together in bed.

A hot flash ran through her body at the memories, making her too warm under her knitted dress and thick tights. Clara bit down on her lip. There was absolutely no time for thoughts like that. Not any more.

She was spending Christmas with Ivy and Merry and that was all she wanted in the world. She followed Jacob up the stairs, ignoring the small part of her mind that pointed out that her Christmas with Ivy could be all the more perfect if Jacob was there too. She needed to time things right. There was too much at risk to just rush in and tell him.

'Now, this room I definitely approve of,' Jacob called out, and Clara hurried towards his voice to find out where he'd got to.

Predictably, he'd found the master bedroom—complete with its antique four-poster bed that looked as if it could sleep twelve and the heavy velvet hangings that gave the room a sumptuous, luxurious feel. This, she could tell from the moment she entered, was a room for seduction.

But not this Christmas, thank you very much.

'This is the room I'd earmarked for your parents,' she said, stopping him before he got too carried away with thoughts of sleeping there. 'It's the biggest, has the easiest access to the rest of the castle and has the largest en suite bathroom. It's also the warmest, thanks to the fireplace.'

Jacob looked longingly at the bed. 'I suppose that makes sense,' he said.

'Come on. I'll show you the rest.'

The other bedrooms were all impressive in their own way but, Clara had to admit, none had quite the charm of the four-poster in the master bedroom.

By the time their tour was finished, Jacob looked much happier with the set-up at the castle.

'Okay,' he said, rubbing his hands together. 'This is going to work. So, what do we do next?'

'*I* need to do some final checks before I have to head to the hotel for the night. I'll do the decorating and so on tomorrow, before your family arrive. They get in at four, right?'

Jacob nodded. 'Yeah. But why don't you just stay here tonight? It's not like there aren't enough bedrooms.'

For one blinding flash of a moment Clara's brain was filled with images of her and Jacob taking advantage of that four-poster bed.

No. Bad brain.

'I need to check in to the hotel,' she said, trying to banish the pictures from her mind. 'Besides, Merry will be arriving this evening too.'

'Of course. Merry.' What was that in his voice? Could it be…jealousy? No. She didn't remember him ever being jealous about who she'd spent her time with when they were actually properly married. It was highly unlikely he was about to start now.

'Anyway. I need to get on, so you can…settle in, I guess. Work, if you want to.' And didn't he always? She was surprised he'd made it this long without setting up his laptop. 'I can get you the Wi-Fi password if you want.'

'There's nothing I can do to help?' Again, Clara felt that strange tug on her heart as she realised how eager he was to be a real part of the planning.

'I'm mostly just checking that the local supplies I ordered have been delivered, and waiting for the courier company to arrive and unload the boxes. Then I'll grab a taxi down to the hotel and make a few calls to confirm the bits being delivered tomorrow—fresh greenery, fresh food, those sort of things. After that, everything can wait until tomorrow. I've got it all in hand. You really don't need to worry.' It was all there on her time plan.

She checked her watch. In fact…

The knock on the door, precisely on time, made her smile.

'That will be Bruce,' she announced.

Jacob frowned. 'Who is Bruce?'

'Bruce the Spruce,' Clara said with a grin. 'Your perfect Christmas tree.'

CHAPTER NINE

It was easy to busy herself in getting the castle ready for Christmas. All she needed to do was stick to her schedule, count the courier boxes that had arrived and ignore Jacob hovering near her shoulder, checking up on everything she was doing. At least then she had a chance of making it to the hotel before Ivy's bedtime. Maybe she could stay up a bit later than normal…

'I do know how to do this, you know,' she snapped finally, when she turned to put the box with the Christmas lights in by the tree ready for the morning and almost crashed into him. 'It's my job.'

Jacob stepped back, hands raised in apology. 'I know, I know. I just feel like I should be doing something to help, that's all.' Clara bit back a laugh. All those months of marriage she'd spent complaining that she wanted him to stop working and spend time with her, and the one time *she* wanted to be left alone to work she couldn't get rid of him! Even Clara could appreciate the irony.

But their conversation in the car had got her thinking. Maybe that had been part of the problem—she hadn't had anything except him in her life so she'd clung too desperately to him. She'd been lopsided, like a Christmas tree with decorations only on one side. She needed decorating all the way around. And now, with Perfect London, and Ivy and even Merry, she had that. Well, almost. There might be a few branches still in need of some sparkle. Or some love…

Could Jacob provide that? Did she *want* him to? Clara had been so focused on what he might mean to Ivy, she had barely paused to consider what it might mean for *her* to have him back in her life.

'Can't I start decorating Bruce or something?' Jacob asked, bringing her attention back to the cold, undecorated castle hallway.

'Bruce needs to settle in overnight,' she explained. 'To let his branches drop, and let him suck up plenty of water to keep him going. I'll decorate him in the morning.'

'Then what *can* I do?' Jacob asked.

'I told you—go do some work or something.'

'I don't want to.'

Clara stilled at his words. What she would have given to hear him say that about work when they'd been married. Now it just made her suspicious. What was he playing at?

'I don't need you dancing attendance on me, Jacob. I'm not your guest—I'm here to work. You're not responsible for me, you know.'

Something flashed across Jacob's face. Was it…relief? Relief that he could get back to work, she supposed.

But he surprised her. 'Fine. But this is still my Christmas. I want to help. Give me something to do.'

Clara shrugged. If that was what he wanted… Flipping through the stack of paper on her clipboard, she pulled off a sheet and handed it to him.

'Box Seventeen?' he asked, reading the title.

'It's that one over there.' Clara pointed to a medium-sized brown box liberally labelled with the number seventeen on all sides. 'Check through it and make sure that everything on that list is in there.'

'Didn't you check them when you packed them?' Jacob slit open the box and Clara tried not to stop breathing as the scissors went a little deeper through the tape than she liked.

'Three times,' she confirmed. 'And now we check them again.'

'Were you always this hyper-organised?'

'I may have got worse since starting Perfect London,' Clara admitted. 'But pretty much, yes.'

Another thing that had set her apart from her own family. Her mother had always been the spontaneous, play-it-by-ear type. The day Clara had left for university—a date circled in red on the calendar for months in advance—her mother had decided to take the rest of the family on an impromptu trip to the seaside. Leaving Clara to find her own way to university with whatever luggage she could carry on the train.

Conversely, the only spur-of-the-moment thing Clara had ever done was marry Jacob.

'So, I guess this must be pretty weird for you,' Jacob said, looking up from his box.

'Weird? Working with a client?' Clara said. 'No, not at all. I mean, it's not the way we usually—'

'I meant setting up Christmas with your ex-husband,' Jacob interrupted her.

'Oh. Well, yes. That is a little more unusual,' she admitted. 'I mean, it would have to be, wouldn't it? I've only ever had the one husband. And technically you're not even officially my ex yet.' Great. Now she was waffling, and drawing attention to the fact that he'd spent five years not agreeing to a divorce, just when he was finally offering to do exactly that. And she was starting to wonder if she really wanted him to… *Could* he be the father Ivy needed?

And what about the husband she needed? Surely that was a dream too far.

'Yet,' Jacob repeated, his voice heavy. 'Actually, that's one of the reasons I wanted you to travel up with me, so I could talk to you.'

'Oh?' That really didn't sound good at all. 'What about?'

'My father… He's very sick.' The words came haltingly, as if Jacob was still only just admitting this truth to himself.

'So I understand.' That was, after all, the only reason she was in this mess at all. And they'd already spoken about it.

This wasn't news, which meant there had to be something more. Something worse.

'He was always very fond of you,' Jacob said.

'I was always very fond of him too,' Clara admitted with a small smile.

'Fonder than you were of me, as it turned out.' Jacob flashed her a quick, sharp grin to show he was joking, but the comment sliced at her heart anyway.

'That was never the problem,' she murmured, and regretted it instantly. She'd just given him an opportunity to ask her again why she'd left. He wasn't going to leave that just hanging there. Not if she knew Jacob at all. And, as her dreams reminded her on dark, lonely nights, she had really thought she did.

'I always thought you were going to come back, you know,' he said after a moment.

So did I. But that had been before a positive pregnancy test had changed her life forever.

Clara would never regret having Ivy in her life, not for a single moment. But she knew falling pregnant had cost her Jacob, and that thought still haunted her sometimes.

'Your note said you needed time to think,' Jacob went on when she didn't answer.

'I did.' She'd thought and thought, working her way through every possible outcome, every potential reaction that Jacob might have to her news. But she'd always come to the same stark conclusion.

Jacob Foster didn't want kids. Not ever.

'So you thought. And…?'

'And I realised that our marriage was never going to work,' she said, as simply as she could. 'I wasn't happy, and you weren't in a position to make me happy.'

It was only later that she'd realised that no man could ever make her happy. She had to find that happiness in herself. And she had—by building her own career, her own family, her own *life*. Finally, she relied on herself, not others, for her own happiness.

But sometimes, alone at night, she couldn't help but wonder if she'd become a little *too* self-reliant in that area.

'I seem to recall making you pretty ecstatic more than once,' Jacob joked, but there wasn't any levity in his words. She could hear the concern underneath and that mantra she knew he lived by: *What did I do wrong? How can I fix it? I will not fail at this...*

It was an exhausting way to live. And it had been just as exhausting being the one he was trying to fix, the person he wanted to win, to succeed at being with, all the time.

'That was sex, Jacob. Not life.' Except, at the time, it had felt like both. It had felt as if their entire existences were tied up in the way they moved together, the way she felt when he touched her, his breath on her skin, her hair against his chest… It had been everything.

Until suddenly it hadn't been enough.

'Maybe that's where we went wrong,' he said. 'Too much sex.'

Clara laughed, even though it wasn't funny.

'Maybe it was,' she said. 'Or rather, too much time having sex, not enough talking.'

'Talking about what?' Jacob asked.

Clara rolled her eyes. 'Everything! Anything! Jacob, we met in a bar on Christmas Eve and we barely came up for air until March.'

'I remember.' The heat in his voice surprised her, after all this time. Did he still feel that connection? The one that had drawn them together that night and seemed to never want to let them go.

She bit her lip. She had to know. 'Do you? Do you remember how it was? How we were?'

'I remember everything.' Clara's body tightened at his words. 'I remember how I couldn't look away from your eyes. They mesmerised me. I remember I was supposed to go home for Christmas the next day but I couldn't leave your bed. Couldn't be apart from you, no matter what day it was. I thought I might go insane if I couldn't touch your skin…'

So he did remember. She'd thought she might have embellished the memory of that connection over the years, but he described it just the way she remembered it feeling. Like an addiction, a tie between them. Something she couldn't escape and didn't even want to.

'What went wrong for us, Clara?' Jacob asked softly.

She shook her head, the memory dissipating. 'That connection… It wasn't enough. We didn't ever talk about our lives, about what we wanted, about who we really were.' All these years, she'd thought their problems had been simple: Jacob had loved work more than her, and he had never wanted a family. She'd wanted his love, his attention…and his baby. They were just incompatible. But now…she wondered if she'd had it wrong all along. Maybe they would have had a chance if they'd built on that connection to really get to know each other instead of burning it up in passion. 'How did we expect to build a life together when we didn't even know what the other person wanted, let alone if we could give it?'

'I couldn't give you what you wanted—is that what you're saying?' He sounded honestly curious, but Clara knew he'd be beating himself up inside.

'I'm saying that I didn't know what I wanted when I married you,' Clara explained. 'And by the time I did…by the time I realised I wanted more than just fantastic sex and nice parties and too many houses…it was too late.'

'I wanted more than just that, you know. I wanted forever with you.'

Clara's heart contracted. How had this happened? How had she ended up somewhere in the Highlands having this conversation with her ex-husband? A conversation she'd been avoiding for five long years.

'I know,' she admitted. 'And I wanted that too.' She couldn't tell him that, sometimes, she still did. Because having forever with Jacob would mean not having Ivy, and that was simply not possible.

This was her moment, her chance to tell him about his daughter. Her hands shook as she turned back to the box she was unpacking, trying to focus on the exquisitely wrapped gifts and shiny paper. She needed to tell him. But his family would be arriving tomorrow and she had work to do and… She could make excuses forever. The truth was, she was scared.

She took a breath, trying to slow her heart rate. January; that was the plan. She needed to stick to her plan. The New Year would be on them soon enough.

'You were talking about your father,' she said, suddenly aware they'd been diverted from his original topic. 'Was there…? It seemed like there was something more you wanted to say about him.'

'Yes.' Jacob glanced over at her, long enough for her to see the indecision in his eyes. What on earth was he going to ask?

Much as she dreaded it, Clara had to know. 'So…?'

Jacob set his list aside, abandoning Box Seventeen completely. 'Like I said, he's always been fond of you. I think… I know that he'd really like it if you could be here for this, his last Christmas.'

'Here…at the castle? With you?' She'd really hoped he'd been teasing when he'd mentioned it earlier. The idea didn't bear thinking about. 'It's your family Christmas, Jacob. I'm pretty sure ex-wives don't get invited.' Not to mention the fact that there'd be a distraught little girl at a hotel a couple of miles away, wondering where her mother was on Christmas morning.

'Ah, but as you pointed out, we're not actually exes yet. Not officially.' Her own words were now coming back to haunt her. Great. As if the Ghost of Husband Past wasn't enough of a Christmas present.

'We haven't been together for five years, Jacob,' she said. 'I think we qualify under these terms.'

'Still. You're putting together this perfect Christmas. Don't you want to stay and enjoy it too?'

No. She wanted to have her own perfect Christmas, with Merry and Ivy. With a new bike and champagne at breakfast and maybe a snowball fight after lunch.

She did *not* want to spend Christmas with Jacob's mother and sister glaring at her over the turkey.

'I don't think that would be a very good idea,' she said in what she hoped was a diplomatic manner. It occurred to her that this would all have been a lot easier if she'd just told him about Ivy the day he'd walked back into her life. He'd probably have run for the hills and she wouldn't be in Scotland at all. 'I mean, I'm sure your family aren't so fond of me any more. I can't imagine they've forgiven me for walking out on you.'

'Maybe not,' Jacob conceded. 'I mean, you broke my heart. Families tend to get a little upset about that sort of thing.'

'I imagine so.' Not that she'd really know herself. 'Most families, anyway.' She'd never even told hers she was getting married in the first place, let alone that she'd left Jacob.

'Not yours?' His gaze flicked towards hers, then back down again. Clara shook her head. If she'd managed to not discuss her family with Jacob when they were actually together, she wasn't going to start now.

'So, probably not a good idea,' Clara said. 'We're agreed.'

'Well, I agree it wouldn't be a good idea if they still thought you broke my heart.' Clara's breath escaped her. What did he mean? That he'd found someone new so he wasn't heartbroken any more? Because on the one hand she really wanted to be the bigger person and be happy for him. But on the other… There wasn't a chance she was spending her Christmas with Jacob, his family and his *new girlfriend,* no matter how ill his dad was.

'Don't they?' she said, wishing she could breathe properly again but knowing it wouldn't be possible until she had her answer.

'They won't if we pretend we're back together,' Jacob said, and Clara lost the ability to breathe altogether.

'I…I don't…'

Jacob didn't think he'd ever rendered Clara so speechless before. Well, maybe once. That night on the balcony of the Los Angeles house, after that party, with her only half wearing that gold dress…

But that wasn't the point.

'It would make the old man's Christmas just to think we were even trying to make our marriage work again,' he said, pushing home with the guilt. He needed her to agree to this. Surely she *owed* him this. He'd given her the world, and she'd given him a note asking for time to think and then divorce papers, two months later. All because they hadn't talked enough? That, Jacob had found, was usually more easily solved by *staying in the same country as someone.*

Clara owed him more than a fake relationship for Christmas.

'But it wouldn't be real,' she said. Clara's eyes darted around desperately, as if she were searching the castle for secret passageways she could escape through.

'No. We'd just play happy families for Dad's sake.'

'Until…' She trailed off, and he realised she was avoiding saying the words *Until he dies?*

'Until after Christmas,' he clarified. 'All he wants is to know that there's a chance. That we're trying.' And if it delayed the inevitable divorce until it was too late for his father to worry about it that would be a bonus.

'I can't… I can't stay for Christmas Day, Jacob,' she said, finally finding the words. 'No. I'm sorry.'

She didn't sound very sorry. She sounded like this was a punishment he was somehow inflicting on her, instead of spending Christmas with people who had once been her family.

'Just think about it,' he said. 'That's all I ask.'

'There's no point,' Clara said. 'I can't do it, Jacob. I have…other obligations.'

Other obligations. Jacob's mouth tightened. He could only imagine what they might be. Through all their conversations she'd conspicuously failed to rule out another man in her life. And what was Merry transporting up here on the train? Some perfect gift for Clara's perfect man?

'You never said,' he bit out. 'Where are you spending Christmas?'

'Merry and I have booked into a hotel a couple of miles away,' she said, not looking at him. 'Roaring fire, haggis for breakfast, that sort of thing. I wasn't sure we'd have time to get back to London after all the set-up on Christmas Eve, so this seemed like the best option.'

'Just you and Merry?' he asked, dreading the answer.

'I think the hotel is fully booked, actually. We only just managed to get the last two rooms.'

Two rooms. But who was Clara sharing hers with? That was what Jacob wanted to know.

'That's not quite what I meant.'

'Really? Then I can't imagine what you did mean.' Clara turned to look at him at last, her eyes fierce. 'Since my life, my Christmas and who I choose to spend it with are absolutely none of your business any more.'

She was right; that was the worst thing. He wanted her to be wrong, wanted to claim that the piece of paper that announced they were still technically married meant it *was* his business. But that was a low move, even he knew that. Five years apart. He couldn't honestly have expected her to stay celibate that whole time.

He just wanted to know…

'Look, all I'm asking for is a couple of days,' Jacob said, aware he was getting perilously close to begging. 'Just stay and make Dad happy. Make me happy. Then I'll give you your divorce.'

'No. A wife is for life, not just for Christmas, Jacob.'

'Really? Where was that bit of trite philosophy when you walked out on me?'

'Where were you?' she asked. 'It was Boxing Day, for heaven's sake. The day after Christmas Day. And you hadn't been home in sixteen hours by the time I left. If you're suddenly all about Christmas being a time for family, answer me this—why weren't you there to spend it with me?'

'I…I had to work.' It was the lamest excuse in the book, and he knew it. But it was all he had.

Clara sighed. 'Jacob, you've made it very clear you don't want *me* at all. Just the appearance of a wife to prove to your father that you've got your life in order.'

'Hey, you're the one who left me,' he pointed out. 'If anyone has made it clear they wanted out of this marriage, it's you.'

Clara shook her head. 'I thought…just for a moment, I thought you might have changed. Grown up. But it's all still an act to you, isn't it? Be honest. You married me because all the other top-level businessmen you worked with had the perfect wife at home and you wanted it too. The sex was just a bonus. You never even *asked* what I wanted out of our relationship. And I was so stupidly desperate for any affection at all that I didn't even question it. Our marriage wasn't a relationship—it was a business merger.

You sealed the deal then went back to work, and left me wondering what I was supposed to do next.' She grabbed her bag and threw her coat over her arm.

'I won't be in another fake relationship with you, Jacob,' she said and for a moment his heart clenched the same way it had five years ago, as he'd read her note and realised that she had left him again. 'All we have left now really *is* business. I'll see you tomorrow.'

And then she was gone.

CHAPTER TEN

CLARA WRAPPED HER COAT tighter around her shivering body as she scanned the darkening road down from the castle towards the village for any sign of headlights. The taxi she'd called had promised it wouldn't be long. She checked her watch. If it made it in the next ten minutes she could be at the hotel waiting to greet Merry and Ivy when they arrived.

That was what she was focusing on. *Her* family. *Her* perfect Christmas. Not Jacob's.

She couldn't think about him now. Couldn't let herself stop and absorb the realisation that all she'd ever really been to him was a useful accessory, like a laptop or a briefcase. She'd felt neglected when they were married, sure. Even unwanted, or unloved towards the end. But she'd never felt as unimportant to him as she did today—at the very moment when he was telling her he needed her to stay.

But not for herself. Not for Clara. For what she represented—his own success. To show his dad that he wasn't a failure. That was all.

He'd made her think he wanted her. For one fleeting moment, she'd almost believed that he still loved her. But it was all still just a game to him, the same way their whole marriage had been. It was the game of life—a game Jacob was bound and determined to win.

She'd asked him why he hadn't stayed for that Christmas night, but she'd known the true answer before he'd spoken. He'd said he had to work, of course, but she knew what that really meant, now.

He hadn't considered her part of his family. Just like her own parents hadn't, in their way. Just like her stepdad hadn't. She hadn't been important to him either—certainly not as important as his work, or her stepbrothers. She hadn't mattered at all.

But she mattered to Ivy. She mattered now. And he could never take that away from her.

How could she have thought that he'd changed? That he might be *worthy* of knowing his incredible daughter?

Jacob Foster would never know the true value of love, of family, of relationships—of her. Not if he was willing to use her just to prove a point to his father.

Ivy didn't need that kind of person in her life. She didn't need a father who would swoop in and show her off when it benefitted him and ignore her the rest of the time. She needed someone who would show her that she mattered every day of her life.

And so, Clara realised as she finally saw the taxi's headlights approaching, did she.

Alone in the castle that evening, Jacob stared up at the monstrously large Christmas tree in the hallway, obscuring the suit of armour, and wondered if this whole thing had been a massive mistake.

Not Christmas in general, or even bringing his family together for this last perfect Christmas. But asking Clara to organise it.

He couldn't have done it all himself, he knew. He had many skills and talents but organising the details of an event like this weren't among them. Clara, on the other hand, seemed to thrive on such minutiae. He'd caught a glimpse of her clipboard while she was debating the exact position of the tree, and discovered that she had everything planned down to the minute. She knew exactly what needed to happen every hour of every day until Christmas was over. She'd probably leave them a timetable for festive fun when she headed back to the hotel tomorrow.

She'd even named the Christmas tree. Who called a tree Bruce, anyway?

No, he couldn't have done it without her, but still he wondered if he should have asked someone else. Or if she should have said no. If seeing her again was only going to make things far worse in the long run.

Maybe he should just have given her a divorce five years ago, when she first asked, and skipped this current misery.

Had she really meant everything she said? That he'd not just neglected her but *used* her? And he'd been thinking she owed him for walking out. Perhaps he owed *her* more than he thought.

Sighing, Jacob sank down to sit at the bottom of the stairs. He'd known all along that the chances of him being a good husband—a good man—were slim, no matter how hard he tried. He'd proved that before he'd even turned eighteen. That disastrous night… Burned into his mind was the memory of his mother's face, wide-eyed with horror and disbelief, and the stern, set jaw of his father that night, all mingled with the sound of the ambulance tyres screeching up the driveway on a winter night…

But worse, far worse, was the image of Heather's tiny body, laid out on a stretcher, and the sobbing wrenched from his own body.

He forced it out of his mind again.

He should never have got married in the first place. He should have known better. He'd let himself get swept away in the instant connection he'd felt with Clara and had told himself what he needed to hear to let the relationship carry on far past the point he should have ended it. It should have been two weeks of intimacy, a wonderful Christmas holiday memory to look back on years later.

Because he didn't deserve anything more, anything deeper than that.

He'd reassured himself that Clara was an adult, that she

could take care of herself. But it seemed a heart was even easier to break than a body.

Jacob buried his head in his hands, his fingers tightening in his hair. His father had known, he realised. James had known that marriage was beyond him—he'd practically said it when Jacob had brought Clara home to meet the family! All his talk about responsibility… What he'd meant was: *Do you really think you can do this?*

And Jacob had proven he couldn't.

He'd been all Clara had, it dawned on him now, too late. He'd been given the gift of her love and all he'd had to do in return was take care of it. She was wrong about one thing, at least—he *had* loved her. She'd never been a convenience, an accessory, even if apparently that was how he'd treated her.

He'd broken her. Let her down. He'd pulled away because he'd been scared—scared of how deeply he felt for her, and scared of screwing it up. That he wasn't up to the responsibility of being a husband.

Maybe he still wasn't. But he liked to think he was a better man at thirty-one than he'd been at twenty-five, and a world better than he'd been at sixteen. He was improving, growing. He might never be a good man, but he could be a *better* one.

And a better man would apologise to the woman he'd hurt.

Jumping to his feet, Jacob grabbed his car keys and his coat and headed out to find Clara's hotel.

It wasn't hard to find; the twisting road down from the castle didn't have much in the way of buildings along it and the Golden Thistle Hotel was the first he came to.

Swinging the door open wide, he stepped inside and… promptly realised he had no idea what he was going to say. Clara hadn't answered him when he'd asked who she was staying with. What if she really was there with another man? The last thing she'd want was her ex-husband storming in, even if he was there to apologise.

'Can I help you?' the teenage girl behind the reception desk asked.

'Um…' Jacob considered. He was there now, after all. 'Are you still serving food?' At least that way he'd have an excuse for being there if Clara stumbled across him before he decided on his next move.

The receptionist cheerfully showed him through to the bar, where he acquired a snack menu and a pint and settled down to study his surroundings.

It wasn't entirely what he'd expected. Not that he'd given it a huge amount of thought. But he'd imagined Clara to be staying in a wildly romantic boutique hotel, with no kids and plenty of champagne and roses. The Golden Thistle Hotel, while lovely, seemed a rather more laid-back affair. The roaring fires were cosy and the prints on the stone walls were friendly rather than designer. The low, beamed ceilings and sprigs of holly on the tables made it feel welcoming, somehow, and somewhere in the next room someone was belting out carols at a piano.

But there was no sign of Clara, or Merry. And the longer he sat there, the less inclined Jacob was to look for them. How would he find them, anyway? Explain to the nice receptionist that he was looking for his estranged wife? That was likely to get him thrown out on his ear if the woman had any sense.

He shouldn't be here. She had been right. It wasn't any of his business who Clara chose to spend Christmas with. Not any more. And maybe she'd been telling the truth; maybe it really was just her and Merry. Perhaps she just wanted to get away from him. And, given his current actions, who could blame her?

She'd left him once. He really shouldn't be surprised if she kept trying to repeat the action.

Jacob drained the last of his pint and got to his feet. Never mind the bar snacks, or his wife. He'd head back to the castle, eat whatever had been left in the fridge for him and go to bed. And tomorrow he'd be professional, adult and considerably less of a stalker.

He'd apologise when she arrived for work. They'd get through Christmas and they'd be divorced in the New Year. He'd give Clara her life back, at least, to do whatever she wanted with it.

Without him.

Glancing into the next room on his way past, he saw a small girl standing on the table, singing 'We Wish You A Merry Christmas' at the top of her lungs and turned away. A perfect Christmas—that was what he was here for. Not to reconcile with his wife, or even exact some sort of revenge on her for leaving him. This weekend was about his family, not his love life.

Clara was his employee now, not his wife. And once this Christmas was over, she wouldn't be his anything at all.

He had to remember that.

Clara arrived at the castle bright and early on Christmas Eve, wrapped up warm and in full warpaint make-up, ready to be professional, aloof and totally unbothered by Jacob Foster. Today, he was her client, not her ex, and all they had to discuss were Christmas plans and decorations. Nothing to do with their marriage—and definitely nothing to do with Ivy.

She'd caught a taxi up to the castle, loaded full of the last few essentials that her friend had brought up herself, not trusting them to the courier company. Namely, the Foster family antique decorations and Jacob's Christmas presents to his family. Everything else she figured she could replace or improvise if the courier company let them down.

But they hadn't. All the boxes had arrived, just as they'd

packed them. The tree was in place, the final food delivery was expected within the hour from the local butcher and deli. All she had to do now was 'Christmasify' the castle. And that was Clara's favourite part.

Normally, she'd have Merry along to help her, but today her business partner had taken Ivy off into the local town to do some last-minute Christmas shopping in the hire car Merry had picked up at the station the day before. Hot chocolates had also been mentioned. Clara was trying very hard not to feel envious; she needed to work and Ivy understood that. Plus, spending time with Aunt Merry was always a special treat for her daughter.

At least they'd all managed to have a wonderful evening together last night at the Golden Thistle Hotel, when she'd finally got done at the castle. She hadn't been completely sure when Merry had suggested the place, but it was the closest and easiest hotel on offer. As it turned out, though, it was wonderful. The staff had welcomed Ivy in particular with open arms, and they'd spent the evening eating chips and then mince pies in the bar while one of the locals played Christmas carols on the old piano there. It hadn't been long before Ivy had been singing along too, much to everyone's delight. All in all, the evening had been the ideal respite after the hideous few hours with Jacob at the castle.

Had he honestly believed that Clara would spend Christmas there, just to make his father a tiny smidgen happier? He couldn't honestly believe that James would care all that much about his ex-daughter-in-law being there, could he? Clara was pretty sure that as long as Sheila, Jacob and Heather were there, everything would be perfect as far as James was concerned.

And as long as she had Ivy and Merry, Clara knew the Golden Thistle would be perfect for her too. In fact, she couldn't wait to get back there this evening and spend Christmas Eve with her girl. The owners had already said that Ivy was welcome to hang her stocking by the main fire, to make it as easy as possible for Father Christmas to find her that night. Ivy had positively vibrated with excitement at the thought.

Yes, Christmas was here and it was wonderful. All Clara had to do was hope that Jacob had come to his senses, get through a few more hours of setting up the castle for the Fosters, and then she could start enjoying herself. This year, she'd decided, would be the one to make up for all those miserable childhood Christmases—not to mention the last lonely one with Jacob.

She shivered as she stepped out of the car onto the frosty castle driveway. There was no snow yet, but the forecast said there would be overnight. All the more reason for Clara to get the job done and get out. The air around her was bitterly cold, cutting into every centimetre of exposed skin, and Clara was thankful for her scarf and gloves, and even the woolly hat Ivy had pushed onto her head before she'd left.

'You don't want to catch a cold, Mummy,' she'd said sternly, and Clara had given up worrying about what it might do to her hair.

Letting herself in to the castle, a box of decorations balanced on one hip, Clara wondered whether she should call out to Jacob. He could be sleeping, she supposed, or working. Either way, she probably shouldn't interrupt him. Besides, she'd work quicker on her own.

By the time he appeared, dressed in jeans and a jumper and heavy boots, she'd already brought in all her boxes and waved the taxi off, unpacked the fresh food delivery, and twined freshly cut greenery all the way up the twisting banister. She was just adding the ribbons and baubles to the stair display when she heard his voice.

'What are you doing?' he asked from the top of the stairs. He sounded amused, which she hoped meant that he planned to ignore the way they'd parted the day before too. The only thing for it, as far as Clara was concerned, was to get back to being client and organiser as soon as possible.

Clara glanced up, one end of the ribbon she was tying still caught between her lips. 'Decorating,' she said through clenched teeth. It came out more like 'Echoratin' but he seemed to get the idea.

'Need a hand?' He jogged effortlessly down the stairs and Clara allowed herself just a moment to appreciate the way his lean form moved under his winter clothes; the clench of a thigh muscle visible through his jeans, the way his shoulders stretched the top of his sweater. Call it a Christmas present to herself.

Then she turned her attention back to her ribbon before he caught her ogling. The man's ego did not need the boost, and she didn't need him thinking he might be able to find a way out of their divorce agreement.

'You could start on Bruce, I suppose,' Clara said doubtfully. Then she realised that Jacob Foster probably had no idea about the right way to decorate a tree and changed her mind. 'Or maybe the table decorations.' They, at least, were already made up and just needed putting in place.

'Or I could make you a coffee and fetch you a mince pie?' he suggested. 'As an apology for yesterday. And, well, our entire marriage.'

'Tea,' she reminded him. 'But actually, that sounds great.'

He returned a few minutes later with a mug and plate in hand. Clara took them gratefully and sat down on the nearest step to eat her mince pie. The early start had meant forgoing breakfast at the hotel, and she realised now that might have been a mistake. Decorating was hungry work.

'I *am* sorry,' he said, standing over her. 'About everything. Not just asking you to fake a relationship for the sake of my pride, but for not giving you what you needed when we were married.'

Clara shrugged, swallowing her mouthful of pastry. 'Forget it. I guess it was inevitable that some old thoughts and habits would come up with us working together. But in a few hours I'll be out of your hair and you can get on with your Christmas and forget all about me.' Now she said it out loud, the thought wasn't actually all that appealing.

'I don't want to forget about it,' Jacob replied. 'Not yet. I…I wasn't made for marriage. I should have known that and not let myself give in to what I wanted when I'd only hurt you in the long run.'

Not made for marriage? Because he cared more about his work than people? Clara supposed he might have a point. Still, she couldn't help but feel a little sad for him, if work was all he'd ever have.

'I should have talked to you more,' she admitted. 'Explained how I felt. But it was all tied up in my family and I…'

'Didn't want to tell me about them,' Jacob guessed. He sat down on the step below, those broad shoulders just a little too close for comfort. Clara could smell his aftershave, and the oh, so familiar scent sent her cascading back through the years in a moment. So much for forgetting. As if that was even possible. If she hadn't forgotten him throughout those five long years apart, why would she begin now, just because he finally signed a piece of paper for her? 'Why was that?'

Clara looked down at her plate. Suddenly the remaining half of her mince pie seemed less appealing.

'You don't have to tell me,' Jacob added. 'I know it's none of my business any more. I'd just like to understand, if I can.'

'My mother… She fell pregnant with me when she was sixteen,' Clara said after a moment. Was that the right place to start? *I was born, I wasn't wanted.* Wasn't that the six-word summary of her life? 'I was an accident, obviously. Her parents demanded that she marry my dad, which was probably the worst idea ever.'

'Worse than our marriage?' Jacob joked.

'Far worse. At least we had a few months of being happy together. I don't think they even managed that.' She sighed, remembering the fights, the yelling. Remembering the relief she'd felt, just for a moment, when her father had left and her mother met someone else. Until she'd realised what that meant for her place in the family. 'My mother always said that I was the biggest mistake she'd ever made in her life.'

Jacob's sharp intake of breath beside her reminded her exactly where she was, who she was talking to. A client, not her ex.

She flashed him a too bright fake smile. 'Anyway. Needless to say, they don't miss me. My father left when I was seven, my mum remarried a few years later and started a new family. One she really wanted. I became…surplus to requirements. That's all.'

'Clara…I'm so sorry. If I'd known…' He trailed off, presumably because he knew as well as she did he wouldn't have done anything differently. Except maybe not marry her in the first place.

She shrugged. 'I'm a different person now. I don't need them.' *Or you.* 'I have my own life. I'm not the girl I was when my dad left, or the teenager being left out by her new family. I'm not even the person I was when I married you. I don't even drink coffee any more!' She tried for a grin, hoping it didn't look too desperate. Anything to signal that this part of the conversation was over. She didn't need Jacob feeling sorry for her.

He took the cue, to her relief. 'So what turned you off coffee, anyway? Some sort of health kick?'

'Something like that.' Clara gave him another weak smile. Why on earth had she chosen that as her example? She couldn't exactly explain about the morning sickness, or the fact that caffeine was bad for the baby, could she? 'I guess I'm just out of the habit now.'

'Funny. You used to swear it was the only thing that could get you going in the mornings.' At his words, another memory hit her: Jacob bringing her coffee in bed before he left for work in the morning and her distracting him, persuading him to stay just a few more minutes… She bit her lip, trying not to remember so vividly the slide of her hands under his shirt, or the way he'd fallen into her kisses and back into her bed.

She couldn't afford to let herself remember. Couldn't risk anything that could lead her back there, back to the girl she'd been when she married him. She'd moved on, changed. And Ivy needed her to be more than that girl. She needed her to be the Clara she'd grown up into. Ivy's mother.

And she couldn't take the chance of Jacob seeing how much of him she still carried in her heart either. She had to shut this conversation down. Fast.

'Now I get up excited to live my life,' she said bluntly and lifted her mug to her lips to finish her tea. It was time to get back to work. 'Things are different.'

'Yeah,' Jacob said, his expression serious, his eyes sad. 'You're happy.'

Clara's heart tightened at the sorrow in his words. But he was right; she *was* happy in her new life. And she needed to cling on to that.

So she said, 'Yes, I am,' knowing full well that she drove the knife deeper with every word.

CHAPTER ELEVEN

How had he not known? How could he have loved a woman, married her even, and not known how she had grown up? That her biggest fear had been being unwanted, unloved?

This was why he couldn't be trusted with people. He'd had a whole year with Clara and he'd never learned even this most basic truth about her. And he'd hurt her deeply because of it.

The Foster family prided itself on success, on not making the stupid sort of mistakes others made. And in business Jacob was the best at that.

In his personal life… Well, all he could do now was try and avoid making the same mistake twice. He didn't imagine that would be much of a problem. Since Clara had left, there'd never been another woman he'd felt such an instant connection with. There'd never been anyone he'd been tempted to stray from his limits for. He couldn't honestly imagine it happening again.

He'd had the kind of love that most people searched a lifetime for and he'd ruined it. The universe wasn't going to give him that kind of luck twice.

Perhaps it was all for the best. This Christmas project had given him a chance to know his wife in a way he never had when they were married. He knew now for sure that she was happier without him. Yesterday, when they'd talked, for a moment he'd seen a hint of that old connection between them, the same heat and desire he remembered from their first Christmas together. But today Clara was all business, and all about the future. She'd moved on and it was time for him to do the same.

As soon as they made it through Christmas.

Clara drained the last of the tea from her mug and jumped to her feet again.

'Back to work,' she said. 'I'm about to add your family baubles to the tree, if you want to help.'

'Is that at all like the family jewels?' Jacob jested, knowing it wasn't funny but feeling he had to try anyway. Had to do something—anything—to lighten the oppressive mood that had settled over them. 'Because if so…'

'Nothing like it,' Clara assured him. He took some small comfort from the slight blush rising to her cheeks. 'Come on.'

The tree—Bruce, as Clara had christened it—was magnificent, rising almost the whole way to the ceiling even in the vast castle entrance hall. He smiled, remembering the trees they'd had as children. Heather had always insisted that the tree had to be taller than her, so as she had grown so had the trees.

He suspected his parents had been secretly pleased when she'd finally stopped growing, just shy of six foot.

'Do we have a ladder?' Jacob asked, staring up at the topmost branches.

Clara nodded. 'I think I saw one in one of the cupboards off the kitchen. I'll fetch it.'

She was gone before he could offer to help.

That was another change, he mused, pulling out the box of baubles he'd retrieved from his parents' house for the occasion and starting to place them on the tree. Not that Clara had ever been particularly needy or helpless, but he didn't remember her being so assertive and determined either. Whenever anything had come up throughout the planning process—even choosing Christmas presents—she'd taken charge as if it were inevitable. As if she were so used to having to deal with everything alone—make every decision, undertake every task—that it had become second nature.

The bauble he picked out of the box now caught the

lights from the tree, twinkling and sparkling as he turned it on its string. Those baubles had hung on his family's tree for every Christmas he could remember. As far as he knew, they weren't particularly expensive or precious. But they signalled Christmas to him.

And this would be his father's last one. He needed to focus on the real reason they were here—not dwell on his past failures as a husband.

Jacob hung the bauble in his hand on one of the lower branches and stood back to admire his small contribution to the decorations. And then he headed off to help find that elusive ladder.

The least he could do for Clara was decorate the stupid tree. Even he couldn't screw that up.

Clara swore at the bucket as her foot got stuck inside it, then at the broom as it fell on her head. She had been so certain there was a ladder in this cupboard somewhere, but so far all she'd found had been murderous cleaning utensils.

With a sigh, she hung the broom back on its hook, disentangled her foot from the bucket, ignoring the slight throb in her ankle, and backed out of the cupboard. Carefully.

Well, there had to be a ladder somewhere. She'd seen one. Unfortunately, since she'd explored every square inch of the enormous castle the day before, exactly *where* she'd seen it remained a mystery—and a mystery which could take quite a lot of searching to solve.

She could ask Jacob for help, she supposed, but even the idea seemed a little alien. She was just so used to doing things herself these days, not just at work but at home too. At four, Ivy was becoming a little more self-reliant, but she still needed her mummy to take care of the essentials. After four years of tending to another person's every need—and knowing that you were the only person there to look after them—doing what was needed had become more than second nature. It was just who she was now.

She hadn't been like that when she was married to Jacob, although that was only something she'd realised later. Shutting the cupboard door, she tried to remember that other person, the one Jacob had married, but it was as if that woman, that other her, was a character in a play she'd acted in once. A person she'd pretended to be.

Clara knew without a doubt that the person she was now—Ivy's mother—was the one she'd been meant to be all along.

But that didn't help her with the ladder. With a sigh, Clara set about checking all the other cupboards off the kitchen and then, when that didn't get her any results, extended her search to the rest of the ground floor.

She was just about to give up, head back to the hall and try upstairs, when Jacob found her.

'Did you find a ladder?' Jacob's words made her jump as they echoed down the dark stone-walled corridor.

'Not yet,' she said, her hand resting against her chest as if to slow her rapidly beating heart.

'Don't worry. I found one.'

Of course he had. Because the moment she was congratulating herself on being self-reliant was exactly the time her ex-husband would choose to save the day.

It's a ladder, Clara, she reminded herself. *Not a metaphor.*

Unless it's both.

She followed the sound of his voice back down the corridor, through the dining room and back into the hallway.

'What do you think?' Jacob asked, beaming proudly at the half-decorated tree. Apparently he'd found the ladder early enough to have hung the rest of his family's decorations haphazardly across the huge tree. Clara thought of her carefully designed tree plan and winced. Still, it was *his* perfect Christmas…

'It looks lovely,' she lied. 'Help me with the lights? Then we can add the rest of the decorations I brought.'

Crossing the hall, she reached into the carefully packed boxes and pulled out the securely wrapped lights; they'd been unpacked for testing back in London, then rewrapped so they'd be easier to set up once she arrived. Merry had also added a bag of spare bulbs and two extra sets of fairy lights, just in case.

And, underneath those, was the apple-green project folder she always brought with her. The one with the Wi-Fi password on the front, apart from anything else. But there was one more note she didn't remember adding. Clara pulled the file out and read the stocking-shaped note stuck on the front: *For when it's all done!*

Frowning, Clara opened the file. On top, before all the contract information and emergency contact details, sat her divorce papers, just waiting for Jacob's signature. Of course. That would be Merry's idea of a brilliant Christmas present.

But for Clara it was growing harder and harder not to imagine both futures—the one she could have had with Jacob and the one she was living now—and wonder what the first would have been like if they'd ever really opened up to each other. She accepted now that she'd never let him in, had never wanted to open herself up that way. What if he had been doing the same? She'd always known Jacob had held his own secrets close to his chest. There were some things they just didn't talk about and she'd accepted that, not wanting to push him and have him push back.

She'd never told him why his behaviour hurt her so much. And she'd never asked him *why* he didn't want children. Was it just a knee-jerk reaction, the fear of a young man, which he might grow out of? Or had there been something deeper there? His reaction to her pregnancy scare told her there was. Was it too late to find out what that problem was?

And would it make a difference when she told him about Ivy?

She needed to tell him. And she was starting to think it couldn't wait until January.

Maybe it was just the Christmas sentimentality getting to her. Didn't every single person have a wobble around the festive season and start wishing that maybe they had someone to share it with?

Well, everyone except Merry. Her best friend was very firmly anti-relationship. Something that worked very well alongside Clara's resolve to give Ivy a stable, secure and loving upbringing, even if that meant being a one-parent family rather than introducing her to potential step-parents who might not hang around.

Could Jacob give her that security? Clara still wasn't sure. But she realised now she wouldn't ever be sure unless she opened up to him.

'Everything okay with the lights?' Jacob asked from just over her shoulder.

Clara slammed the folder closed and shoved it back into the box, hiding it under some emergency ribbon for the tree.

'Fine.' She grabbed the fairy lights and turned, stumbling back slightly on her heels as she discovered Jacob was even closer than she'd realised.

He reached out to steady her and Clara could feel the warmth of his hands even through her light sweater. She bit the inside of her cheek and stepped away.

She'd let her guard down. Let herself appreciate the way he looked at her—the way he looked in his jeans and jumper. She'd let her imagination enjoy the moment. And she couldn't afford to do that, not any more.

Especially not when he had that hot look in his eye. The one she remembered all too well from their wedding night.

She had to focus on getting the job done and getting out of there. The connection between them might still be there, but giving in to that attraction was exactly how they'd ended up as man and wife without knowing the most basic things about each other. She couldn't let that happen this time. She needed to tell Jacob about Ivy before she could even *think* about what it might mean for their relationship.

Swallowing, Clara found her voice again. 'Let's string some lights.'

CHAPTER TWELVE

JACOB FLICKED THE SWITCH on the lights again, smiling when every single bulb lit up. Clara's excessive testing at least meant he didn't need to hunt for the missing ones and replace them, like he always found himself doing at home.

Maybe it truly was a perfect Christmas.

The thought soured even before he appreciated it as he remembered the folder in the decorations box. She'd been fast to close it, but not so quick that he hadn't seen enough to know what it contained.

Divorce papers. The very ones he'd been avoiding signing for five years.

Who brought divorce papers to a Christmas celebration?

But this wasn't *Clara's* celebration, no matter how much he'd tried to convince her to join it. For her, this was still work. And his signature on those papers was part of her payment.

She'd earned it. More than earned it. She deserved to be free of him.

Except… The hardest thing was knowing how good things *could* be between them. Yes, their marriage had lasted less than a year, and yes, he'd screwed up. And Clara was right—they'd spent more time in bed than they had talking. They hadn't known each other the way they'd needed to.

But that time in bed… He'd been working so hard to forget it, until the moment she'd stumbled against him and it all came flooding back. The feel of her body pressed against his, however fleeting, had been so familiar, so right, his own had immediately reacted the way it always did when Clara was near.

And now all he could think about was that four-poster bed, going to waste upstairs.

But no. He needed to keep his distance. Set her free. Sign her blasted papers.

It was just that it had been five years. Five long years he'd hung in there, not quite letting her go. Now he just couldn't imagine saying goodbye without kissing her one more time. Without showing her that however much she'd thought he hadn't wanted her when they were married, he had, and he still did. For all the distance he'd put between them, trying to keep her safe from him, he wanted to stride across it now and hold her, kiss her, touch her.

Love her, one last time.

'Just a few more decorations and I think we're done here,' Clara said, unnecessarily cheerily, in his opinion. 'I'll be able to leave you to enjoy Christmas with your family.'

Jacob checked his watch. His parents and Heather were due at four, only another hour away. Clara was cutting it fine and, from the way she scurried around the tree adding decorations, she knew it. She'd already packed up everything else. Clearly, she planned on making her escape the first chance she got.

Only he wasn't sure he could let her go. Not forever. Not like this.

'Are you sure you won't stay?' he asked. 'Not even for a sherry and a mince pie?' That was the polite, proper thing to do on Christmas Eve, wasn't it? And Clara wouldn't want to be impolite… 'I know my family would like to see you again, however briefly. To thank you for everything you've done setting up this weekend, if nothing else.'

Clara paused, halfway through hanging a silver bell on the tree. 'You told them you were working with me on this project?'

'Of course I did.' Maybe not entirely intentionally, but he'd told them. Jacob wasn't one of those people who told his parents everything that was going on in his life and he was pretty sure they wouldn't want to know. But when it mattered, he kept them informed. Mostly.

'And they weren't…weird about it?'

'Why would they be?'

Clara raised her eyebrows at him and Jacob interpreted the look as meaning: *Ex-wife. Remember?*

'They were fine,' he said, skipping over his mother's concern. Mothers worried.

'Really?' Clara asked, disbelief clear in her voice.

Jacob sighed. He'd never been able to get away with lying to her when they'd been married either. He'd thought that made them a great match, at the time. But clearly Clara had been much better at hiding the truth. Otherwise he'd have realised how unhappy she was long before she'd left.

He'd honestly thought she was coming back. That it had been just another of their spats—a minor retaliation for the fact he'd had to work on Christmas Day. He hadn't believed she'd really meant it.

Not until she still hadn't come back a month later.

No wonder his mother worried. He'd been the poster child for denial at the time.

'They just want me to be happy. And I want them to be happy. And you staying for sherry and a mince pie would make us all very happy.'

With a small, tight smile on her lips, Clara shook her head again. 'I'm sorry.' Reaching down, she picked up her bag.

She was actually leaving him. Again. And this time he was under no illusions that she would come back.

He had to let her go. But not like this. Not when he was so close to understanding everything that had gone wrong between them. To knowing her the way he never had before. Maybe it wouldn't have made a difference, but maybe it would. And he just knew, deep down, that there was more here. Something she wasn't saying.

This was his last chance to find out what that was.

Jacob swallowed his pride.

'Please. Stay.'

'I can't.'

Those words again. He hated those words.

He stepped closer. 'Why?'

'I told you,' she said, frustrated. 'Merry is waiting for me at the hotel.'

'Merry. I don't buy it.' He didn't want to have the same argument again. Wasn't that the definition of insanity—doing the same things and expecting different results? But then, Clara might actually be driving him insane. Even if she left again, even if they finally got divorced, even if he never had another chance with her…he needed to know the truth. The truth about it all. He now knew why she'd left but not why she hadn't come back. He knew now how he'd hurt her but there was more, he could tell. He wanted to know everything.

Starting with why she wouldn't stay.

'Merry wouldn't be enough of a reason for you to be this determined not to stay,' he said. 'Tell me the truth, please. I'm not asking to start a fight, or to judge you or anything else. I just need to know. Is there someone else? Is that what you're not telling me? Are you afraid I won't give you the divorce if there is? Because we had a deal.' It might break his heart into its final pieces but if she was truly happy with another man he'd give her the divorce. She'd made it clear that he couldn't make her happy and goodness only knew somebody should. Clara deserved all the happiness in the world.

She stared back at him, her beautiful dark eyes so wide he could almost see the battle going on behind them. Would she tell him the truth? Or would he face more evasion?

Eventually, she shook her head. 'That's not it. I almost wish it was.'

Jacob frowned. 'What do you mean?'

'It would be so much easier to just lie. To tell you I'd fallen in love with a lumberjack from Canada or something. Because the truth is…' She sighed. 'There's no one else, Jacob. There never has been. It's only ever been you.'

Jacob reeled back as if he'd been hit. Five years. Five years he'd spent trying not to imagine her with other men, and failing miserably. Five years torturing himself with thoughts of her falling in love again, of her pressing him for divorce because she wanted to remarry. Five years of thinking he hadn't been enough for her, that she'd needed to go and find something else, someone better. And all this time…

'No one,' he repeated. 'There's been… You mean, you haven't…'

That was a game changer.

Clara's cheeks were bright red. 'I shouldn't have told you that.' She brushed past him, heading towards the door, and he grabbed her arm to stop her.

'Yes. You should.' Because that meant something, didn't it? It had to. Five years, and no one else. That wasn't nothing. Those weren't the actions of a woman who was desperate to get away from him.

'Why?' she asked, sounding anxious. 'Why does it even matter now?' She pulled her arm away but he reached out and took it again, more gently this time—a caress rather than a hold.

'It matters.' The words were rough in his throat. He couldn't even put a name to his emotions but he knew it mattered. Knew he cared, still. Knew that the sense of relief flooding through him as he realised there really wasn't another man waiting for her at the hotel meant something.

No other man had touched her. No one had run their

hands over that pale, smooth skin the way he had. She'd been a virgin when they'd met, when she was twenty-one and he twenty-five, so he knew now that he was the only man she'd given herself to. Ever.

And that definitely meant something. The primal urge to take that again rose up strong within him.

Clara shook her head, looking down at the stone floor. 'It's over, Jacob. None of it matters any more.' Her voice was small, desolate and, despite her words, he didn't believe it.

'It doesn't have to be.' For the first time he was almost convinced. He knew her now in a way he hadn't before. He was older. Better. Maybe this time he could make her happy.

Stepping closer, he ran his hand up her arm, wrapping his other arm around her waist. 'Stay, Clara.'

'I can't.' Always those words. He was starting to wonder if they really meant what he thought they did.

'Because you don't want to?' Raising his hand to her chin, he nudged it up so she had to look at him and her eyes were wide and helpless as they met his.

She wanted to. He could see it. So what was stopping her?

'No,' she admitted, swallowing visibly. At least she wasn't lying to him now. It was a small victory, but he'd take it.

'Then why?'

She bit her lower lip, her small white teeth denting the plump flesh. Oh, how he wanted to kiss her…

'You can tell me,' he assured her, shifting just a little closer.

Her gaze dropped again as she gave a small hollow laugh. 'I really, really can't.'

'If you don't tell me, I'll be forced to guess.' He tried to make it sound like a joke, but it really wasn't. Not knowing was driving him crazy.

Looking up, she rolled her eyes at him. 'Fine. You want to know the real reason? Because our marriage is over, Jacob. I have the divorce papers in my bag, ready for you to sign. And I know you. If I stay, you'll try and convince me to give things another shot.'

'And you don't think you'll be able to say no?' Something wasn't right here. Apart from the fact he knew full well that Clara was of course capable of saying no to him—and she knew he'd respect that—the bitter, hard words didn't match the desperation in her eyes. She was making excuses.

She *was* still lying to him.

Clara looked up and met his eyes. 'Of course I can say no. *I left you*, remember?'

As if he could ever forget. 'And why am I starting to think that maybe you regret that decision?' It was a stab in the dark, a wild guess. But there hadn't been anybody else… What if she really did still have feelings for him? *Could* he make it work this time? Could he be the husband she needed?

'It was the best decision I ever made.' Her words were clear, bright and true, echoing off the walls of the castle. She meant every word, Jacob could tell.

The hurt in Jacob's eyes was palpable as his arms fell away from her and Clara regretted the words as soon as she'd spoken them. It was true, of course—if she hadn't left Jacob, then Ivy wouldn't have been born into a loving home, even if that home only had one parent.

Leaving had been the right decision—for her, for Ivy and even for Jacob, although he didn't know it.

But that was the point. He *didn't* know. And without that context her words were harsh, hurtful. Cruel.

And Clara tried hard never to be cruel. Cruelty was

something she knew too much about to knowingly inflict it on another person.

She had to tell him the truth. Now. But how?

This wasn't the plan. The plan was to get the job done then meet him privately in London, somewhere public but discreet, and have the conversation. Not in a secluded castle in the middle of nowhere with his family due to arrive within the hour!

But how could she not tell him now?

Swallowing, she stepped forward and placed a hand on his arm. 'I'm sorry. I didn't mean...'

'Yes,' he said, the word coming out raspy. 'You did. I can tell when you're lying to me, Clara. And you meant that.'

Hysterical laughter bubbled away in her throat. If he really could tell when she was lying then they were both doomed. 'I... Being married to you... For a time, it was the best thing that had ever happened in my life.'

'But not for long enough.'

'It took me a while,' she said, feeling her way to the right words. 'But I realised that we both wanted different things.'

'You never told me what you wanted!' Frustration flew out from Jacob's words, and the tension in his shoulders and the tightness of his jaw. She was doing this all wrong. 'If I'd known you wanted to run your own business, I'd have helped you! We could have worked together. And if I'd known about your family—'

'I know, I know. I should have told you, should have opened up to you more,' Clara said. 'But Jacob, that's not what I'm talking about.'

'Then what? If not that, then what on earth did you want that I couldn't give you?'

'A baby.'

Jacob froze, his eyes wide and scared, his face paling by the second as if he was turning to ice. 'You...you never said,' he stuttered eventually.

'Because I knew how you felt about kids.'

'I can't have them.' As if he needed to confirm it all over again now. 'I can't.'

'Can't?' Clara asked, eyebrows raised. From her experience it seemed to be much more of a *won't.*

'I'm not meant to be a father, Clara.' Jacob scrubbed a hand over his hair. 'Jesus. You're right. We really should have talked more. I always assumed that you were happy with it just being us. But if you really wanted…that. Then yeah, I get why you left. Finally.' He gave a small, sad half laugh then looked up at her, his eyes narrowing. 'Wait. If you wanted a baby, why haven't you done anything about it? Five years, Clara. You could have met someone else in that time, started a whole tribe if you'd really wanted. You're gorgeous, caring, wonderful… Don't tell me you didn't have offers.'

And this was it. Confession time. Clara sucked in a deep breath.

'I didn't need them. You see, when I left you…I was already pregnant.'

This time, Jacob didn't freeze. He was all movement—staggering back away from her, his mouth falling open. 'You…'

'I should have told you, I know. But I knew how you felt. When I left, I thought I'd come back again, same as every other time. But then I took the pregnancy test and I knew…you wouldn't want me if I did. You wouldn't want her. And Jacob, I couldn't let my daughter—she's a girl… we had a girl… I didn't say—and I couldn't let her go through what I did, growing up with a parent who didn't want her. I couldn't.' The words were tumbling out of her mouth, too fast for her to think them through. 'But I always meant to tell you eventually. And when you came back… I thought this would be my chance to see if you wanted to get to know her.'

'To know her?' he echoed, sounding very far away.

'Ivy. I called her Ivy. And she's the best person on the planet.' If Jacob only ever knew two things about his daughter, it should be those.

'I don't…' He shook his head as if he were trying to shake away this new reality he found himself in. 'I can't…'

Clara nodded. 'I know—it's a shock. And I'm sorry. I'll go. Let you… Well… I'll just go.'

She stumbled backwards, fumbling for the door handle and yanking the door open. As she did, there came a sound like a feather mattress falling to the floor with a *whoomp.* Suddenly Clara was pulled back and she came to the realisation that Jacob's arm was around her waist, tugging her safely out of the range of the huge bank of snow that had fallen from the castle's crenellations. It must have been building up all day, Clara thought, amazed. She hadn't even known it was snowing out there.

But now, when she looked out of the door, she saw a blanket of snow covering the land—deep and crisp and even.

But mostly deep. Really, really deep.

CHAPTER THIRTEEN

'LOOKS LIKE YOU might be spending Christmas with me after all,' Jacob said, his voice faint even to his own ears.

She'd lied to him for five long years. She'd let him believe that he'd screwed up—and maybe he had, but not in the way he'd always believed. She'd planned to come back. She'd planned to keep trying. Until she'd found out she was pregnant.

He was a father. How could that even be possible? Why on earth would the universe *allow* him to father a child?

He stared out at the snow. Somewhere out there, in the dark and the cold—well, actually she was probably nice and warm at the hotel, but that wasn't the point—somewhere out there was a little girl who belonged to him. That he was responsible for.

Just like he'd been responsible for Heather.

The thought chilled him far more than the weather ever could.

'I have to get out of here.' Clara spun on her heel and stared at him with wide, panicked eyes. 'I have to get back to Ivy. We can dig your car out. I saw a shovel somewhere...'

Probably in the same place as the mythical ladder she hadn't been able to find. And, given that he could only just make out the windows of his car and the tyres were completely snowed in, he thought she was being a little optimistic. The snow was coming down faster than they'd be able to shovel.

'Wait, Clara. You can't. You need to—'

'What? Stay here with you?' She gave a high shrill laugh. 'Not a chance. I know that look, Jacob. That hunted, panicked look. I recognise it distinctly from the first time

I thought I was pregnant, thanks. It's fine—you're off the hook. Ivy doesn't know you exist and now she never has to. You never even have to meet her—but you *do* have to help me get home to her *right now*!'

She was losing it, Jacob realised. He needed to calm her down. He could have his own breakdown about being a father later. He'd waited five years, apparently. Why rush it now?

'How do you plan to do that?' he asked, ignoring the rest and focusing on the part that was clearly making her crazy right now. 'That road back to the hotel isn't going to be passable even if we could dig out the car.' He remembered the steep stretches and sharp turns. There wasn't a chance of either of them driving it in this weather.

'Then I'll walk,' she said. She was so stubborn. How had he forgotten that?

'In those shoes?' The fur-lined boots she was wearing looked warm enough but, unless he was mistaken, they were suede and the soles looked too thin for any decent grip. Definitely fashion items rather than practical.

'There might be some boots around here somewhere.' Clara cast a desperate glance around the hall as if she was expecting Santa himself to appear and furnish her with some, but even she had to know her arguments were growing weaker and weaker.

'If we didn't find them looking for that ladder then they're not here,' Jacob pointed out. 'Look, Clara, it will be fine. Your…' he swallowed '…*our* daughter, she's with Merry, right? At the hotel?' She nodded. 'Then she's safe. And we're safe. That's the important thing. The moment they clear the roads, I'll drive you back, I promise. But for now…you're stuck here with me, I'm afraid.'

Clara glared at him. 'You do realise that if I'm trapped here, there's no way your family can get here either.'

A chill settled over him that had nothing to do with the

snow. He'd been so busy focusing on Clara that he'd forgotten, just for a moment, what the weather would mean for his parents and Heather.

'They'll get here.' They had to. It was their perfect Christmas. One way or another they had to make it to the castle, or everything would have been for nothing. He'd have failed his father one last time, and he might never get the chance to put it right.

That was unacceptable.

'How?' Clara asked, incredulous. 'If I can't drive or walk out of here, what have you got planned for your family?'

'Helicopter,' Jacob suggested desperately. 'I'll make some calls…'

'They won't fly in this weather.' Clara tilted her head as she looked at him, as if she was studying his reactions. 'You know that. Are you sweating? Jacob, it's zero degrees out there.'

'I'm not sweating.' But he was. He could feel the cold clamminess of the moisture on the back of his neck, under his jumper. Like always, it was all about his father. 'I'm thinking.' Thinking *How can I put this right?* And *How am I going to tell him I got Clara pregnant?*

Given his father's reaction to the news of Jacob's marriage, and his emphasis on responsibility, Jacob could only imagine how James Foster would take the news that he was now a grandfather—and that Jacob had taken no responsibility so far at all for his daughter.

'Well, when you figure out a way to get them here, we can use the same method to get me out. I've got my own Christmas I need to get to. Mine and Ivy's.'

One he hadn't been invited to share. One he was pretty sure he didn't want to share.

But he couldn't help but wonder… *Does she look like Clara or like me?*

Hands visibly shaking, Clara held up her phone. 'I need

to find some reception in this place and call Merry. I need to know that Ivy is okay.'

She disappeared up the stairs, as quiet as the falling snow. Jacob waited until he knew she must have reached the bedrooms, then sat heavily at the foot of the stairs.

He was trapped in a castle with his ex-wife, he'd just discovered he was a father and the perfect Christmas he'd worked so hard planning was ruined. What would his father be thinking now? He wouldn't blame Jacob for the weather—the man wasn't irrational. But that didn't change the fact that in the annals of Foster history this would go down as his mistake. Jacob's failure. He had been the one who'd decided to host Christmas in the Highlands, after all. *Ha!* He'd even asked Clara for a white Christmas.

Seemed like she couldn't help but deliver, even when she didn't want to.

His shaky laugh echoed off the lonely stone walls and he dropped his head into his hands, his fingers tugging at his hair as they raked through it.

The difference was that, this time, there'd be no years to come for his father to bring this up, to tease him for his stupid plan. This was going to be his last Christmas and Jacob had ruined it.

His throat grew tighter as he remembered that long-ago Christmas, and another screw-up. One that no one ever mentioned, especially not as a joke. One that he never needed to be reminded of anyway.

He had a clear visual every time he saw the scars on Heather's arms. He knew just how badly he'd failed his family in the past.

And now he'd done it again.

What could he do now?

Clara made sure the master bedroom door was closed behind her before she let her shaky legs give way. The fire she'd lit in the grate earlier burned bright and merry but she couldn't stop shivering. She couldn't think of anything except Ivy, stuck in a strange hotel with her aunt Merry, waiting for her mum to arrive for hot chocolate and Christmas presents.

Except Clara wasn't going to be there.

Damn Jacob and his stupid perfect Christmas. How had she let herself get dragged into this in the first place? A ridiculous desire to prove to her ex-husband that she was better off without him, she supposed. To prove it to herself too.

If only she'd stayed in London with Ivy, where she belonged, she wouldn't be in this mess.

And she'd told him. She'd told him everything—although how much he'd taken in, what with the shock and the snow and everything, she wasn't sure. They'd have to talk again later, she supposed.

If they really were snowed in for the duration, they'd have plenty of time for that conversation.

She made a sound that was half sob, half laugh as she realised there was another, more pressing, conversation she needed to have first.

Clara fumbled with her phone, holding it up towards the window and praying for reception. There it was. Just a single bar, but hopefully enough for her to reach Merry.

She dialled, held her breath and waited.

'Clara? Where are you? I've been trying to call all morning, ever since the snow started, but I couldn't even get through to your voicemail.' Merry sounded frantic. Clara didn't blame her.

'I'm so sorry. Reception here is terrible. And I was so busy getting things ready…I didn't notice the snow.' If she had, she'd have called a taxi and headed straight out of the castle before the roads became impassable. 'Is Ivy okay?'

'Wondering where you are. Clara, are you even going to be able to get back in this? The roads look bad.'

Clara's heart hurt at the idea of her little girl watching out of the window of the hotel, waiting for her to come home. This was exactly what she *never* wanted Ivy to feel—as if she'd been abandoned for a better option. That there was something else that mattered more than her. Because there really wasn't, not in Clara's world.

'They look worse from this end,' she admitted, her throat tight. 'We can't even dig Jacob's car out, Merry. And the road…' She stared out of the window at a vast blanket of white. 'I can't even see where it should be.' Somewhere in the distance, beyond all the falling flakes, was the Golden Thistle. Clara wished more than anything in the world that she could be there now.

'Hang on,' Merry said. Clara heard her murmuring something, presumably to Ivy, then the sound of a door closing. 'What are you going to do? It's Christmas Eve!'

'I know!' Clara rubbed a hand across her forehead and tried to blink away the sudden burn behind her eyes. 'I wanted to walk but I don't fancy my chances. And Jacob's family can't even get here. He was talking about trying to find a helicopter or something but… I think I'm stuck here. And Merry…that's not the worst of it.'

Her best friend must have sensed that Clara was on the edge because suddenly the note of panic was gone from Merry's voice and she became all business again. They had a rule at Perfect London: only one of them could fall apart at any given time. And it was definitely Clara's turn.

'Tell me what happened,' she said briskly. 'Tell me everything, and I'll fix it.'

Clara let out a full-blown sob. 'Oh, Merry, I'm so sorry. But I have to tell you something. Something I should have told you years ago.'

'That Ivy is Jacob's daughter?' Merry guessed, calm as anything.

Holding the phone away from her ear, Clara stared at it

for a moment. Then she put it back. 'How…how did you know?'

'It doesn't take a rocket scientist, Clara. Not when you've seen the two of them. She's very like him.' Merry gave a low chuckle. 'Besides, you never were the one-night stand type. So I always wondered… Did you tell him?'

'Yeah. It went…badly.'

'Then he's an idiot,' Merry said simply. 'Ivy is the coolest kid in the world. He should be so *lucky* as to have her as a daughter.' Clara relaxed, just an inch. Maybe Ivy didn't need a father at all. Not when she had an Aunt Merry.

As long as Aunt Merry forgave Mummy for lying to her, of course.

'Are you mad?' Clara asked in a tiny voice.

Merry paused before answering, and Clara's heart waited to beat until she spoke. 'I understand why you wanted to keep it a secret, I think. I hope you know that you could have trusted me with it but…I guess we all have our secrets, don't we? So no, not mad. But I *do* want a full retelling of everything, with wine, the moment we get you out of there.'

'*If* we get me out of here,' Clara muttered, but she couldn't help a small, relieved smile spreading across her face. Despite everything, she still had Merry. Her best friend still wanted to be exactly that.

'Okay, let's fix that first,' Merry said, businesslike once again. 'How stuck is stuck? And what do you want me to tell Ivy?'

'I don't know.' The words came out practically as a wail.

'Let me check the weather forecast. Hang on.' Clara heard the tapping of laptop keys in the background. 'Okay, it's deep and treacherous right now, but there's no more snow due overnight. Snowploughs will be out as soon as it stops, then we can look at getting you out of there. So tomorrow morning, if we're really lucky. The next day if we're not.'

'But tomorrow is Christmas,' Clara whispered. Oh, poor Ivy. How was she ever going to explain this to her?

'Not this year it isn't,' Merry said firmly. 'This year, Santa is snowed in up at the North Pole too, and will be coming tomorrow night. Then we'll celebrate Christmas once you're back here.'

'I'm pretty sure Father Christmas can't get snowed in,' Clara said dubiously.

'Well, as long as your daughter doesn't know that, we should be okay,' Merry replied. 'Look, I'll fix it, okay? You've fixed things for me often enough—our own business, as a case in point. Let me fix this for you.'

She sounded so sure, so determined, that Clara almost began to feel a little better. 'What are you going to do?'

'I'm going to talk to the staff here, and the other guests,' Merry explained. 'I reckon they'll all buy in to postponing Christmas until Santa—and you—can get here.'

'But it's their Christmas too,' Clara protested. 'Some of them were only staying until Boxing Day night. We can't ruin it for them just because I screwed up.'

'You didn't screw up—you were doing your job. Besides, we can have a practice Christmas tomorrow. As long as Ivy believes that the real deal is the next day, it doesn't matter anyway.'

'Do you really think you can pull it off?' If Merry managed it, then Clara would still have Christmas with her daughter. It might not be perfect, but it would be pretty wonderful all the same.

For the first time ever, Clara cared a whole lot less about perfect. She just wanted to be with Ivy for Christmas. Whatever day they decided that was.

'I can do it,' Merry promised her. 'Just leave it with me. Now, do you want to speak to Ivy?'

'Please. And Merry…'

'She can't know about Jacob. I know.'

Clara waited until she heard her daughter's high-pitched voice coming closer, feeling her heart tighten with every second.

'Mummy?'

'Hi, sweetheart. Everything okay there?' Clara tried her best to sound light-hearted. She knew from past experience that Ivy would pick up on any slight tension in her voice.

'It's brilliant here. Auntie Merry and I went shopping and we bought you—' Clara heard a shushing noise from the background '—something I'm not allowed to tell you about yet. And then we went for hot chocolates.'

'Sounds wonderful. I wish I could be there.'

'Are you coming home soon?' Ivy asked. 'It's really, really snowy out there.'

'I know. And I'm afraid the snow is very deep where I am too. It's half way up the door!' She made it a joke, even though it meant that no taxi would drive to the castle in this, and she had no means of escape. The most important thing was that Ivy continued to believe this was all one big, fun adventure.

Ivy let loose a peal of laughter. 'How are you going to get home?'

'Well, it looks like I might have to wait for the snowploughs to clear the roads.' Now came the tricky bit.

'Will you be home before Santa comes?'

'Actually,' she said, dropping her voice to a secretive whisper, 'I just heard—Father Christmas is snowed in too!'

'Nooo...' Ivy breathed, amazed.

'Yes. So he's postponing Christmas! I can't remember the last time that happened!' Because it never had. But Ivy didn't know that yet.

'Does that mean he won't be bringing my presents?' Ivy asked, obviously anxious.

'Of course he will! You've been such a good girl this year, he wouldn't not bring you presents. It just means that he might have to come tomorrow night instead of tonight. And I'm sure I'll be back by then.' If she and Jacob hadn't killed each other before Boxing Day.

'What are we going to do tomorrow then?' Ivy sounded confused but hadn't expressed any disbelief yet. Clara took that as a good sign.

'Have a practice Christmas, of course!' She injected as much fun as she could into the words. 'You and Auntie Merry can practise opening a few presents, eating Christmas dinner, pulling crackers, wearing the hats and telling the jokes…all the usual things. Then, when I get home, we can do it all again for real, once Santa has been!'

'So I get two Christmases this year?'

Clara let out a small sigh of relief at the excitement in her daughter's voice. 'Exactly!'

'Brilliant!' There was a clunk, the familiar sound of Ivy dropping the phone as she got bored and wandered off. In the distance, Clara heard her excited chatter. 'Auntie Merry! I get two Christmases this year! Did you know? Santa's stuck too!'

Clara waited, listening to the plans for the Christmas she was missing, and wiped a rogue tear from her cheek. She didn't have time to break down now, not with Jacob here.

Although, until those snowploughs made it up here, she had nothing *but* time.

Eventually, Merry came back on the line. 'Okay?'

'Seems to be.' Clara sniffed. 'Tell her I love her, yeah? And you'll be okay tucking her in? You know she likes to sleep with—'

'Blue Ted,' Merry finished for her. 'I know. I've babysat for her a hundred times. We'll be fine.'

'I know you will. I just wish I was there.'

'And you will be. Really soon,' Merry said soothingly. 'Now get off the line so I can phone whoever is in charge of snowploughs around here and work out how to postpone Christmas.'

'Thank you, Merry.'

'For you, anything. Go and make your ex-husband and the father of your child miserable. That should cheer you up.'

Clara gave a watery chuckle. Merry had all of the best ideas.

CHAPTER FOURTEEN

JACOB STARED AT THE bottle of brandy. It stared back. Well, probably it didn't but he'd drunk a good quarter of it now so it felt as if it might.

'So…your latest solution to the snow issue is getting drunk?' Clara's voice from the doorway made him spin round—too fast, as it turned out. It took a good thirty seconds for the rest of the room to catch up.

'I called Heather,' he informed her. 'Before the brandy.'

'Are they all okay?' Sitting down across the table from him, she poured herself a small measure into a clean tumbler. She'd never been a big drinker, he remembered. Apparently being snowbound in a castle with him was driving her to it.

'Fine. They're actually in a hotel in Inverness at the moment. They're hoping to travel up tomorrow morning, meet us here if the snow has cleared enough.' So his father would be spending his last Christmas driving on treacherous Scottish roads, trying to save his only son from his own stupidity. Just the way he wanted it, Jacob was sure.

Time for another brandy.

Clara moved the bottle out of his reach as he moved across the table to grab it. 'You're a terrible drinker, Jacob. You're plastered after about two pints.'

'I might have changed.' As he said the words, he thought of all the ways he had changed, or might have changed since she'd left. Drinking wasn't one of them but she didn't know that.

'Apparently not.' The certainty in her voice told him she wasn't just talking about alcohol. 'But anyway. Here's to a perfect Christmas.' Clara raised her glass and took a long swallow. 'Somehow I don't think you're going to be giving me a top recommendation after this.'

'I don't blame you for the snow, Clara,' he said. For many other things, sure. But not the snow.

'But I bet you're blaming yourself, aren't you?' Her eyes were too knowing, and she saw too deep. He glanced away the moment her gaze met his. How did she always manage to do that? Pick up on his biggest insecurity and dig right in to it?

'I was the one who wanted Christmas in the Highlands. The part of Britain voted most likely to get snow at Christmas.' It was his fault. His failure.

'And I was the one who brought you to a castle on top of a hill,' Clara countered. 'Place least likely to get its roads gritted, or cleared by the snowploughs first.'

'It's what I asked for.'

'What if I told you I had an ulterior motive for bringing you here?' Clara asked.

Suddenly, Jacob's mind filled with exotic scenarios. Had she brought him here purposefully to punish him? Or, more likely, to tell him about his daughter… 'What ulterior motive?'

'I'd booked this place for another client.' Clara took another sip of brandy, her eyes warily peering over the rim of the glass, watching to see how he'd react. 'They pulled out and left me liable for the reservation fee, thanks to a contract screw-up. Holding your Christmas here meant I wasn't out of pocket after all.'

'I see.' It wasn't what he'd expected but part of him had to admire her business sense. 'So it really *is* your fault that we're snowed in and stranded in a castle at the top of a hill.'

'Hey, you asked for a white Christmas.'

Jacob couldn't help it; the laughter burst out of him before he could think. Somehow, tossing the blame for their predicament back and forth had defused some of the awful tension that had been growing between them since they'd arrived. After a moment Clara joined in, giggling into her brandy. Jacob marvelled at her. For once, she looked just like the Clara he remembered. The woman who, he knew now, had fought back against a childhood that could have left her bitter and cruel and instead had chosen to find joy in the world. He'd been scared that being married to him had taken that away from her.

He'd always thought her capacity for joy the most beautiful thing about her.

'I'm sorry,' she said once she'd calmed down again. 'Believe me, I really never intended for this to happen.'

'Oh, I believe you,' Jacob said with a half-smile. 'After all, you've made it very clear you'd rather be anywhere else than here with me.'

'Not anywhere.' She gave him an odd look, one he couldn't quite interpret. 'I just… I'm supposed to be elsewhere tonight. That's all.'

'With Ivy.' It was the child-sized elephant in the room.

'That's right.'

'She must be…four now?' Even simple mental arithmetic was proving tricky. 'Is she okay? With Merry?'

Clara raised her eyebrows. 'Suddenly concerned for the child you didn't know existed an hour ago? The one you made it rather clear you don't want in your life?'

'I didn't say that.' His reaction might have strongly hinted at it but he hadn't actually said the words. 'And you're worried about her. I'm just worried about you.'

'Don't.' Clara sighed. 'Ivy's having the best slumber party ever with one of her favourite people in the world and, thanks to a story about Santa getting snowed in, is potentially having two Christmases this year, if we don't get out of here in time. She might be missing me but she's fine.'

She was a good deal better than Clara was, by the sound of things.

Jacob reached across, took the bottle of brandy and poured a small measure into both of their glasses. 'Since we're stuck here…we should talk about it. Her, I mean.' Clara pulled a face. 'We're never going to get a better opportunity than this,' he pointed out.

'I know. And you deserve to know everything. I realised this week…it wasn't just that we didn't talk when we were married. We didn't let each other in enough to see the real people behind the lust.' She waved her glass in the air as she spoke. 'We thought we had this epic connection, this unprecedented love. But we never really knew the true heart of each other. We never opened up enough for that.'

Jacob stared down at the honey-coloured liquid in his glass. She was right, much as he hated to admit it. He'd wanted to believe that he could be a success as a husband, that he could be what she needed, so he'd only let her see the parts of him that fitted his vision of what that meant—working hard, taking responsibility, earning status, being a success. Everything his father had always done.

He'd hidden away the other parts, the bits of him he wanted to pretend didn't exist. All the parts that made his family ashamed of him.

Would it have made a difference if he'd shown them to Clara? Or would they just have made her leave him sooner?

'I always knew,' he said slowly, 'that something was different the last time you left. I just never guessed it could be this. I always thought that it was me and that I'd let you down. And I had, I know. But that's not why you didn't come back to try again. That was because…'

Clara finished the thought for him. 'Ivy mattered more.'

'And that's why I could never have children.' Jacob gave her a wonky smile then tilted his glass to drain the last few drops. 'I never did seem to grasp the concept of other people mattering more.'

'What do you mean?' Clara asked, frowning. 'Do you

want me to tell you you're selfish? Because you are a workaholic who often forgets there's a life outside the office…or at least you used to be. I think this Perfect Christmas project of yours shows that you're definitely capable of thinking of others when you want to.'

Jacob's mind raced with warnings to himself. With all the things he'd never told Clara—all his failures, the acts and mistakes that would strip away any respect she'd ever had for him.

Why tell her now? Except it was his last chance. The last opportunity he might ever have to explain himself to her and to make her understand the sort of husband he'd been and why.

Should he tell her? He gazed into her eyes and saw a slight spark there. Was he imagining the connection that still existed between them? The thread that drew them together, even after all these years?

Would the truth be the thing that finally broke it? Or maybe—just maybe—could it draw her in to him again?

'I made a mistake once,' he started.

'Just the once? Jacob, I've made hundreds.' She was joking, of course, because she couldn't know yet that this wasn't a laughing matter. Not for him and not for his family.

'Only once that counts,' he said and something in his tone must have got through to her because she settled down in her chair, her expression suddenly serious.

'What happened?'

'My parents… They left me in charge of Heather one evening while they were at a friends' Christmas party. I was sixteen. She was six. I resented it. I wanted to be out with my friends and instead I was stuck in, babysitting.' Across the table, Clara's eyes were wide as she waited, even though she had to know that the story ended as well as it could. Heather was still with them.

Just.

'I was messing around in the kitchen,' he went on, hating the very memory. He could still smell the scent of the Christmas tree in the hallway, the mulled wine spices in the pan on the stove. 'I was experimenting. I used to think I wanted to be a scientist, did I ever tell you that?'

Clara shook her head. 'No, you didn't. Like your father, you mean? What changed?'

'Yeah, like my dad.' That was all he'd wanted: to be like his father. To invent something that changed people's lives for the better. At least he had until that night. 'And as for what changed…' He swallowed. 'I sent Heather up to bed early because I didn't want her getting in my way. I was trying some experiment I'd read about—a flame in a bottle thing—when the phone rang. I turned towards it, moving away from the table.' The memory was so clear, as if he was right there all over again. A familiar terror rose in his throat. As if it were happening again and this time he might not be able to stop it…

'I was far enough away when I heard the explosion. And then I heard Heather scream,' he went on, the lump in his throat growing painfully large. But still he struggled to speak around it. 'The experiment… The fire should have been contained in the bottle, burning up the methanol. But I screwed it up, somehow. It exploded. And when I turned back…Heather…'

'Oh, Jacob,' Clara whispered and reached out across the table to take his hand. He squeezed her fingers in gratitude.

'She'd come downstairs to see what I was doing,' he explained. 'She was right by the table when it happened. Her arms…'

'I'd seen the scars,' Clara admitted. 'I just never thought… She always kept them covered, so I didn't like to ask. I should have.'

'No, you shouldn't. We don't… Nobody in my family likes to talk about it. We like to pretend it never happened.'

Even though there hadn't been a day since when Jacob hadn't thought about it, hadn't wished he'd acted differently. 'Dad only ever refers to it as our lucky escape. Heather put her arms up to protect herself when the bottle exploded but her pyjamas caught fire. I grabbed a throw blanket and smothered her with it to put the flames out but…' He swallowed. This was the part of the memory that haunted him the most. 'The fire chief said that she would have been burnt beyond recognition if I'd been a moment slower, if her hair had caught fire. It could have taken her sight too. And she might have…'

Clara's fingers tightened around his. 'But she didn't. She's fine, Jacob. She's out there right now with your parents, waiting for this snow to clear. She's fine.'

She's alive. Some mornings, that was the first thing he said to himself. Whenever he worried about the day ahead, about a deal that might go wrong or a business decision he had to make, he just reminded himself that Heather was alive, and he knew anything was possible. But nothing had ever been the same since. His parents had never looked at him the same way. They loved him, he knew. Forgave him even, maybe. But they couldn't love him the same way they had before he'd hurt their baby girl. And they couldn't trust him, not with people.

He'd been lucky—far luckier than anyone had any right to be, his father had said. But Jacob knew he couldn't ever rely on that again. He'd used up his allocation of good luck and all he had left was hard graft and determination.

A determination never to let his family down like that again. A resolution never to put himself in a position where he was responsible for a child again.

He couldn't be trusted. He should always focus on his own dream, his own ambition, instead of another person's welfare. He couldn't take the risk of hurting another kid that way again.

He'd thought that maybe he could manage marriage, as long as it was on his terms. And when he'd met Clara he'd known he had to try.

But in the end he'd only let her down too. He'd neglected her the way he'd neglected Heather that night, but the difference was that Clara had been an adult.

When he'd hurt her, Clara could leave, and she had done exactly that.

And he couldn't ever blame her.

Clara held Jacob's hand hard and tight, her whole being filled with sympathy and love for that younger version of her husband. A teenage boy who'd been acting exactly like sixteen-year-old boys always would—foolishly—and had almost destroyed his family.

'It wasn't your fault, Jacob,' she said and his gaze snapped up to meet hers.

'How can you say that? It was entirely my fault. Every last bit of it.'

The awful thing was, he was right. 'You were a child.'

'I was sixteen. Old enough to be responsible, at least in my parents' eyes. I let them down.'

And he'd never forgiven himself, Clara realised. He'd held this failure over himself for years and it had coloured every single thing he'd ever done since.

Even his marriage to her.

Clara sat back, her fingers falling away from his as the implications of that washed over her. In her mind, a movie reel replayed their whole relationship with this new knowledge colouring it.

Suddenly, so many things made sense in a way they never had before.

This—*this* was why he was so determined to succeed, every moment of every day. Why he'd worked so hard to never let his father down, ever again. Why he did everything he could to bring glory and money and power to his family—to try and make up for the one time he'd got it wrong.

Finally she understood why he was so adamant that he never wanted children. Because the one time he'd been left in charge of a child something had gone terribly, almost tragically wrong.

He'd spent almost half of his life carrying this guilt, this determination not to screw up again.

Clara knew James Foster. He was a good man, a good father—but he demanded a lot. He was an innovative scientist who'd achieved a great deal in his lifetime and expected the same from his children.

She could only imagine how that sort of expectation, weighted down by his own guilt, had driven Jacob to such lengths to succeed.

She focused on her almost-ex-husband again, seeing him as if through a new camera lens. Suddenly, the man she'd thought she'd known inside out had turned out to be someone else entirely.

Someone she might never have had the chance to get to know were it not for an ill-timed snowfall and a castle in the middle of nowhere.

He was the father of her child. The man she'd always believed had no interest in kids or a family because he had other priorities—namely, chasing success. But that was only half of the truth, she realised now.

He wasn't chasing success; he was running away from failure. Because Jacob Foster was scared. Deathly afraid of screwing up. That was why he'd worked so hard to show her the trappings of success, not knowing that what she really wanted was to have her husband with her. This was why he'd avoided a family, not realising what Clara herself had only learned once Ivy had come into her life: that children, family and the love they brought were what made failure bearable, what made every setback something you could recover from.

Jacob had missed out on four years of Ivy's life. But, if Clara was right, if she could convince him that one teen-age mistake didn't have to ruin his whole life, was there a chance that he might not have to miss any more?

And did she have the courage to find out? She wasn't sure.

'All these years,' she said slowly, choosing her words with great care, 'you've been blaming yourself for this?'

'It was my fault,' Jacob reiterated. 'Of course I have.'

'Does Heather hold it against you? Your father? Your mother?' Clara knew the family, and she thought she knew the answer to two of those questions. But she wasn't quite sure about the third.

'Heather… I'm not even sure how much she remembers. And Mum won't talk about it, ever, so I don't know how she feels.' Clara felt sure that they would have forgiven him long ago. But that wasn't enough, not if Jacob hadn't for-given himself. And if Sheila wouldn't talk about it… Clara could understand that. Of course Sheila would want to pro-tect her daughter, and try to block out the memories of her being hurt. But, by refusing to talk about it, she might not have realised how badly she was hurting her son.

'What about your father?' James Foster was a fair man usually, but one with exceptionally high expectations. Why else would Jacob have gone to such trouble putting together a perfect Christmas for him?

'I… Like I said. He calls it our lucky escape,' Jacob said. 'I think it reminds him of how quickly things can change. Once Heather was home from the hospital…he made me make him a promise. A promise to never screw up like that again. And I haven't.'

He'd lived his whole life trying not to fail. What would that do to a person? What had it done to Jacob?

'At least, not until you walked out that last time,' he added.

The words flowed like cold water over her. He considered their marriage his personal failure. Well, of course he did; she could see that now. But before today…she hadn't been sure he had cared that much at all.

'Me leaving…that wasn't just *your* failure, Jacob. We were too young—we wanted different things. That's all.' Except now she was imagining the life that they maybe could have had, if she'd known his secret sooner. If she'd understood, been able to convince him that blaming himself wasn't getting him anywhere… Was it too late for that now?

'I really thought we were supposed to be together, you know.' The wistful tone of his voice caught her by surprise. 'That's the only reason I risked it. I knew I couldn't take responsibility for a child again, but I thought that maybe, just maybe, I could take care of you. But I was wrong.'

Clara's heart twisted. She couldn't leave him like this, believing this. She had to help heal Jacob's heart, even if it was the last act of their marriage. But dare she try to show him another life, one where he didn't have to be so scared of failure? Where love could be his, no matter what went wrong? Where forgiveness was automatic?

Did she even believe that love was possible any more?

She wasn't sure. But, for Ivy's sake, she knew she needed to find out for certain.

One night. That was all she had to give. One night to find out if there really could possibly be a future in which Jacob might choose to be a part of his daughter's life and maybe even forgive Clara for keeping her existence a secret from him.

One night to find out if their marriage had a future after all.

By the time the snow cleared she needed to know for certain, one way or the other.

She was almost scared to find out which it would be. But, for her daughter, she'd take the risk.

Clara swallowed around the lump that had formed in her throat.

'Come on,' she said. 'I've lit the fire in the main sitting room. Let's take some food and drinks through there where it's more comfortable. We've got a long, cold night ahead of us.'

CHAPTER FIFTEEN

JACOB SCRUBBED A HAND over his face as he stared at his reflection in the bathroom mirror. He needed to get a grip. Clara was waiting out there, probably with a glass of something, definitely with a romantic fire lit and festive food. He needed to focus. He needed to figure out how not to mess up whatever happened next.

It was too late for Heather. The scars he'd caused would be with her for life; he'd accepted that long ago. He was just thankful she was here. And as for his father… Jacob had limited time. He would never be able to make up for the mistake of his youth, and he couldn't personally change the weather forecast, as much as he might want to right now.

All he could do was work with what he had. And right now that was…Clara.

Why had he never told her about Heather before? Perhaps because he didn't want his wife to know his deepest regrets and mistakes. She'd always looked at him with such love and adoration before their marriage. Awe, even.

It was only once the vows had been spoken that she'd discovered exactly the sort of man he was. And she'd left him, without even knowing his deepest shame.

Maybe she'd always had a better understanding of who he really was than he'd given her credit for.

Could he change that?

He needed to ask her about Ivy, he realised. It was strange; he'd only known that he was a father for a couple of hours but already that knowledge was buzzing at the back of his head, every moment, colouring his every thought. He just didn't quite have a handle on how he felt about it yet—at least, not beyond the initial terror.

At least Clara understood at last why he couldn't be a father.

And now…what? What did Clara want from him now?

And would he be able to give it?

It was time to find out.

'I've put the oven on for some nibbles,' Clara said, smiling at Jacob as he opened the door. 'Remind me to go and put them in to cook when my phone buzzes?'

'Sure.' He took the glass of wine she offered him and returned her smile as well as he could.

'I figured that maybe we should go for something a little more easy-going than the hard spirits, seeing as it is still only barely half past four,' she said.

'Ah, but it is Christmas Eve,' he pointed out. 'Everyone knows that wine o'clock comes earlier on Christmas Eve.'

'Which is why we're having wine. Not brandy.'

'Fair enough.'

She grinned, raised her glass, and the last of the tension he'd felt lingering from the emotional exchange in the kitchen evaporated. How did she do that? Clara had always been able to make him relax, but usually it had involved a rather different range of techniques. But now he was starting to think it had just been her, that the massages or the sex or even the wine had just been accessories, a mask, even, that was hiding the truth.

Clara just made him feel better.

How had he forgotten that over the past five years? How had he forgotten how it felt to be the centre of her world? To have her focus all that love and attention on him?

And, more to the point, what had he done to earn it back now?

'So, we're stuck here,' Clara said, settling onto the sofa in front of the promised roaring fire. 'At least until tomorrow at the earliest.'

'Are you okay with that?' he asked, suddenly more aware

that this wasn't just his own personal disaster. Clara had Christmas plans that had been ruined too. It might have taken him a while to catch up, but now he needed her to know that he wasn't just thinking about himself.

'Not really.' Clara plastered on the most falsely cheery smile he'd ever seen. 'But it's the situation, and we can't change that. So we just need to figure out how to make the most of it.'

Her smile settled into something a little sadder but more real. Something more familiar too. And suddenly he had an idea of exactly what they might do to pass the time…and it wasn't very in keeping with their divorce plans.

'What did you have in mind?' he asked, clearing his throat as he tried to disperse the images filling his head. But really… Secluded castle, snowed in, roaring fire… There was even a sheepskin rug in front of it, just waiting for naked bodies.

But not his and Clara's bodies. Because that would be wrong. Somehow.

Why would that be wrong again?

Clara's teeth pressed against her lower lip before she answered, and Jacob's mind wandered on a little field trip again.

'I thought maybe you might want to hear a little about Ivy.'

He swallowed, hard. *Ivy.* His daughter. Fear rose in his throat once more at the thought. 'I'd like to know a little more about what happened. After you left, I mean.' Facts, those he could control, could understand. So he'd focus on the events—what happened and when. 'What did you tell people?'

'What people?' Clara asked with a half-smile. 'Once I left you…I didn't have anyone. Until Ivy came along, and until I met Merry.'

He hated the thought of her all alone in the world. But

it had always been her choice. 'What did you tell Merry? The truth?'

Clara shook her head. 'I told her that I'd had a one-night stand after I left you, and that he didn't want anything to do with the result.' *The result. A daughter.* 'That's what I told anyone who asked about Ivy's dad.'

'What did you tell her?' He swallowed. 'Ivy.' *His* daughter.

'That I loved her father very much but he couldn't be with us.' Her gaze locked onto his. 'So, the truth. That's why I couldn't come back. I took that pregnancy test and…I knew I couldn't have both. I could have you or a baby. And I chose Ivy.'

Of course she had. Wasn't that what any reasonable human would do? Any loving mother?

'You chose to lie to me,' he said, his voice hard. 'You chose to take away *my* choice. To take away the rights of my parents to see their grandchild, to even know that they had one. You made a decision that wasn't just yours to make.' It didn't matter that her choice had been the right one. It should have been his too.

'It was my body. My choice.'

'My daughter.' Hearing it out loud was even more frightening. 'Five years, and you never even told me she existed.' Never gave him the chance to understand what had really happened between them.

'You didn't want a family—you made that crystal-clear to me from the outset. Or at least once we were married, when it was too late for me to do anything about it.'

'So what? I'm allowed to make that choice. What did you think I would do? Did you think I'd order you to get rid of the baby?' Even the thought made his skin crawl. If she truly believed that about him, then she'd never known him at all. Their whole marriage had been a mistake.

'No!' Clara's eyes grew wide with shock. 'I didn't… I

knew you wouldn't do that. No, Jacob. It wasn't that.' He shouldn't feel relieved—everything was still such a mess. But a very small part of him relaxed just a little bit at her words.

'Then what? Why didn't you talk to me at the time?'

Clara ran a shaky hand through her dark hair. 'I didn't find out until after I left. I took a dozen pregnancy tests in a hotel bathroom, just to be sure. But… I'd already left you, Jacob. Again. And I realised that was all we'd been doing since the day we'd got married: pulling apart until we snapped back together again. Everything would be perfect, then you'd get caught up in some project and I wouldn't see you for weeks. I'd get lonely, I'd walk out to get your attention…and then you'd win me back and it would be all flowers and romance. But only for a while, until it started all over again.' She sighed. 'I knew that even if by some miracle you changed your mind about having a family—which you wouldn't have done—we couldn't have brought up a child like that. So I made the decision not to come back.'

'And since then?' He didn't want her answers to make sense. And even if they did, he was still furious. Not because she was wrong—he couldn't say he would have changed his mind about wanting a family. He still hadn't, even though he apparently had one. But because she'd taken away his chance to decide. She'd made him powerless. He felt the same helplessness he'd felt the night Heather had been hurt. And he couldn't forgive that. 'It's been five years, Clara. Did you really at no point think, "Ooh, maybe I should let Jacob know about *our child*"?'

'Of course I did!'

'Then what stopped you?' Because that was the part he really couldn't understand. Maybe a child meant that they couldn't be together any longer; maybe she was right that their marriage couldn't have taken that. But that was still no reason not to tell him.

'You did.' Her words were soft but heavy. Full of meaning. And he understood them instantly. He hadn't been good enough. He'd failed as a husband and Clara had known he'd fail as a father—and so had he! That was exactly why he'd been so adamant about not becoming one.

But hearing her say it out loud, seeing it come from those same lips he'd been thinking about kissing… Jacob felt his heart break, just a little.

'I see.'

'I'm not sure you do.' Clara twisted her hands together as she stared up at him. 'I knew you didn't want a child. Knew that Ivy was the last thing you wanted in your life. You'd made that very clear.'

'So you were sparing me the knowledge? It was for my own good?' he asked, incredulous. Not even Clara could believe that.

'No. It was for Ivy's. I couldn't let you reject her, and let her live her life knowing that she wasn't wanted. I wouldn't do that to her. Not even for you.'

Jacob looked away. 'I can understand that, I guess. And…as much as I hate it, you made the right decision. For both of us.'

'Did I?' His gaze snapped to her face as she spoke. 'I always thought so. But after this week…I'm not so sure.'

'What do you mean?'

'I mean…I thought it was all over for us, the moment I left.' Clara's gaze met his and he felt it deep in his soul. He was missing something here. And he had a feeling he couldn't afford not to listen to her this time. 'But you never would sign those divorce papers.'

It was a risk. A calculated one, but a risk nonetheless. Still, the more she thought about it, the more she wondered. Yes, it had been five years. And yes, she understood now that Jacob's fear of failure must have played into his reluctance to actually give her the divorce. But surely the easier choice would have been to move on, to start over and succeed with someone else, if that was all it was.

There had to be something more. A bigger, better reason why he'd never really moved on from their marriage. From loving her.

Clara knew she had the advantage there. She'd never been able to move on completely, or leave Jacob behind, because his eyes had stared at her every day over the breakfast table, looking out from their daughter's face. She could never cut him out of her memories, even if she'd done her best to cut him out of her life.

But Jacob… Once they left here, that could be it for him. As soon as the snow melted, he could sign those papers and walk away for ever. Never see Ivy. Never see Clara again.

If that was what he really wanted. But she was starting to suspect it wasn't.

'What do you want from me?' Jacob asked, pulling back to put a little more distance between them. 'I've given you all of my secrets now. You know everything. So, what do you want?'

'I want you to know you have a choice,' Clara said slowly, thinking it through as she spoke. 'You have a daughter, and you know that now. You can choose to ignore that fact, but you can't deny that you know it. So you have to decide—do you want to be a part of Ivy's life?'

She held her breath while she waited for his answer.

'You'd let me? If I wanted?'

'Of course.' Clara nodded. 'But there are conditions.'

'I thought there might be.' He folded his arms across his chest. 'Go on, then.'

'If you want in, you have to be one hundred per cent sure. Because once she meets you…you're her father. You have to be there for her, for everything she needs. You can't let her down.'

'And if I can't commit to that?'

'Then you walk away now and Ivy will never know that you exist.' It was just what she'd planned, the way she'd lived for so long. So why did the idea feel like such a wrench to her heart now?

'What about you? You'll always know. And what about us? Is our marriage part of this deal?'

Clara shook her head. 'I don't know. It depends.' She couldn't think beyond Ivy right now.

'Depends on what?'

She looked up and met his gaze again. 'On why you never signed the divorce papers.'

He made a huffing sound that was almost a laugh and put his wine glass down on the table. Clara watched the firelight dancing across his skin and wondered if she really could let him go again without touching him one more time…

'If I signed them,' Jacob said, the words slow and precise, 'I knew, once they were signed, that there was no chance of you ever coming back. And I wasn't ready to face that.'

'Because it would have meant you'd failed?'

'Because I couldn't imagine my life without you in it, even when you weren't there.'

The breath caught in Clara's throat. Had he spent the past five years the way she had, imagining a parallel life in which they were still together? Another universe where they were happy?

'I couldn't let go of us either,' she admitted quietly. 'That's one of the reasons why I never pushed back when your lawyers put obstacles in my way.'

'I wondered.' Jacob shifted closer, just near enough so that his sleeve brushed against hers. Barely touching, but still she felt it like a lightning strike through her body. It was as if everything she'd ever been missing was finally coming home. 'I hoped.'

'I guess it's not as easy as all that to just leave a year of marriage behind,' she said, swallowing hard as she saw the heat in his eyes.

'Oh, I don't know. The marriage part was only ever a piece of paper. It was *you* I couldn't bear to be without.' Not the status. Not the band on his finger that showed his clients that he was serious, grown up, able to take care of business.

Her. Just Clara.

He wanted her, the way that her own family never had. And even if he decided to walk away tomorrow, she owed herself one more night of being wanted like that.

She knew now the real reason why she'd never signed those papers either. Because she still wanted him too. She'd been waiting for him to confirm that it was over.

And suddenly it wasn't. It wasn't over at all.

She couldn't say which of them moved first, but in a blink of an eye the distance between them disappeared and she was close enough to feel his breath against her lips. Her tongue darted out to run over them, as if she could taste him there already.

Jacob groaned, low, in the back of his throat, and then the millimetres between them vanished altogether.

The kiss felt just as Clara remembered—like love, and home, and warmth—and she wondered how she'd lived without this for five long and lonely years. How she had ever believed, even for a moment, that things could be over between them.

She knew now, in that instant, that things could never be truly finished between her and Jacob. Whatever happened next, however large the distance between them might grow, it would never be the end. She would always be connected to this man, in a way far more elemental and real than a mere marriage certificate. It wasn't even only Ivy who held her tied to him; it was her own heart.

And that, she'd discovered, she couldn't organise and order into submission. Her heart had a life of its own, a love of its own, and it had chosen Jacob six years ago and had never let go.

She knew now it never would.

Jacob pulled back, just enough to look into her eyes, his forehead resting against hers and his breath coming as fast as her own.

'Okay?' he murmured.

'Just fine,' Clara replied, her mouth strangely dry.

She knew there were questions to be answered, things to consider and decisions to be made, eventually. But, right in this moment, her world had shrunk to little more than just the two of them and the snow falling outside that had kept them together on Christmas Eve, six years to the day after they met.

Then her phone buzzed and she remembered the oven warming and the food waiting to be cooked. She pulled back but Jacob's hand shot out and he wrapped his fingers around her waist.

'Ignore it,' he whispered.

'Aren't you hungry?' Clara asked.

'Not for anything you can cook.' Jacob gave her a slow, hot smile and Clara knew that dinner would be several hours away.

And by that time she would be ravenous.

This time, it was Clara who leant in to kiss him first and that kiss led to many, many more, each more wonderful than she'd remembered, or ever dreamt she'd feel again.

CHAPTER SIXTEEN

JACOB STRETCHED OUT across the sheets of the four-poster bed, luxuriating in the warmth of the fire burning in the grate, the wonderful ache in his muscles from a night of loving his wife and the feel of Clara's smooth, bare skin beside him.

Well.

That wasn't quite what he'd had in mind when he'd envisioned the perfect family Christmas, but now it was here…

He'd forgotten how in tune they were, physically. They might not have been able to communicate all the issues they had between them in their marriage, and in their pasts, but physically they'd always been able to express themselves totally. The way their bodies moved against each other, the way their fingers sought out sensitive places, the way their mouths moved across skin… That was beyond conversation, beyond language, even. It was innate. It was special.

It was something Jacob knew he'd never find with another living soul, no matter how hard he looked.

Maybe that was the real reason he'd held up the divorce. Maybe it hadn't been his need not to fail, or to prove something, or to make Clara as miserable as she'd made him by leaving.

Maybe it had been as simple as knowing that Clara was his only chance at true happiness.

Only an idiot would give that up without a fight. But when Clara had left she'd denied him that fight, taking the battleground far away, somewhere he couldn't reach.

But now he had his opportunity.

His last chance to win back his wife.

But if he wanted that chance, he had to make a decision—

the biggest he might ever make. He couldn't rush it, just because sex with Clara was so good. This mattered—Ivy mattered. Even if he couldn't be her father, he still knew she mattered more than anything, especially to Clara. So he had to get this right. He wouldn't hurt another child—physically or emotionally.

One night with Clara wasn't enough to brush away all of his fears, and he'd be an idiot if he thought it could. But Clara believed in him. That counted for something.

It counted for a hell of a lot, in fact.

But was it enough?

Only Jacob could make that decision. And he wasn't sure where to start.

Clara woke to the glorious pressure of Jacob's lips against her skin and let herself just enjoy the moment for almost a full minute before reality came crashing down around her.

She'd slept with her ex-husband. She'd let herself get carried away by the connection between them before they'd come to any decision about Ivy—just as she'd promised herself she wouldn't do.

She hadn't even worked on persuading him that having a child in his life would not be the terrible, horrible thing he imagined.

She'd done nothing to convince him that Heather's childhood accident shouldn't affect his whole life, or to deal with the issues that had spanned their marriage and led to her leaving in the first place. Instead, she'd just taken what she'd wanted, selfishly and greedily, and without thinking about what would happen in the morning.

But now it was morning.

She sighed, puffing air out into the pillow. They had talked, they'd covered all sorts of secrets and she'd given him her terms. That wasn't nothing. She understood him a lot better now. She'd just have to hope it was enough and that he knew what he was committing to if he chose to be part of Ivy's life.

Jacob's hands ran up the length of her body, his fingertips skimming her skin and making her shiver. She almost didn't want to move, didn't want to give any sign that she was awake, because the moment she did the night would be over and they would have to deal with the hard decisions to be made in the cold light of day. If Jacob said no, if this really was the end for them, she just wanted one more moment in his arms…

But Ivy was out there waiting for her.

Opening her eyes, Clara realised that they hadn't even managed to close the curtains before falling into the massive four-poster bed the night before, and the winter sun that Jacob had been so sure that Scotland never saw was streaming in through the glass.

'It's stopped snowing,' Clara said, blinking in the light.

'Mmm-hmm,' Jacob murmured, his lips busy working their way across her neck. 'So it has.'

Suddenly, Clara's mind overruled her body and she twisted around in his arms to face him, even as her skin called out for more. 'If the snow has stopped they might be clearing the roads.'

Jacob's hands fell away from her. 'Are you still that keen to get away from me for Christmas?'

'No! I just…' *I'm desperate to get back to our daughter.* 'Ivy will be waiting. Besides, I put a lot of work into setting up your perfect Christmas, you realise. I want your family to be able to enjoy it, if at all possible.' She tried to insert some levity into her words, even though inside, her heart ached.

With a groan, Jacob rolled out of bed, naked despite the cold morning air, and crossed to the window. 'I think I can see the ploughs working their way up from the bottom of the hill.'

Clara swallowed. That meant that she'd be able to get home to Ivy soon, and the relief she felt at that realisation was huge. She just wished it wasn't also tinged with the sadness of having to leave Jacob.

'So,' he asked, sitting on the edge of the bed and pulling the blanket back over him. 'You're the planner. What happens now?'

Nothing like an approaching snowplough—and ex-in-laws—to get the brain working fast in the morning.

'Well, if they're still at the bottom of the hill we probably have an hour or more before the roads are clear enough to drive. You should call your family, see where they are and if they're willing to drive over now. I can get things going downstairs—get the turkey in the oven and so on. Most of the food is ready prepared so it won't take too much effort to get the meal cooking. I can't imagine the staff I hired are going to make it here now, anyway, but we can do it between us, I'm sure.' She wished she had her handbag with her, with her planner inside. She needed her lists. But they had been the last things on her mind when she and Jacob had retired to the bedroom the night before... She checked her watch. 'Lunch is going to be rather later than is traditional at this point, but at least it will happen. The presents are all ready, under the tree, and the... What?' she asked, suddenly aware that Jacob was barely containing his laughter. 'What's so funny?'

'You,' he said, grinning. 'You sitting there, naked, in total professional mode.'

'You think me being professional is amusing?' Clara asked, bristling.

'No, I think it's hot as hell,' he admitted. 'But when I asked what happens now... I wasn't talking about the perfect Foster family Christmas. I was talking about us.'

His grin faded away as he finished speaking, and she stared down at her hands to avoid his gaze. Talking about work was *so* much easier than discussing their mess of a relationship. Of a marriage.

'Unless you already knew that and were avoiding the subject.' There was no laughter in Jacob's voice now.

'No, I wasn't. It's just that whatever happens next… It's up to you, Jacob.' Apparently there was no putting it off any longer. 'I know you haven't had much time, and we were, well, busy for a lot of it. But have you thought about whether you want to meet Ivy?'

Jacob blew out a long breath. 'Yeah. It's pretty much *all* I've been thinking about since you told me. Well, on and off.' He flashed her a smile that told her she'd been a pretty good distraction.

'And?'

'Honestly? I'm scared, Clara. I never planned this. I didn't even get the usual nine months to get used to the idea.'

'I know. I'm sorry.'

'But…' She held her breath, waiting for him to continue. 'I'm not willing to give this—us—up. Not yet. Not without trying.'

But trying wasn't good enough. 'Jacob, if you step into her life you can't just—'

'Step out again, I know,' Jacob said. 'But I've got an idea, if you're willing. A compromise.'

Clara gave a slow nod. 'Okay. Go on.'

He wrapped an arm around her bare waist and pulled her close. 'Bring Ivy and Merry up to the castle for Christmas. We don't need to tell her, or my family, anything just yet. Just…give me a chance to meet her, spend time with her. See if I can manage that without a full-blown panic attack.' He made it sound like a joke but Clara suspected it wasn't. Not entirely, anyway. 'Break me in gently. Then we can decide if we should tell her.'

We. We can decide. Clara liked the sound of that. The two of them. Just like it should have been from the start.

She nodded. 'Okay. I'll call Merry.'

'In a moment.' Jacob darted forward, capturing her lips with his own again. 'How long did you say we had until the roads were clear?' he asked between kisses.

'Sadly, not long enough,' Clara said.

He kissed her one last time, hard and deep and full of promise. Then he pulled away with a groan. 'Then I suppose we'd better make ourselves respectable.' With a wink back at her, he strolled towards the bathroom, whistling.

Clara gave herself one whole minute lying back in bed, replaying the events of the last day in her head. Maybe, just maybe, this could all work out okay. Maybe she didn't have to choose between her two futures any more. Maybe they could be a real family at last.

She smiled to herself. Maybe this would be the best Christmas ever, after all.

Then she sat up and called Merry.

CHAPTER SEVENTEEN

JACOB STOOD AT THE open front door of the castle and watched as the large SUV his father had hired weaved its way up the hill towards him. Heather had texted earlier to say they were waiting at the hotel down the road for the snowploughs to finish clearing the way, and that they had coffee and Christmas cake and carols so Christmas was off to a brilliant start. He wondered if they'd met Merry and Ivy already.

Somehow it seemed that, despite the huge odds stacked against it, he might actually pull off the perfect Christmas after all.

Perfect for more than just his dad, now that Clara was there too. Jacob was apprehensive still, about meeting Ivy. But Clara had promised to introduce him just as 'Jacob'—no pressure, no expectations, just a chance to get to know the little girl he'd helped to make, if not to raise.

And if that went well…who knew? If Clara thought he could be a father, a real husband again, maybe it was possible.

For the first time since his father's diagnosis, the future looked like a place he could bear to live in, even if he knew the inevitable losses coming his way would still be soul-destroying. With Clara at his side, he had faith that he could make it through them.

Everything seemed possible when Clara was with him.

'Are they nearly here?' Clara appeared from the kitchen, a festive apron still wrapped around her waist, and she wiped flour from her hands onto it. 'Have I got time to wash up?'

'Nope.' Jacob pointed down the path. 'That's Dad's car.

They'll be here any moment.' The excitement thrumming through his veins was only partly to do with the festivities and pulling off the whole plan. Mostly, he suspected, it had something to do with Clara standing beside him, smelling of cinnamon. He hadn't felt this kind of excitement at Christmas since he'd been about ten.

'Oh, no. I look a state.'

'You look beautiful.' He snaked an arm around her waist and kissed the top of her slightly floury hair. 'What have you been making?'

'Last-minute mince pies,' she said, absently. She peered out of the door. 'There's Merry's hire car too, just behind them.'

Merry. And Ivy. Jacob's chest tightened and he focused on breathing in and out, creating steam in the frosty air. He could do this. 'Nearly time, then.'

'For our perfect Christmas.' Clara's small hand sneaked into his and he felt her warmth throughout his body.

'Ours,' he echoed.

The SUV pulled up onto the driveway with a crunch of snow. 'And here they are! Merry Christmas!' Stepping out into the glorious winter's day, he helped his mum down from the car and held her tightly before hugging Heather and shaking his father's hand.

'We made it!' Heather said, beaming. 'Jacob, this place is incredible!'

'Isn't it? Come on in. Clara's waiting to see you all!' He realised that the second car had pulled up beside the castle too. 'And we've got some other special guests today too.'

Clara's business partner, Merry, stepped out of the car. And behind her walked a small girl. The girl who must be Ivy. His daughter.

A chill settled into Jacob's bones as he watched her smile and bounce out into the snow.

She looked exactly like Heather had as a child.

* * *

'Mummy!' Ivy yelled and raced across the snow into Clara's arms. Dropping to her knees, Clara held her daughter tight and, just for a moment, refused to think about what might happen next. It was Christmas morning and she was with her daughter. That was all that mattered.

'Hello, sweetheart,' Clara murmured. 'I'm so happy to see you.'

'Clara?' Jacob asked, and she could hear the nervousness in his voice.

'We should get everyone inside the castle. It's cold out here,' she said, straightening up to stand again. 'But first… Ivy, this is Jacob. He's the one who planned this whole Christmas in a castle for his family and for us.'

'And then your mum organised it all,' Jacob said, still standing a metre or so away.

Ivy turned her big, blue eyes on him then stuck out a hand. 'I'm Ivy.'

Clara watched Jacob's jaw tighten as he reached out to take his daughter's hand. 'Hi, Ivy. It's brilliant to meet you.'

A bubble of hope floated up inside her. Maybe, just maybe, this might all work out.

Christmas dinner went as well as she could have hoped. Merry kept up a constant stream of inconsequential conversation, for which Clara was eternally grateful. And when James turned to her over Christmas pudding and said how pleased he was to see her again, and how he hoped she'd become a permanent fixture of the family once more, Clara even managed a polite smile.

'It's very kind of you all to let us impose on your family Christmas,' she said. 'Especially since we were caught here by the snow. I know it's been very special for Ivy.'

'It's been very special for us spending time with Ivy too.' James's pointed look was knowing, but Clara ignored it.

She didn't want to give anyone false hope about the future of their families.

Least of all herself.

'Time for presents!' Heather announced, jumping to her feet, seeming more like a child than a twenty-something.

'But I thought Father Christmas got snowed in at the North Pole,' Ivy piped up and Clara winced.

Heather smiled down at the girl and Clara realised that Merry must have primed everyone on the story they'd told her. 'Well, if the roads here got clear enough for us to make it to the castle for Christmas, maybe Father Christmas was able to get out too. If he's been, I reckon there'll be more presents by the fireplace next to the tree. Shall we go and check?'

'Okay.' Ivy reached up to take Heather's hand and followed her into the hallway. Moments later, they all heard a gasp, and Ivy came racing back into the dining room. 'Mummy! Mummy! He's been! He must have come while we were eating dinner!'

'Really? Fantastic!' Clara caught Merry's eye over Ivy's head and mouthed *Thank you,* but Merry just shrugged.

They all made their way into the hall, where seven red stockings hung by the fire, each with a name tag hanging from it.

'It's a Christmas miracle,' Jacob said drily, but he squeezed Clara's hand when no one was looking. She squeezed back. Really, he was coping surprisingly well. A lesser man might have been driven to distraction by Ivy's many questions over the dinner table, but he'd answered every one thoughtfully and patiently. He'd even lost some of the slightly panicked air that had surrounded him since Ivy had stepped out of the car.

Clara had seen photos of Heather as a child; she knew exactly what he must have been thinking. But that was why today was so brilliant an opportunity for them to meet.

Heather was right there with them, happy and whole and alive.

The whole set-up was just asking for a happy ever after.

Clara smiled to herself as she watched Ivy dig through her stocking. She unwrapped the bike lock, helmet, knee and elbow pads that Clara had bought for her, then reached into the bottom to find an envelope. She tore it open, then frowned at the ornate letters printed on the card. Merry leaned over her shoulder.

'It says *Look outside*.'

Ivy dropped her haul and dashed out of the front door, squealing with delight. 'It's a bike! A purple bike, just like I wanted!'

'How on earth did you get that up here without her noticing?' Clara asked as they followed her outside.

'Trade secret,' Merry replied, tapping the side of her nose. 'Plus we bumped into Jacob's family at the hotel before we drove up. That helped.'

'Mummy! Come see!' Ivy called, and Clara went to watch her daughter wobble across the snowy ground on her new bike. Then Ivy yelled, 'Jacob! Come watch me ride!'

But Jacob wasn't there. Clara frowned; he'd been beside her before they'd come outside. What had happened to him?

'I'll go find him for you, sweetie,' she told Ivy and, leaving Merry in charge of supervising the bike riding, headed back through the giant wooden doors into the castle.

'All I'm saying is, Clara has taken on a lot of responsibility, raising that child alone.' James Foster's voice echoed off the stone walls, and Clara's frown deepened as she followed the sound. She didn't like the idea of her father-in-law discussing her in her absence—especially when it involved a subject he knew nothing about.

'Dad, I know that. And if…well, if things had been different…' Jacob sounded more stressed than he had since the moment they'd realised they were snowed in the day before. Clara disliked that even more.

Stepping through the doorway into the kitchen, she coughed loudly to announce her presence. 'Jacob?' she added for good measure. 'Ivy's looking for you. She wants you to see her riding her bike.'

Jacob spun round, apparently surprised to see her there. 'Right. I'll be right there.'

But his father's hand was already on his arm. And James was murmuring something more, something she couldn't hear.

She'd always been fond of Jacob's father. But, right now, she wondered if she hadn't paid enough attention to James's relationship with his son.

Jacob nodded and stepped away, taking Clara's hand and turning her back the way she'd come. 'Come on then,' he said, flashing her a smile that didn't reach his eyes. 'Let's go see your girl cycle.'

Clara has taken on a lot of responsibility.

His father's words echoed through his head as he watched Ivy gleefully cycling up and down the same stretch of driveway. The snow was still piled up in banks on either side, but they'd cleared enough that she could ride in one big circle around the cars.

Raising that child alone.

He'd wanted to explain—tell him how he hadn't known about Ivy. How, if he had, he'd have done things differently. But the truth was, he didn't know for sure if that was the truth.

Today had been wonderful. He'd honestly enjoyed Ivy's company, loved hearing her questions and answering them as best he could. He'd loved watching the pure joy on her face as she'd opened her presents. Loved standing with Clara, seeing her bursting with pride for her girl.

Their girl. Their child.

But Christmas Day wasn't like any other day, was it? And life wasn't all Christmas Days. It was balancing work and family, and looking after each other, and too many other everyday things he didn't even know how to imagine yet. Could he do *that?* He didn't know.

He wouldn't know unless he tried.

And now that you're in that child's life? his father had asked in a murmur, while Clara had stood waiting. *I hope that you will live up to* your *responsibilities, Jacob.*

Could he? And could he risk it, not knowing for sure?

He wanted to; he knew that much. He wanted to try, for the first time since Clara had walked out. He wanted to try for something he wasn't sure he could succeed at, something he was certain he didn't deserve. But did that make it the right decision?

'Look at me, Jacob!' Ivy called out to him and he waved to show her he was watching. Taking in every second of her gleeful, happy ride.

Could he walk away from this? Maybe that was the question he should be asking.

When it happened, it happened in slow motion.

Ivy was still waving back, riding one-handed as she wobbled along on her stabilisers, not looking where she was going. She couldn't have seen the rock, hidden under the snow bank. As he watched, her front wheel bashed into it, jerking her to a halt, sending Ivy flying over the handlebars into the snow.

Jacob darted forward but he was a full second behind Clara, too slow to reach Ivy first. And too slow to warn them about the wedge of snow, dislodged from the castle walls above as it slid down towards them.

He shouted to them to move, but Clara was too busy pulling Ivy up out of the snow bank, holding her close as she cried. Without thinking, he dived forward and yanked them both aside, shielding them with his body as the snow landed, hard and cold and wet against his back, even through his coat.

'What… Where did that come from?' Clara asked. 'The roof?'

Jacob nodded, too winded still to speak.

'You saved us.' Ivy stared up at him, her eyes wet with tears, but filled with a look of trust and hope that was all too familiar. Jacob felt it like a stab wound to the heart.

That was how Heather had looked at him when she was a child. Before the accident.

He didn't deserve Ivy's trust. And he'd only betray it in the end if he stayed. He couldn't let her believe otherwise, not when he knew how badly he could fail.

He couldn't be her father.

He stumbled backwards, almost losing his footing on the snow. 'I need to go…dry off.' Turning away, he headed back into the castle, head down.

He needed to escape. He needed to get away from those eyes. From that faith and expectation and responsibility.

From everything he'd always failed at before.

'Ivy's fine.' Clara leant against the bedroom door frame, watching Jacob towelling off his hair. 'Your mother is feeding her mince pies and hot chocolate. She's been so spoilt today she's never going to want to leave, you realise.'

But they were going to have to leave. They had to go back to London, to the real world and their real lives.

And, from the way Jacob had just run from them, Clara had a horrible feeling they'd be going alone.

Jacob looked up, guilt shining in his eyes. 'I'm glad she's not hurt.'

'Thanks to you.'

He shook his head. 'I should have got her out of the way sooner. Or stopped her from falling. Told her to keep both hands on the handlebars, watch where she was going. Something.'

'She's a child, Jacob,' Clara said, sitting on the edge of the bed. 'Children have accidents all the time. It wasn't anyone's fault.' Never mind that her own heart had stopped for a moment as she'd watched it happening. She couldn't let Jacob blame himself for this.

'Maybe not. But that just makes it worse.'

Clara frowned. 'How?'

'I couldn't keep her safe, Clara. She was my responsibility for half a day and she got hurt. I wasn't paying enough attention.'

'You know how crazy that sounds, right? It was an accident, Jacob, that's all.' She reached out to touch his arm but he pulled it back, out of reach.

'I can't do this Clara.'

And there it was. The words she'd dared to believe might not be coming. But there they were, out in the world like a final sentence. His last words.

'Because of one stupid accident?'

'Because I'm not the right person for this. I never was. I thought… When I married you, I convinced myself that I could be a good husband just because I *wanted* it so much. Wanted *you* so much.' He ran his fingers through his damp hair, a look of agony on his face. 'And I almost made the same mistake again. I wanted to be with you, with Ivy, so much I thought I could be what you need. But I can't. And it's not fair to Ivy to take that risk. She deserves everything—including a wonderful father. And that's just not me.'

'You're giving up,' Clara said quietly. 'Giving in. Because you're scared.'

'You're right I'm scared. I'm terrified, Clara. And that's a sign. I shouldn't be doing this.'

Anger rose up inside her, the flames licking her insides.

'You're wrong. If you're scared, it's a sign it's worth fighting for.'

Jacob laughed, and it came out harsh and bitter. 'Like you fought for us? You walked out without a backward glance, Clara. And you know what? *You were right.* I admit it. So now it's my turn to do the same.'

'And you never came after me! You wouldn't let me go, wouldn't divorce me, but you wouldn't come after me either. Why was that, Jacob? Because you were too scared to lose me—but too scared to love me too. Too scared to let me in, let me close.'

'And you weren't?'

'Maybe I was. But you know what? I've grown up. I've opened up to you, told you everything. And I took a risk; I gave you a chance. A chance at the best thing you could ever have—being Ivy's father. And you're turning it down?' She shook her head sadly. 'You're an idiot.'

'Maybe I am,' he said, his voice soft. 'But Clara, I'd rather hurt you both now than risk breaking you later.'

She stared at him. He was really doing this. After everything they'd shared, said and done, he was pushing her away again.

'One day you're going to realise,' she said. 'Keeping people at arm's length doesn't keep them safe, Jacob. It only keeps them lonely.'

He didn't answer.

Clara turned and left, closing the door behind her, alone once again. Alone, not because he didn't want her, or even because he didn't love her, but because he didn't have the courage to be with her and Ivy.

She wasn't sure if that was better or worse.

'So that's that, then?' Merry asked, and when Clara looked up she saw her best friend standing a little way along the corridor.

'You heard?'

'Enough,' Merry confirmed. 'What do you want to do now? Sheila has invited us to stay here for the night, and Ivy looks close to falling asleep on her feet.'

'I know.' Clara chewed her lip. Part of her wanted to get out of there the first chance they got, but another larger part didn't want to do anything to ruin Christmas Day for the others. She couldn't stay but she couldn't run either. Not just yet.

'Let's put Ivy to bed,' she decided. 'Then we can clear up down here.'

'And then?'

'Then, the moment everyone else goes to bed, we get Ivy in the hire car and drive back to London,' Clara said.

Christmas was nearly over.

It was time for her new life to begin again.

CHAPTER EIGHTEEN

'I ONLY ASKED if you'd spoken to her,' Sheila said, throwing up her hands defensively. 'There's no need to snap.'

'I didn't snap,' Jacob said, knowing full well that he had. But really, it had been four days. No, he hadn't spoken to Clara. And no, he had no intention of doing so.

His family hadn't taken Clara's departure in the middle of the night well, or the note that she'd left explaining that she and Merry had work back in London they needed to return to. Jacob, who was more used to being walked out on in the middle of the night, had simply crumpled the note up and thrown it on the fire.

He'd made his decision. He couldn't blame her for abiding by it. Not this time.

'Is Dad in his study?' Jacob asked, looking past his mother down the hallway at Honeysuckle House. The Christmas decorations were still up and he wanted nothing more than to tear them down. Wasn't it New Year yet? Couldn't they move on?

He was ready to start his new life, without Clara. Without Ivy. He just needed the world to stop reminding him of them both.

Both. That was the biggest surprise. He'd expected to be haunted by Clara's memory—he had been often enough over the past five years to have grown almost used to it. But Ivy… Jacob had spent less than a day with her, and yet everywhere he turned he seemed to find reminders of her. A girl on a bike, a small red coat, a too bright smile, a Christmas cracker like the ones she'd insisted on pulling with everyone. Even the Christmas lights made him think of her.

Clearly he was losing his mind.

'Yes, he's upstairs, I think,' Sheila said, answering the question Jacob had almost forgotten he'd asked.

'Right.' He made for the stairs, his mind still occupied by thoughts of an empty castle, and a note he never wanted to see again.

He'd hoped that a business conversation with his father would take his mind off things, as well as giving him a chance to check on James's health after the trek to Scotland and back. But, instead, he found his dad in a pensive, family orientated frame of mind. Which was the last thing Jacob wanted.

'Come in! Sit down!' James motioned towards the visitor's chair. 'Pull it up over here. I'm just looking through some old photo albums.'

Jacob's stomach clenched as he saw the open page, filled with photos of Heather as a little girl, through from babyhood to a final one of her with bandages wrapped around her arms and scratches and cuts on her face. Why had they even taken that picture? Who wanted to remember that moment in time?

He reached across to try and turn the page but James stopped him with a gentle hand on his wrist. 'She really did look uncannily like Ivy, don't you think?'

'Yes. And no, before you ask, I haven't spoken to them.'

'Why?' James asked. 'Really, Jacob. Why haven't you gone after them?'

'Because we decided it would be best for Ivy if I wasn't part of her life.' The truth was always easier than a lie. 'I can't commit to being a father right now.'

'And whose decision was this, exactly? Yours or Clara's?'

Jacob looked away. 'Does it matter? She kept Ivy's very existence from me for five years. I think we can assume that Clara agrees I'm not the right person to be a father.'

'I think she was scared. Maybe even as scared as you are right now.'

Jacob looked up to meet his father's gaze and found a depth of knowing and understanding there that shocked him to his core.

'When your mother first told me she was pregnant with you, I was terrified,' James admitted, flipping to the next page of the album as if his words were of no consequence. But Jacob clung to them anyway. 'I had no idea how to be a father—I was a scientist! An academic, at that point. I was the only child of an only child, so there had never been any babies around when I was growing up. I hadn't the first idea what you should do with one.'

'So what did you do?'

'I learnt,' James said bluntly. 'Because I knew that being a father was the one thing in life I couldn't afford to fail at. So I learnt everything I could.'

'It worked,' Jacob said with a bitter laugh. 'You were an excellent father. Far better than I could ever hope to be.'

'No, I wasn't.'

Jacob looked up at his father in shock. 'You're wrong. I…I couldn't keep my sister safe, or my wife happy or by my side, or even stop Ivy from falling off her bike! But you, you kept our whole family together, all these years.'

James shook his head. 'It's not enough. I think maybe our fear for Heather, after the accident… We focused so hard on her, on keeping her safe, maybe we ignored your needs. I should have told you…so many things. That I'm proud of you. That no one ever blamed you for what happened. It was a freak accident. You didn't *mean* to hurt her. I should have told you that nothing you ever did could make me less proud of you.'

'Dad… You don't have to…' Jacob felt as if his heart was growing in his chest as his father spoke. As if years of armour built of fear and shame were falling away from his shoulders, leaving him lighter than he could remember feeling since he was a child.

'Yes. I do.' James reached out and took Jacob's hand. 'I'm dying. We both know that. And people say you have all sorts of revelations at the end of your life. But that's not what this is. These are all the things I should have told you years ago—that I should have been telling you every day and didn't.'

'And you've said them. Thank you.'

'But that's not all. Son, you have to know…it's okay to fail. It's okay to screw up and make mistakes. As long as you *try again*. When I was inventing, for every thing I created that worked, I made a hundred—a thousand!—that didn't. But I still didn't give up, no matter how many times I failed. That's the key to the things that matter in life. You just have to keep trying.'

'I tried, Dad, with Clara. We both did. Time and again. It just didn't work.' Whatever he did, she was always going to leave him.

'What about with Ivy? Isn't it worth trying again for her?'

'Not if I'm just going to mess it up again.' He'd seen the look on Clara's face when she'd spoken about not wanting Ivy to feel unwanted. He knew where that came from—knew how scared she was of Ivy living through what she'd had to. And maybe she was right not to take that risk.

'As long as you keep trying, you can't get it wrong,' James promised him. 'Look at me. I've been messing up your upbringing for over thirty years, and I'm still trying to make it right. So let me try. And help me succeed.'

'What do you want me to do?'

'I want you to be happy,' James said simply. 'I want you to think about the last time you were truly happy, and do whatever it takes to get you there again. And then I want you to try your best to stay there. Can you do that?'

The last time he had been happy. In bed with Clara at

the castle. Except…no. There was one more moment after that, one more second when he'd felt pure happiness.

Watching Ivy's face when she'd found her bike outside the castle.

Jacob swallowed, hard.

'I think I can,' he said. 'And I'm definitely going to try.'

James clapped him on the shoulder. 'That's my boy.'

Clara was officially pampering herself. Or at least that was what Merry had instructed her to do when she'd shown up to whisk Ivy off to see a pantomime earlier that afternoon.

'You've been working flat out ever since we got back from Scotland. You need a day to relax and get yourself ready for the Charity Gala tonight. To get ready for the new year to start and for you to begin your awesome new life,' Merry had said. 'And you can't do that while you're busy putting on a brave face for Ivy or working too much so you can pretend you haven't just had your heart broken. So we're going out. Take a bath or something.'

'But what about the gala? There's last-minute stuff to sort—'

'All delegated. That's why we have staff.'

'What about the last table? The cancellation?' One last-minute cancellation had left them with an empty table—or, at ten grand a plate, one hundred thousand pounds less money that had been raised. That wasn't acceptable—and it definitely wasn't Perfect London.

'Sorted. I sold it this morning.'

'Seriously?'

'I am a miracle worker. I have planned and fixed everything. Now, go run that bath.'

Merry probably hadn't planned on the knock on the door, however.

Clara sighed into the bubbles around her. Then, as whoever was waiting knocked again, she hauled herself out of the bath and wrapped a towel around her.

'Mrs Clara Foster?' the delivery man at the door asked.

Clara blinked. 'I suppose so.' Even if no one had called her that in five years. 'For now, anyway.'

'These are for you.' He motioned to the large stack of boxes in his arms. 'Shall I bring them in?'

Clara nodded. He set them on the table, then discreetly disappeared again, leaving Clara to open them in peace.

Fixing her towel more tightly around her, she opened the largest box, lifting out the most beautiful ballgown Clara thought she had ever seen. It was dark red velvet, sprinkled with sparkles on the bodice and overlaid with lace on the skirt. She held it against her and imagined dancing in it at the gala that night. She'd never worn anything half as beautiful. Even her wedding dress had been grabbed off the rack at the shop next to the Vegas chapel.

The next box held matching shoes, then a bag and smaller boxes with discreet silver and garnet jewellery—earrings, a necklace—and a silver bangle studded with garnets, and with a message engraved on the inside: *She believed she could, so she did...*

Someone knew exactly what she liked. Clara pulled out the card last, and held her breath as she read it.

I chose the presents myself this time.
I'll see you tonight.
Both of you.
Love, J x

She blinked. *Both of you?*

A second knock rattled the door and she dashed across to answer it, half expecting Jacob to be there himself. But instead it was another delivery man, carrying another stack of boxes, all a little smaller than the first.

'I'm looking for a Miss Ivy Foster?' the delivery man said.

Clara bit back a smile. 'She's not here right now, but I can take those for you.'

This time, she reached for the card first.

Ivy,
I can't wait to carry on our conversations at the ball tonight. I hope your mum might still let me tell you something very important.
Love, Jacob x

Clara grabbed her phone, hoping to catch Merry before the pantomime started. 'Who exactly did you sell the last table to?' she asked when her friend answered.

'Ah,' Merry said. 'It's a funny story…'

Clara fell into her chair and laughed, her heart lifting for the first time since she'd left Scotland.

CHAPTER NINETEEN

THE BALLROOM AT THE Harrisons' mansion was bedecked with sparkling white fairy lights. Perfectly laid tables were dressed with crisp white linen and glistening crystal chandeliers hung from the ceiling. Jacob tugged at the collar of his tuxedo and hoped, not for the first time in the last few days, that this wasn't all a huge, huge mistake.

He'd already let Clara down. He'd played right into her worst fears and walked away just when she thought she could rely on him to be there for her and Ivy. It was asking a lot to want to come back from that, and all he really had to work with was a couple of fancy ballgowns, a ridiculously expensive dinner and—he glanced behind him at the three people sitting very expectantly at a table set for ten—his family.

'This could be a huge mistake,' he told them, taking his seat. His mother pushed a bread roll towards him and Heather motioned a waiter over to bring him a glass of wine. 'I mean, she's running this event. She could actually have us thrown out.'

'She won't,' his father said, totally calm. 'Patience.'

'Where is she?' Jacob craned his neck to try and spot her in the crowd, but there were so many people filling the ballroom it was almost impossible to pick out any one person.

Of course, if she was wearing the dress he'd sent, he had a feeling she'd be hard to miss.

'She'll be here,' his mother reassured him. 'Eat some bread. You should never go into a stressful situation on an empty stomach.'

'It's not stressful!' Heather said, reaching for her own

wine. 'It's romantic. He's paid *thousands* to be here tonight to tell her he loves her and he wants to be a family again.'

'You make it sound easy.' Meanwhile, just thinking about it made his hands shake with nerves. God, what was it about Clara that could drive him to such panic? He was never like this before a big business meeting.

'It is! All you need to do is tell her, "I love you, I'm sorry, can we try again?"' Heather said.

'I think it might take a bit more than that.' Such as an entire personality change from him. Oh, no, this was *such* a bad idea.

'I think you'll be surprised.'

Before they could argue the point further, a small girl in a dark green velvet dress, complete with satin sash, came barrelling through the crowd towards them, a harried-looking Merry hurrying behind.

'Jacob!' Ivy squealed, throwing herself into his arms. 'You came! Thank you for my dress—I love it!'

Jacob let himself savour the feeling of those tiny arms around his neck, the scent of clean little girl and a sweetness he suspected had something to do with Merry sneaking her chocolate. He looked up at Clara's business partner.

'Clara's double-checking things in the kitchen and briefing the entertainment for later. She'll be here soon. Can I leave Ivy with you guys for dinner?'

'Absolutely!' Jacob's mum beamed. Then, belatedly, she looked across at Jacob. 'That's fine, isn't it, darling?'

His first parental moment, pre-empted by his mother. He supposed it was inevitable.

'Ivy will be fine here with us,' he told Merry. 'And, uh, if you see Clara…'

'I will surreptitiously nudge her in this direction.' Merry rolled her eyes. 'It's not like she doesn't know you're here, you know.'

'So she's avoiding me?'

'She's working,' Merry said, looking amused. 'I'd have thought you would have appreciated that.'

Jacob returned her wry grin. He hadn't been able to focus on work since Christmas.

But then he looked up and saw Clara across the room, the dark red velvet dress he'd chosen for her clinging to her very familiar curves, and he knew he'd never be able to focus on anything else but her again.

'Ivy? Are you okay staying here with Heather and my parents while I talk to your mum?'

Ivy, who was already pulling a cracker with Heather, nodded.

'Right. Then I'll…go and do that.' He paused for a moment.

'Go on, son,' his father said, placing a hand on his shoulder. 'You can do it.'

Yes. He could. He hadn't been sure in Scotland, but now…he knew exactly what he needed to do.

Heather's words came back to him. *All you need to do is tell her, 'I love you, I'm sorry, can we try again?'*

He could do that.

'Clara?' He crossed the ballroom towards her and lost his breath when she turned and faced him. It wasn't just her beauty—formidable though it was. It was the connection, the instant spark of recognition he felt when their eyes met. The link that told him that whatever happened, however he screwed up, they were meant to be together. Always.

Clara's smile was hesitant. 'Jacob…it was kind of you to buy the last table tonight. I know the Harrisons appreciate your generous donation. And I hope it means that maybe we can work something out between our families. I know Ivy would love to see more of Heather, and your parents.'

'But not me?' Jacob finished for her.

'Well, that rather depends on you,' Clara said, meeting

his gaze. 'And whether you've changed enough to make the commitment we need from you.'

This was it, Jacob realised. His second chance. And he might not have the perfect plan but he had a heartfelt one. One that was good enough to make a start with, anyway.

And if he screwed it up he'd just have to try harder.

Jacob took a deep breath and prepared to change his life for ever.

Clara smoothed her hand over her dress, the weight of her ballgown giving her small courage as she waited to hear what he'd say. He'd paid a lot of money to be there. It couldn't be the end of everything, as she'd thought. But could there really be a way through for them? She still wasn't sure.

And she knew it all hinged on Ivy.

She glanced across and saw her daughter pulling a cracker with Jacob's father and smiled. Her daughter had been so delighted with the dress Jacob had sent, so excited to be allowed to go with her this evening. The Harrisons had thought it a charming idea and, with Merry delegating so efficiently, Clara had very little to do at the gala but enjoy the evening.

Right then, all she could see was Jacob, gorgeous and nervous and smiling in his tux.

'I keep seeing children. Everywhere.'

Clara blinked at his words in confusion.

'There are…quite a lot of them in the world?' she said.

'Yes. But I never noticed them before. Not until I met Ivy.' He took her arm and led her to the window, out of the way of the flow of the other guests. Outside, more lights flickered in the trees, bright and full of hope for the year ahead.

Maybe Clara could be hopeful too.

'And now?' she asked.

'Now I can't stop seeing them. Can't stop wondering if they're older or younger than Ivy. What she was like at their age, or what she will be like. Whether she likes the same things. Obviously she's prettier and cleverer and more wonderful than all of them… I can't understand it, though. I only spent one day with her and suddenly she's everywhere.'

'She gets under your skin,' Clara said. 'Once I knew I was pregnant, I saw babies everywhere. And once she was born… She's my first thought every morning when I wake up, and my last thought before I go to sleep.'

'You used to say that was me,' Jacob said, but he didn't seem disappointed. More…proud?

'It was,' Clara admitted. 'You were all I thought about. But being a parent, it changes you. In all sorts of good ways.'

'You were everything to me too,' Jacob said. 'All that I could think about, any time of the day. I know you thought I ignored you and that I focused too much on work, but really I never stopped thinking about you, not for a moment. It was…everything. And terrifying. Because I didn't know if I could cope if I hurt you, lost you.'

'So you kept me at arm's length.' Just like he'd tried to do again at the castle.

'Yeah. I think so.'

'What about now?' Clara asked.

'Now…I'm still thinking about you. But not just about losing you. I'm thinking about all the possibilities we have, instead. I'm thinking about Ivy. I'm thinking about the life we could have together.'

'I thought you didn't want that.' In fact, her entire existence for the past five years had hinged on the fact that the last thing he wanted was a family.

'So did I,' Jacob agreed. 'Right up until the moment I

realised that you had gone again, and this time you'd taken Ivy with you.'

Clara grabbed hold of the window frame behind her. The world must be spinning off its axis because she felt a fundamental shift somewhere underneath everything she knew to be true. 'What are you saying?'

'I've spoken to my real estate agent. I'm selling the houses—all those white, soulless designer places you hated. We'll choose a new home together, the three of us. And I'm speaking with the board, working out a more family friendly schedule. One that will work with your business commitments too, I hope.

'Basically, I'm saying…I love you. I'm sorry. Can we try again?'

Clara shook her head. 'Jacob, we tried. So many times.'

'Yeah, but this time we've got a better reason to succeed.'

'What happened to you?' Clara asked. 'What changed? Because…I want to believe you. But I need to know why.'

Jacob stood beside her and took her hand. 'It was my father, mostly. He told me that success nearly always starts with failure. That the key is to keep trying for the things that matter. And you, Clara…you matter more than anything. You and Ivy. You're all that matters.'

'You never wanted to be a father.'

'I was too scared to be a father. Too scared that I'd screw it up.'

'Everyone screws it up. That's what being a parent is all about.' Hadn't she learned that the hard way, over the past four years?

'So my parents tell me,' Jacob said with a wry smile. 'And the thing is…I think, if we were screwing up and trying again together, if it wasn't just me on my own, scared to death of failing…if it was *us,* I think I could do it.'

'You have to be sure, Jacob. Ivy can't take maybes. She's four. She needs to know you'll always be there.'

'And will you?' Jacob asked. 'Will you be there for me, as well as her? Because if we do this…I need to know you won't leave again.'

Clara looked down at her hands, at where her wedding ring used to sit. 'I will. I realised, this time…I can't spend my life running away. I wanted to be wanted, and when I thought I wasn't, I left. But with Ivy, I'm not just wanted, I'm needed. And that's so much more important.'

'She's not the only one who needs you,' Jacob said. Clara looked up to meet his open gaze and saw the truth of his words there. 'I need you in my life, Clara. I need you there to pick me up when I fall, to hold me when things fall apart, to cheer me on when things are going well and to love me, all the time. And, most of all, I need you to let me do all those things for you too. Because I love you, more than I ever thought I could. More than I ever realised I would. You're part of me and I can't risk losing that part again. I need it. I need you.'

Clara let out a choked sob and he pulled her against him, his arms warm and safe around her. 'I need you too,' she admitted. 'Not because I can't do it on my own—I know I can. It just doesn't mean as much without you there.'

'Then I'll be there. For you and for Ivy. Whenever you need me. I promise.'

'And I'll be there too. I won't leave again.'

'And when we both screw up?' Jacob asked. 'Because I have it on good authority that we will. Things won't be perfect all the time.'

Clara shook her head. 'They don't need to be perfect. We just need to try. And when we screw up, we'll try harder. Together.'

'Together,' Jacob echoed. Then he smiled. 'Look,' he said, nudging her chin upwards. 'Mistletoe.' She smiled.

Apparently Merry had known what she was doing when she'd insisted on hanging it in all of the window alcoves.

'Well, you'd better kiss me then,' Clara said, her heart full to bursting. 'And then we'll go and tell Ivy that she just gained a family.'

'She had us all along,' Jacob said. 'I just didn't know it yet.'

'And now that you do?' Clara asked, in between kisses.

Jacob grinned down at her under the mistletoe. 'Now…' he said. 'This is officially my perfect Christmas.'

* * * * *

"Maybe I should invite myself to dinner," Matt said lightly.

Olivia looked at him. "Seriously?"

"Seriously." He grinned. "Single guys don't get many home-cooked meals."

Once again, she hesitated before answering, "Well, I know Thea will be thrilled if you stay to dinner."

"Only Thea? What about you?"

"Are you digging for a compliment?"

"Everyone likes compliments."

"Okay. I'm glad you want to have dinner with us. There. Are you satisfied?"

Now that the tone of their conversation had changed, he decided to make one more attempt to burrow through her defenses. "I was hoping you'd say you liked me, too."

"Of course I like you, Matt. You're part of the family."

Because they were now approaching her mother's house, he let the comment go without answering.

* * *

The Crandell Lake Chronicles:
Small town, big hearts

THE MAN SHE SHOULD HAVE MARRIED

BY

PATRICIA KAY

MILLS & BOON

First Published in Great Britain 2016
By Mills & Boon, an imprint of HarperCollins*Publishers*
1 London Bridge Street, London, SE1 9GF

ISBN: 978-0-263-92026-0

23-1016

Our policy is to use papers that are natural, renewable and recyclable products and made from wood grown in sustainable forests. The logging and manufacturing processes conform to the legal environmental regulations of the country of origin.

Printed and bound in Spain
by CPI, Barcelona

Having formerly written as Trisha Alexander, **Patricia Kay** is a *USA TODAY* bestselling author of more than forty-eight novels of contemporary romance and women's fiction. She lives in Houston, Texas. To learn more about her, visit her website at www.patriciakay.com.

This book is dedicated to all the amazing women in my life. I don't know how any woman survives without girlfriends. Your friendship and support has meant the world to me. I love you all!

Chapter One

Crandall Lake, Texas
Mid-October...

Olivia Britton grinned at her cousin, the newly married Eve Crenshaw. "I'm so happy you're here!"

Eve laughed. "You've already said that at least ten times."

"I know. But I *am*. I've missed you." In fact, Olivia couldn't believe how much she'd missed Eve.

"Oh, come on, Liv. I've only been gone six weeks. And we've texted and talked on the phone almost every day."

"It's not the same," Olivia insisted. "You're not here. We can't meet for lunch or have dinner together or just sit and talk for hours. And Thea misses you, too!" Thea, short for Dorothea, was Olivia's four-year-old daughter.

Eve nodded. "I know. But no matter where I am, I'll always be here for you...*and* Thea. You know that." She drank some of her wine, then reached over and squeezed Olivia's knee. "And I'm here now."

The cousins were sitting on either end of the sofa in Olivia's living room. Their children were settled upstairs for the night and it was blessedly quiet, so Olivia hoped they were all asleep. They should be. It was after eleven, and she and Eve could finally talk without curious ears.

Olivia sighed. Eve wasn't just her cousin. She was also her best friend, someone Olivia had always looked up to, someone she'd known was just minutes away for a hug, a shoulder to cry on or a listening ear. The only person in the world who knew everything about her—well, *almost* everything—and could be completely trusted.

But now Eve would be spending the majority of her time in either Los Angeles or Nashville, where her new husband (and the twins' birth father), the famous and fabulous Adam Crenshaw—composer and lead singer of the band Version II—had two magnificent homes.

Eve, along with her twins Nathan and Natalie, had come back to Crandall Lake for the weekend to join in the family celebration of Olivia's mother's birthday.

Olivia sighed again. She was thrilled for Eve. Her cousin had waited a long time for some true happiness. But Olivia also loved seeing her daughter with her older cousins, both of whom Thea adored. And now that Eve and the twins had settled in Los Angeles for the school year, nothing would ever be the same again, no matter what Eve said.

Eve was still talking, still making an obvious attempt to reassure Olivia. "I'll be coming to Crandall Lake a lot. And you'll be visiting us wherever we are. And you know, I've been thinking. If you want to, you and Thea can even travel with us when Adam has a concert and we're able to go with him."

"I have a job, you know." But wouldn't it be wonderful to be free of everything tying her down and just take Thea and go, the way Eve was suggesting? "Besides, I don't think I should leave my mom." Norma was newly diagnosed as a diabetic—something their family seemed to be genetically disposed to—and was having some trouble dealing with the disease.

Eve gave Olivia a sideways look. "Stella's here." Stella was Olivia's younger sister and she lived within walking distance of their family home. "You said yourself she's really stepped up to the plate and has educated herself about the disease so that she can help your mom."

"I know, but…" Olivia evaded Eve's gaze.

"Let's talk about the *real* reason. You're afraid Vivienne would make trouble for you if you moved."

Olivia made a face. Her mother-in-law hated her in direct proportion to the possessiveness she felt for Thea, her only grandchild, the daughter of her perfect younger son, who had died so tragically in the crash of his Black Hawk helicopter in Afghanistan.

"Am I right? Or am I right?" Eve pressed.

"You're right."

"She's a piece of work, isn't she?"

"That's a kind way of putting it."

"I'll never understand her." Eve finished her wine and set the glass on the coffee table in front of them.

"I'm not sure anyone does." Olivia got up and retrieved the still-half-full bottle of Merlot she'd opened earlier. She poured more into Eve's glass. "Even Matt says she's just used to getting her own way, and when she doesn't, look out."

She was referring to Matt Britton, her brother-in-law, Vivienne's oldest son. He'd always been good to Olivia, in spite of his mother. In fact, since Mark's death, Olivia wasn't sure how she'd have coped with her mother-in-law if not for Matt.

From day one, Vivienne Britton had been furious that Mark, her obvious favorite child, had wanted to marry "a nobody" like Olivia Dubrovnik instead of Charlotte Chambers, the daughter of the Brittons' oldest friends. Charlotte was "our kind" and "perfect for you" as she'd told Mark many times, once even in Olivia's hearing. It still amazed Olivia that Mark had defied his mother, because in all other things he had always done what she wanted him to do.

"Let's not talk about her anymore." Olivia poured more wine into her own glass and sat down again, curling her bare legs under her.

Eve smiled. "Good idea. Instead, let's talk about you dating again."

"I'm only *thinking* about dating again," Olivia corrected. "I haven't really decided. Besides, it's not like there's a line of eligible men out the door."

There *was* one person who interested her, and for a moment, she was tempted to tell Eve about him, but pushed the urge away, because the situation was impossible. She felt a bit guilty about *not* telling Eve, because normally she told her everything, but in this case, her gut told her it was best not to put her feelings into words.

"The reason guys aren't lining up is because no one knows you're ready," Eve said.

"I can hardly make an announcement."

"No, but I can get the word out."

Olivia stared at her. "What are you going to do? Put

a notice in the *Courier*?" Eve had worked for the *Crandall Lake Courier* before marrying Adam in August.

Eve grinned, a sly look in her eyes. "No, but I just might mention it casually to Austin when we see him Sunday morning."

"Austin!" Olivia was startled. Austin Crenshaw was one of Adam's younger brothers. A successful lawyer, he took care of all Adam's personal and professional legal and financial matters. "Why would *he* care?"

"Surely you saw how he was checking you out at the wedding," Eve said. Austin had been Adam's best man, and Olivia had served as Eve's matron of honor.

"That's ridiculous!" Olivia said. "He was just being polite to his new sister-in-law's cousin."

Eve shook her head knowingly. "Nope. He's interested. I know the signs. And he'd be perfect for you."

"That's crazy. I am *so* not in his league."

"Why are you constantly putting yourself down? He couldn't *find* anyone better if he tried!"

Olivia loved that her cousin was always so loyal, but she had to face facts. "C'mon, Eve. If he'd really been interested, as you say, why hasn't he called me or something?"

"I don't know. But I'm going to find out."

"No, no. Please don't say anything to him."

"I'll just casually bring up your name Sunday."

"No! Please, Eve. I really don't want you to."

"It's not a big deal," Eve insisted. "Austin and I have a great relationship. Since Adam and I got married, I've really gotten to know him. We've sort of bonded. And he's a really great guy."

Olivia knew, just from the determined look on Eve's face, that she was not going to be dissuaded. It was useless to keep trying. Because, if she did, Eve would eventually wonder why. "Okay, but don't say anything in front of the kids." Eve and her twins were meeting Austin for breakfast Sunday.

"Don't worry." Eve smiled, happy now she'd gotten her way. "I'll be discreet. The kids won't hear me."

"Thing is, I don't want him to think I put you up to talking to him." The very idea made Olivia cringe. Why had she even mentioned she was thinking about dating? She should have known Eve would latch on to that and start suggesting possible candidates. She gave a mental sigh. Austin *did* seem nice. Plus he certainly was easy on the eyes. All the Crenshaw men were. And since the one man who *did* interest her was completely and totally off-limits…

"Quit worrying," Eve said. "That's my job, remember?"

Olivia smiled. Worrying *was* Eve's job, always had been. She was the conservative one, the cautious one. Olivia had always been more impulsive, more willing to take a chance.

But that was before she'd had Thea.

Before she was a mother.

Now her first priority would always be her daughter, and that meant she had to think carefully before she did anything that might negatively impact Thea's life in any way.

"Seriously, Eve," she said, "I'm not in any hurry. If I do get into another relationship, he'd have to be pretty special…after Mark." It made her sad to think about Mark, who was her first love. They'd only been married months before he went to Afghanistan. They'd had so little time. His life had been cut so short, and he'd died so young. And without ever holding or knowing his daughter, except for photos and images on Skype.

"I know," Eve said. "You have plenty of time, and I'm

sure, once the guys around here—Austin included—know you're ready, there'll be no shortage of possible candidates."

Olivia rolled her eyes. She wasn't anywhere near as confident as Eve that men would be lining up to take on a widow with a small child.

The cousins continued to talk for another hour or so, but when the Wedgewood clock on the mantel chimed one o'clock, Eve yawned and stretched. "I'm beat."

"Me, too. We'd better get to bed. Tomorrow's a big day." Olivia got up and took Eve's glass. "You can use the bathroom first. I'll take these out to the kitchen and be there in a minute." The cousins were sharing Olivia's bedroom and the king-size bed she and Mark had so happily purchased together.

As she rinsed out the wineglasses and put them in the dishwasher, Olivia decided she was going to make the most of the weekend. She wasn't going to think about her mother-in-law or about Eve going back to LA or the way Olivia's own life had not turned out the way she'd once imagined it would.

She was just going to relax, have fun, eat some salty and sugary junk food, and thoroughly enjoy having Eve and the kids home again.

No matter what.

"It's a gorgeous day, isn't it?" Eve exclaimed. "I love autumn in the Hill Country."

"Me, too," Olivia said, linking her arm through Eve's.

The cousins were strolling through the grounds where Crandall Lake's Fall Festival, an annual celebration featuring music, food, games and rides as well as various craft items for sale, took place every October.

Norma Dubrovnik, Olivia's mother, and her older

sister, Anna Cermak, Eve's mother, were walking up ahead. Between the older women and the two younger women were Nathan and Natalie, with Olivia's Thea between them. Each twin had one of Thea's hands, and every few steps they'd lift their little cousin and swing her out, then set her back on her feet again. Thea's delighted giggles peppered the air.

"Liv, Eve, hurry up! You're so poky!" Olivia looked around to see her younger sister Stella waving and calling to them.

"We're coming," Eve said as they caught up to where Stella stood.

"I thought you'd gone home or something," Olivia said. "You disappeared."

"I spied my boss by the pizza booth, and I went over to talk to her," Stella said. She was laughing, her fresh face and bright eyes a clear sign that life hadn't yet dealt her any devastating blows. Olivia hoped it never would.

Just as Eve and Olivia reached the rest of their group, who were now gathered by the crowded booth where hot funnel cakes were cooked and sold, Olivia's mother said, "It's so hot." She was mopping at her forehead with a tissue.

Olivia frowned. It wasn't hot. In fact, the weather was perfect. Sixty-eight degrees and sunny, according to her phone just thirty minutes earlier.

"I don't feel good," her mother continued. Her face had drained of color, and she swayed.

"Norma," Eve's mother said, reaching out to put her arm around her sister. "C'mon, let's go sit on that bench over there." She met Olivia's eyes. "She's shaking."

Alarmed, Olivia said, "Mom. What's wr—" But she never had a chance to finish what she was going to say because at that moment Norma just seemed to fold in on herself and slumped to the ground. “Mom!” Olivia dropped down to where her mother lay.

“Norma!” This came from Eve’s mother, who knelt next to Olivia.

People around them buzzed with concern and several onlookers crouched down.

“Mom,” Stella said, patting Norma, who was struggling to sit up. “What happened?”

“I—I don’t know. I just feel so weak.”

“Did you eat breakfast this morning?” Olivia asked.

“What’s going on here?” said an authoritative male voice.

Olivia looked up. She knew that voice. It was Dr. Groves, Thea’s pediatrician. “Dr. Groves, this is my mother. She said she was hot and she was sweating, but her face was white. Then she just collapsed. I think it’s a low blood sugar reaction. She’s a diabetic. Newly diagnosed.”

“On oral meds or insulin?”

“Oral,” Stella said. “She takes them in the morning and again at night.”

“When did she eat last?”

“I—I had some toast for breakfast,” Norma said weakly.

“Nothing since? No protein?” Dr. Groves asked.

Stella shook her head. “I don’t think so. We’ve been here since ten o’clock.”

Olivia mentally sighed. Her mother still didn’t seem to realize the importance of eating at regular intervals and keeping her meals balanced, even though they’d already had several discussions about the potential consequences.

“She needs sugar, fast,” Dr. Groves said. “She’s having a low blood sugar reaction. This happens when diabetics are on meds and don't eat the right things often enough."

"She can have my funnel cake," one of the onlookers said. The woman, someone Olivia didn't know, thrust forward her paper plate containing a sugared funnel cake. "I just got it."

"That's good," the doctor said, "but some orange juice would be faster acting. Once we get her blood sugar stabilized, she'll need something more substantial, with protein, like a hot dog or one of those chicken drumsticks they're selling."

"I'll go get some orange juice," Nathan piped up. "There's a juice stand right over there." He pointed to one about a hundred feet away. "I have tickets!" He held up a strip of the tickets used in lieu of money at all the booths.

In all the confusion Olivia had lost track of Thea, and she looked around as Nathan ran off, and Dr. Groves continued to monitor her mother, but she didn't see Thea. She saw Natalie, though, and called to her. "Where's Thea, honey?"

Natalie frowned and looked around. "She…she was just here."

Olivia's mother was now sitting on a nearby bench, with her sister, the doctor and Stella in attendance. They were feeding her some funnel cake. Olivia, who wasn't yet alarmed, figured Thea was simply hidden by one of the members of the group of people waiting on funnel cakes or lured by the earlier commotion of her mother's collapse. She headed toward Eve, who still stood near the booth with Natalie. At the moment, the young girl seemed a lot older than her almost-twelve years, with her worried face and frightened eyes. She took her responsibility of watching after Thea very seriously.

"Thea!" Olivia called as she walked through the clusters of people. "Thea, honey, where are you?"

Eve frowned and hurried toward Olivia. "What's wrong?"

"I don't see Thea anywhere." Now Olivia's voice held an edge of fear.

"Natalie?" Eve said, eyeing her daughter.

Natalie looked stricken. "Mom, I—I don't know where she is."

"But you were holding her hand, honey. You and Nathan said you were going to watch her today."

"I know, Mom, but Auntie Norma fainted and…and I must have let go of her hand. I—I don't know where Thea went." The last word was a wail, and Natalie's eyes filled with tears. "I'm sorry."

"Oh, my God," Olivia said. Her heart had begun to hammer, and full-blown panic had set in. Now she looked around frantically. "Thea! Thea! Where *are* you?"

By now, several people had stopped whatever they were doing and were staring at her. One of them said to Eve, "What's wrong?"

Eve quickly explained. "She's probably just wandered off, but–"

"But what if she hasn't?" Olivia cried. "What if…" She couldn't even finish the thought. Horrible images flashed through her mind in the space of seconds. Thea was so little. So sweet and innocent and trusting. And so very beautiful with her blond curly hair, the exact shade of her father's, and her shining brown eyes, just like Olivia's own. Olivia closed her eyes, also thinking how inquisitive her daughter was, how *interested* in things, the way she would talk to strangers. "Please, God," she whispered. "Please, God, let her be okay."

Her greatest fear was losing Thea. Losing Mark had been hard enough, but losing Thea was unthinkable.

"Liv, she's okay, I know she is," Eve said. "Let's look methodically. Think, Natalie, did she say anything?"

Natalie's tear-stained face screwed up in thought. "I—I think she said something about a kitty right before Auntie Norma said she didn't feel good."

"A kitten!" Olivia said. "Maybe…maybe she saw a kitten." She looked at Eve. "You know how she loves cats. She…she's been begging for one for months." Olivia had been waiting, thinking she'd surprise Thea at Christmas.

"Let's get some of these people looking. She can't have gone far," Eve said. She turned to one of the nearby groups. "Her little girl's wandered off. We need help looking for her."

"I'll notify security," a man said, taking out his cell phone. "I know the man in charge. What's the little girl's name?"

Within moments, Eve had organized a search party armed with Thea's description and information, the head of security had arrived and been briefed, and 9-1-1 had also been called.

Olivia felt sick with fear. It was all she could do not to break down completely, but she knew if she did, she'd be useless. She forced herself to take deep breaths… and *think.* Thank God for Eve. And thank God, Olivia's mother didn't know what was happening, because Thea was *her* only grandchild, too, and totally adored.

But it wouldn't be long before Norma would find out about Thea, because Olivia could see two police officers coming toward them, and the head of security here at the festival had just told her they were going to get an announcement on the loudspeaker so that everyone attending the festival would be on the lookout for Thea.

"Olivia?" The oldest police officer, a man Olivia recognized as Tom Nicholls, looked at her. His wife, Betty, was a nurse at the Crandall Lake Hospital where Olivia worked in Admitting and Registration. "It's your daughter that's missing?"

"Yes." Olivia stepped forward, with Eve and Natalie right behind.

For the next five minutes they gave Tom Nicholls all the information he asked for. Natalie was also questioned, and then Nicholls got on the phone and fired off orders. A dozen more search parties were organized, and throughout, Olivia fought against the panic threatening to paralyze her. She very nearly gave in to it when she wanted to join one of the search parties and Nicholls wouldn't let her.

"You need to be at the security tent," he said. "That's going to be our command post and where Thea will be brought when she's found. And she'll need you then. You can't be off somewhere searching." Without waiting for her to protest, he beckoned to another officer. "Officer Wilkins here will take you to the security tent."

"I'll go and tell your mom and the others what's happening. Then I'll find you," Eve said, giving her a quick hug. "It's going to be okay, sweetie. I love you."

Olivia bit back her tears and allowed herself to be led off. She couldn't help remembering how, the night before, her last thought before going to bed had been about how much fun today was going to be.

What a fool she was.

She had tempted fate.

And now fate was showing her, once again, that she had no control over anything.

Chapter Two

Matthew Lawrence Britton wondered for about the thousandth time if he really *did* want to run for the US House of Representatives. He'd been greeting possible supporters at the festival for less than two hours, and he was already sick of it. And the election he was aiming for was more than two years away! He hated having to ask people for money, but without money—big money—no one, no matter what your name was, had a chance of winning an important election anymore.

Even more to the point, and the main thing that had been bothering him, was the fact he enjoyed his job as an assistant criminal district attorney for Hays County. And he was good at it. He might even have a shot at district attorney when his boss retired—something that was rumored to happen fairly soon.

But everyone, friends and family alike, seemed to think a more national stage was the road he should take.

They had been pressuring him for a while now, ever since the idea had been floated by an influential former law professor of his. Even his sister-in-law, Olivia, had weighed in, saying he'd make a wonderful representative for their district. He guessed he'd better make a final decision soon.

With all this on his mind, he was just about to approach Wylie Sheridan, an old family friend, when the loudspeakers dotted around the festival grounds crackled to life.

"This is an emergency message. May I have your attention, everyone?" boomed an authoritative male voice. "We have a missing child. Four-year-old Thea Britton has been separated from her family. Thea has curly blond hair and brown eyes. She's wearing blue denim pants, red sneakers, and a red-and-white-striped long-sleeved T-shirt and has a red bow in her hair. If anyone sees her now or remembers seeing her recently, please come to the security tent next to the main pavilion or call this number." He went on to give the number, then say that Thea had last been seen by the funnel cake booth. "She may have been chasing after a cat or kitten."

Matt had his phone out and had pressed Olivia's cell phone number before the announcement was finished. Thea was Matt's godchild, and even if she hadn't been the daughter of his late brother, Mark, Matt would have loved her. Thea was special—smart and sweet, loving and beautiful.

Just like her mother.

The thought, which had come more and more often lately, still had the power to make him feel guilty. He knew this emotion was ridiculous. Mark was gone. And he would have been the first to want Matt to take care of Olivia. Wouldn't he?

"Olivia?" Matt said when she answered. "I just heard the announcement about Thea. Where are you?"

"I'm at the security tent. The police want me to st-stay here." Her voice broke in a sob. "Oh, Matt, I'm so scared. She was right *there*, then she just *disappeared*!"

"I'm coming. I'll be there in two minutes." He was already running, his heart racing along with his feet. "It'll be okay. We'll find her."

When he reached the security tent, Olivia was pacing outside the door. She looked so forlorn, and so beautiful. Without thinking whether he should or shouldn't, he pulled her into his arms. Her slight body trembled, and more than anything, he wished he could tell her how he felt about her, how much he wanted to take care of her.

But this wasn't the time…or the place. And even if it was, he had no idea how she would react to this kind of declaration. He refused to think what he'd do if he confessed his feelings and she shot him down. Once he'd put those feelings into words, he knew they could never go back to their present relationship of caring brother-in-law to his brother's widow.

"Matt, oh, Matt," she sobbed. "I'm so afraid. The woods, the river, the lake. Who knows how far she's gone? You know how she is. How she always wants to investigate things. The questions she asks. What if…if someone…took her? But the police… I—I wanted to look for her, too, but they said I needed to stay here." Her body shuddered.

Matt inhaled the subtle fragrance of her silky hair as he held her and said over and over, "They'll find her. You've got everybody looking. They'll find her." But his mind was whirling as he imagined all the things that could have happened to Thea. He loved her as much as he had finally admitted—to himself if to no one else—he loved her mother.

Sometimes he wondered if he had always loved Olivia. Always wanted her. There was something about her that had touched him from the moment he was introduced to her when she and Mark were dating. Matt had always championed the underdog; it was simply part of his nature, and Olivia—in terms of how his parents viewed her, anyway—was definitely the underdog.

Matt's mother, in particular, disliked her daughter-in-law intensely and criticized her constantly: she wasn't raising their granddaughter to the standards of a Britton; she plopped the child in day care instead of allowing Vivienne to hire a nanny and have Thea raised in her grandparents' home under proper guidance and supervision; and worst of all, Vivienne considered Olivia to be one of the major reasons Mark was killed—because, in Vivienne's view—Olivia wasn't the wife he needed and kept him distracted and worried about his family instead of focusing on his job as a Black Hawk pilot. Unsaid was her bitter disappointment that the son she had imagined doing great things after fulfilling his service to his country, the son she'd envisioned going up the political ladder to high office, possibly the *highest* office, was gone forever. Olivia had been, and still was, a convenient scapegoat.

Matt's father was more tolerant than his wife and might have been okay with Olivia's entrance into the Britton family, but Vivienne ruled in the elder Brittons' home, and it was always easier for her husband to keep the peace and just go along. Actually, if Matt were being really honest with himself, he'd admit he'd long known his father was weak. That as long as he was able to live his privileged life, he didn't seem to care how that life was obtained or maintained.

Olivia finally withdrew from Matt's embrace and raised her tear-stained face to look at him. Her soft brown eyes met his. "I'm so glad you're here. I—I thought about calling you, but in all the confu—"

"It's okay. I know. C'mon, let's go sit down." He gestured to a nearby bench. When she hesitated, glancing back at the security tent, he said, "Don't worry. I'll let them know you're right here. If they want you, they'll come out and get you."

For the next hour, both Matt and her cousin Eve tried to keep Olivia calm as people came and went, as the security team and the police department officers combined their efforts and the search parties combed the nearby grounds and questioned dozens of people.

Olivia eventually just looked numb. Her eyes clouded with worry and fear, she kept biting her bottom lip and twisting her hands. She couldn't sit still, and every ten minutes or so she'd jump up and start pacing again. Or her phone would ring and she'd either talk or she'd say, "I can't talk! I have to keep the line clear in case..." Then her voice would trail off and she'd have to sit down again.

Matt and Eve, whom he'd met several times—and liked very much—exchanged a lot of concerned looks. He knew what Eve was thinking, because he was thinking it, too. The longer it took the searchers to find Thea, the more likely it was the outcome of the searching wouldn't be good. His own fear felt like a huge weight in his chest, and it was all he could do to keep that fear from showing.

Olivia needed him...and Eve...to be strong.

He thought about calling his parents, but he didn't.

The last thing Olivia needed was for his mother to come charging over to the festival with her accusations and criticisms.

But after more than two hours had gone by, and one by one the search teams reported in with no success, Matt knew he could no longer delay notifying his parents. He waited until Olivia was busy with Officer Nicholls, and then he walked a few feet away and placed the call.

His mother answered. "Hello, Matthew," she said. "To what do I owe this pleasure?"

Matt gritted his teeth at this subtle dig. She never missed a chance to let him know he wasn't living up to her expectations. "Listen, Mom. I need to tell you something. Now, don't get hysterical, but I'm at the festival, and… Thea is missing. The police are here, and—"

"I see," his mother said, interrupting. "And just how did *that* happen? Just exactly how did my granddaughter go missing?"

Matt blinked. What was wrong with his mother? She didn't sound the least bit upset, just disdainful.

"What happened is," he said in the most measured tone he could manage, "Olivia's family is here celebrating her mother's birthday, and her mother felt sick and fainted, and in all the commotion, Thea wandered off. The authorities organized search parties, but they haven't found—"

"Of course they haven't found her."

"What the *hell*?" Matt said, losing his temper. "Aren't you even *upset*? Your only grandchild is missing and all you can do is imply the security people, the police, aren't doing their—"

"Do not swear at me, Matthew," she said, interrupting him again. "I'm not upset because Thea is here."

"She's *what*?"

"You heard me. She's here. Where she *should* be. Safe and sound. More than I can say for when she's in her so-called mother's so-called care."

If his mother had been physically in his presence, Matt knew he might have choked her, he was that angry. "And just how did she happen to be there? Did someone find her and bring her to you?"

"I found her. I was at the festival myself, earlier, and I saw her wandering all alone, that *family* of her mother's nowhere to be seen, so I did what any grandmother would do. I scooped her up and I brought her home. She's even now upstairs playing happily in the nursery. In fact, I can hear her talking. I think she's on Buddy Boy." Buddy Boy was the name of the rocking horse that had been in Vivienne's family since *she* was a child. "You know how she loves Buddy Boy and how she talks to him, just like her father did when he was a boy. Now if you'll excuse me, I must get back—"

"I'll be there in fifteen minutes," Matt said, doing his own interrupting now. His heart was once again hammering, but not in fear this time. He felt murderous rage, mixed with disbelief. How could his mother be so downright cruel? He was appalled by Vivienne's behavior and the way she had so callously disregarded the fear and worry Olivia and her family were feeling. Hell, that *he'd* been feeling! And all those people who had been searching for hours. The police, the security people…it all boggled his mind.

He disconnected the call and strode to where Olivia was still talking to Tom Nicholls. "Call off the search party," he told Tom. "Thea's been found. She's at my mother's."

Ignoring Nicholls's startled expression and the inevitable questions, Matt took Olivia's arm and said, "C'mon, let's go get her. I'll explain everything on the way."

Eve, who had heard the exchange, met Matt's eyes. She looked stunned, but didn't say anything.

"She'll call you, or I will, after we get Thea," he said. "Tell the others."

Eve nodded and Matt knew she'd take care of things there.

"Where'd you park?" Olivia asked, her face beginning to portray her conflicting emotions. Matt still found it hard to believe his mother had done this unspeakable thing. To take Thea home and never call Olivia to tell her where Thea was defied every standard of decent behavior. He'd always known how manipulative and controlling his mother was—and how insensitive to the feelings of others when they interfered with what she wanted—but he'd never imagined she was actually heartless and devoid of compassion for a fellow human being.

"On Waterside," he said. "This way." Grabbing Olivia's hand, he led her through the crowd and together, they hurried to where his BMW was parked. He hit his remote, the doors unlocked, and Olivia was in the passenger seat before he could even think of helping her. In minutes, they were on their way.

As he drove, he quickly told her a sanitized version of his conversation with his mother. From the way Olivia's throat worked, he knew what she must be feeling, yet all she said was, "I don't really care why your mother did what she did…or what she said. I'm just thankful Thea is okay. And I just want to get her and take her home."

"I know." But he also knew when she'd had time to really think about this, Olivia would feel differently. In fact, he wouldn't be surprised if she ended up forbidding his mother to see Thea again. Hell, if he was in Olivia's shoes, he might consider moving away from Crandall Lake to put as much distance between her and his mother as she could.

Even the thought that Olivia might move away made him want to do something terrible to his mother.

Barely twelve minutes had elapsed since his phone conversation with Vivienne before Matt and Olivia were pulling into the long drive leading to his parents' stately home. Matt parked in the front turnaround, and again Olivia was out of the car and dashing up the shallow front steps before he managed to get out himself.

Olivia jabbed at the doorbell, but Matt, who had a key to the house, shoved it into the lock and opened the door himself. The first thing he saw was his mother, looking coolly elegant in tailored black pants paired with a black-and-white geometric top, her expertly colored blond hair in a chin-length style she'd recently adopted. Vivienne was halfway down the curving staircase that led to the second floor. She stopped at their entrance and lifted her head defiantly. Her blue eyes met Matt's. She ignored Olivia.

"I've come for my daughter," Olivia said, her voice only betraying a tiny tremor.

Vivienne turned her icy glare to Olivia. "You're wasting your time, because I won't allow you to take her. It's quite obvious she's not safe with you, and I can't have you putting her in danger again."

Matt attempted to interrupt her, but she ignored him and kept going. "I'm not surprised, though. I've always known you weren't a fit mother. You're just lucky I'm the one who found her. That some crazy person didn't abduct her."

"Mother—" Matt stopped, took a deep breath to keep

his voice calm in case they could be heard upstairs. "You can't keep Thea here. Olivia is her mother, and she has every right to take Thea home with her. Now before—"

"Before *what*?" his mother said, her voice rising a notch. "Are you going to physically manhandle me? Threaten me? Your own *mother*? You'd better be careful, Matthew, or I will—"

Before Vivienne could finish her sentence, Olivia ran to the stairway and pushed past his mother, nearly causing Vivienne to lose her balance, but she managed to grab the banister in time. Matt didn't hesitate. He, too, went up the stairs, taking them two at a time. He didn't look at his mother as he passed her. He didn't trust himself. He couldn't remember ever being this angry.

Olivia had already entered the old nursery where both he and Mark, as well as their younger sister, Madeleine, had spent the major part of their childhood. By the time Matt caught up, he sensed rather than saw his mother a few feet behind him.

Amelia, who had been the Britton family housekeeper since before Matt was born, sat in a child-sized chair as she watched Thea, sitting across from her, happily putting together a puzzle. "I'm sorry, Mr. Matt," Amelia said, looking up as he entered the room. "But she wouldn't listen to me when I told your mother she should call Miss Olivia."

"I know this isn't your fault," Matt said as Olivia, with a cry, ran to Thea. She picked her up and kissed her over and over again.

"Mommy! Stop!" Thea said, looking at Matt. "Unca Matt!" She tried to squirm out of her mother's grasp, raising her arms to Matt.

"Oh, sweetheart! I thought you were lost," Olivia said. "I'm just so happy you're not."

"I wasn't lost. Mimi found me." *Mimi* was the pet name Vivienne had insisted Thea call her, saying the title of grandmother implied she was old. Matt had rolled his eyes when he heard that one.

"Good. I must thank Mimi," Olivia said, still hugging Thea.

"Mommy, let me down," Thea said again.

"We're taking her home now," Matt said to his mother, who stood behind him.

"You're going to be sorry for this," Vivienne muttered under her breath.

Matt knew she was keeping her voice down because she didn't want to make a scene in front of Thea. Nor did he, and he knew Olivia felt the same way. They might have their issues with his mother, and she might be extremely misguided, but she was still Thea's grandmother, and Thea loved her Mimi and Poppa.

"Mommy!" Thea shouted. "I said I want Unca Matt!"

Olivia, meeting Matt's eyes, finally let Thea loose, and she ran into his arms. Matt picked her up and held her close. Laughing, she wrapped her little arms around him and snuggled in. If someone had asked Matt how he felt at this moment, he wasn't sure he would have been able to put his emotions into words. His heart was too full. Right here in this room were the two people in the world who meant the most to him, and somehow, some way, he had to figure out how to keep them both safe forever. But at the present moment, he just needed to get them out of here.

"Where's Dad?" he asked his mother as he motioned for Olivia to precede him out of the room.

"Playing golf," his mother said coldly. "Where else?"

"Tell him I'll call him later."

When she didn't answer, just gave him another icy stare, then turned and walked down the hall toward her bedroom, he sighed and followed Olivia down the stairs and out to the car.

As Matt drove Olivia and Thea back to the festival to pick up Olivia's car, he apologized in an undertone for the things his mother had said.

"Forget it," she said. "Thea is safe, I have her back, and that's all that counts."

That was the most important thing, yes, but Matt knew there were going to be repercussions to this episode. However, no matter what it cost him, he'd already decided he'd do everything in his power to make sure none of those repercussions affected Olivia. The guilt for this debacle lay at one door, and that door wasn't hers.

When they reached Olivia's car, she thanked him. "I don't know what I'd've done if you hadn't been with me today. I—I would have put off calling your mother because..." Her voice trailed off.

"I know." He wondered how long his mother would have kept Thea without notifying Olivia. He wanted to think she would have relented and done the decent thing, yet would she? Surely, when his father arrived home she would have had to tell him what she'd done.

But maybe not. Maybe she'd have made up some story and his father would have been none the wiser. It wasn't as if Thea had never spent the night with his parents. Olivia had been generous, even when his mother had not. That quality—Olivia's generosity—was one of the many things about her he'd grown to admire.

"I'll always be there for you and Thea, Olivia," he said, reaching out and squeezing her shoulder.

That brought a smile to her face. "Thanks, Matt. Eve said something similar last night. I'm lucky to have you guys, I know that."

Not that lucky, he thought. But he smiled, too. "That's the Olivia I know. A glass half-full girl."

"Yeah, that's me. A cockeyed optimist."

"Nothing wrong with that."

"Mommy, put me down," Thea said, struggling to get out of Olivia's arms once again.

"Thea, you know you have to be belted into your seat," Olivia said. "So you can be safe, and we can go home."

"I don't wanna go home. I wanna go back to the festable. With Unca Matt."

"Festival," Olivia said.

"That's what I said! Festable!"

Matt wanted to laugh. Thea might be sweet and loving most of the time, but she was also a very bright, very determined and very stubborn four-year-old with definite opinions of her own. "I'm not going back to the festival, honey. I'm going home and you're going home, too, because your Grammy and Aunt Stella and everyone is waiting for you. I think you're having birthday cake, right?"

"Uncle Matt's right," Olivia said. "Grammy will need help blowing out her candles."

"Candles!" Thea said with a delighted smile, obviously forgetting all about the festival. "Presents, too?"

"Yes, presents, too," Olivia said.

"For me!"

"No, honey, not for you. You're not the birthday girl today. Grammy is."

Thea gave her mother a look that said that didn't seem fair. "Unca Matt's coming, too."

"No, sweetheart, I can't." He wanted to say he hadn't been invited, but he knew that wasn't fair. He'd be putting Olivia on the spot.

Thea looked as if she was going to protest that, too, but she didn't, and finally allowed Matt to get her buckled into her seat and kissed him goodbye.

Once Thea was safely settled in her Camry, Olivia turned to him. "Thanks, again, Matt." She lowered her voice. "Do I need to call anyone, do you think? Like Chief Donnelly? Apologize for everything?"

Barton Donnelly, the chief of police in Crandall Lake, was a crony of Matt's father. Matt would be sure to apprise him of what had actually happened. No way was he letting Olivia take the fall for any of this. "I'll take care of it," he assured her. "Don't worry. Just enjoy the rest of the weekend with your family, and we'll talk tomorrow night after Eve's gone. She *is* leaving tomorrow, right?"

"That's the plan," Olivia said. "Luckily for her, she has her husband's plane and pilot at her disposal."

Matt could see the weariness returning to Olivia's face. The stress of everything that had happened today had exhausted her. He gave her a quick hug, careful to make it brotherly and not lover-like, then stood watching as she walked around to the passenger side of her car, got in and drove away.

As always, when they parted company, the world seemed less bright with her gone. If only he could always be there for her in the way he wanted to be, but if today had shown him anything, it had shown him how hopeless his situation actually was. For even if Olivia should ever feel the same way about him that he felt about her, the only way they could ever be together would be for him to break all ties with his family, and for him and Olivia and Thea to leave Crandall Lake behind forever.

And that was impossible.

For them…and for him.

Wasn't it?

Chapter Three

Olivia wasn't quite as forgiving as she had pretended to be. She just hadn't wanted to cause any more trouble between Matt and his mother. Because if Matt kept siding with her against his mother, things would only get worse. His parents weren't just Thea's grandparents. They were one of the most influential couples in the state.

Hugh Britton was the president of a large commercial real estate and investment firm Vivienne's great-grandfather had founded, and the family owned thousands of acres of property around Texas and parts of Oklahoma, including the oil and mineral rights in places that continued to add to the family coffers. The Britton family influence was vast, their resources unlimited, and Olivia, no matter how angry and upset she was over what Vivienne had done today, did not want to worsen an already touchy situation.

In addition, even though she hadn't admitted this to anyone, including Eve, Olivia had begun to have feelings for Matt—feelings that extended beyond those of family ties. She knew it was unwise, she knew what she felt for him could never go anywhere—in fact, he could never even *know*—but she couldn't seem to help herself. More than any other member of Mark's family, she had been drawn to Matt from the first day they'd met. Perhaps it was because he was so kind and welcoming, such a contrast to his mother. As she'd gotten to know him better, she'd realized he was a genuinely good man and well respected, in addition to being handsome and smart and fun to be with. She didn't know exactly what it was about him that drew her. All she knew was, the admiration and connection she'd felt for him as her brother-in-law had morphed into something else in the last year.

So the last thing she wanted was to cause any problems for him. It was bad enough he had helped her today. Vivienne would probably make his life hell because of it.

Oh, Matt, why can't we just be two normal people? Why do we have to have this complicated relationship that spells only trouble for us?

This question…and more…lay heavy on her mind as she called Eve to tell her they were on their way.

"We're at your mom's house, waiting," Eve said.

"Be there in ten."

"Is everything okay?"

Olivia sighed. "We'll talk later."

When Olivia pulled into the driveway at her mother's house, Eve and the twins were waiting on the front porch. The cousins exchanged looks as the twins boisterously greeted Thea.

"I'll tell you everything tonight," Olivia murmured as the screen door opened and the rest of the family emerged. While her mother, Eve's mother and Stella hugged and kissed Thea and told her not to ever scare them like that again, Eve just watched and smiled. But she covertly took Olivia's hand and gave it a comforting squeeze.

"So I guess this was all a big misunderstanding?" Eve's mother said carefully.

"Yes," Olivia said in an equally even tone, "Thea's Mimi couldn't find us, so she made sure Thea was safe, didn't she, sweetheart?"

Thea nodded happily. "Mimi said you wouldn't care, Mommy."

"Well, I did care, and I was worried because Mimi didn't call me, but I'm just glad you're okay. We all are."

Olivia knew they all understood what she wouldn't say in front of the children, so the subject was dropped, and the matter of the birthday cake and presents were introduced, much to the excitement of Thea. The twins gamely joined in the fun, and Olivia was able, for a little while at least, to relax and just enjoy being with the people she loved most in the world.

Like Thea, she did wish Matt could be there, though. She wished she could have invited him, but her family, especially Eve, were too sharp, too aware of Olivia and her emotions, especially since Mark's death. It was hard enough to keep the right tone and distance when it was just the two cousins together, but Matt amongst her family? Olivia was afraid she'd somehow give herself away. And having her family know how she felt about Matt would make a tough situation impossible.

"Auntie Norma, Mom said this is a special birthday," Natalie said after the cake and ice cream had been consumed and Norma was preparing to open her gifts.

Olivia's mother beamed. "It is. It's my social security birthday, so I can retire now, if I want to."

"You mean from your job at Dr. Ross's?" asked Nathan. Dr. Ross was a popular veterinarian in Crandall Lake, and Norma was his office manager.

"Yes," Norma answered.

"Are you going to, Grandma?" Natalie persisted.

"I don't think so. Not yet, anyway," Olivia's mother said. She grinned. "I like my job. I'd miss the animals."

Nathan nodded. "I thought so. And Grumpy would miss *you*."

They all laughed, agreeing. Grumpy was a rescue cat Dr. Ross had adopted, and he'd turned into the office mascot, living there 24/7. All the pet owners who visited the office enjoyed Grumpy.

Olivia hoped her mother stuck to that decision. Sixty-seven was too young to retire nowadays. Plus it wasn't as if her mother was wealthy. She had some savings, Olivia knew, and some insurance money left from when Olivia's dad died, but her mother could live another twenty years…or longer. No, it was better if her mother stayed on the job as long as she could, and not just because of finances. Everything Olivia knew from her hospital job showed that remaining engaged and active was good for older people, that they lived longer and healthier lives because of it.

Olivia continued to think about her mother while Norma opened her presents. When she finished, it was time to gather everyone and head for home.

"Will we see you at church in the morning?" Eve's mother asked as Olivia, Eve and the children said their goodbyes.

After agreeing they would, the cousins took their leave and headed for Olivia's house, just minutes away.

It took nearly forty minutes, but finally the twins and Thea were settled in the living room with the movie *Frozen*, although Nathan was also playing a game on his iPad. Olivia and Eve headed for the kitchen, where Olivia put the kettle on so they could have tea.

"Tell me everything," Eve said quietly.

So Olivia did. By the time their tea was ready, she'd finished with her blow-by-blow account of the scene at the elder Brittons' home.

"She's unbelievable," Eve said, shaking her head. "I just don't know what she thought she was accomplishing by keeping Thea there and not telling you."

"With her twisted logic, she probably thought she was reinforcing her belief that I'm an unfit mother."

"Doesn't she realize you could keep her from seeing Thea *at all*?"

Olivia shrugged. "She probably knows I wouldn't do that unless there was no other alternative."

"But why not?" Eve said. Her blue eyes flashed with anger as she stirred milk into her tea.

"Oh, Eve," Olivia said resignedly, "you know why not. If I tried to keep Vivienne away from Thea, she'd make a world of trouble for me." She drank some of her tea. "I just… Life can be hard enough. I can't deal with constant stress and all the drama that comes with any conflict with my mother-in-law."

"So you're just going to ignore what she did today? Listen, why don't I ask Austin to—"

"No! You're not going to ask Austin to do anything. Matt said he'd take care of things…talk to his dad and to Chief Donnelly."

"Yes, but that's just today. What about tomorrow?

What about next week? What about *you*? What if this vendetta against you escalates? She seems to be capable of anything!"

Olivia rubbed her forehead. "Eve, please. Can we talk about something else? I'm so tired of thinking about Vivienne."

Eve looked as if she wanted to protest, but all she did was sigh and give Olivia a reluctant nod. "Okay. I'm sorry. I just…well, I hate this for you. After all you've been through, it sucks."

"I know you worry about me, and I love you for it." Olivia smiled at her cousin and thought about how grateful she was that Eve was here today.

"I want you to promise me something, though," Eve said.

"What?" Olivia said warily.

"If she tries anything else, *anything*, you'll call me immediately. Okay?"

Olivia shook her head. "Eve, what can you do about it? You'll be a thousand miles or more away."

"Just promise."

"Oh, all right, I promise."

"Good." Eve's eyes narrowed. "I'm not without resources, either, you know. As Queen Vivienne will soon find out if she messes with you again."

On that note, the conversation turned to Olivia's mother, then to what the cousins might feed their offspring…and themselves…for dinner. Soon Olivia was laughing and had managed to temporarily wipe Vivienne out of her mind.

But down deep, she knew Vivienne would always be a threat to her peaceful existence with her daughter.

And unfortunately, for now at least, there wasn't a thing Olivia could do about it.

* * *

Matt decided golf game or no golf game, he would try to reach his father on his cell phone.

His dad answered almost immediately. "What is it, Matt? I'm playing golf."

"I know that, Dad. Just wondered when you'd be finished."

"I don't know. Around five, I guess."

"Can we meet for a drink before you go home? I need to talk to you."

"Can't you just come to the house?"

"No. I'll explain later."

Matt heard his father sigh. "Where do you want to meet?"

"How about The Grill?" He'd named a popular restaurant and bar near the golf course.

"I'll call you when I finish here," his father said.

"All right."

Good, Matt thought as they hung up. He wanted to be the first to tell his father what had transpired today. Certainly before his mother got a chance to, since she would spin the story in her favor. Even so, Matt knew his father was too smart not to realize Vivienne's stories were *always* spun in her favor.

Matt had tolerated the way his mother treated Olivia because he'd known any interference would only make Vivienne more vindictive toward her daughter-in-law. But today's debacle had changed something in the way Matt saw things. Something had to be done before his mother escalated to something even worse than she'd done today. And the only way anything *could* be done was if he could somehow persuade his father to join him and unite against her.

Would his father go along with that?

Matt would just have to wait and see.

* * *

Vivienne was furious. How dare Matthew take that woman's side against his own mother? The fact Olivia wasn't fit to raise a Britton grandchild was indisputable—anyone with any sense could see it—especially after what had happened today. Yet Vivienne's own son refused to see the truth. Vivienne gritted her teeth. She could just scream.

Matthew had always taken Olivia's side, from the very beginning when Mark brought her home to meet them. Vivienne had seen through the girl immediately. A wannabe. Someone not fit to shine the shoes of her youngest son, let alone marry him. But neither Mark nor Matthew would listen to her. And now look where they all were. Her beautiful Mark was dead, struck down before he'd had any chance of showing the world how special he was. And her willful oldest son—who really couldn't hold a candle to Mark—was still defending Olivia.

Well, Vivienne had warned him. And he'd ignored the warning. Matthew would be sorry. Very sorry. Did he really think he could get elected to the US House of Representatives without his parents' support? If he did, he was going to be sorely disappointed, because it wasn't possible. All Vivienne had to do was talk to a few people, drop a few hints that Matthew would not have his parents or his parents' money behind him, and the race would be over before it ever began.

Did he think she *wouldn't* oppose him? Ha. He had another think coming. She would not only oppose him, she would actively work to see he was defeated by openly and financially backing his opponent, whomever that turned out to be.

Not only that, she would make sure both her and

Hugh's wills were changed. They'd been changed once, right after Mark married that…*woman*…and they could be changed again. *Would* be changed again, because Hugh would do whatever she told him to do. He liked his easy, no-questions-asked life too much to buck her, not when she and she alone controlled the purse strings.

And…if Matthew changed paths and decided not to run for the House but instead to go for the district attorney's slot when Carter Davis retired…well, Vivienne would have something to say about that, too. No one, absolutely no one, opposed Vivienne Marchand Britton and survived to tell about it.

It was exactly five fifteen when Matt's cell rang.

"Matt?"

"Dad? You done?"

"Yes. I'll be at The Grill in about fifteen minutes."

"Okay. I'm leaving now, too."

Matt pulled into the parking lot of the restaurant just before his dad's Lexus. Getting out of his car, Matt walked over to meet his father.

At sixty-two years old, Hugh Britton looked a good ten years younger. Tall, tanned, still slender and fit, with a thick head of salt-and-pepper hair, he was the picture of health. Matt often wondered just how his dad had managed it, especially married to Matt's mother. Then again, Matt knew how. Hugh took the path of least resistance. As long as he could live the way he wanted to live and Matt's mother turned a blind eye to the other women Matt suspected his father of being involved with over the years, he didn't seem to care what she did.

"What's up, son?" Hugh said as they walked into the entrance to the bar side of the crowded place. "Problems with the campaign already?"

"No. Problems with Mom."

His father frowned. "Matt, you know I try to stay out of—"

"This isn't something you can ignore."

His father pointedly looked at his watch. "I only have about twenty minutes."

Matt waited until they were seated and had ordered their drinks before telling his father an abbreviated version of the story.

Hugh toyed with his drink. "Is Thea okay?"

"Thea's fine. She didn't even know anything was wrong."

"Well, then—" Hugh shrugged. "All's well that ends well."

Matt stared at his father. "All's well that *ends well*? Dad! Olivia was sick with worry. So was her family. And possibly a hundred other people, not to mention the police, were involved. This time, Mom's gone too far."

His father didn't meet his eyes.

After a few seconds of silence, Matt said, "Don't you think we need to do something? You know she won't listen to me, but can't you make Mom understand that she can't continue this vendetta against Olivia? You know, if Olivia wanted to, she could get a court order barring both of you from even *seeing* Thea. Any judge, hearing about today's incident, would be hard-pressed *not* to rule in Olivia's favor if she decided to go that route."

His father finally looked at him. "Would Olivia do that?"

"In her shoes, I would."

"You haven't suggested anything like that, have you?"

Matt shook his head. Not that he hadn't felt like it.

His father sighed heavily. Drank more of his Scotch.

Then turned worried eyes to Matt. "I just don't know what you want *me* to do."

"Confront Mom. Tell her you won't stand for any more of this unfair treatment of Olivia."

"Easier said than done," his father muttered.

"C'mon, Dad. Can't you at least *try*? Maybe if you tell her what could happen if she doesn't stop this behavior, she'll think twice next time she's tempted to do anything else."

His father still didn't look at him. "I can't promise anything, but I will try." So saying, he finished off his drink and looked around for their waiter. "I need to get going. Your mother will be upset if I don't get home soon. She said the Hoopers were coming for dinner, and I still have to shower and change."

Matt said he'd settle the bill and watched as his father left. A few minutes later, as Matt left, too, he didn't feel optimistic. Oh, he figured his father *would* try, but Matt could pretty much predict that his mother would roll right over Hugh and, ultimately, nothing would change.

Olivia and Eve and their children went to nine o'clock Mass at Saint Nick's, the church where they'd both made their First Holy Communion and their Confirmation. It was also the church where Eve and Bill Kelly, her first husband and the man who had raised the twins as his own, had been married, and where the twins and Thea had been baptized.

After Mass, Eve and the twins left to meet Austin Crenshaw for breakfast, while Olivia and Thea headed to the activity center where coffee, juice and doughnuts were being served. Once they got there, Olivia looked for her mom and Eve's mom.

"You know, honey," Olivia's mother said once they

were all seated at one of the tables, "I've been thinking about what happened yesterday, and it really bothers me."

Olivia shook her head in warning. "Little pitchers," she said under her breath.

"I just think you should do something about it."

"Mom…"

"Okay, fine. But let's talk later."

Olivia should have known her mother wouldn't be content to drop the subject. And, as it turned out, neither was Eve. Later that day, after Olivia and Thea were back home and Eve and the twins had returned from their breakfast with Austin, Eve suggested they drop the children off at the local multiplex, where a new Disney film was showing. "We can sit in the food court while they're seeing the movie," she said, "have something to drink and be free to talk."

Olivia wasn't surprised to find Vivienne was the subject uppermost on Eve's mind.

"I can't go back to California unless I know you're going to be okay," she said once they were settled with Frappuccinos from Starbucks.

Olivia sighed. "Eve, please stop worrying. I can handle Vivienne. Haven't I *been* handling her for years now?"

"Seems to me her campaign against you is escalating. What she did yesterday is atrocious. And both your mom and mine agree with me. That woman is out of control."

"She does seem to be getting worse."

"At least Matt is on your side," Eve said. Then, shocking Olivia, she added, "You do know he's in love with you?"

Olivia stared at her. "That…that's crazy. He's just a friend. He's…he's Mark's *brother*!"

"So?" Eve said. "It's not like he's *your* brother."

"You're wrong," Olivia insisted. "He doesn't think of me that way." But inside, she was trembling. Did he? Was it possible?

"I'm not wrong, and you're blind. Actually, your mother agrees with me."

"My *mother*? When did you talk to her about this?"

"Yesterday, before you arrived at the house. She said she's been thinking this for a while now. My mother agreed."

"No. It's crazy."

"Why is it crazy?"

"Because…it just is. He…he's never acted like anything but my brother-in-law. Anyway, even if he *was* interested in me, in that way, it could never work out."

"And why not?"

"You know why not. One word. *Vivienne*."

Eve laughed. "Oh, Liv, think about it. It would be so perfect! I can't even imagine the look on her face if you and Matt should—"

"Stop it!" Olivia said. "Just stop it. Matt is *not* in love with me."

"Actually, I'd be surprised if he *wasn't* in love with you. After all, you're beautiful and smart and the two of you get along like a house afire. Plus, he adores Thea…"

Olivia scoffed. "Matt is around beautiful and accomplished women all the time. Much more beautiful and accomplished than *me*." She couldn't help but think of Jenna Forrester, a fellow attorney whom Matt had dated for nearly a year until their breakup in the summer. Jenna was gorgeous!

"Why are you constantly putting yourself down?" Eve persisted.

"I'm not. I'm…just being realistic."

"Uh-huh, just like you were being realistic when you said Austin wasn't interested in you. And you were totally wrong there, too."

"What do you mean? Did you *say* something to Austin today? Eve, you promised you wouldn't."

"I promised I wouldn't mention you were ready to date again. I did not promise I wouldn't even mention your name."

Olivia closed her eyes. What had Eve said?

Eve started to laugh. "Come on, Liv. It's no big deal. I didn't say anything other than telling him what happened at the festival."

"You told him *that*?"

"Why not? It isn't as if no one else knows. There must have been a hundred people involved in looking for Thea."

"I know, but—"

"Don't you want to know what he said?"

Olivia sighed. "What did he say?"

"He said if you have any more trouble with Vivienne—anything at all—to call him. He said he would be happy to represent you, if it ever came to that."

"Why would he say *that*?"

"Why?" Eve said. "Because he's a nice guy."

"No, that's not what I meant. Did you somehow *suggest* I might take legal action against Vivienne?"

"Liv, you know I wouldn't do that. It's just that he's a lawyer. That's the way lawyers think." Eve smiled. "He also asked if you were dating anyone."

"Really?"

"Really."

"What did you tell him?"

"I told him you hadn't been, but I thought you might be ready."

Olivia guessed she couldn't be mad at Eve for that. But still, she felt uncomfortable.

"Don't you want to know his reaction to that?"

Olivia rolled her eyes. "Whether I do or not, I'm sure you're going to tell me."

"He asked me if I thought you'd go out with him." Eve grinned. "See? I told you he was interested in you."

Olivia wasn't sure what to think. "And what did you say?"

"I told him I didn't know, that he'd have to call you and find out on his own."

Olivia had begun to feel as if everyone, Eve included, was pushing her in a direction she wasn't sure she wanted to go. Unfortunately, she also didn't know how to stop this momentum.

"What's wrong now?" Eve said.

"Nothing."

"Look, no one's forcing you to do anything. If you don't want to go out with Austin, just say no when he asks."

Olivia bit her lip.

Eve frowned. "What?"

"I don't know. I guess I'm just feeling a bit pressured."

Eve threw up her hands. "I don't understand you, Liv. What's the problem? Honestly, I don't care if you go out with Austin…or anyone, for that matter. I just thought that's what you wanted."

She hadn't said, *make up your mind*, but Olivia knew that's what Eve thought. And actually, she'd have a right to feel that way. Because Olivia *had* been blowing hot and cold. Trouble was, she just wasn't comfortable moving back into the world of dating. In fact, it scared the you-know-what out of her to even contemplate dating again.

She made a face. "I'm sorry, Eve. You're right. And I'm not mad at you or anything. I guess I have to make up my mind what it is I really want right now."

"Yeah, you do."

Olivia took a deep breath. "And I will."

"Good. And, Liv…"

"What?"

"Austin's a good guy. You could do a lot worse."

"I know."

"But if you decide you're not interested in him, it's okay. I won't be upset with you. Just…be nice. Let him down gently."

"I promise I will."

"Okay, good." Eve looked at her watch. "And now I think it's about time to go get our kiddos."

As the cousins headed toward the theater, Olivia's thoughts were all over the place, and she wasn't sure about much. But one thing she *was* sure about was how her life was changing, whether she wanted it to or not.

Chapter Four

"Mommy?"

"Yes, sweetie?" Olivia finished tucking Thea into bed. Eve and the twins had left for home earlier, and Olivia had just finished giving Thea her bath.

"Nathan and Natalie have two daddies." She pronounced Natalie's name "Natlee."

Gazing down into her daughter's brown eyes, Olivia felt her heart swell with love. "I know."

Thea's forehead knitted in thought. "Why do they?"

Olivia sat on the side of the bed and took Thea's hand. "I explained that to you, honey. It's because their daddy Bill married someone else and now their mommy is married to their daddy Adam." Olivia had decided this was the only explanation Thea could understand right now. When she got older, Olivia would explain the situation properly.

Thea thought about this for a few minutes, then said, "My daddy died."

Olivia swallowed. "Yes, he did."

"But he loved me a lot."

"Yes, honey, he did. Your daddy loved you so much."

"Mommy, tell me the story about my daddy."

By now Olivia had to blink back tears, but she managed to keep it together and launch into the familiar story of the handsome daddy who was very brave and very strong and who had loved his little girl more than anyone else in the world. "And your daddy is now watching over you from Heaven," she finished with a tender smile.

"He's my garden angel," Thea said, beginning the ritual that always followed the "daddy story."

"Yes, he's your guardian angel."

"And he'll always keep me safe."

"Always."

"I have his hair." Thea touched her golden curls.

"You do."

"And his nose." Now Thea was giggling, pointing at and mashing down her nose.

"Except it's not as big," Olivia said, laughing in spite of the lump in her throat.

"And his ears!" Thea tugged at both her ears.

"Except they're not as big, either."

"If he was here, he'd smother me with kisses!" Thea exclaimed, an expression of delight already on her face as she waited for what was coming.

Olivia drew back. "I'm his messenger. Ready or not, here they come." Then, with an exaggerated laugh, pretending to be a dive-bomber, she buried her face in her daughter's warm neck and began kissing her.

"Mommy, that tickles!"

Olivia finished by kissing the tip of Thea's nose and murmuring, "Good night, sweetheart."

Thea sighed happily. "Good night, Mommy."

"And good night to Daddy…" Olivia began.

"Up in Heaven," Thea finished.

Olivia got up and dimmed the carousel lamp on Thea's dresser. She stood there for a long moment watching her child drift into sleep. Then, whispering softly, "Sweet dreams, my beautiful girl," she left Thea's bedroom and headed downstairs.

Matt waited until nine thirty Sunday night before calling Olivia. He knew Thea's bedtime was normally at eight, but figured he'd give Olivia some time to unwind from her hectic and emotionally chaotic weekend before fulfilling his promise to check in with her.

"How are you?" he asked when she answered.

"I'm okay."

But he could tell just by her tone that she wasn't okay. He wasn't surprised. Olivia was strong, much tougher than his mother imagined, but she was only human. It would be hard *not* to be affected by the treatment his mother had dished out.

"Eve and the kids get off okay?"

"Right on time. She was anxious to get back to Adam. Newlyweds, you know."

In her voice, he heard many things, and he knew she was already missing Eve, but more than that, there was a deeper sadness. "What's wrong, Olivia? Did something else happen since I saw you? Or are you thinking about my mother and what she did?"

Silence greeted his question, followed by a barely perceptible sigh. Just when he thought she wasn't going to answer at all, she said softly, "When I was putting Thea to bed, she asked me why Natalie and Nathan have two daddies."

The words, filled with pain, hit Matt somewhere in the vicinity of his solar plexus. He didn't know what to say. Groping clumsily, he finally said, "Life sucks sometimes."

"Yes," Olivia said in a weary voice.

"Liv, do you want—"

"You know what," she said before he could finish his half-assed question, "I can't talk about this right now. I'm so tired. I just want to go to bed. I'm sorry, Matt. I'll call you tomorrow."

And then she was gone.

Matt sat staring into space for a long time after that disconnect. Two emotions were warring inside. The first was anger at his mother and the second was the fierce love he felt for Olivia and Thea.

When he finally got up and went into the compact kitchen of his mid-rise condo near the county offices where he spent most of his waking hours, he had made up his mind. No matter what the outcome of his father's attempt to talk some sense into his mother, Matt would do whatever it took to protect Olivia and Thea from any more pain…or loss. And if that meant a complete break from his family, so be it.

Olivia had a hard time falling asleep. She kept thinking about Thea and reliving the day she'd gotten the news about Mark and his death. She'd thought she was recovered from his loss, and had accepted what had happened. She'd believed she was fully ready to move forward.

But tonight's bedtime ritual with Thea, always bittersweet, had been more painful, more filled with an almost overwhelming sense of loss. Was it always going to be this way? Would she never be able to feel entirely happy again?

Of course, you'll move forward. Of course you won't always be sad. This is a normal progression of grief you're feeling. Remember how you felt when your dad died? Magnify that by about ten, and that's what you're dealing with now. When you lose someone you love, it's always two steps forward, one step back.

The voice in her head wasn't hers. It was Eve's. And Olivia's head knew Eve was right. But her heart was having a hard time tonight.

That's because Thea showed you a part of her heart. We can always deal with our own sorrows and regrets, but when it comes to our children, it's tougher. We want to protect them from everything. And we can't.

Eve again.

Olivia almost laughed. Eve was like her alter ego or something. Or her twin. They just understood each other.

Eve was right. Olivia needed to quit beating herself up because she'd taken a step backward tonight. Thea hadn't known it. Olivia had soothed her and reminded her of how loved she was and always would be. By Olivia, by everyone, and especially by the father guarding her.

More tranquil now, Olivia's thoughts finally segued into what Eve had said about Matt. Was it possible Eve was right about that, too? *Was* Matt in love with her?

The idea thrilled her, but it also terrified her. Because she knew she was right, too. No matter how much they might care about each other, nothing could ever come of an attraction between them. It was hard enough living with Vivienne now. If Olivia and Matt should become involved in that way, there would be all-out war.

Vivienne would never sit still for another son of hers tying himself to Olivia.

So there was no point in thinking about Matt. If he *did* harbor feelings for her, he'd get over them. Especially if she discouraged him the way she had involuntarily done tonight by cutting off their conversation. She'd felt bad afterward, but now she realized the way she'd ended tonight's phone call might be the first step in distancing herself. Even so, she didn't want to hurt him. So what else could she do? She couldn't say anything, could she? No. Not unless he said something first.

You could date someone else.

Now that voice inside her was Eve again! Yes, Eve, she mentally answered, that would probably discourage him.

If Austin calls you, you should go out with him. And you should make a point of telling Matt.

Olivia closed her eyes. It saddened her to think of doing something so underhanded, but what other choice did she have?

On and on her thoughts went, replaying the phone conversation she'd had with Matt earlier, replaying everything she and Eve had discussed, going over and over the possibilities of how she could move forward with her life, perhaps build a new family with a daddy for Thea, yet somehow keep from causing Thea another loss, this time of her Britton grandparents—until finally Olivia fell into a fitful sleep.

Her dreams were as scrambled with emotions and people and events as her thoughts had been. Thea calling "Daddy!" Eve and Austin beckoning to her. Vivienne spewing hateful words. Her mother fainting. Erotic images of Matt. Those were the most vivid. Matt, kissing her, touching her, making love to her. The images of

Matt, so real and coming as they did just before dawn, caused her to awaken gasping, her heart pounding.

Later, after a long shower that soothed her and brought her back to reality, dressed and ready for the day, she stood at the kitchen counter in her blue scrubs waiting for her coffee to be ready and told herself that for her sake and for Thea's, she had to focus on going forward toward what was possible, even if it wasn't what she really wanted.

But it didn't really matter what *she* wanted, did it? Thea's welfare was far more important. So Olivia needed to suck it up and put ideas of Matt out of her mind for good. Because, unfortunately for her *and* for him, if he really did harbor romantic feelings toward her, her association with the Britton family had mostly brought her unhappiness and heartache and it didn't look as if that would ever change. It certainly wouldn't change if she and Matt became a couple.

Olivia was done with unhappiness. Done with heartache. She wanted something different in her life, something that promised peace and calm, happiness and security for both her and Thea.

And the only way to achieve that was to move on.

With someone other than a Britton.

"Say that again?" Matt couldn't believe he'd heard his father correctly.

"I said, your mother thinks we should petition family court for primary custody of Thea," his father repeated.

"I can't believe this. What possible grounds could you have?"

"Your mother feels this latest incident at the festival, added to the other incidents she's documented, will show that Olivia is an unfit mother."

"Other incidents? What other incidents?"

"Your mother's been keeping a list. Dates, times, circumstances, witnesses. She showed it to me, Matt. It's pretty incriminating."

"Dad, this is ridiculous. I can't believe you're in agreement with this."

"That list is bad, Matt. Your mother's right. Olivia doesn't seem responsible, just like your mother says."

Matt was appalled that his father could be taken in so easily. "This is the craziest thing I've ever heard. You know what? I'm coming over. I want to talk to both you and Mom together."

"Matt, I don't think that's a good—"

"I'm coming." He broke the connection.

Thirty minutes later, he was knocking at his parents' door. His father answered.

"Matt." He took Matt's arm, "I really wish you'd—"

Matt shook his father off. "Where's Mom?"

"She's in the sunroom, but—"

Ignoring his father, Matt strode straight back to the sunroom. He found his mother seated at the glass-topped table in front of the windows that looked out over the garden.

"Hello, Matthew," she said, looking up. She didn't smile.

"We were just about to eat lunch, son," his father said.

"And you were not invited," his mother said.

Before she'd finished speaking, Phoebe, their long-time cook, entered the room with a laden tray. "Oh, hello, Mr. Matt," she said. "I didn't know you were here. I'll get another plate."

"No need," his mother said in a clipped voice. "He's not staying."

"Oh, okay."

"Vivienne..." his father said.

She gave Matt's father one of her chilling looks, and whatever else he might have said died on his lips. He avoided Matt's gaze.

Matt sighed. He knew his mission was doomed to fail, but he had to at least try. He wouldn't be able to count on his father, though, that was obvious. He waited until Phoebe had unloaded the food: a bowl of shrimp salad, sliced tomatoes, French bread, butter and a pitcher of lemonade.

"That's all, Phoebe," his mother said, and Phoebe, who had hesitated, nodded and left the room, but not before giving Matt an apologetic glance.

Vivienne began filling her plate. "Sit down, Hugh."

Matt's father, whose role in their family had been determined long ago, shrugged and took his seat.

Matt, not about to allow his mother to cow him, too, pulled out one of the other chairs and joined them.

She turned toward him and narrowed her eyes. "I thought I made myself quite clear when I said you were not invited to stay."

"I have no intention of leaving until we talk about this latest craziness of yours."

"I beg your pardon?"

"I can't believe you are really going to try to take Thea away from her mother."

"Believe what you want."

"Mom, this is just wrong."

His mother put down her fork. "Matthew, I don't really care what you think. I will do what I know is best for my granddaughter. End of discussion."

"You're really willing to drag the Britton name through the mud? The *Marchand* name? Have everyone in Crandall Lake know your business?" Appealing to her family pride seemed the only avenue open to Matt, since it seemed to be highest on her list of priorities.

"*My* name won't be the one sullied, because I'm not the one who's unfit to raise Thea." So saying, she picked up her fork again and ate some of her shrimp salad.

Matt thought of ten things he could have said in rejoinder, but what was the use? Nothing would change his mother's mind, and his father didn't have the backbone to oppose her. "Fine. You're obviously determined to go down this path. But I won't be a party to it, and if you proceed, I won't help you."

"You would go against us?" his mother said in disbelief. "You would side against your own parents? Surely, even in your misguided state, you have to agree that Thea would be better off with us."

Matt shook his head. "No. I don't agree. Olivia is a good mother, and she doesn't deserve what you're doing to her." He pushed back his chair and stood. "She was Mark's *wife*, for God's sake. Think about what *he* would say if he were alive."

Her eyes narrowed. "I'm warning you, Matthew. Leave your brother out of this. And *you* stay out of it. Because if you don't, you will live to regret it."

With that last threat ringing in his ears, Matt turned and walked out of the room, leaving his parents to their lunch...and to each other.

But as he drove back to his office, he knew he had to warn Olivia. So after parking his car, and before heading inside, he took out his cell phone and called her work number.

"Registration and Admitting."

Matt didn't recognize the voice. "May I speak to Olivia Britton, please?"

"She's on her lunch break. Would you like to leave a message?"

"No, thanks. I'll call her cell."

Olivia answered on the second ring. "Hi, Matt."

"Hi. I called your work number first. I know you're at lunch. Can you talk?"

"Sure. I'm sitting outside, enjoying the beautiful day and eating my tuna sandwich."

"Well, I don't want to ruin your lunch hour for you, but something's come up that you need to know about."

"Oh?"

"Look, there's no way to sugarcoat this. My mother plans to petition family court for primary custody of Thea."

"What?"

The alarm in Olivia's voice was evident. Matt sighed. "I know. I was just as shocked as you are."

"On what grounds?"

"That you're an unfit mother."

"Oh, my God. You mean, because of Saturday?"

"Not just Saturday, apparently. My father says my mother's been keeping a list of incidents, with dates and times and witnesses."

"Incidents? What incidents?"

"I don't know. I haven't seen the list, and since I'm now persona non grata with my mother, I doubt I ever will." Actually, he was kicking himself for going on the attack with his mother before finding out exactly what *was* on that list.

"But, Matt—"

"I know, it's crazy. I went over there on my lunch break, tried to talk to her about it, but you know how she is. She just barreled right over me. Wouldn't listen. In fact, she threatened me."

"Threatened *you*? Why?"

"Because I sided with you. Told her I wouldn't go along with this."

"Oh, Matt, I don't want to cause any more trouble between you and your parents."

"You're not causing trouble. The trouble was there long before you came along."

"Is that true?"

"Yes, it's true. You remember the scandal involving Chet Parker? My mother bragged about bringing him down—she was actually proud of herself. And I've always thought she had a hand in Rosalie Harris's downfall. Someday I'll tell you all the gory details. But right now, we have more important things to worry about. I think we need to talk in person. Can you get your mother to watch Thea tonight? Maybe go out to dinner with me?"

"Um, yes, I'm sure I can, but…"

"But what?"

"Don't you think I need to do something to prepare? Like, immediately?"

"That's what I want to talk to you about."

"Oh, okay."

"How about if I pick you up around six thirty? Would that work?"

"Yes. That's perfect."

"All right, see you then."

"See you then," she echoed.

Matt sat in his car for long minutes after disconnecting the call. He knew he was on the precipice of something very dangerous, and that if he stepped off that cliff, he could never go back.

But if he didn't step off, if he allowed Olivia to fight

this on her own, he would never have any chance with her at all. There really wasn't any choice, was there?

He loved Olivia.

So he would do whatever it took to help her, no matter what else that path might cost him.

Because he knew, without any doubt at all, that without Olivia, his life would be meaningless anyway.

Chapter Five

Olivia still had ten minutes before she had to be back at her desk, so she used it to call Eve.

"Oh, my God," Eve said. "The woman is certifiable."

Olivia couldn't help laughing. Eve never did mince words. "We think so, but there are plenty of people who follow her lead."

"Tell you what, hon, as soon as we hang up, I'm going to call Austin. He's a top-notch attorney, and I know he'll represent you."

"Don't you think I should wait till I talk to Matt tonight?"

"No. I think you should line Austin up immediately. After all, we both know Matt can't represent you in this. He can be on your side privately and he can help from the sidelines, but he can't oppose his parents in court. I mean, think about it. If he fights her openly, your mother-in-law will just become more vindictive toward you."

Olivia did know that. It was one of the primary reasons she knew she could never have a romantic relationship with Matt, despite what Eve thought. She hesitated a moment, then said, "I would have to use some of Mark's insurance money to pay Austin, and I hate to do that. I wanted to keep it intact for Thea."

"Don't worry about the money, Liv. I'm paying his fee," Eve said. "And I don't want any argument about that, either."

"I can't let you do that."

"You're not letting me. I'm doing it, period."

"But—"

"No buts. Seriously. Adam has put so much money in my 'fun' account, as he calls it, I couldn't spend it all if I wanted to. Please let me do this for you."

Olivia's eyes filled with tears. "I love you, Eve."

"I love you, too. I'll let you know what Austin has to say."

"I don't want to talk about this while I'm at work. And I have to go back in a few minutes."

"I'll text you instead. And we can talk later tonight. After you've had dinner with Matt."

"All right."

They hung up then, and after Olivia tossed her trash, she headed back inside the hospital. She was filled with so many mixed emotions: disbelief and anger over Vivienne, gratefulness and relief over Matt's and Eve's support, and worry over the future.

She wondered what Mark would think if he knew what his mother was doing. He would be disgusted, she was sure. After all, he'd stood up to his mother when she tried to discourage him from marrying Olivia. Yes, Mark would be on her side. Of course, if Mark were alive, Vivienne would never even think of doing something like this.

Maybe not, but she'd have done her best to ruin your marriage.

Oh, God. What a mess everything was.

For the rest of the afternoon, Olivia couldn't give one hundred percent of her concentration to her job. How could she? At the back of her mind was always the thought of what could happen if Vivienne followed through on her threat. Even with Austin representing her, Olivia knew there was always the chance Vivienne could win, because the Britton family name carried tremendous influence in the county. In fact, Olivia had heard Vivienne had several judges in her pocket. Some of that was just gossip brought about by envy, but still... if there even a grain of truth in what was said, Olivia could be in for a rough ride.

I could lose. She could take Thea away from me!

Dear God. That couldn't happen. Eve was right. Olivia needed to be prepared with the best legal representation she could find. And aside from Matt, who was off-limits, Austin Crenshaw *was* the best. But what if Austin no longer wanted any part of this? Olivia wouldn't blame him if he didn't. After all, he had to live and work in Hays County, too, and Vivienne Britton could make a lot of trouble for him. *What will I do if he says no*?

She kept checking her phone, but Eve hadn't yet texted her. Olivia told herself that didn't mean a thing, that Eve had probably not been able to contact Austin yet, but still she worried.

Finally, at three thirty, a text came in.

Call Austin when you're free. He will take your case. XXOO, Eve.

A giant wave of relief crashed through Olivia. Thank God for Eve. What would Olivia do without her? Not wanting to wait, Olivia told her supervisor she was taking a break, and she headed for a quiet corner of the cafeteria where she placed a call to Austin's office. His secretary put her right through.

"Olivia, hi," he said warmly. "Eve told me what's happening with your in-laws."

"Yes, and she said you're willing to represent me."

"I'll be happy to represent you. But you know, it may not come to that."

"What do you mean?"

"Well, your mother-in-law may change her mind. Sometimes people threaten things, then back down when their lawyers tell them what they're contemplating is not in their best interests. Or that they can't win."

Olivia wished. "You don't know Vivienne. She never backs down."

"In that case, we'll be prepared. I'd like to meet with you to go over everything. When would be convenient?"

"I'm off tomorrow."

"Great. Tomorrow afternoon works for me. Could you come here to my office? Say about two?"

"I'll be there. And, Austin, thank you. I can't tell you how grateful I am to have you in my corner."

"Like I said, happy to do it. I'd been meaning to call you anyway." He hesitated a moment. "See if maybe I could take you to dinner some night."

Olivia could hear the smile in his voice. He really was so nice. Eve was right. Olivia could do a lot worse. She resolutely pushed all thoughts of Matt out of her mind. Matt had nothing to do with this. *Could* have nothing to do with it. She needed to remember that. She especially needed to remember it tonight. Because even if she were willing to take on the wrath of Vivienne Britton, she could never do that to Matt.

Olivia was still thinking about Matt and how to let him know, without ever saying anything directly, that there could never be anything more to their relationship than there was now, when he arrived to pick her up for dinner that evening.

"Right on time," she said as she answered the door.

When he smiled at her, her traitorous heart skittered. Why did he have to be so handsome? So sexy? And those eyes of his. An inky blue, they reminded her of the ocean at twilight. A girl could drown in their depths. He was everything a man should be. Not just sexy and good-looking, but strong, smart and kind. It still bewildered her that Matt had gone so long without marrying.

You could tell he was a Britton. There was an unmistakable resemblance between him and his siblings, although Matt was taller and darker than Mark had been. His hair was more chestnut, whereas her late husband's had been blond like Vivienne's.

Matt looked more like his father. So did Madeleine, the youngest of the family, who lived in Austin. Olivia was sure that's why Vivienne had favored Mark; he was the only one of her children who clearly belonged to her.

"You look very nice," Matt said now. His gaze swept her in admiration, taking in the black pencil skirt, the pretty pale blue silk sweater Eve had given Olivia for her birthday, and the black heels that fostered the illusion Olivia was taller than her actual five foot two.

"Thank you."

"Shall we go?"

"I'm ready."

"I thought we'd go to the inn."

Olivia frowned. "Are you sure you want to do that?" She knew he'd understand she was referring to the fact The Crandall Lake Inn was a favorite spot of his parents and their friends.

"I refuse to sneak around," he said firmly. "Unless you'd prefer to go somewhere else?"

"Actually, I would. Do you mind?"

"Of course not. What about Sam's Steakhouse?"

Olivia smiled. Sam's was a popular spot preferred by the younger set and was located nearer San Marcos than Crandall Lake. She doubted they'd see any of the Brittons' crowd there. "That sounds perfect."

Sam's wasn't as crowded on weekday nights as on the weekends, so they had no problem getting a table. And although all the window tables were occupied, Olivia actually preferred the quieter, more secluded corner table they were shown to.

Once they'd been seated, and their waiter had introduced himself, taken their drink order, and brought them their water and a basket of the warm rolls and herbed butter Sam's was known for, Matt said, "All day I've been thinking about my parents and what they're proposing to do."

"I know. Me, too. In fact—" But before she could finish, their waiter approached once more, this time bringing their drinks.

"What did you start to say before?" Matt asked when he left.

"Let's wait to talk until after we order our food."

"Okay."

It took a while to study the menu and decide what

they wanted, but finally their orders were placed, and Olivia could relax for a bit. "What I started to tell you before is that I've hired an attorney to represent me if your parents follow through on their custody threat."

Matt seemed taken aback. "I thought you'd wait till we talked. In fact, I have a recommendation for you."

"I *was* going to wait, but Eve arranged this for me. Her brother-in-law is taking my case. I'm sure you know him. Austin Crenshaw?"

"Of course I know Austin. He's a great lawyer. But he doesn't specialize in family law. I doubt he knows much about it. You need someone who not only knows case law, but also knows the judges and other lawyers who work in the field. You'll be at a disadvantage otherwise."

Olivia hadn't expected this. When Eve had suggested Austin, Olivia had been thrilled. On her own she never could have afforded a lawyer of Austin's caliber. But was Matt right? Was Austin a poor choice? Matt wouldn't say these things unless he meant them, would he? Now what should she do? She'd already told Austin she wanted him.

"I'm looking out for your best interests, Olivia," Matt said quietly.

"I know you are. But Eve is, too." Olivia thought about telling him Eve was also paying Austin's fees, but admitting that would be embarrassing, so she said nothing.

"Even if you've already agreed to hire Austin, I think you should reconsider," Matt said. "Paul Temple is a friend of mine, and he's just about the best family law attorney in the county. If I asked him, I know he'd take your case and do a terrific job for you."

"If he's that good, maybe your parents have already signed him up."

"No, they've hired Jackson Moyer."

"How do you know that?"

"I asked around."

Jackson Moyer was famous in Hays County. He'd handled every high-profile case in recent memory. His name graced the pages of not just local newspapers, but the wire services and national network news shows. Olivia swallowed. Her earlier fear returned with terrifying clarity. "That's not good, is it?"

Matt started to answer, but just then, their waiter appeared with their food—the house special rib eye for Matt and the shrimp and scallops for Olivia. Matt waited until the waiter had left them alone again, before saying, "I knew my mother would want the best, so I wasn't surprised to find out they'd hired Moyer. But Paul Temple is just as good. Maybe not as showy, but totally on top of things. Moyer won't be able to run roughshod over him the way he does some attorneys."

When she didn't answer, he said, "Look, if you're worried about telling Crenshaw you've found someone else, I'll do it. I'll call him and talk to him. He'll understand."

"I appreciate your concern, Matt, I do. But I'm sure Austin will do a good job for me. After all, he represents his brother in all his dealings, and those are *huge* cases. Eve tells me no one likes tangling with him because he always wins."

"Yes, he's got a good reputation, and he's smart. But family law and family court are different animals, and it's not his specialty."

Olivia sighed. "I know, but I can't go back on my word."

"Olivia, this is too important for you to worry about

hurting someone's feelings. This is about Thea. She matters more than anything else, doesn't she?"

"Yes, of course, but—"

"Look, how about this? I'll ask Paul Temple if he'll assist. There's no law against you having a team of lawyers. I'm sure Jackson Moyer will have several assistants. He usually does."

"I don't know… I—" Cornered now, Olivia decided to tell Matt the truth. "I don't think I can afford more than one lawyer, Matt."

"Let *me* do this for you, Olivia."

"I can't. It…it wouldn't be right. And if your mother ever found out…"

"First of all, of course it's right. I'm Mark's brother. He would expect me to look out for you. And I'm Thea's godfather. And as far as my mother finding out, she won't. But even if she did, I really don't give a damn. I'm so tired of her and her machinations—"

"I appreciate the offer, Matt, but I can't accept. I—I won't come between you and your parents."

"I'm telling you, they won't know."

"This kind of thing always gets out, you know it does."

He sighed heavily, laying his fork down. "All right, Olivia. You win. But you're making a mistake, and I wish you'd reconsider."

Olivia knew he was disappointed in her. She wanted more than anything to reach across the table. To take his hand. To say she was sorry and admit that Eve was footing the bill for whatever this possible lawsuit would cost her. To add that his concern for her meant the world to her.

But she could say none of that.

If she did, he would view it as encouragement, and who knew where that would lead?

Remember, she told herself again, *you are not good for Matt. You will ruin whatever relationship he still maintains with his parents. And you will ruin his career in the process. In fact, you should not be here with him now. You absolutely* must *discourage him. No matter what it costs.*

"I wish none of this was happening," Matt said. "I still can't believe my parents are even thinking of doing this to you."

"I'm not really surprised," Olivia said. "I've always known your mother hates me."

"You took Mark away from her. She can't forgive you for that." He cut a piece of steak and ate it.

"Do you suppose she'd have felt that way about any girl he fell in love with?"

Matt shrugged. "The only girl she seems to approve of is Charlotte Chambers." He made a face. "Lately she's been pushing her on me."

"On *you*?" Olivia hoped the sudden stab of envy his words had caused didn't show in her face.

"Yeah. Ridiculous, I know."

"Not so ridiculous." Charlotte Chambers was everything Olivia was not. Tall, blonde, model beautiful, wealthy and a graduate of all the best schools. She had a pedigree a mile long and a name worthy of linkage with the Brittons.

"She doesn't interest me one iota," Matt said, eating more of his steak. "I find her bland and boring."

"Bland and boring!" Olivia very nearly started laughing. "How can you say that? She's perfect." She speared part of a scallop.

"That's the problem. She's so perfect, she feels she

doesn't have to say or do anything to be interesting." He drank some of his wine. His eyes met hers over the rim of the glass. "I prefer my women to be more down-to-earth," he said, setting the glass down.

Olivia couldn't seem to look away, and for a long moment, their gazes held. She knew suddenly that Eve had been right. He *was* interested in her. Right now he was telling her something he couldn't say out loud. She only hoped she hadn't done or said anything to encourage him. Oh, Matt, she thought. Why did your name have to be Britton?

After a few more seconds pregnant with unspoken tension, Matt sighed and shook his head. "Tell Austin Crenshaw if he needs anything, anything at all, to call me."

"Matt, I don't want you sticking your neck out for me. You have a lot to lose, and if your mother—"

"You have more to lose than I do. And never mind. You don't have to tell Austin anything. I'll call him myself."

A tremor passed through Olivia as their gazes met again. Right now she felt as though an avalanche was on its way, and no matter what she did, she would not be able to avoid its destruction.

Olivia dreamed of Matt again that night. The two of them were somewhere warm, an island maybe. In her dream, they were making love on a rumpled bed, with the sound of the ocean somewhere near.

A warm breeze ruffled the sheer curtains, and wooden shutters were open to the fragrance of tropical flowers. Birds sang, and somewhere in the distance lilting guitars played irresistible melodies.

She moaned as his hands explored and caressed her.

The dream was so vivid, so real, that when they came together, she called out his name and woke up.

Heart pounding, she sat up in bed. Disappointment coursed through her. She was alone, the same way she'd been for more than four years now. The lovemaking hadn't been real. It could never be real. Not with Matt.

She looked at her bedside clock. It was 4:48 a.m. She would never get back to sleep, she knew she wouldn't. She had to get up at six o'clock anyway. Sighing, she tossed aside the light blanket, turned off the alarm and reached for her robe.

Downstairs, moving quietly so as not to awaken Thea, she fixed herself a cup of coffee and took it into the living room where she sat in her favorite chair and watched the sky slowly lighten. By the time she was ready to go upstairs and shower, she'd come to a decision.

Avalanche or no, she did not intend to allow anything to harm Thea, including her own foolish heart. She had to face it once and for all: loving Matt would come to no good.

In fact, it would destroy them all.

She couldn't allow that to happen. She *had* to begin pulling away from him. It was the only option she had.

"Oh, there you are. I've been looking for you."

Matt turned at the sound of Jenna Forrester's voice. As always, she looked impeccable and every bit the ideal ACDA—Assistant Criminal District Attorney—in her dark blue suit, tailored yellow blouse and sensible blue pumps, with her red hair swept back in a neat twist and secured by a gold clip. She was beautiful, smart and charming. He knew people felt she was the perfect partner for him. At one time, he'd thought so, too. Somehow, though, being perfect for him hadn't been enough. He'd needed passion, too, and it hadn't been there, no matter how much he might have wished it were.

"Hey, Jenna. What's up?" he said now.

"Wanted to give you this." She handed him a blue bound document.

He quickly scanned it: a motion to suppress evidence found during a search of the home of a defendant he was prosecuting. "How'd you happen to have this?"

She shrugged. "Guess they thought we were working together on the case."

Normally, they would have been. She had often been his second chair. But he'd been avoiding her since their breakup in August. "Thank you."

"You're welcome." She studied him for a moment. "You know, Matt, I'm not the vindictive sort."

"I know that."

"So stop avoiding me, then."

"Sorry. I thought it might be easier for everyone if—"

"Easier for you, you mean," she said, interrupting. Her smile was wry. "Seriously. There are no hard feelings."

He nodded, feeling like a bit of a heel. "I appreciate that."

"After all, why would there be? I mean, you can't help how you feel. Or don't feel. It's just my bad luck, right?"

Now there was an edge to her voice. Maybe she wasn't quite as understanding as she'd been pretending to be. "Why don't you just say it? I'm an idiot."

She chuckled. "You said it, not me."

"I'm sorry things have turned out this way, Jenna. You deserve better."

"Yes, I do. And I'm sorry, too. But I meant what I said. There are really no hard feelings."

"Thanks."

Their eyes met again, she gave him one last crooked smile, then waved goodbye and walked away.

Matt sighed again. Damn. Why was life so messy? Jenna really *was* perfect for him, unlike his mother's choice of Charlotte Chambers. Of course, Vivienne hadn't thought so, because Jenna wasn't in the same social circles. But none of that mattered, because neither woman was Olivia. And that was the problem, and always would be. Now that Olivia was in the same world and free to marry again, she was the only woman he wanted.

He hated that she'd hired Austin Crenshaw to represent her. He hadn't been able to stop thinking about it ever since she'd told him. Last night, as they'd said good-night at her front door, he'd been tempted to bring up the subject again, but he'd held off because he didn't want to upset her any more than she already was. Bad enough his mother bullied her. Olivia didn't need him bullying her, too.

But today, he decided he at least needed to reassure himself that Austin Crenshaw really would do a good job for her. So as he walked back to his office, he pulled out his cell and called Olivia. The call went directly to voice mail. She was probably still at work herself.

"Hey, Olivia, I was thinking. You said you were meeting with Austin Crenshaw tomorrow? I'd like to sit in at that meeting, because I'll know what questions to ask him, and you might not. Also, I'll be able to provide other information he might need. Call me back, okay?"

Because he was disciplined and because he took pride in his work, he managed to mostly put her and the custody suit out of his mind until he heard back from her.

She returned his call at six thirty. "I got your message."

He loved hearing her voice. "So it's okay if I go with you tomorrow?"

"I'm actually relieved you offered, because I probably *wouldn't* know the right questions to ask. My appointment is for two o'clock at Austin's office. Does that work for you?"

Matt would have to juggle some appointments, but that was okay. "No problem. Why don't I pick you up? We can go together."

She hesitated a few seconds. "Okay."

"I'll be there by one thirty."

He was smiling when they hung up. She needed him, whether she knew it yet or not. And he was determined to make sure that didn't change.

Still smiling, he decided since he'd be gone several hours tomorrow afternoon, he'd better stay late tonight and make sure everything for the Murphy trial was ready for next week's opening arguments.

Chapter Six

The smile had barely faded from Matt's face when there was a knock at his office door. Matt looked up as the door opened and his boss, Carter Davis, walked in.

"I'm glad I caught you," Davis said. "Thought you'd probably already gone for the day. Then I saw your lights on."

Matt smiled. He liked Carter. More important, he respected him. "I still have some stuff I need to do before I call it a night."

Carter lifted some files off the leather chair facing Matt's desk, put them on the floor and sat down. He studied Matt for a long moment.

Matt wondered what was up. Usually, when Carter wanted to see him, he summoned Matt to his office.

"Been wanting to talk to you about something," Carter finally said. His tone had turned solemn.

"Okay."

"You made any final decision about running for the House?"

Not sure where this was going, Matt decided to hedge. "I'm still mulling it over."

"But you're leaning toward doing it?"

Matt shrugged. "Truthfully? I'm not sure."

Carter nodded. "It's a big step."

"Yes."

The two men looked at each other. Carter hesitated, tented his hands, then said, "I don't like putting pressure on you, Matt, but I need you to make a decision, and soon. I've decided to retire the first of the year."

Even though Matt had expected something like this eventually, he was still a bit stunned. Carter had held the DA's position for twenty-eight years. He was practically a fixture in Hays County.

Seeing the expression on Matt's face, Carter smiled. "The governor will ask for my recommendation on a replacement to fill in until the next election. My pick would be you. And I know he would appoint you in the interim, but if you decide to go for the House and don't want to be DA, then I'll recommend someone else."

Matt let out a breath. Although he'd heard the rumors, he hadn't really expected Carter to retire this soon. That was one of the reasons he'd been receptive to the run for the House seat instead. *At least be honest with yourself. You were receptive because you were flattered. But now the flattery part has worn off, and reality has set in.*

"I know people have been speculating, so you must have thought about this possibility," Davis said.

"Yes."

Davis studied him a few seconds longer, then got up.

"I'll give you a week or so to think about it, but I'd like your answer fairly soon. Need to get that ball rolling."

In that instant, Matt knew what his answer was going to be. To hell with what his family wanted…or what his friends thought. This was his life, the only life he had. And everything he really wanted was right here, in Crandall Lake, not thousands of miles away.

But Matt wasn't the type of person to jump into anything. So he'd take a few days to think everything over thoroughly before giving Carter his answer.

But he couldn't help feeling excited about the way his career situation was shaping up. Now if only his personal life would keep pace, he would be one happy man.

Why had she agreed to let Matt go with her? Especially after what she'd decided this morning.

Yes, he'd be a help at the meeting, but she needed to begin standing on her own two feet, without relying on Matt so much. The more time she spent in his company, the harder it was to pretend they were only in-laws. She was afraid that one of these days she would give herself away by a word or a look. And then what?

Even if Eve had been right and Matt *did* care for her the way she'd begun to care for him, it was a go-nowhere situation. And no one knew that better than Olivia.

Why can't you stick to your convictions? You should have told him no today.

And yet, how could she? She didn't want to hurt him. And really, he'd been right. It *was* a wise thing to have him along with her today, because she didn't have a clue about what to ask Austin or whether he really *was* her best choice as a lawyer. Matt would be an invaluable help to her.

And wasn't Thea's welfare and keeping her daughter safe more important than anything else right now?

Of course, it was.

So all Olivia had to do was put on her big-girl panties, keep that thought uppermost, and she would be fine.

Matt left his office at one o'clock Wednesday and pulled into the driveway at Olivia's house shortly before one thirty. He'd barely rung her doorbell when the door opened. His heart squeezed at the sight of her. To him, she was more beautiful than any actress or model. Today she wore a dark blue dress with a simple string of pearls. The color emphasized the creaminess of her skin and the warmth of her eyes. It took all Matt's willpower to stop him from reaching for her. He wanted, more than anything, to pull her into his arms and kiss her. He wanted it so badly, he was sure she could feel the need emanating from him.

"Goodness," she said, smiling a little. "You look so official." Her gaze took in his dark pin-striped suit, white shirt and gleaming black shoes.

"My work uniform," he said, trying for a tone as casual as hers, even though the desire to touch her hadn't diminished. He managed to assuage that a bit by helping her into his car and breathing in her subtle scent.

"How's work going?" she asked once he was buckled in and had started the car. "You hardly ever talk about it."

"In the office, we refer to our work situation as OOU."

"OOU? What does that mean?"

He smiled. "Overworked, overwhelmed and understaffed."

She nodded. "Kind of sounds like the hospital."

"Just seems to be a fact of life most places nowadays."

"Can you afford to take this time off, then?"

"I have personal time coming to me."

She didn't answer, and Matt shot a glance at her. She was biting her lower lip. "Don't worry about it, Olivia. It's not a big deal." He considered telling her about Carter Davis's visit the previous evening, but decided this day was about her—her and Thea—not about him.

After a moment, Olivia smiled. "Thank you. I appreciate your doing this."

"I'd do anything for you…and Thea. You know that, don't you?"

"I… Yes. I do."

"So quit worrying." He knew she was always thinking about his mother and about not causing him trouble. One of these days, when the time was right, he would tell her everything, and do his best to make her understand that nothing she did or didn't do would make one bit of difference to the way his mother felt about him—*really* felt about him. It never had. And it never would.

It was a short drive to Austin Crenshaw's Crandall Lake office on the fourth floor of the First National Bank building on Main Street. They were silent as Matt pulled into the garage and parked. Five minutes later, they stood in Austin's office, ten minutes early for Olivia's appointment. The receptionist said she'd let Austin know they were there and disappeared into an inner sanctum.

A few minutes later, Austin walked into the waiting room. He seemed taken aback to see Matt sitting there, but he recovered quickly and gave Matt a smile, although he greeted Olivia first, taking her hand and saying, "It's good to see you again, Olivia. I'm only sorry about the reason."

"Thanks, Austin. I'm sorry, too."

Matt wished the man didn't seem so damned confident. He looked every inch the successful lawyer in a midnight blue suit that was obviously a designer label, paired with a dark red tie. Austin Crenshaw also had the good fortune to bear a marked resemblance to his famous brother, with the same dimpled smile and lanky grace. The only differences Matt could see were his short, professional haircut and the color of his eyes—hazel instead of Adam's much-written-about gray.

"I feel sure everything will be all right, though," Austin said. He was still holding Olivia's hand. Still smiling down into her eyes.

Matt had a childish urge to hit him. The feeling was so strong, he was afraid the emotion would show on his face.

Austin finally let go of Olivia's hand and turned to him. "I'm surprised to see you here, Matt," he said. "Since you're a member of the opposition camp."

"I don't happen to share my parents' feelings. I'm on Olivia's side all the way in this and will do whatever I have to do to help her."

"All right, then. Good. Let's go into my office, shall we?"

Austin took Olivia's arm, leaving Matt to follow them. Matt gritted his teeth. Austin's office was subtly elegant, with a jewel-toned Oriental carpet covering most of the hardwood floor, and classically designed furniture gracing its environs. Guiding Olivia to a rose-hued Queen Anne chair that was part of a grouping to one side of a shining mahogany desk, Austin took its mate next to her, leaving Matt to sit on the sofa facing them.

This put Matt at a disadvantage because he was seated lower than they were—part of the group, yet not part of it. His resentment grew, even as he understood Austin's strategy. The man was showing Olivia he was in charge, not Matt. In his shoes, Matt would have done the same.

Now, along with the desire to punch out Austin's lights, was a reluctant admiration. Clearly, Austin was a worthy adversary and certainly no fool. That he was interested in Olivia as more than a client was also evident because he hadn't taken his eyes off her more than a few seconds since they'd arrived, and his gaze was filled with warmth and undisguised admiration.

Although Matt was willing to concede the opening salvos to Austin, he knew it was time to take charge of this meeting and score his own points. "I'm sure you've done your research," he said. "So you know that my parents have hired Jackson Moyer."

Austin grimaced. "Yes, I know."

"I have to be honest with you, Austin. I don't think you're the best choice to represent Olivia. I think she needs an attorney more familiar with family court and the issues involved. Someone closer to Moyer's caliber. In fact, I recommended Paul Temple."

"I understand. But I can bring something to the case that Temple can't." Austin's gaze rested on Olivia. He smiled at her. "I care about Olivia personally and her case will be my top priority."

If Matt wasn't convinced before that Austin was thinking of Olivia as far more than a client, he was convinced of it now. And he also knew if he wanted a prayer of success with her himself, he didn't have long to make his move. Although she might shoot him down, wasn't that better than never taking a chance at all?

For the next hour and a half, both he and Olivia gave Austin all the information he asked for, plus some he hadn't. And Matt promised he would try to find out exactly what kind of "evidence" his mother had compiled against Olivia.

"That should be a part of discovery," Austin said.

Matt shrugged. "You'd think, wouldn't you? But knowing Moyer, I'm certain he'll figure out a way to keep it under wraps until we're actually in court. He likes the big reveal, the drama inherent in surprising his opponents." His glance met Olivia's, and he saw the worry in her eyes. "I'll try to get the information, though."

Olivia made a face. "I don't know, Matt. Your mother knows you don't agree with her. I doubt she'll tell you anything. And you'll just make things worse between the two of you."

"I agree she probably won't tell me, but my father might."

"I hate this," Olivia said. "I don't want to cause any more trouble for you."

"You're not causing it. My mother's responsible for that."

"But you're their son…"

"And you're their son's widow. And the mother of his child."

"Your brother-in-law's right, you know," Austin interjected.

Matt felt a moment of irritation. He didn't need Austin's help. Nor did he need him pointing out their relationship. He almost said something, but the moment passed. It would be stupid of him to argue with Austin or try to make his job harder. They both wanted the same thing. To help Olivia win her case and keep her daughter. In this, at least, they were in perfect accord.

"I'll file our response to the complaint tomorrow," Austin said as both Olivia and Matt stood. "And I'll call you when I have anything to report." Once again, he reached for her hand, keeping it in his much longer than necessary. "Actually, I'll call you tomorrow, regardless."

Matt's jaw clenched.

"Thank you. I'm feeling more hopeful now that we've all talked," Olivia said. She withdrew her hand and smiled at him.

Austin seemed reluctant to turn to Matt. They shook hands, and they all said their goodbyes, with Austin reiterating he would call Olivia. As Olivia and Matt rode the elevator down to the parking level, they were both silent, and he wondered what she was thinking about. Was she worried about the upcoming custody battle? Or was she thinking about Austin and his attention to her?

Matt wasn't sure. In fact, the only thing he was sure about was that he had no time to lose. Today, for the first time, he could feel her slipping away from him, and he couldn't let that happen.

He had to think of ways to spend more time with her. To maybe bring their situation to a head without seeming to pressure her.

"So did you mean what you said in there? You do feel more hopeful now that Austin's on the case?"

"Yes, I do. What about you?"

They had reached Matt's car by now, and he unlocked it and helped her in before answering.

"I'm still not convinced he's going to do as good a job as Paul Temple would do," Matt said once they were on their way. "One thing was clear today, though."

"What?"

"He likes you. In fact, I'd say he likes you a lot. So I'm sure he'll do his best to impress you." He glanced over at her to see her reaction.

Just from her body language and her hesitation in answering, he knew she was probably uncomfortable. Maybe even blushing. Olivia blushed easily. In fact, most of the time she wore her emotions for all to see. That was another thing he loved about her. There was never any subterfuge with Olivia. She was genuine through and through.

"He was just being nice, that's all," she finally said.

"You know," Matt replied carefully, "I don't blame him for being interested. Why wouldn't he be? You're a beautiful woman. And Mark's been gone a long time."

"First of all, I'm not beautiful. And second, yes, Mark *has* been gone a long time, but I can't think about anything like that right now, Matt. I have to concentrate all my energy on this lawsuit."

"You *are* beautiful, Olivia. I've always thought so."

"I..." She stopped, looked out the window. "Can we please change the subject? You're...making me uncomfortable."

"Sorry. I didn't mean to."

"I know. It's just that... I'm not ready for a discussion about dating."

He knew he'd pushed as far as he could right then. "Fair enough. New subject. Want to grab an early bite to eat before I take you home?" He had lightened his tone, but he felt encouraged, because he sensed something in the way she had reacted to him. Something that told him maybe, just maybe, he had a chance.

"Thank you, but Thea and I are having dinner at my

mom's. She's making one of our favorites—*haluski*." She pronounced it ha-loosh-key.

"Haluski?" He'd never heard of it.

"It's an ethnic dish, basically noodles and cabbage, fried with lots of onions and butter. I made it for Mark a couple of times. He loved it."

"Maybe I should invite myself to dinner," Matt said lightly.

Olivia looked at him. "Seriously?"

"Seriously." He grinned. "Single guys don't get many home-cooked meals."

Once again, she hesitated before answering. "Well, I know Thea will be thrilled if you stay to dinner."

"Only Thea?"

Suddenly Olivia laughed. "My mother will be thrilled, too. She likes you."

"What about you?"

"Are you digging for a compliment?"

"Everyone likes compliments."

"Okay. I'm glad you want to have dinner with us. There. Are you satisfied?"

Now that the tone of their conversation had changed, he decided to make one more attempt to burrow through her defenses. "I was hoping you'd say you liked me, too."

He could feel her looking at him, but he kept his eyes on the road.

After a long moment passed, she finally said, "Of course I like you, Matt. You're part of the family."

Because they were now approaching her mother's house, he let the comment go without answering. Because she was sending mixed signals, whether she knew it or not.

"Think it's okay for me to park in the driveway?" he asked a few seconds later.

"Sure."

Olivia didn't knock first or ring the doorbell. She simply opened the door and walked in, beckoning him to follow. "Mom," she called out, "we've got company for dinner."

Norma Dubrovnik, looking like an older version of her daughter, emerged into the hallway. She was flushed, wearing an apron, and it was obvious she'd been cooking. She smiled when she saw Matt. "Oh, hi, Matt. It's good to see you."

He smiled back. He liked her. She was just the kind of woman he wished his mother was. "Hi, Mrs. D. I hope you don't mind, but I invited myself to dinner."

"I don't mind at all. I always make enough for an army."

Just then, Thea came running out from behind her grandmother. "Unca Matt!" she exclaimed as they entered the house. "I'm getting a kitten!" Her smile lit her entire face.

"You are?" he said, scooping her up and twirling her around.

She giggled. "Yes!

"You're a lucky girl," Matt said, nuzzling Thea's cheek.

"I know!" Thea said, squirming out of his arms and running down the hall where she was out of earshot.

"She's talked of nothing else since I told her we'd go soon," Olivia said. She frowned. "But if we get a kitten, I don't know what we're gonna do on the days Thea has to go to day care. She won't want to leave the kitten at home."

"Maybe I could take a leave of absence from work," Norma said. "Then you could bring them both here instead of taking her to day care, especially while all this other mess is going on." She'd dropped her voice, although Thea had disappeared into the kitchen again.

Olivia's mouth dropped open. "A leave of absence? What will Dr. Ross say? Who will do your job? Thea is my responsibility, not yours."

"Dr. Ross can get a temp the way he does when I'm on vacation. I know if I talked to him he'd understand," Norma said.

"No, I don't want you to do that. Besides, Mom, you do enough as it is, picking her up from day care and keeping her when I work the afternoon shift."

"What do you think, Matt?" Olivia's mother said, turning to him. "Wouldn't Olivia's case be stronger if Thea wasn't in day care at all anymore?"

Matt hated to disagree with Olivia, but he thought her mother was right. He nodded reluctantly. "Your mom has a point, Olivia."

Olivia sighed. "I'll think about it. Maybe *I'm* the one who needs to quit working."

By now, they'd moved into the kitchen, and Matt, lured by the good smells wafting from the big cast-iron skillet on the stove, walked over and peered at its contents. "Looks great," he said. "Smells great, too." He was a sucker for any kind of pasta.

"Wait'll you taste it," Olivia said.

"I made sausage, too," her mother said.

"Better and better," Matt said.

"Maybe, since Matt's here, we should eat in the dining room," Norma said.

"Mom, don't fuss. Matt doesn't care," Olivia said.

"I'd rather eat in the kitchen," he said. "It's cozier."

Norma was still making noises about the dining room as Olivia got Thea settled into a booster chair, but finally the food was on the table and the four of them had taken their seats. Matt grinned when he saw the size of the serving bowl containing the cabbage and noodles.

"You weren't kidding about feeding an army, were you?" he teased Olivia's mother.

She laughed and brushed her hair back from her forehead. "It's ingrained. In our house, growing up, putting a lot of food on the table showed you cared about your family."

"Actually," Olivia interjected, "it showed you could afford to *feed* your family. Right, Ma?"

Norma gave her a sheepish smile. "Yes, that's true."

Matt couldn't help but think about how different his own home had been. He couldn't ever remember a homey scene like this one. All Britton meals had been served in the dining room, and certain dress and behavior were de rigueur.

Just then, Thea hit the table with her spoon. "I'm hungry!" she announced.

They all laughed, and Olivia took her plate and filled it with the noodles. Then she cut up a piece of sausage and transferred half of it to Thea's plate, as well. Thea immediately dug in as the rest of them served themselves.

Matt couldn't remember anything tasting so good. He knew part of his enjoyment had to do with the company he was with, but the food really was great. So was the talk and laughter and genuine love among them. Matt had always known something was missing from his own family, and now he fully understood what it was: the knowledge that these people cared for him more than any other people in the world.

His heart felt full as he looked around the table. Right now, at this moment, he was home.

And home was where he wanted to stay.

Chapter Seven

Olivia knew what she was doing and feeling was crazy but having Matt there with them made her happier than she'd been in a long, long time. It just felt so right, so natural. And she knew she wasn't alone in feeling this way. She could see how much her mother liked him. And, of course, Thea loved him.

And I love him. That's the problem. That's why it's so impossible to stick to any decision that has to do with easing him out of my life.

She had been so uncomfortable in the car today when Matt said those things about Austin. And about her. She'd wanted to say there was only one man who interested her in that way, and that man wasn't Austin. But how could she?

If only things were different.

If only Matt wasn't a Britton.

If only Vivienne was a normal mother-in-law, someone who loved her and wanted her to be happy.

Much of Olivia's happiness faded. Vivienne *wasn't* normal. And Olivia wasn't free to love Matt. To even *hint* at how she felt. Her love would cost him his family. And possibly his career.

Don't ever forget that.

Perhaps her eyes or her expression betrayed her thoughts, because Matt's eyes met hers and he frowned. Olivia made a determined effort to smile and pretend everything was just as good as it had been moments before, but she was afraid she hadn't succeeded, because his eyes remained curious and his own smile seemed strained.

Thank goodness for her mother. Norma stood and said, "Is everyone ready for dessert?"

"Ice cream!" Thea shouted.

"Not ice cream," Norma said. *"Kolache."*

"Kolache!" Now Thea laughed happily. "*Kolache and* ice cream!"

"She's got you there, Mom," Olivia said. Turning to Matt, she added, "You'll love my mother's *kolache*, Matt. She makes one kind with walnuts. And another kind with apricots. They're both wonderful."

"And sometimes poppy seed," Norma said.

He grinned, the strain gone. "I can't wait."

Olivia got up and began clearing the table. Surprising her, Matt stood, too, and helped.

"Sit, sit," Norma said. "Our guests don't do kitchen duty."

"This guest does. I invited myself, remember?" He turned to Thea. "Let's get you cleaned up a bit, princess."

"You're silly. I'm not a princess." But she allowed him to wipe her face and hands.

"You're *my* princess," he said, ruffling her hair.

Thea giggled.

Olivia's heart squeezed at his tender words. He would make a wonderful father because it was easy to see he loved Thea. In fact, he'd shown time and again that he really liked kids, not just Thea. Some men only pretended to, but with Matt it was genuine, and kids responded accordingly. He even helped coach a Little League baseball team and had once said he couldn't wait until he had a son of his own to coach. Yes, he'd make a terrific father.

If only… But she cut the thought off. "Time for dessert," she said brightly instead.

Minutes later they were all settled around the table again. The adults had fresh coffee with their slices of *kolache*, and Thea happily ate Blue Bell Homemade Vanilla ice cream to go along with hers.

"This is the best *kolache* I've ever had," Matt declared.

"It's different than what you usually find in Czech communities," Norma said, "but it's the way my grandmother made it."

She was referring to the fact she baked long jelly-roll-like pastries, then sliced individual servings. Most Czech bakers made stand-alone fruit *kolaches*, with a well in the middle containing fruit or jam.

"Well, they're wonderful," Matt said.

Olivia made a determined effort not to let her thoughts stray into dismal territory again, and for the most part, she felt she was successful. After they'd finished their dessert, Olivia and Matt cleaned up the kitchen. He even allowed Olivia to give him an apron.

"I'm not going to be responsible for you ruining that suit," she said, knowing it was expensive.

"Slave driver." But he was laughing.

She laughed, too, especially when she saw how cute he looked in the frilly apron. "That suits you." She pretended to reach for her phone. "I think I need a picture. To post on Facebook."

"I'll kill you if you take one." He wielded a wooden spoon as if it were a weapon.

Still laughing, she mock-ducked.

After more silly banter, the kitchen was clean and Norma suggested they go into the living room "where it's more comfortable."

They passed another pleasant hour talking and watching Thea play with the Lego set Norma kept in a toy box for her beloved granddaughter. But at seven o'clock, Olivia reluctantly said she thought it was time to go. No matter how much she loved this part of the day, it couldn't last forever. "Put the Lego away, sweetie," she said to Thea.

"I don't want to," Thea said, pouting.

"Thea," Olivia said.

Thea's lower lip protruded.

"I mean it."

With a long-suffering sigh, Thea began to very slowly put each Lego piece in the toy box.

Olivia considered saying something about speeding it up, but didn't. It was enough that Thea was obeying.

"Need some help with that, princess?" Matt said, getting down on the floor with her.

"Matt… "

He looked up, and when his eyes met hers, the rest of what Olivia was going to say died on her lips. There was something undeniable in his eyes, something Olivia knew she was going to have to deal with. The only question was, how? Because here…and now…she knew it wasn't going to be easy to walk away from him, no matter how much she knew it would be the right thing to do.

Why does he have to be so wonderful? And why am I so attracted to the absolute wrong man?

Heart pounding, she looked away and began gathering her things.

Finally they were ready to leave.

At the door, when Norma hugged Olivia goodbye, she whispered, "He would make Thea a wonderful father."

"Mom!" Olivia whispered back. What if Matt had heard her?

But he hadn't. He'd instead picked up Thea and was allowing her to sit piggyback, which she loved to do. She was giggling and he was pretending to be a horse, complete with neighing sounds as he transported her outside to the car.

All the way home—which was only minutes away—Olivia couldn't get her mother's comment out of her mind. Hadn't she thought the same thing earlier? That Matt *would* make a wonderful father? And he'd probably make an even more wonderful husband.

And lover.

That thought made her breath catch, almost as if she'd said it out loud. She glanced over at Matt, but he wasn't looking at her. Thank God. Even though she'd not voiced that thought aloud, her eyes might have betrayed her.

When they reached her house, she turned to say goodbye to him at the door, but he said, "I'll come in. Help you get Thea ready for bed."

"You don't have to do that, Matt. I know you have things to—"

"I want to."

What could she say? *I don't want you to.* That would be a lie because she did want him to. The fact was, she wanted even more. She wanted, after they'd gotten Thea ready for bed and settled her into her room, to take Matt's hand and lead him into the master bedroom. She wanted him to stay the night. She wanted him to undress her and make slow love to her, not once, but several times.

She remembered that old song from the oldies station her mother used to listen to—the one about slow hands.

She swallowed.

Just thinking about what she wanted made her stomach feel hollow.

It had been so long. So very long. She could hardly remember what it had been like to be held, to be loved, and touched, and cherished. She and Mark had been too young, really. Their lovemaking had been fast and impatient, the way young lovers are. Mark had never had the chance to grow with her.

She was so lonely.

Her loneliness hadn't been so bad when Eve was living there, when they'd been in the same boat, but now Eve had found love again. A wonderful, passionate, grown-up love. All you had to do was look at her to see how happy she was. How fulfilled.

I want that, too. I deserve that, don't I?

Why was she torturing herself? She knew what she wanted couldn't happen. That's all her neighbors would need. To see Matt's car in her driveway all night long. The entire gossip network of Crandall Lake would be on overtime tomorrow!

And Vivienne.

She would go ballistic.

Olivia actually shuddered, thinking of it.

"What's the matter?" Matt said. By now they'd settled Thea into her bath and were sitting watching her. "Are you cold?"

Olivia shook her head.

"You sure?"

Olivia tried hard to make her smile genuine. "Yes, I'm sure." She could feel his eyes on her as she looked away.

After Thea's bath was finished, Olivia dressed her in her pj's and got ready to read her a story. She hoped Thea wouldn't ask for the daddy story tonight, because she wasn't sure she could handle that kind of emotion right now. Not in front of Matt.

But Thea surprised her, saying in her stubborn voice, "I want Unca Matt to read to me, Mommy."

Olivia looked at Matt, who stood in the doorway.

He smiled. "I'd love to."

Olivia sat in the rocking chair in the corner while Matt sat next to Thea on her bed and read her *Pigtastic!*, one of her favorite stories. Olivia loved looking at him, loved seeing the way Thea responded. It was clear he was enjoying himself, that none of what he was doing was pretense. No one was that good an actor. With every moment that passed, Olivia realized anew what she would have if she could have Matt.

By the time he'd finished, Thea's eyes were closing. It had been a long, full day, and she was obviously tired.

Olivia got up and went over to the bed. "Say good-night to Uncle Matt, honey."

"'Nite, Unca Matt."

"Good night, sweetheart." He bent over and kissed Thea's cheek.

Then Olivia kissed her daughter, too, saying, "Sweet dreams, pumpkin. I love you."

"I love you, too, Mommy."

Olivia turned off the carousel lamp, leaving only the night-light on, and she and Matt where almost out of the room when Thea said, "Unca Matt?"

He stopped, turning to look back at Thea. "Yes, sweetheart?"

"I wish you were my daddy."

Olivia's startled eyes met his. For a long moment, their gazes held. Then Matt, still looking at Olivia, said, "I wish that too, sweetheart."

Thea's words and Matt's answer thundered in Olivia's mind as they left Thea's room and walked to the front of the house. Olivia knew she should say something, but she couldn't think of anything. She could barely look at Matt, let alone make conversation.

"I guess I'd better go," he said.

"Yes," she murmured.

When they reached the door, he turned to her. "Liv."

She finally raised her eyes. Her heart felt unsteady.

"I meant what I said. I do wish I was Thea's father. Just as I wish you were…mine."

Then, shocking her, he drew her into his arms, lowered his head and captured her mouth in a kiss that sent lightning bolts all the way to her toes.

Knowing he'd stunned her, Matt almost said he was sorry. But he wasn't sorry. And Olivia had responded to his kiss, opening her mouth and allowing him in for long seconds before pushing him away. That had to mean something.

"Matt, we…we can't do this." Her troubled eyes met his as she backed away from him.

He reached for her, taking her hand. "Why not?"

"You know why not."

"What I know is, I'm tired of pretending to just be your brother-in-law when I'd like to be so much more. And I think you *want* me to be more."

"I just… I don't see how you *can* be more. You know how your mother feels about me. She'd go crazy if she thought there was anything between us."

"That would be *her* problem, wouldn't it?"

"It would also be our problem."

"Not mine. I don't care what she thinks. Think about it, Olivia. She's going to go crazy when I testify as a character witness for you, so what's the difference?"

"You're planning to be a *character* witness for me?"

"Of course I am."

"You can't do that, Matt."

"I can, and I will."

"But—"

"No buts. I'm doing it. You and Thea are more important to me than anyone else in the world, and I don't care who knows it."

Olivia sighed shakily. "Knowing that means a lot to me, Matt. But are you sure? Your mother won't sit still for this."

Matt shrugged. "Let her do her worst."

"I…" Another shaky sigh. "Matt, you have to give me some time. This is a lot to process."

"I know it is. I don't expect you to make me any promises. I just wanted you to know how I feel." He didn't add that he'd wanted to make sure he staked his claim before Austin Crenshaw started working on her.

Their eyes met again, and he could see all the confusion and doubt and fear raging through her. At that moment, he could have cheerfully strangled his mother. This mess was all her doing. If Vivienne was a normal person, with normal feelings, she would want her son's widow to find happiness again. She would *encourage* her. And if that happiness was with her other son, she would be ecstatic. But Vivienne wasn't normal. And, for some reason Matt had been trying to figure out all his life, she didn't have the same feelings for him as she'd had for Mark.

"Just tell me one thing," he said.

"What?" Olivia said softly.

"Do I have a chance?"

She closed her eyes. "Oh, Matt…"

"Do I?"

"I—I do care for you. In fact, I more than care for you, but I…" Her face twisted. "I don't want a life filled with tension and estrangement from family. It was hard enough with Mark…before Thea. I just can't go through all of that again. And it would be worse now. I know it would. If…*when*…I win this custody case, I want something different. I—may have to move away to get it. I don't want to do that, but if that's what it takes for a peaceful life, that's what I'll do."

His heart sank. He could see the truth of what she was saying in her eyes. And he felt it in his bones. "Please don't make any decisions yet. Just wait. Okay? Will you promise me that? Anything can happen."

She slowly nodded. "I promise I'll wait. I won't decide anything for sure yet. I need time. And as I said before, if your mother follows through on filing for custody of Thea, I'll need to focus every bit of my energy on defeating her."

"And I'll do everything in my power to help you do that."

"Thank you," she whispered. Then, as if to take the sting out of what she'd said earlier, she rested her head against his chest and hugged him. "Good night, Matt. And thank you for everything."

He allowed himself to hold her for a long moment, then kissed the top of her head, inhaling its clean, fresh fragrance, and whispered, "I love you," and left.

As Matt walked out to his car, his thoughts were in turmoil. But one thing he was sure of. He might lose, but that didn't mean he wouldn't give everything he had into fighting for Olivia.

Even if it meant he would have to walk away from everything here and begin again somewhere new.

Olivia leaned against the door after Matt left. His kiss, and everything he'd said, had shaken her to her core. She'd wanted to tell him that being with him today had meant everything to her, that having him as her husband and as Thea's father would be the answer to all her prayers.

But that couldn't happen.

Because no matter how she felt, she'd meant what she told him. She did want something different. She wanted a close, warm, loving relationship with both her family and a potential husband's family. And that would never happen with Matt and the Brittons. Vivienne would never accept her. Even if she mounted a fight to gain custody of Thea and lost, Vivienne would continue trying to undermine Olivia. She would continue fighting her and finding fault with her and working to make her life miserable.

But Olivia had to be strong. She could no longer allow her mother-in-law to do these things. For the longest time, Olivia had felt she had to do everything in her power to keep communication with Vivienne as pleasant as possible, no matter what the older woman said or did. But this probable suit against her, Vivienne's threat to wrest Thea away, had proven to Olivia that nothing would ever change. And if she allowed Vivienne to continue in this spiteful vein, it would impact Thea's life in ways Olivia couldn't...*wouldn't* tolerate.

So for everyone's good, but most especially Thea's, Olivia would need to start a new life...probably somewhere far away from Crandall Lake and everything Britton.

Olivia was still turning all these thoughts over in her mind thirty minutes later after changing into her pajamas and pouring herself a glass of wine, with the intention of putting her feet up and watching the latest recorded episode of *The Good Wife*, one of her guilty pleasures, when her cell rang.

Olivia smiled; it was Eve.

"I wondered how your meeting with Austin turned out," Eve said. "But I gave up on you calling me, so I decided I'd call you."

"It's been a long day," Olivia said. She sank into her favorite chair and put her bare feet on the matching ottoman.

"Well? How'd it go?"

Olivia gave her an abbreviated version of the meeting.

"Has Matt come around to agreeing Austin's a good choice for you?" Eve asked.

"Sort of." Olivia hesitated, then decided it would be good to have Eve's opinion of everything that happened after the meeting. "He said it was clear Austin would work hard for me because Austin likes me."

"Oh, really? Did he mean *likes* you as in wants to date you?"

"Yes."

"And what did you say?"

"I said I wasn't sure I was ready for that and that I needed to put all my energy into this court case."

"Is that what you're going to tell Austin if he asks you out?"

"I don't know." Maybe it would be best to go out with Austin if he asked her. Maybe that would be the only way to make Matt forget about her. "Um, something else happened today. Later on."

"I'm all ears."

"Matt invited himself to dinner at Mom's. And then afterward, he came in to help put Thea to bed. And after he kissed her good-night, she said she wished he was her daddy."

"Oh, Liv."

"I know."

"What did you say?"

"I was too rattled to say anything. But then Matt was leaving to go home, and he said he wished the same thing. And that he wished I was his, too. Then he…he kissed me."

"Wow."

"Yeah."

"Did you kiss him back?"

"I couldn't help myself. But then I pushed him away."

"See? I *told* you he felt that way about you."

"I know you did." Olivia sighed.

"So what happened then? After you pushed him away?"

Olivia repeated the rest of the conversation between her and Matt. "I'd give anything if things were different, Eve. But they aren't. And I meant what I said. I don't want a repeat of my marriage to Mark."

"I totally understand. And you deserve that. Frankly,

I don't think a relationship with Matt could survive the continuous onslaught of viciousness Vivienne would subject you to. Not to mention she could totally ruin Matt's career."

"I know."

Eve was silent for a few seconds. Then, thoughtfully, she said, "You know, Liv, you should seriously think about moving out here. Adam was just saying today that he desperately needs to hire a secretary/assistant to take care of things here, not just for his career, but for our personal lives, too, which would mean basing someone here in the house, but he didn't know how I'd feel about having a stranger among us. But if it was *you*…oh, my goodness, that'd be perfect. And you'd be perfect for the job. Oh, Liv, think about it, will you? I know you'd have to wait till the custody hearing is over, but after that… it's the ideal solution. There's even a separate place you could live and have your privacy. We have a guesthouse adjacent to the pool. It has two bedrooms and its own kitchen! The previous owner's mother lived there, so it's entirely self-sufficient. And we have tons of room in the house. There are six bedrooms! Your mom, my mom, Stella, they could all come to stay, whenever they wanted to. It would be wonderful. I would love it. The kids would love it!"

Later, as Olivia settled into bed, she couldn't stop thinking about Eve's suggestion. Everything in her felt sick at the thought of leaving Crandall Lake and Matt. But in her heart of hearts, she knew she was close to a place where she could no longer handle Vivienne and her vindictiveness.

Nor did she want Thea exposed to it, grandmother or no grandmother.

Maybe moving away was the only choice left.

Chapter Eight

Matt waited until Monday morning to call Carter Davis's office. "Is he free to see me for a few minutes?" he asked Mary, Carter's longtime secretary, now officially called his admin.

"Let me check." A few seconds later, she said, "He said to tell you he's got twenty minutes before he has to leave for an appointment in Austin."

Two minutes later, Matt accepted a cup of coffee from Mary and settled into one of the chairs in front of Carter's desk. "I've come to a decision," he said.

"Okay." Carter put down the pen he'd been using to sign some documents.

"I'm not going to run for the House seat. I'll notify my biggest supporters today."

Carter seemed surprised. "You're sure about this?"

"Very sure."

"I have to admit, I wasn't certain you'd go this way. But I'm glad. I think you're the best person for the job.

It'll make stepping down a lot easier for me, knowing I'm leaving everything in your hands."

"Well," Matt said, "I still have to win an election next year."

"No doubt in my mind that you will."

"Nothing's a sure thing when voters are involved."

"You'll have me in your camp." Carter stood, extended his hand, then clapped Matt on the back as he walked him out.

Heading back to his own office after leaving Carter's, Matt felt a twinge of guilt. He knew he should have been completely open with Carter and told him there was a possibility he would not be able to follow through on running for district attorney in the next election, that there was a chance—a slim one, but still a chance—that he might actually have to move to another state, and why. But he hadn't said anything because he hoped matters would never come to that. And he'd known if he confessed this possibility to his boss, no matter how slim, Carter would not have felt comfortable recommending him to the governor.

Damn his mother. Why couldn't she be a normal mother, someone who was proud of him and wanted him to be happy?

He tried to wipe the entire problem out of his mind as he reentered his office and began to deal with the day's schedule, and he was nearly successful until his phone rang an hour later and the caller turned out to be his mother's favorite candidate for a daughter-in-law, Charlotte Chambers.

"I haven't seen much of you lately," she said, "and decided to take matters into my own hands and give you a call."

"I've been buried in work," he said. "I'm buried now." Maybe she'd take the hint.

"I figured as much, especially since you're getting your ducks in a row for your campaign for the House seat."

"Yes, lots of things going on," he answered smoothly. He wasn't ready to advertise the fact he didn't intend to run for the House seat. Not until he'd had a chance to talk to the people who had been supporting him. He owed it to them not to say anything to anyone else before notifying them. He especially didn't want Charlotte to even suspect. Knowing her, the first person she'd call would be his mother.

"Surely you can take a break now and then," Charlotte said in a flirty voice.

He made a noncommittal sound. Good thing she couldn't see his expression.

"Anyway, that's why I'm calling," Charlotte continued. "I was hoping to persuade you to accompany me to the Harvest Ball next week." The Harvest Ball was one of the biggest charity events of the year, with the proceeds going to the new women's health center that would serve the entire county.

"Thanks, Charlotte, but I can't. I have another commitment."

"Oh, darn. I'm disappointed. It would have been good for your campaign to be seen there."

"I'm sure you're right. But it can't be helped." He knew she wanted to know what his commitment was, but he refused to fall into the trap of trying to explain. Especially since there was no commitment. But mostly because he didn't owe her an explanation.

"I'm sorry for another reason," she said, her voice

softening. "I miss you. I've barely seen you in the last few months."

"That's what happens when you're trying to raise money for a campaign as well as holding down a job that requires sixty- and seventy-hour weeks. Your friends get neglected."

She didn't say anything for a long moment. When she did, her voice turned coy. "All right. You get a pass this time. But I think you owe this friend a rain check, don't you? In fact, I know just how you can make it up to me."

Matt mentally thought a bad word.

"My sorority is having a casino night the Friday after Halloween. It's loads of fun and all the profits will be donated to the children's museum. You can be my date that night."

"I can't promise anything, Charlotte. I'll check on some things and get back to you. I may be out of town that weekend."

"Now, Matt, I'm not going to listen to any more excuses. You work far too hard."

What was he going to have to do? Come right out and tell her he was not interested? He couldn't help comparing her to Olivia. Hell, there *was* no comparison. Olivia was a beautiful, warmhearted, kind woman and Charlotte was all flash, no substance. However, she seemed to have the hide of an elephant. Hints didn't make a dent. In fact, in this regard, she bore a decided similarity to his mother. With a mental sigh, he knew he could no longer postpone the inevitable.

"Look, Charlotte," he said, keeping his voice as pleasant as he could manage, "we're both adults and I know you're the kind of person who would prefer honesty. The truth is, I'm involved with someone else. And it's serious."

For a long moment, there was only silence on the other end of the phone. Finally, in a voice almost as icy as his mother's could be, she said, "I see. Well, it's your loss."

Then she hung up.

Matt looked at the phone, then returned it to its holder. Had he actually managed to get rid of her? He knew there would probably be repercussions as a result of their conversation, but he no longer cared.

He managed to put Charlotte and her phone call out of his mind and was deep into an analysis of a lengthy crime report when there was a knock at his office door, followed by the entrance of his sister.

He smiled in greeting. Of all his family, Madeleine was his favorite, the only one he felt completely comfortable with, the only one he felt loved him unconditionally. She looked wonderful, as always. Tall, slender, glowing with good health, she was the picture of the all-American girl with her long golden-brown hair, her large green eyes—a throwback to their great-grandmother Britton—and her bright smile. At twenty-seven, she was an accomplished and talented artist who worked for the largest advertising agency in Austin.

"What're you doing here?" he said, getting up to hug her.

"I have to give a presentation to a potential client at one o'clock and hoped I could persuade you to have an early lunch."

Matt thought about all the work he had to do and the fact he'd taken off early yesterday. "Nothing I'd like better," he said. "What did you have in mind?"

"You know me. I could eat Tex-Mex five times a week."

Ten minutes later, after a short walk, they were

seated at a window booth in a locally owned restaurant that happened to be one of Matt's favorites. After their waitress had given them their iced tea and set a basket of warm chips and a bowl of salsa on the table, Madeleine said, "What I really wanted to talk to you about is Mom."

"Not my favorite subject."

"I just can't believe what she's doing to Olivia."

"I know."

"It's just wrong, Matt. Olivia is a wonderful mother."

"I agree."

"She called me this morning and said her attorney filed an official petition with family court Friday afternoon."

Damn. Matt had figured this was coming, but it was still a blow. He wondered if Olivia knew yet. They had only talked on the phone over the weekend because she and Thea spent the weekend in Dallas with friends where Thea enjoyed Halloween festivities and Olivia had been able to forget, at least for a little while, what was happening at home.

"Can't you talk to Mom?" Madeleine said.

"I've tried. It doesn't do any good. Reason doesn't work with our mother. Not where Liv is concerned."

Madeleine shook her head. "This whole thing is just crazy."

"It is, but now that she's set this in motion, our mother will see it through to the bitter end, no matter who she hurts or how much harm she does."

"And there's nothing you can do? I mean, couldn't you talk to the people at family court? Pull some strings?"

"I wish I could, Maddie, but Mom and Dad have a hotshot attorney and now that they've made their charge official, everything is set in motion. At this point, the only way it would stop is if they changed their minds and withdrew their petition. And trust me, there's not a snowball's chance in hell of that happening."

Madeleine's eyes clouded. "I feel so bad for Olivia."

"Yeah. Me, too."

"I want to testify on her behalf."

"I figured you would." He reached across the table and took her hand, giving it a squeeze. "You sure you can handle the fallout? It won't be pretty."

"I can handle it."

"Good. I intend to testify on Olivia's behalf, too."

"Oh, I never doubted *that*."

Something about his sister's tone told him she suspected how he felt about Olivia. He gave her a quizzical look.

"C'mon, Matt. It's obvious how you feel about her. At least, to me it is."

He started to answer, but just then their waitress brought their food: fish tacos for Madeleine, the house enchiladas for Matt. With unspoken agreement, they waited till the waitress was out of earshot before resuming their conversation.

"Does Olivia know how you feel?" Madeleine asked as she picked up one of her tacos.

So even though he'd never intended to say anything to anyone about what had happened between him and Olivia, especially last Wednesday night, he found himself telling Madeleine everything.

Her eyes were filled with sympathy when he finished. "You can't blame her for wanting calm instead of constant storms, Matt," she said softly. "If Mom wasn't my mother, I wouldn't want any part of her, either."

He sighed. "I don't blame Olivia. I understand. Hell,

don't you think *I'd* like some peace and quiet for a change? Dealing with our mother is like picking your way through a minefield every day. You never know when something is going to explode under your feet."

Because the subject of Vivienne had depressed them both, Matt asked his sister what was new in her life, and she gave him an update while they ate. Afterward, they walked back to his building and hugged goodbye.

"Call me if you need me," Madeleine said.

"I will."

"I love you, big brother."

"Ditto, kid."

Madeleine waved and headed to the parking lot and her car, and Matt went inside. Once he was settled at his desk, he called Olivia.

She answered the phone almost immediately. He could hear squeals and giggling in the background.

"You're at home," he said. "I thought you'd be at work."

"I'm on the four-to-midnight shift this week. I have to drop Thea at day care soon."

"She sounds happy. What's she doing?" He knew he was stalling, but he hated to give her the news about the petition if she didn't already know it.

"Playing with the kitten we picked out this morning."

"I thought maybe you'd changed your mind."

"No, I couldn't do that. She's so excited, Matt. Listen to her. And the kitten is so cute. Oh, and guess what she's named her?" Olivia was laughing.

"I have no idea."

"Kitty Kat!"

He made himself laugh, too, even though he felt murderous. Damn his mother. Olivia should always be laughing. "Well, it makes sense."

"It does, doesn't it? I'm spelling *cat* with a *K*, though."

"Send me a picture."

"Okay. I will."

He couldn't put off telling her any longer. "I hate to bring up bad news, but has Austin called?"

"About your parents filing their petition Friday?"

"So he did call."

"Yes. Last night."

"Did he explain the next step will be for a caseworker to come and interview you? Inspect your home?"

"Yes."

When she didn't say anything more, he realized she didn't want to talk about this while Thea was in hearing distance. "You okay?" he asked softly.

"I'm fine. Resigned. Besides, I've got a more immediate problem."

"Oh?"

"Yeah, my mom always picks Thea up at day care when I fill in for the afternoon shift, and today she can't. Eve was always my backup, so now I guess I need to call Stella and see if she can do it."

Matt made a quick decision. "Don't call Stella. I'll pick Thea up. What time do I need to be there?"

"No, Matt, I don't want you to have to do that. I can—"

"I don't *have* to do it. I want to do it. I'm her godfather, remember? What time?"

She started to protest again, and he interrupted her a second time. "C'mon, Olivia. This is not a big deal. In fact, it'll be fun for me. What time should I be there?"

"Um, around five thirty? Is that too early?"

"Five thirty is fine," Matt said, already mentally juggling his schedule. He could bring work home with him, do some reading after Thea was asleep. "Will you let the day care center know I'm coming?"

"If you're sure..." She still sounded doubtful.

"I'm sure."

"Okay, I'll call the director and tell her you'll be there."

"Good."

"But, Matt, I won't be home until after midnight."

"No problem. I'll enjoy having Thea to myself. We'll have fun. She likes pizza, doesn't she?"

"She *loves* pizza. No meat, but lots of cheese."

"A girl after my own heart."

"Don't forget, you'll have the kitten, too. And the litter box."

"Not a big deal. Remember, you're talking to a criminal prosecutor."

"Thea will want the kitten to sleep with her."

"Is that all right with you?"

He could hear her resigned sigh. "I guess."

"So we're good?"

She finally agreed, saying, "I'll write some instructions and put them on the counter in the kitchen. And I'll leave a key for you out back. I'll put that in Thea's little red bucket. In her sandbox."

Matt smiled. He'd like to see the burglar who could figure *that* one out. "Good. We're all set."

Her voice softened. "I'll owe you one, Matt."

He waited a heartbeat, then answered just as softly, "I've told you before that I'd do anything for you, Liv. You *and* Thea. Don't you believe me?"

For a moment, he didn't think she was going to answer. Then, in a whisper so soft, he nearly missed it, she said, "Yes, I believe you."

And then she disconnected the call.

* * *

She shouldn't have agreed to let Matt pick up Thea. What was wrong with her that she couldn't stick to her decisions? She knew there was no future for her and Matt. She knew it was best she distance herself from him. Yet at the first small problem, what did she do? Like a drowning woman, she latched on to Matt as if he were the only life preserver around. She was hopeless.

What she should do, like it or not, was quit her job and stay home and be Vivienne's version of a proper mother to Thea. If she'd done that in the beginning, and not gone back to work until Thea started school, she wouldn't have to worry about Vivienne and her accusations. In fact, Vivienne wouldn't have a leg to stand on.

Even if Olivia didn't quit entirely, she could stop filling in for the afternoon shift when they were short-handed. So what if she got paid extra when she did so? It wasn't as if she was financially destitute. She had Mark's insurance money, after all. Yes, she wanted to keep it intact for Thea's education and more, but if she had to use some of it to ensure Thea had a stable, happy childhood, it wouldn't be the end of the world, would it?

Around and around Olivia's thoughts went after her conversation with Matt. Several times, she almost called him back to say she'd changed her mind and wouldn't need his help, after all.

But then Eve called, and after they talked, she felt better. She always felt better when she talked to Eve, who seemed able to put things into perspective when Olivia was looking at them too emotionally. By the time they ended their conversation, Olivia had settled down and decided to let things stand the way they were.

But tonight, when she saw Matt again, she needed to make sure he understood their relationship couldn't be a romantic one. She had to be strong, no matter how much she wished circumstances were different.

Because if she *wasn't* strong, if she yielded to her loneliness and the growing desire between them, she was just asking for more heartache.

The first thing Olivia saw when she walked into the kitchen after work that night was the gorgeous vase of flowers sitting in the center of the kitchen table. For a moment, she thought they were from Matt, but then he entered the kitchen and said, "I brought them in from your front stoop. I guess the florist thought it was okay to leave them there."

"Oh. Thank you." Olivia frowned. Who on earth had sent them? And why? It wasn't her birthday…or any other kind of holiday. She eyed the card.

"Go ahead," Matt said, giving her a crooked smile. "Read the card."

Olivia hesitated the briefest of seconds. She wished Matt wasn't standing there. His presence made her feel self-conscious. She wished she could casually say, *Oh, the flowers can wait, how'd things go with Thea?* Yet she couldn't. So with an inward, resigned sigh, she reached for the envelope containing the card.

It wasn't sealed. Had Matt already read it? Her heart picked up speed. No, he wouldn't do that. He was too much of a straight arrow. He would never violate her privacy.

She opened the card.

Don't let Friday's events upset you. We will prevail.
Austin

Looking up from the card, her eyes met Matt's. She swallowed, putting the card back in its envelope. Now her heart was beating hard.

"The flowers are from Austin Crenshaw, aren't they?" he said.

She nodded.

"See? I knew he viewed you as more than a client."

"He...he's just trying to make me feel better. Not worry." Why was she sounding so apologetic? She hadn't done anything wrong.

"I'm sure he is."

"It... The flowers don't mean anything." Oh, why had she said *that*? She was an idiot. She never knew when to be quiet. Her heart sped up as their gazes locked. Why did Matt have to look so sexy standing there? He still wore his work clothes, but he was barefoot and he'd taken off his tie and rolled up his shirtsleeves.

"We both know that's not true, Olivia."

Because she was so flustered, but mainly because her wildly conflicting emotions and lack of willpower where Matt was concerned frightened her, she went on the defensive. "Why are we even discussing this, Matt? It's not important. They're just flowers. Here. You can read the card. It's perfectly professional." She thrust the card into Matt's hand.

He didn't even look at it. Just placed it on the table behind her. Then, looking deep into her eyes, he pulled her into his arms.

She couldn't look away. She could barely breathe.

"Why are you so mad?" he said.

She swallowed. What could she say? The truth? *I don't know what to do or say because I want you so badly. I want what isn't possible.*

For a long moment the only sounds in the room were the ticking of the clock on the wall and their own breathing.

Still holding her gaze, he said, "I want to kiss you, Olivia. If you don't want me to, say so now."

"I—" She stopped, unable to continue. To say no would be lying. Of course, she wanted him to kiss her. She'd been wanting that ever since she'd admitted to herself how she felt about him. The one kiss he *had* given her hadn't been nearly enough. It had only whet her appetite for more. Much more. *Don't do this. It's foolhardy.*

"So it's okay?" he said.

Dear Heaven. Knowing she was lost, her eyes answered for her. And when his lips met hers, she sighed deeply, opening her mouth and her heart to him. Every sensible and rational objection she might have made was buried under an avalanche of feeling, a torrent of emotion and desire and need and loneliness. The kiss went on and on, overpowering everything except how much she loved and wanted this man.

When his hands dropped down to cup her bottom and pull her closer, she felt his heat, and her body responded with a fire of its own.

"I want you so much," he muttered, burying his face in her neck. "I wish—"

"Don't talk," she whispered. "Just make love to me."

"But I don't have a condom with me. I didn't expect—"

"It doesn't matter," she said, yielding to the moment, rationalizing it through her emotions, feeling rather than reasoning that if this was the only chance she'd ever have to be with Matt, she was going to take it. Besides, she knew she wasn't ovulating. Her period was due to start in two days.

Grabbing his hand, she pulled him toward the hall and her little study, where there was a daybed. She wouldn't take him upstairs, not with Thea asleep in the bedroom next to hers.

"Are you sure?" he said, giving her one more chance to back out.

"I said, don't talk."

Later, she wouldn't remember getting undressed. Somehow, in the middle of all the kissing, they managed to shed their clothing, which ended up in puddles on the floor. And then they became a tangle of arms and legs on the daybed, with only the light from the hallway spilling into the room.

He was a wonderful lover—thoughtful and generous. He gave her body his full attention, kissing her everywhere, touching her and stroking her and exploring her. When she would have responded in kind, he whispered, "Not yet. Let me love you first."

So she closed her eyes and gave herself up to the sensations. She didn't allow herself to think, only feel. It felt so right to be there, to allow him to care for her the way he wanted to. When he finally turned his attention to that most intimate part of her, she gasped, and her body responded immediately. Her back arched, and it was all she could do not to cry out, especially as his fingers delved. She tried to push him away, not wanting to reach that peak without him, but he wouldn't allow her to. Instead, his mouth covered hers, shutting off her protest, and his fingers moved more urgently.

Her body, denied release for so long, built to a crescendo, then exploded. Waves and waves of intense pleasure pummeled her, leaving her breathless and so weak, she could barely move. And it was then, and only then, that he slowly entered her.

The feel of him, his strength and heat, caused her to gasp. And as he began to move, she felt her own strength returning, and she moved with him. Soon they found their rhythm and within moments, she could feel herself climbing once more, desire building to another peak, and when she felt him stiffen, then shudder as he reached his own release, she allowed herself to let go once again, and she held tightly to him and gave herself up to the painful pleasure of loving him.

Chapter Nine

Later, the two of them covered by the quilt she kept on the daybed, nestled spoon fashion in Matt's arms, Olivia knew this was where she belonged, the place where she felt safe and loved and protected, the place she always wanted to be. Yet nothing had changed, even though everything had changed.

"You're not sorry, are you?" Matt murmured, tightening his arms around her, kissing her shoulder.

"Never," she said. She sighed deeply, contentment in every pore. She could lie there, in his arms, forever. She didn't even care that his car was parked in her driveway. That her neighbors, if they happened to be awake, would know that at one o'clock in the morning, he was still at her house. And she knew she *should* care. Because if Vivienne should somehow find out… Well, that possibility didn't bear thinking about.

"What's wrong?" Matt asked.

"Nothing."

"Don't lie to me, Olivia. I felt you tense up. Something is bothering you. What?"

Sighing, she said, "Just your mother. What she'd do if she knew about us. About this."

"Maybe we should just tell her."

That statement made Olivia turn in his arms so she could look at him. "No, Matt. We can't do that."

"Why not? We haven't done anything wrong. And I certainly don't intend to pretend things are still the same between us. Not after tonight. I love you, Olivia. I want everyone to know that. I want to declare that love openly. I want to marry you."

His words thrilled her even as they terrified her. "But Matt, we can't do any of that. I—I'm not convinced there will ever be any kind of future for us, and telling the world right now, while this custody suit is going on, would be crazy. It's just asking for more trouble."

"What if we informed the judge who will handle the case that we intend to get married? It would be very hard for anyone, my mother included, to say Thea would be better off with her and Dad than with you and me."

Oh, it was tempting. But what if he was wrong? What if Vivienne already had the judge in her pocket? That wouldn't surprise Olivia, because Vivienne had boasted in the past about her powerful friends, and how she could get anything she wanted, whenever she wanted. And Olivia had seen her do just that. So had Matt.

"But Matt, you know how dangerous your mother is. Why give her more ammunition? We would be taking a terrible chance. I'm not willing to gamble with Thea in the crosshairs. We at least need to wait and see what happens with the custody case. If things go my way, then we can talk again. But in the meantime—"

His arms tightened around her. "Don't say we can't see each other again. I won't agree to that."

"Matt..."

"No, Olivia. There's not a thing wrong with us spending time together. Even my mother can't make that seem wrong, because it isn't. After all, we've always spent time together. We're family."

Because she hadn't the strength to keep arguing with him, Olivia let his reasoning go unchallenged, because essentially, he was right, yet inwardly, she couldn't rid herself of her foreboding. She knew some people might think she was paranoid where Vivienne was concerned, but that didn't make her fears any less real. But instead of saying anything more, she simply threw off the quilt and attempted to get up.

"Where are you going?" He tried to hold her back.

"I'm sorry, Matt, but it's late. It's time for you to leave and for me to go up to my bedroom. Thea sometimes wakes up in the night, and I don't want her to think I'm not here."

But instead of letting her go, he pulled her back. "I don't want to leave," he said softly.

"I know. I don't want you to, either. But you have to."

He sighed and finally released her.

Ten minutes later, both dressed again—and now he had his shoes and jacket on—she said goodbye to him at the front door. He kissed her lingeringly and held her close for a long moment. "I love you," he said again, resting his head against hers.

She understood he wanted to hear her say she loved him, too, and part of her wanted to say it, but something stopped her.

"I'll call you tomorrow."

"Okay."

After one last kiss, he said good-night, and walked out the door.

"I'm thinking of quitting my job." It was Wednesday morning and five days since the Brittons' petition had been filed in family court.

"But why?" Olivia's mother said.

"Because if I'm a stay-at-home mom, Vivienne's case against me will be a lot weaker."

"But, honey, you really like your job. And there's not a thing wrong with you working. After all, you're a single mother."

"I know that and you know that, but what's going on right now with Vivienne's case is more important. And once Thea starts kindergarten, maybe I can go back to school myself." This idea had come to her after Matt had gone home early Tuesday morning, and Olivia hadn't been able to fall asleep because she couldn't shut off her brain.

"You'd go into nursing?"

"Yes, I think so." When she'd become pregnant with Thea, Olivia had put her dream of becoming a nurse on hold. But now maybe becoming a registered nurse would be a possibility for her.

Her mother smiled. "That would actually be wonderful, I think. I mean, you talked about being a nurse from the time you were about five years old."

"I know." Olivia smiled, too. "And once Thea's in school, I'd have the freedom to do that." She wondered what Matt would think of her idea, and had a feeling he would like it. In fact, she couldn't imagine Matt preventing her from doing anything she wanted to do. He simply wasn't like that.

"Have you talked to Eve about this?"

"Not yet. Why?"

"Well, I know from what Anna has said, that Eve hopes you'll move out to LA and work for Adam."

"She told her mother that?"

"Yes."

"And you like the idea?" She wished she could see her mother's expression, but the two women were talking by phone while Norma was on her lunch break.

"Not really," her mother said, "but I wouldn't have made a fuss if that's what you truly wanted to do. I mean, the idea does have merit. A change might be really good for you, and removing Thea from Vivienne's constant interference would certainly make your life easier. And, as Anna pointed out, I could come out and visit you as often as I wanted."

Olivia couldn't believe her mother was actually advocating for such a radical change.

"I'm not saying I think you should move, honey. I'm just saying if you wanted to, I wouldn't make it difficult for you. I want what's best for both you and Thea, you know that."

"I do know it, and I love you for it." Olivia thought, not for the first time, how lucky she was to have a mother like Norma. To have a family who loved her and only wanted the best for her.

And now you have Matt, too.

If only Matt wasn't a Britton. If only he, too, had a family like hers.

She wondered if she should tell her mother what had happened between them. Not about the sex, of course. That was private. But about the fact that Matt had proposed to her. That she loved him, too, even though she hadn't told him.

Yet something stopped her. And it wasn't just that they were talking on the telephone and this seemed news that should be discussed in person. Mostly, she said nothing because maybe it was too soon. Maybe, as she'd advised Matt, she should wait till this whole custody thing was over. Once that was behind her, once she no longer had that to fear from Vivienne, then she'd confide in her mother.

"So you're okay with picking Thea up tonight?" she said instead.

"I'll be there."

"I love you, Mom."

"I love you more."

Olivia was smiling as she disconnected the call.

Olivia had only been on her shift for a little more than an hour when her cell rang. She didn't recognize the number, so she let the call go to voice mail. She could deal with it on her break.

The call turned out to be from the caseworker assigned to do a home evaluation and interview with her prior to the hearing at family court. The woman, whose name was Joan Barwood, left a number for Olivia to call. Taking a deep breath, telling herself there was nothing to fear, Olivia placed the call.

"Joan Barwood."

"Hello, Ms. Barwood. This is Olivia Britton returning your call."

"Yes, hello, Mrs. Britton. I was calling to see if we could set up a convenient time for me to come and visit your home and talk with you and Thea."

"I'm free every morning for the next three days."

"How about Friday at ten, then?"

"That's perfect. You have my address?"

"I do."

"And you want Thea to be there?"

"Yes, I do."

"All right. I'll see you then."

Olivia's hands were shaking when she disconnected the call. She had promised to call Austin and let him know when she'd been contacted. He answered almost immediately.

"I'm glad you've heard from the caseworker," he said. "I was hoping they'd visit quickly, not make you wait."

"Yes, I'm glad to get it over with quickly, too," she agreed.

"I'll check on Ms. Barwood tomorrow. See what I can find out about her. I'll call you after I do."

"That would be great, Austin." She would also ask Matt what he might know about the woman. "Oh, and I meant to tell you, thank you so much for the beautiful flowers. That was very thoughtful of you."

"I'm glad you like them. And listen, don't worry too much, okay? You'll do fine with the Barwood woman. Just be yourself. She won't be able to help liking you."

"I'll try. It's just that the whole idea is nerve-racking. That some stranger is coming into your home to evaluate it...and you."

"I know. But try to relax. She's a professional. Trained to be objective. It's not like she's your mother-in-law's paid assassin or anything."

"I know." But Olivia couldn't help feeling that the unknown Ms. Barwood might actually be just that. Perhaps she was someone Vivienne already knew and had already influenced.

"You don't sound very convinced."

Olivia sighed. "I'm sorry. I'm trying. It's just that all of this is so scary. This woman could hold my fate, Thea's fate, in her hands."

"She's not going to give you a bad report. How could she? You don't do drugs. You don't leave Thea alone. You don't run around or hang out in bars. You've never been arrested. You work in an honest profession. You have a close family. And Thea is obviously a healthy, well-adjusted, happy child."

"Yet her grandmother says I'm an unfit mother. And supposedly has proof." She still had no idea what this so-called proof was.

"Vivienne Britton is just used to getting her own way. And threatening people has always worked for her."

Olivia nodded, then felt silly because of course, he couldn't see her. "I know."

"But it's not going to work now," he said firmly.

"No." But even though she said it, she couldn't help feeling scared.

"Look, I've dealt with people like her…and worse than her…since Adam's career took off the way it has. She's a bully. I know how to handle bullies."

They talked awhile longer, then just as she was about to say goodbye, he said, "Let me take you to dinner Friday night. We can go over everything."

"Oh, Austin, I'm sorry. I can't. Friday is my last day on the afternoon shift."

"Saturday, then."

"Um, I just—"

"Don't say no, Olivia. It'll be the perfect way for us to catch up on everything. You can tell me how the home inspection went and we can go over our strategy for court."

She really didn't want to go, not after what had happened with Matt, but she didn't know how to get out of it gracefully, either, because she certainly couldn't tell Austin the truth. So she finally agreed, and he said he'd pick her up at seven.

She sighed after they hung up. She hoped her mother would be able to babysit again. It seemed as if Olivia was always asking her, and that didn't seem very fair. If Vivienne wasn't doing what she was doing, Olivia would have called *her*, but of course, now that option was out of the question. Maybe she should call Austin back and tell him to just plan on having dinner there at the house, with her and Thea. No, not a good idea. Thing was, if they were out to dinner, she could more easily control the length of time they spent together. If he was there, in her home, it would be hard for her to end the evening if he seemed the least bit reluctant to leave. Maybe she should just ask Stella.

Stella was always her last choice because, after all, Stella was young and had a life of her own. She loved Thea wholeheartedly and she never acted reluctant to help out, but Olivia knew she could easily take advantage of Stella's good nature and generosity, and she never wanted to do that. Especially since there was little she could ever do for Stella in return. However, "needs must" as Olivia's grandmother Dubrovnik always used to say.

Before she changed her mind, she placed the call to her sister.

"Hey," Stella said. "What's up?"

"Sorry to bother you at work, but I need a sitter for Saturday night. You available?"

"You're in luck. I am. Why don't you let Thea come to my place and spend the night?"

Olivia smiled. "She'd love that, but, um, I have a bit of a problem, and it would be better if you were here."

"Why's that?"

"Austin Crenshaw is taking me to dinner, and I don't want to come back here to an empty house. If you're here, he won't suggest coming in."

"Olivia…"

"What?"

"Austin Crenshaw is *hot*. Most women would give their right arm to go out with him. And invite him in afterward."

"I'm not most women. And Austin is my attorney."

"So?"

"Mixing business with pleasure is not smart."

"Oh, c'mon. It's not like the two of you work together, or anything. He's just handling your case, which will soon be over."

"I'm just… I'm not interested in him that way. And I'd like to avoid potential awkwardness on Saturday."

"Why aren't you interested in him? Are you blind?"

"No. I realize he's attractive and sexy and all that, but you know, I'm just not…interested," she finished lamely.

"All right, if that's your final word. But I think you're nuts."

"That's my final word. Besides, don't you need to get back to work?" Stella was a sales rep for a software-related company.

Stella laughed. "Nice way to change the subject. Okay, fine. What time do you need me on Saturday?"

"Can you come by at six?"

"Sure."

"Thanks, Stella. I'll owe you one."

"Yes, you will."

After exchanging "I love you," the sisters hung up.

Olivia sat there for a long moment, then, with a sigh, placed her final call.

"Good morning," Matt said when he answered.

She couldn't help smiling. "Yes, it is."

"If you're calling to thank me, it's not necessary."

"Thank you? For what?"

He chuckled softly. "For great sex?"

"Matt!" She could actually feel herself blushing.

"What? My door's closed. No one can hear me. And it *was* great, wasn't it?"

"Yes, it was." Her stupid heart was beating too fast.

"Maybe we could have a repeat performance."

Now she laughed. "I told you. We have to be cool. We can't do anything to jeopardize the custody suit. Which brings me to the real reason I called. The caseworker phoned me. She's going to come and do her interview and home inspection Friday morning."

"Good. Glad it'll soon be over."

"I thought maybe you could check her out for me. See what kind of reputation she has."

"What's her name?"

"Joan Barwood."

"I've heard of her. I'll do some checking today and call you later."

"Okay. Thanks."

"So when is the afternoon shift over?"

"Friday's my last day. I have the weekend off, then go back on days Monday."

"How about letting me take you and Thea somewhere fun on Saturday?"

"Matt, I don't think that's a good idea. Besides, I have a prior commitment on Saturday." She hoped he wouldn't ask what the commitment was because she didn't want to lie to him, but she also wasn't in the mood for any kind of argument.

"How about Sunday, then?"

"What did you have in mind?"

"Maybe a picnic at the park. Or we could drive to San Antonio, take a boat ride on the river, have some good Mexican food. Maybe look around at El Mercado."

Because Vivienne wasn't likely to hear about a visit to San Antonio, and Olivia loved going there, she agreed to this plan, and Matt said he'd come by and pick them up around ten.

By the time their phone conversation was over, it was time for her to get ready for work. Hopefully, when she got there, it would be so busy she wouldn't have time to worry about anything.

Chapter Ten

For at least the tenth time, Olivia checked the house to make sure she'd left nothing undone. The furniture shone with polish, the floors were immaculate, the air smelled fragrant with the scent of freshly brewed coffee mixed with the tempting richness of the pumpkin muffins she'd taken from the oven only minutes earlier, and Thea was happily playing with her dollhouse—a birthday gift from Eve and the twins.

Everything was ready for the caseworker's visit.

The thought had no sooner formed than the doorbell rang. Olivia's heart knocked painfully. She took a deep breath before going forward to answer the door. *There's nothing to be nervous about. Just be honest and straightforward with the woman. You have nothing to fear.*

So why then did she feel as if she were headed to the guillotine? Actually, she knew why. It was because so much was at stake. If this interview went well, the Barwood woman would recommend the court let Thea remain with her mother. If it didn't go well, who knew what could happen?

Forcing herself to smile normally, Olivia opened the door. Standing on the stoop was a tall, thin woman with a narrow face, wispy brownish-blond hair pulled back into a tiny bun and a too-long nose. She was dressed in a drab brown skirt, white blouse and olive green jacket. Olivia's heart sank. The woman didn't inspire confidence.

"Hi," Olivia said. "I'm Olivia Britton. And you're…"

"Joan Barwood," the caseworker said. She smiled.

The smile changed her face, made her seem much warmer and friendlier. Olivia's spirits lifted a fraction. "Come in," she invited.

The Barwood woman stepped inside and looked around. "Lovely," she said. "I liked the look of the house from the outside, too. Small but inviting."

"Yes, that's what Mark and I thought when we bought the house. It looked like a happy family would live in it." The memory caused Olivia a twinge of sadness, but she shook it off. "May I take your jacket?"

"Thank you." Joan Barwood removed the jacket and handed it to Olivia, who hung it in the tiny coat closet in the foyer.

"I thought we could sit in the living room," Olivia said, gesturing toward the open doorway to Ms. Barwood's left.

"It would be easier if we sat at the kitchen table. I have forms that need to be filled out as we talk." Ms. Barwood looked into the living room as she spoke. "Oh, I see your daughter is playing in there."

Olivia smiled. "Yes. Thea, honey? Come out and

meet Mommy's friend." She breathed a sigh of relief when Thea immediately obeyed. Lately, it wasn't a certainty that she would. She'd begun showing quite a streak of independence.

"Hi," Thea said, grinning up at Ms. Barwood. "I'm Thea. I'm four years old."

"I can see that. Quite a big girl, aren't you?"

Thea nodded proudly. "I look like my daddy."

"Do you? Well, you seem to have your mommy's eyes."

"But I have his hair and his nose and his ears."

Joan Barwood smiled. "He must have been a very nice-looking man, your father, because you're a very pretty little girl."

"I know," Thea said.

Both Olivia and Joan Barwood chuckled at the remark.

"She's not shy, I see," Joan Barwood said. Her pale blue eyes met Olivia's.

"No. Not in the least. In fact, sometimes she's too friendly. I've been warning her about that tendency."

"Mommy says I shouldn't talk to strangers," Thea said. "But I like talking to people. They're inner-esting."

"Interesting," Olivia said.

Thea gave her a long-suffering look and sighed dramatically. "That's what I *said*, Mommy."

"A mind of her own, too, I see," Joan Barwood said.

"Yes," Olivia said. "Thea, why don't you go back to playing with your dollhouse while Ms. Barwood and I go into the kitchen to talk."

"Okay." But Thea seemed reluctant, because she frowned a little. But she turned and went back to her toys.

"This way," Olivia said.

A few minutes later, with Joan Barwood settled at the kitchen table, her paperwork on the table in front of her, Olivia poured two cups of coffee and brought them, plus a small pitcher of half-and-half and a bowl of sugar to the table. "I have fresh muffins," she offered. "They're still warm."

"No, thank you," Joan Barwood said. Then, softening a bit, she added, "Maybe later."

Olivia sat across from her. Their eyes met again.

"I like your home," the caseworker said. "Is it paid for? Or do you have a mortgage?"

"It's paid for. Mark bought a separate insurance policy to cover it, just in case." Olivia thought about how she'd argued against doing that because the premiums were so high. But when Mark had been killed, she'd been very grateful to him for his thoughtfulness.

"That was smart."

"Yes, he was pretty sensible when it came to me."

"And you have a full-time job?"

"I do. At the Crandall Lake Hospital. I'm in Admitting."

"On the day shift, right?"

"Yes, but I do fill in for the afternoon shift when they're shorthanded."

"Is that a requirement of the job?"

"No, but it pays time and a half, so that really helps financially. My mother watches Thea when I take those shifts."

Barwood nodded thoughtfully. "But I would have thought your husband left you quite well off. I mean, the Britton family is very wealthy."

"Yes, but that's his parents. Mark had other insurance—aside from the policy that paid off the house—and it was substantial, and Thea gets social security until she's eighteen, but my working is really helpful. I really hope to keep his insurance intact for Thea. To finance her education, and to help her get a good start in life when she's older."

"That's commendable, but surely the complainant, her Britton grandparents, would provide for her, if necessary? She's their only grandchild, isn't that correct?"

"Yes, that's true. But—" Olivia hesitated, then plunged ahead. She had to be honest. She didn't know any other way *to* be. "But if they were paying, they would want to control everything. As Thea's mother, I'd have no say. And frankly, Ms. Barwood, I'm not sure Thea would, either. I don't want that for my daughter. I want her to continue to grow up strong and independent, and to form her own ideas and opinions, not be told how to live and what to think."

Now that Olivia had begun to explain, she couldn't seem to stop. "Anyway, Thea loves going to day care. And I don't think it's harmful. She's learned to share and get along with other children. She's very social, and she's made so many friends."

Joan Barwood nodded, then made some notes on her forms. When finished, she looked up again. "The complainant, your in-laws, have stated that you aren't as careful about Thea's welfare as you should be. That she fell and split her lip last year and had to have stitches because you had left her alone in your backyard."

"I didn't leave her alone. I simply walked into the kitchen to get the sandwiches I'd made for our lunch. I wasn't inside for more than two minutes."

Glancing again at her notes, Barwood said, "Yet in that two minutes, she fell and cut her lip and knocked out a tooth."

Olivia sighed. She still remembered how frightened

she'd been when she'd seen the blood gushing from Thea's mouth. "Yes, but accidents happen. I wasn't neglecting her. Why, her father told me that he once fell off the sliding board in his backyard. Actually, he said he jumped. He thought he was Superman because he was wearing a Superman cape. Was that his mother's fault? I mean, she was sitting right there and she couldn't stop him falling and hurting himself. He broke his arm! Had to wear a cast for weeks."

"I don't know the circumstances of Thea's father's accident. But we're not discussing that. We're discussing what happened to Thea."

Olivia should have known that episode would be on Vivienne's list of grievances against her. "What else do my in-laws say about me?" she said, trying not to sound bitter.

Barwood consulted her notes again. "They mention an incident last year where Thea darted into the street where she could have been struck by a car."

Olivia wanted to scream. Vivienne had been out of sorts that entire day because it was Thea's birthday and she'd wanted to have an elaborate party for her at the Britton home. But for once, Olivia had stood up to her mother-in-law and held the celebration at her mother's house. "Did they also mention that they were both with us at the time? And that Thea had spied a baby rabbit? And that none of us were able to grab her in time to prevent her running after it?"

Barwood's eyes again met Olivia's. "No. That detail isn't here."

"Well, they *were*. And I immediately went after Thea and caught her before any harm came to her." She'd brought her back to their group kicking and screaming, but Olivia decided not to say so. Thea's stubbornness was an ongoing problem, and would probably only get worse as she got older. She was a strong-willed child; she would cause Olivia to become prematurely gray, Olivia was sure of it. Yet Olivia wouldn't have her any other way.

"Let's talk about Thea's eating habits," the Barwood woman said after making a few more notes.

"Oh, brother," Olivia said, rolling her eyes.

"Is there a problem?" Joan Barwood said.

Olivia just shook her head. "No. Not for me or for Thea. But I should have known Vivienne would bring up my daughter's food preferences."

"Such as?"

"Well, she doesn't like meat. She's pretty much a vegetarian."

"What about you?"

"I'm not. I like just about everything, and I've tried to get her to at least taste things, but she's got a mind of her own, that one." Actually, not for the first time, Olivia thought that Thea's strong opinions were directly related to the genes she'd received from her paternal grandmother.

"So she doesn't eat any meat at all?"

"No. She likes fish, though, and she gets plenty of protein in beans and nuts and dairy. She has a very healthy diet, despite what my mother-in-law thinks."

Joan Barwood nodded thoughtfully. After glancing at her notes again, she said, "The day care issue seems to be primary. That, and the odd hours you sometimes work. Your in-laws feel Thea would be much better off in their home, with a normal, structured schedule, under the proper guidance of a full-time nanny."

"They're entitled to their opinion, but I don't agree. Thea belongs here, with me, her mother. But if my working really is a major issue, and you agree with that, then I'll quit immediately. Nothing in the world is more important to me than my daughter. Nothing."

The caseworker's eyes met hers. "I worked when my children were small," she finally said.

Olivia breathed a mental sigh of relief. Surely the Barwood woman was telling her something without actually telling her. Wasn't she?

They talked awhile longer, and then Ms. Barwood asked to see the rest of the house, and Olivia showed her around. The woman spent the longest time in Thea's bedroom, looking around, opening the closet door, the drawers to Thea's chest and small dresser, and her toy box. "It's a lovely room," she finally said.

Just as they were ready to go back downstairs, Thea appeared in the doorway. "Why are you in my room?" she demanded.

"Miss Barwood just wanted to see it, honey," Olivia said. "Because I told her how pretty it was."

"It is pretty," Joan Barwood agreed.

"I like it a lot," Thea said, frowning.

"What's wrong?" Ms. Barwood asked.

"It's *my* room." Now Thea's frown grew darker.

Olivia almost smiled. Her daughter was showing her colors right now. And her possessiveness.

"This is where my mommy tells me the daddy story," Thea said. The statement was almost challenging.

"The daddy story?" Ms. Barwood said.

"At night. When I go to sleep," Thea said.

"I always tell her how her daddy is looking out for her, and how much he loves her," Olivia said. She kept her voice neutral, but inside she was angry. Angry that she had to share something so intimate. Something that was no one's business except hers and her daughter's.

Angry that Vivienne had brought this unjustified ugliness into their lives.

"He's my *garden angel*!" Thea said, glaring at Joan Barwood.

The caseworker nodded. Then she knelt down, and took Thea's hand. "I'm sorry if I upset you, Thea. I can see you love your daddy and mommy very much, and that the daddy story is very important to you. Thank you for telling me about it."

Thea's frown slowly disappeared. "You're welcome."

"Such a polite little girl, too," Ms. Barwood said. "Your mommy has done a good job, that's very clear."

Olivia wasn't sure what to say…or do. But Joan Barwood obviously realized this, for she rose, then turned to Olivia and said, "I've enjoyed visiting both you and Thea, Olivia. Thank you for having me. Now I think it's time to get going."

Five minutes later, she was gone. After shutting the door behind her, Olivia felt as if the weight of the world had been lifted from her shoulders. No matter what the Barwood woman recommended, and Olivia was pretty certain the interview had gone well, Olivia was just glad to have this part of the custody suit behind her.

Now all she could do was wait.

After Olivia told him about the interview with the caseworker from Children's Protective Services, Matt decided to do some digging of his own. Knowing Paul Temple, the lawyer he'd wanted Olivia to use instead of Austin, would have inside knowledge of the way CPS worked, he called him to see what he could find out.

"I know Joan Barwood," Temple said. "She's one of the old hands in the department, very thorough, very conscientious and fair."

"Do you know her well enough to ask her about Olivia's case?"

There was a pause on the other end of the line. "I wouldn't normally do that," Temple finally said.

"As a favor to me?"

Another pause. Then a sigh, clearly audible. "Okay, Matt. As a favor to you."

"I'll owe you, Paul," Matt said.

"Yes, you will."

Less than an hour later, Paul Temple called him back. "I just spoke to Joan Barwood. She was hesitant to say anything, but when I pressed her, she admitted that your sister-in-law made a good impression on her. She'll give her a positive recommendation, I'm sure of it."

Matt hadn't even realized he'd been holding his breath until he let it out. "Thanks, Paul. I really appreciate this."

"Don't ask again."

Matt grinned. "I won't."

"I think a couple of bottles of a good red would be a nice payback, don't you?"

Now Matt laughed. "You got it."

After hanging up, he decided while he was out this afternoon would be a good time to make a call on his mother. Maybe, if she knew CPS wasn't going to be on her side, she'd drop this ridiculous custody suit before it went any further. It was worth a try, anyway.

He wouldn't give her any warning. He would just drop by the house on his way back from court. It was nearly three thirty before he pulled into the driveway at his parents' home. Luckily, his mother was in.

"Hello, Matthew," she said coolly.

"Mom," he said, bending over and kissing her cheek.

As usual, he caught the subtle fragrance of Beautiful, her perfume of choice.

"What's on your mind today?" she asked. Still no smile.

"I received some information I thought you might like to know." He kept his voice as pleasant as he could manage.

She lifted her chin. "Oh?"

"CPS sent a caseworker to Olivia's home this morning, and knowing Olivia, I'm certain the woman will give her a favorable recommendation. Are you sure you want to risk that? "

His mother's eyes narrowed, her jaw hardened.

"I thought maybe, under the circumstances, you might be persuaded to drop the custody suit and spare all of us the embarrassment of a public display of dirty family laundry."

"I believe I'll wait and see for myself what CPS has to say. And if they are so misguided as to be taken in by *that woman*, I'm sure Jackson Moyer will have more than one way to counter."

Matt sighed. He wasn't really surprised. His mother rarely backed down from a fight, mainly because she was always so convinced she was right and everyone else was wrong, but he'd felt he owed it to Olivia to at least make one more attempt to end this debacle. "I'm sorry to hear that."

"And I'm sorry to hear that you're still defending Olivia. I don't know how someone as intelligent as you can be taken in by her, but obviously you don't have any more sense where she's concerned than your brother did. He, at least, was *young*, and the young can be forgiven for foolish choices. But *you*, Matthew, should know better."

By now Matt was sorry he'd ever stopped by. He should have known better. His mother wasn't going to back down. Deciding he wouldn't be drawn into a lengthy argument, he turned to go, but her next words stopped him.

"Perhaps you thought I wasn't serious when I said I would withdraw my support for your candidacy for the US Senate."

Looking back at her, he said, "Oh, no. I knew you were serious."

"Good."

"Doesn't matter. I no longer intend to run for that seat."

Her face darkened. "Excuse me?"

"You heard me."

"You would thwart me? Even in this?"

"Thwart *you*? I swear, you live in another world."

"You're doing this out of some kind of misplaced spite. You know how much I wanted this for you."

"For *me*? Come on. That's a joke. You wanted that for *Mark*. You wanted it for *you*. Nothing in this house has ever been about me. From the moment Mark was born, it was like I'd never existed." All the bitterness and loneliness and hurt stored up in Matt over the years brimmed over and the words poured out. "So don't pretend otherwise, because I don't believe you."

Her mouth actually dropped open.

He almost laughed. But it wasn't funny. Nothing in this house had ever been funny.

"You're a fool," she finally said.

He almost told her then about Carter's offer, but an innate sense of self-preservation stopped him. She was entirely capable of calling the governor, with whom she was on a first-name basis, and attempting to ruin that for him, too. "Maybe so," he said softly. "But at least I can look at myself in the mirror every morning and not be ashamed of what I see."

And with that, he walked out the door and didn't look back.

Chapter Eleven

Austin arrived promptly at seven on Saturday. When Olivia opened the door, her first thought was that he was the kind of date most women would be thrilled to have. Her second was that this wasn't *really* a date, but she still hoped Matt didn't find out about tonight's dinner. Then she was mad at herself. Why shouldn't Matt know? And why hadn't she told him? She wasn't doing anything wrong. Austin was her lawyer, and it was completely reasonable that they should have dinner together. By not telling Matt, she was tacitly admitting she felt weird about the evening.

"You look lovely," Austin said, eyeing her wool dress with approval. "I like that shade of red."

She smiled. "It's called cranberry, in honor of the coming holidays."

"It looks good on you."

"Thank you." She reached for her black shawl and

small clutch bag, which she'd placed on the little table in the entryway.

"Where's Thea?" Austin said, looking around.

"At my sister's. Stella will bring her back here at bedtime and stay here till we get home." This had been a last-minute adjustment to their plans because Stella had a pitch to give to a potential client on Monday and wanted to do some last-minute work on it this evening without having to lug her laptop and other materials with her when she came to Olivia's.

Austin stood aside so she could precede him out the door. Soon she was settled in his Lexus and they were off.

"I made a reservation at Hugo's," Austin said.

Olivia raised her eyebrows. "Really?" Hugo's was a relatively new and already top tier restaurant in the lake district. The chef, a James Beard award winner, specialized in French cuisine with a Creole flair. "Wow."

Austin smiled. "I was hoping you'd be impressed."

Olivia didn't know how to respond. She knew he was subtly flirting, and she should be flattered, but instead she just felt even more uncomfortable than she had earlier.

When she didn't answer, his tone became more serious. "I was also hoping you'd be pleased."

"I am pleased, but—"

"What?"

Best to be honest. Or at least as honest as possible, under the circumstances. "I wasn't thinking of tonight as a date. I was thinking of it as a meeting. And Hugo's isn't a meeting sort of place." She made an effort to keep her voice light.

"And I was hoping tonight could be both," he said softly.

Olivia hesitated only a moment. "Until the custody issue is settled, I don't think it's appropriate for me to date anyone. I think I have to keep my head and my life clear of anything that could be construed as an obstacle to my winning."

"I see your point, but seriously, Olivia, I take my clients to lunch and dinner all the time. It's a perfect way to relax and talk and strategize."

"That may be true, but still, Hugo's?"

"All right. Here's the deal. We'll agree that this evening isn't a date. We won't get personal at all. We'll just talk about the case and anything else that might impact it. Does that work?"

Olivia nodded. "Yes. That works." But would he keep his promise? At a restaurant like Hugo's, it would be hard *not* to get personal. From what she'd heard, its entire ambiance invited confidences…and romance.

"Good. But that doesn't mean we can't enjoy wonderful food and a friendly glass of wine, does it?"

"N-no."

"So stop worrying and relax. We're almost there."

Her first impression of the restaurant was exactly what she'd expected: warmth mixed with elegance. It immediately welcomed you and soothed you. She had to admit she loved the atmosphere and the sense that everyone there cared only for your comfort and enjoyment. She sighed with pleasure as she sank into her softly upholstered chair and looked around. She particularly loved the floor-to-ceiling windows that gave diners a view of inviting tree-filled, lighted grounds.

"It's lovely," she told Austin.

"I'm glad you like it," he said, smiling.

Later, after receiving their glasses of Cabernet Sauvignon and placing their orders—the jumbo sea scallops for him, the mushroom risotto with lobster for her—he leaned back in his chair and said, "Now tell me about the home visit."

So she did. She also told him what Matt had found out about the Barwood woman, although she didn't tell him *how* he'd gotten the information.

"I knew the caseworker would like you."

Olivia couldn't help smiling at him. He really *was* so nice. "I'm still scared, though," she admitted. "Vivienne wields a big stick."

"Yes, I know that. Everyone living in Crandall Lake knows that. But her case for custody of Thea isn't strong. Not from what you've told me."

They continued to discuss the home visit and the things the Barwood woman had disclosed to Olivia until their food came. Both dishes were beautifully presented and smelled wonderful. Suddenly Olivia felt hungry and she was glad they'd come.

She had just fully relaxed and taken her second bite of the truly amazing risotto when a flash of red on her right caught her eye. Her heart jumped when she realized the red dress on the woman being seated across from them was worn by Catherine Elliott, one of Vivienne's bosom buddies. Catherine hadn't seen Olivia yet, but her husband, Arthur, had. He smiled and gave Olivia a little salute, causing Catherine to turn around curiously. When her dark eyes met Olivia's, she inclined her head, smiled slightly, and pointedly turned her curious gaze to Austin. Her expression changed the moment she realized who Olivia's escort was.

No, Olivia thought, her heart now sinking. But she kept her expression even and nodded a silent greeting. Then she turned her attention back to her dinner and tried to ignore the fear the presence of the Elliotts had generated.

Austin frowned. "What's wrong?"

Olivia forced herself not to show how disturbed she felt. "Don't look, but the couple just seated across from us are very good friends of my in-laws."

"So?"

"So Vivienne will now get a play-by-play description of our evening."

Austin shrugged. "We're having dinner, Olivia. We're not doing anything wrong. And I *am* your lawyer."

Olivia couldn't help but think how Matt had said the very same thing the other day about them not doing anything wrong. And even though both men were right, somehow Olivia knew Vivienne wouldn't see either situation the same way. Because, with Vivienne, even Olivia's breathing was a punishable offense.

She continued to eat her meal, but the lovely dinner now tasted like sawdust. Why had she agreed to come out with Austin? She knew that now Catherine Elliott would give Vivienne more ammunition to use against her, for no matter how innocent this dinner with Austin was, the two women would somehow make it seem otherwise.

"Stop worrying," Austin said.

But Olivia couldn't. She did manage to get most of her food down, but she refused dessert, and silently implored Austin to get her out of there. He sighed, and had just asked for the bill when Olivia's cell vibrated.

"I have to take this," she said, glancing at the screen and seeing that it was Stella. Excusing herself, she hurried in the direction of the ladies' room.

"Stella?" she said when she was out of earshot of the diners.

"Oh, thank goodness," Stella said. "Liv, I'm so sorry, but I had to call you. Something's happened."

Olivia's mouth went dry. "Is Thea all right?"

"Thea's fine, but…oh, God. We…there was a fire."

"A fire! Where?"

"In my building. We were just getting ready to leave to go to your house. I'd shut down my laptop and was packing my tote with my things. Thea was in the living room, and when I walked in there I smelled smoke. I couldn't imagine where it was coming from." Stella's words were tumbling out, tripping over each other. "For a minute, I thought I'd left the stove on or something, 'cause earlier I'd made her some hot chocolate. Then, a second later, I heard sirens and when I looked outside, I saw a fire truck coming into the parking lot along with emergency vehicles. I grabbed Thea and my tote and opened the apartment door to run out, but the hallway was already filled with smoke, and I couldn't see, so I shut the door again and stuffed my afghan under the door to keep the smoke out. Oh, God, Liv, I was so scared! My heart was just pounding like crazy! But we went out on the balcony where the firefighters could see us and they ended up rescuing us that way."

"The balcony!" Stella's apartment was on the third floor of her building. "Is Thea okay?"

"Yes, she's fine. She thought it was an adventure, actually. She wasn't afraid at all when the fireman took her down the ladder." Stella was calmer now that she'd gotten the story out.

"Ohmigod." Olivia was shaking, just thinking about it.

"She's okay, Liv, I promise. Not a scratch on her. And I'm fine, too, but the apartment building is a mess. The fire started in an apartment on the second floor, almost right below me. There was a lot of damage, both from the fire and the smoke. I don't know about my apartment, but I have a feeling it's pretty much a loss."

"Oh, God, Stell. I'm so sorry. But I'm grateful you're both okay." Olivia was trembling at the thought of what *could* have happened.

"Me, too. Thing is, looks like you or Mom are gonna have company for a while. I'm just grateful the firemen allowed me to take my tote bag with me when it was my turn to go down the ladder. And thank goodness my laptop was in it. If I'd lost that, I'd be in deep doo-doo."

"You can stay with me as long as you need to, you know that."

"Yeah, I know. But it might be easier for everybody if I just go to Mom's. Okay, listen, I'm gonna go. I'll see you when you get home. We're gonna head over to your place now."

"All right. I'll be there in thirty minutes or so. We're leaving the restaurant soon."

Olivia waited outside the ladies' room for a few moments after disconnecting the call. She still felt shaky and wanted to compose herself before going out and possibly being observed by Catherine Elliott. The last thing she needed was for Vivienne to find out that Thea had been at Stella's apartment when the fire broke out. Even though nothing that had happened was Stella's or Olivia's fault, Olivia could only imagine the spin Vivienne would put on the night's events.

But as she headed back toward the dining room, she saw Austin approaching, so she didn't have to see the Elliotts again.

"I got worried," he said. "Are you all right?"

"I'm okay. Have you paid the bill?"

"Yes."

"I'll tell you about the phone call once we're in the car. I need to get home quickly."

He looked as if he wanted to say something else, but he didn't. He simply took her arm and walked outside with her. A few minutes later, the valet parking attendant brought Austin's car around. Two minutes later, they were on their way back to Crandall Lake.

"I don't think you have to worry," Austin said when she'd told him what Stella had said. "Your mother-in-law won't know about Thea being there unless you tell her."

"Don't be so sure about that," Olivia said. "One of the firemen could be someone she knows. Or a bystander might have recognized Thea. Don't forget, Vivienne is very well-known."

"Well, even if she did find out, she certainly can't fault you for the fire. And your sister kept her wits about her, made sure Thea got out safely."

But no matter what Austin said, Olivia couldn't help worrying. Somehow Vivienne *always* heard the things you didn't want her to. And Olivia was sure, if she *did* find out about the fire, she'd find a way to use it against Olivia in the custody suit. Bottom line, tonight's events would be one more incident to show that Olivia didn't keep a close enough eye on Thea or make good judgment calls when it came to her welfare.

When they arrived at Olivia's house, Austin asked if he could come in. "I'd like to talk to your sister. Make sure I have all the facts straight."

"Of course."

Stella must have been watching for them, because she opened the front door before Olivia could use her key.

"Thea's in bed, but she's waiting for you to say goodnight," Stella said.

"I'll go up. Austin wants to talk to you."

"Okay."

When Olivia reached Thea's room, Thea said, "Mommy, Mommy, did Aunt Stella tell you about the fire? I was carried down the ladder by a fireman!"

"Yes, honey, I know."

"It was 'citing. Just like a story!"

"Really? Exciting? Not scary?"

"No, Mommy, I wasn't scared." Thea's eyes shone. She loved drama. "And guess what? I was on television!" Olivia froze. Television? Oh, God. Now Vivienne was sure to find out about tonight. But she managed to tamp down her dismay and listen to Thea's account, then give her daughter a hug and good-night kiss before making her escape.

Austin and Stella were standing in the living room, talking. He turned at Olivia's entrance. "Brace yourself. A television crew was at the apartment, and they filmed Thea being rescued."

"Yes," Olivia said, sighing. "I know. Thea told me. She's all excited about it and probably won't fall asleep for hours."

"I'm sorry, Olivia," Stella said. "I didn't want to tell you over the phone. I knew you'd freak out."

Olivia sighed unhappily. "I can't help but think how Vivienne will just have one more thing to use against me now."

"If you hear anything from your in-laws—" Austin began.

"They won't call me," Olivia said, interrupting him. "I haven't heard directly from either one of them since this whole thing began. Actually, not since the day at the festival when Vivienne took Thea home with her."

"Good. You shouldn't be talking to them, anyway. All exchanges should be through me and their attorney."

"I'm so sorry about this," Stella said.

"It's not your fault," Austin said. Then he turned back to Olivia. "Please don't worry about this. I promise you, I'll take care of it. In fact, maybe I'll jump the gun and call Jackson Moyer myself. In the meantime, I'll be going. I know you're probably exhausted after this. I'll call you tomorrow."

"Okay." Olivia thought about the trip to San Antonio planned with Matt for tomorrow. Should she still go? Or should she stay home and figure out some kind of damage control? Maybe she should call Matt now. Let him know what had happened and see what he thought. She dreaded doing so, though, because she'd have to tell him she was out with Austin, and then he'd wonder why she hadn't told him where she was going to begin with.

Still debating what to do, Olivia, along with Stella, headed back upstairs to make sure Thea was settled down after Austin had gone. Surprisingly, she was half-asleep when they entered her room. Stella offered to read her a bedtime story, and when Thea agreed, Olivia thankfully left the two of them and went into her own bedroom to change into comfortable sweats. While there, she turned on the small television set mounted on her wall because it was almost time for the local news. She had decided to call Matt, but wanted to see what, if anything, was said about the fire before she did.

Her heart sank when she saw it was the lead story, and almost the first image was that of Thea being carried down the ladder from the third-floor balcony. She couldn't help feeling proud of her daughter, who didn't look frightened at all. But along with the pride was a huge dose of fear.

And the awful suspicion that Vivienne might have just been dealt a winning hand.

"Hugh! Hugh! Come and see this!" Vivienne had just settled down into her favorite chair in the sitting room off her bedroom, a glass of her favorite Bordeaux in her hand, and had switched on the local news at ten.

"What is so all-fired important?" her husband said irritably as he entered the room. "I was changing clothes."

"Look! Thea is on the news!"

"What?"

Vivienne even forgot about her wine—a nightly treat before bed—when she realized what the lead story was about. She was partly appalled and partly triumphant. Now everyone would see that she, Vivienne, was not being cruel or unreasonable to ask for custody of that precious child. How could they? Thea had been left at the apartment of that woman's sister, and look what had happened. Who knew who lived in those apartments? That was a totally unsuitable environment for Vivienne's granddaughter. And why was she there anyway? The child should be in bed no later than eight, and Vivienne would bet it was later than that when this all happened. Where was Olivia?

Vivienne bristled with indignation as she avidly watched the newscast. But she couldn't help swelling with pride over how her granddaughter showed absolutely no fear. Well, Vivienne certainly wasn't surprised about *that*. Good genes would always win out in the end. Thea's mother and her family might not possess the best lineage, but Thea's father and her paternal grandparents certainly did, and that was what was apparent now. That old saying about cream rising to the top had once again proven to be true.

"Well, I'll be damned," Hugh said when the segment was over and the newscasters had moved on to the next story.

All Vivienne did was smile. "This incident makes our case even stronger, you know." She finally picked up her wine and took a satisfying swallow. Her mind was spinning. Should she call and check on Thea? Was the child even home now? She wanted to call. She wanted to demand to speak to her granddaughter. She particularly wanted to tell that woman what she thought of her and her irresponsible behavior. But no matter how much she wanted to, she simply couldn't. Jackson Moyer had emphatically instructed them not to contact Thea or her mother directly.

From now on, every communication with or about your granddaughter needs to go through me, he'd said. *Don't forget that or you could jeopardize your chances of winning.*

Although Vivienne understood why he'd given them the directive, she couldn't help chafing under the rule because it wasn't in her nature to let others fight her battles. In fact, she relished the battles. They made her feel stronger and superior to her foes because she was powerful and intimidating, and she knew it, and she could almost always cow an adversary.

"I'm just glad Thea is all right," Hugh said now.

"Of course we're glad she's all right, but surely you see that what has happened is to our advantage."

Hugh sighed. "If you say so."

Vivienne's eyes narrowed. She was so tired of her mealymouthed husband's wishy-washy attitude about everything. For about the thousandth time she wondered what he'd say if he knew the truth. Sometimes she really wanted to tell him. To throw it in his face and see his expression. Would *that* finally get a rise out of him? Make him act like a man? Make her respect him, at least a little? But of course, her better judgment always won out and she kept silent. Her secret would remain her secret because that was in her best interest.

As Hugh walked back into their bedroom to resume changing into his pajamas, she made a decision. She might not be able to call and talk to Thea, but she would call Jackson Moyer tomorrow and make damned sure he knew all about the fire.

She was smiling as she settled back to finish her drink.

Chapter Twelve

Matt didn't see the news, but one of his buddies called him at ten fifteen to tell him about it. After they'd hung up, Matt immediately phoned Olivia.

"Hi, Matt." She sounded tired. "I was just thinking about calling you."

"Nolan Underwood called me and told me about the fire. Were you there? Was that Stella's apartment? Is Thea okay?"

"I wasn't there. Stella was babysitting. And Thea is fine. She considered the whole thing quite the adventure. She told me it was ''citing.' She loved being carried down the ladder."

He grinned. Sounded like Thea. "That's a relief."

"Yes. I was really upset when Stella called me. I'm sure your mother will have a field day over this."

"I'm afraid you're right. Most people would just be glad all's well that ends well, but she'll find a way to blame you even though you weren't there and the fire wasn't Stella's fault, at least according to what Nolan told me."

"No, it wasn't her fault. It started in an apartment below her. Unfortunately, though, her apartment received lots of damage, so she's going to be staying with my mother for a while. Thank goodness she bought rental insurance, so at least the damages will be covered."

"She was smart to do that."

"I actually think she was required to. Um, Matt… there's something I—"

"You're not going to tell me you don't want to go to San Antonio tomorrow?"

"No, I thought about it, but I really don't see any reason why we can't still go. I mean, Thea's fine. But there is something I need to tell you."

He didn't like the tone of her voice.

"I—I was out with Austin Crenshaw last night. We had a dinner meeting. At Hugo's. I should have told you that's where I was going when you asked me about spending the day with me. I don't know why I didn't. I mean, it really was just a meeting. Not a date."

Hugo's? Not a date? For a moment, Matt was flummoxed and couldn't think how to respond. Of course it was a date! Maybe Olivia wanted to believe otherwise, but Matt was sure Austin Crenshaw thought so. No man would take a woman to Hugo's for a dinner meeting. The place, not to mention the prices, literally screamed romance. Besides, Austin hadn't exactly made a secret of his interest in Olivia. "I see," he finally said.

The silence between them seemed to stretch forever.

When she broke it, her voice was pleading. "Come on, Matt…don't be like that."

"Like what?"

"You know like what. You're angry."

"I'm not angry. I'm just…confused, I guess. Hell, I thought after the other night things had changed. I thought we had an understanding."

"We do."

"Yet you had plans to go out with Austin Crenshaw and you didn't mention it when we talked. All you said was you had *a commitment*."

"It *was* a commitment, for a meeting. It wasn't a date."

"If it wasn't a date, you would have told me up front what you were doing. You would have simply said you were meeting with Austin to discuss the case."

When she didn't answer immediately, Matt knew he was right. She'd felt awkward and guilty. That's why she hadn't told him the truth. She'd known going out to dinner on a Saturday night couldn't be anything else *but* a date.

Maybe he was kidding himself. Maybe she didn't feel the same way about him that he felt about her. Maybe she regretted making love the other night and why she hadn't said she loved him, too. Maybe *that's* why she kept coming up with all kinds of excuses about why they couldn't be aboveboard about their relationship. Maybe it didn't have a damn thing to do with his mother.

He had to know. "Are you sorry about the other night?"

"Matt…"

"Just tell me, Olivia. I need to know the truth."

Seconds went by before she answered in a tired voice. "You know, Matt, it's late and I'm exhausted. Let's talk about this tomorrow."

"Thea will be with us tomorrow."

"So, what, then? Do you want to cancel tomorrow?"

He swallowed. "Do you?"

"No, Matt, I don't. But I don't see the point in going round and round on this subject. I'm not sorry about the other night with you and I've told you I don't consider tonight's meeting with Austin a date. And I've apologized for not immediately telling you about it. But you don't seem satisfied, so I don't know what else I can do."

Part of him—the hurt part of him—wanted to say it might be best to have a cooling-off period before seeing each other again, but the other part of him—the part that knew they were at some kind of crisis point in their relationship and that the next few minutes might determine which direction their future would take—told him maybe he was being unreasonable because he was jealous. Maybe, if he was smart, he needed to just swallow his pride.

"You're right," he said, softening his voice. "I accept your apology and think we should just forget about the whole thing. How about I'll pick you and Thea up around ten tomorrow morning?"

"We'll be ready. Good night, Matt."

"Good night, Olivia. I love you."

"I love you, too." This was said so softly, he wasn't sure he'd actually heard it or maybe imagined it because he'd wanted to hear it.

Sunday morning dawned clear and bright, with temperatures in the sixties and the promise of a beautiful day ahead. Unfortunately, Olivia awoke with a headache because she hadn't slept well. It had taken her hours to fall asleep, and then even after she had, she awakened several times in the night, disturbed by tumultuous dreams.

If only she hadn't gone out last night. It had been a really stupid thing to do, all the way around. She should have simply told Austin she'd come to his office in the morning or that she'd meet him somewhere for coffee during the day. Why hadn't she?

She put on her robe, then went downstairs, took some Advil and quietly fixed her morning coffee. Grateful Thea was still asleep, she padded barefoot into the living room and curled onto the sofa.

As she drank her coffee, her thoughts returned to last night and her phone conversation with Matt. In a way, she understood why he'd reacted as he had when she'd told him she'd been out with Austin. But in another way, his reaction still bothered her. Because either Matt trusted her or he didn't. Was it possible that his mother's constant undermining of her had planted seeds of doubt about her in Matt's subconscious? Seeds he didn't even know were there? Seeds that would grow into a kind of poison that would eventually ruin whatever chance they had?

By the time she'd finished her coffee and began to get ready for the day, she decided the time she and Thea and Matt spent together in San Antonio today would be a test. It would give her a clearer picture of how things really stood between them. If Matt seemed back to normal, then she'd do her best to forget about their conversation last night, too. But if he still seemed suspicious of her relationship with Austin or made any comments to that effect, then maybe she'd been right all along, and Matt had no place in her future.

Just the thought made her feel sick to her stomach. But yesterday's events had only brought back all her old doubts. Yes, she knew Matt loved her. And she loved him. Sometimes she ached from loving him and wanting him.

But was love…and desire…enough?

Could she bear being married to Matt when his mother despised her? Was a life filled with constant tension what she wanted for Thea? For herself?

Could she live that way?

Today, she needed to find some answers.

Even if she didn't like what she discovered.

Matt hadn't slept well, either.

He was sorry he'd implied he didn't believe Olivia. It wasn't her fault Austin was pursuing her. And the fact he was her attorney didn't make things easy for her. Instead of Matt piling more stress on her shoulders by criticizing her or inferring he didn't trust her, he should be a better man and totally support her. He *was* a better man. The problem was, he cared too much, and deep down he was afraid Olivia would never fully commit to him.

And realistically, why would she?

Family was of primary importance to her. She was a warm, giving, loving, generous person. Why would she want to remarry into a family headed by his mother? His mother had never given Olivia anything but heartache and grief, and all indications were that this kind of behavior would not only continue into the future, it would worsen.

Matt needed to do something to change this dynamic. But what? Everything he'd tried—talking to his mother, talking to his father, nothing had worked. If only he had something new, some way to persuade and influence his mother.

He was still thinking along these lines when he arrived at Olivia's home a few minutes before ten. But he purposely pushed all thoughts of his mother and his family situation out of his mind when he rang the doorbell. He wanted to give Olivia and Thea a wonderful carefree day, and he would not let his mother and her poison mar it. Later, at home alone again, would be time enough to go back to the problem.

When Olivia opened the door, an excited Thea at her side, love swept through him. He wanted nothing more than to gather both of them into his arms. But with Thea there and possible nosy neighbors, all he could do was smile down at the two females he loved most in the world. "Ready for our adventure?"

"Yes, Unca Matt!" Thea shouted. Then, practically jumping up and down, she said, "Did you see me on television?"

"No, sweetheart, I didn't. But I heard you were really brave."

"I was! And there were 'porters there!" Thea frowned. "But I didn't talk to them."

"'Porters?" Matt said.

"Reporters," Olivia said. "She wanted to talk to them. You know how she likes being in the spotlight," she added sotto voce.

"Maybe she'll be a performer of some sort when she grows up."

Olivia raised her eyebrows. "Don't encourage her."

"I am gonna be a 'porter when I'm big," Thea said, giving her mother a dark look.

Matt laughed. He couldn't help it. Thea was a handful now, at four. He couldn't imagine what she'd be like at fourteen. And at twenty-four. But he knew he wanted to be around to find out. And not just be around. He wanted these two people to be an intimate part of his life. He wanted Olivia as his wife and Thea as his child. And he also wanted more children, brothers and sisters, for Thea.

"How's that kitten of yours doing?" he said. "Did she see you on television last night?"

Now Thea's frown intensified. "Mommy said Kitty Kat has to stay in the laundry room while we're gone today."

"That seems sensible."

"Mommy's being mean," Thea said.

Olivia's eyes met Matt's. "I'm not being mean, Thea. Cats don't like traveling in cars, so we can't take Kitty Kat with us."

"I could hold her!" Thea insisted.

"Kitty Kat will be just fine at home," Olivia said patiently. "She's got her litter box, her food, her water. And she has that nice bed we bought for her."

"She'll be lonesome," Thea said, not appeased.

"Kittens don't get lonesome," Matt said. "She'll probably sleep away the whole day."

"If we don't get going, we won't have enough time in San Antonio," Olivia said, obviously wanting to take Thea's mind in a happier direction.

Her ploy worked. Thea immediately lost her frown. And five minutes later they were all in Matt's car and on their way.

The day turned out to be everything Matt had hoped it would be. They got to San Antonio well before noon, and since none of them were very hungry yet, they decided to take the riverboat tour first. Thea loved it and even Olivia seemed to completely relax and be more like her old self. One older woman said in an aside to Matt, "Your wife and daughter are lovely."

Matt didn't correct her. He simply smiled and said, "I think so, too."

At one o'clock they chose one of the riverside Mexican restaurants and snagged an outdoor table. Thea happily dove into the chips and salsa and, later, into the bowl of queso Matt ordered. Matt and Olivia allowed themselves one margarita each, they enjoyed the excellent food and watching the boats filled with tourists go by, and he felt the day was already a success.

After lunch they walked for a while, then headed for the market where Olivia bought Thea a bright red, embroidered Mexican dress and, for herself, a beautiful woven shawl in shades of blue. Matt bought both of them silver bangle bracelets, and Thea could hardly contain her excitement.

"Mine's just like yours, Mommy!" she kept saying while waving her arm in the air.

"I know, honey," Olivia said. "I love mine, too."

At that moment, with Thea between them, when Olivia's eyes met his, Matt knew he'd never been happier. If only he could stop the moment in time.

Then, on the way out of the market, Thea spied a handmade doll dressed in authentic Mexican costume, and Matt bought that for her, too. At first, Olivia objected, saying it was too expensive and Thea had to learn she couldn't have everything she wanted.

"It's an early Christmas present," Matt said.

"Please, Mommy," Thea begged.

"Please, Mommy," Matt said, smiling.

"Well...okay," Olivia said, relenting.

Thea fell asleep on the way home, and Matt and Olivia finally had a chance to talk about what was in the back of each of their minds.

Olivia introduced the subject after glancing behind

her to make sure Thea was asleep. "Have you forgiven me for yesterday?"

"You're the one who needs to do the forgiving," Matt said. "I shouldn't have reacted the way I did. Actually, I guess *overreacted* is the right word." Before she could say anything, he rushed ahead. He needed to make sure she understood. "I can't tell you how sorry I am, because I don't want you having doubts about us. The times I've told you that you and Thea are more important to me than anything else in my life, I've meant it. That will never change, and I want you to always remember that."

"I will."

He waited, but when she didn't echo his sentiment, he quickly realized she couldn't and tried not to let the omission bother him. Because of his mother, the looming custody case was probably the most important thing to Olivia right now, that and making sure Thea remained in her care. Her feelings for him had to be put on the back burner.

They fell silent for a while, and then Olivia said, "I hope we get word about the custody hearing soon."

"I imagine you will now that CPS has conducted their inspection. I wouldn't be surprised if you got notice tomorrow. If you don't, I'm sure Austin will check into it for you." He wanted to say he'd call Austin and make sure he did, but wisely kept that thought to himself.

A few minutes later, Olivia asked him about his campaign, and Matt belatedly realized he hadn't told her about his decision not to run. So for the rest of the trip home they discussed his promised appointment to temporary district attorney and the possibility of winning that position legitimately later on.

"Are you sure this is what you want, Matt? Your decision…it doesn't have anything to do with me, does it?"

"It is exactly what I want. The minute Carter made the suggestion, I knew it was perfect for me…and for us. So yes, every decision I make has something to do with you. And Thea."

She didn't say anything for long seconds. And when she did, her voice seemed flat. "What does your mother think about all this?"

"I only told her I wasn't running for the Senate. I didn't tell her about the DA's job."

"Why not?"

"Knowing her, she'd try to throw a monkey wrench into the appointment. That's what she does when things don't go her way. She ruins everything she touches." He immediately wanted to take the words back, but it was too late. He could have kicked himself.

Olivia didn't answer, and when he glanced at her, he saw she was staring out her window. Why hadn't he simply said he would tell his parents when the time was right, and drop it at that? Why had he had to remind Olivia of everything she feared in a relationship with him?

Dammit! They were almost home, and this wasn't the way he wanted to end the day.

"Let's talk about something more pleasant," he said almost desperately. "Like ordering a pizza for dinner. Or we could get Chinese takeout."

"I'm not really very hungry after that big lunch," Olivia said. "I'm sorry, Matt, but I think Thea and I will just have soup or something light, and I'll go to bed when she does tonight. I didn't get much sleep last night and I'm on the day shift tomorrow."

Disappointment flooded him. Reality had once again reared its ugly head. Already, the fun-filled day of San

Antonio had been replaced with reminders of the custody suit and what would be in store for them in the coming days here at home.

He silently cursed his mother. Every single negative thing in their lives right now could be directly traced to her. Was there any way to stop her before she ruined their lives completely?

Chapter Thirteen

Olivia decided she would give her notice Monday morning. So as soon as she arrived at the hospital, she told Helena Tucker, her supervisor, that she needed to talk to her.

"Oh, Olivia, I hate to hear this," Helena said, dismay written all over her face. "You're one of the best people I've got on my team. I don't want to lose you."

Olivia sighed. "Thank you, I appreciate that, but something has happened that's made me think about the future sooner than I'd expected to." Although she had not told anyone other than her family about the custody suit, she decided it was only fair to tell Helena.

"Unbelievable," Helena said when she'd finished. "Why, you're one of the best mothers I know. Listen, Olivia, if you need a character witness, you can count on me."

Olivia was touched. She knew her boss liked her,

but she hadn't expected this kind of loyalty. "I can't tell you how much that means to me. I'll keep your offer in mind."

"Well, I'm serious. So don't hesitate to ask. Now, can I count on you to stay on until I can replace you?"

"As long as it doesn't drag on too long," Olivia said. "I'd like to be free after the holidays."

"Oh, that shouldn't be a problem. I'm pretty sure Shari wants to go full-time, and I also have a couple of applications hanging fire."

As Olivia turned to leave, Helena said, "We'll miss you around here."

"I'll miss you, too." But mixed with her regret over leaving a job she loved, Olivia also felt tremendous relief.

It would be wonderful not to have to worry about the days Thea was under the weather and Olivia had to prevail upon her mother to watch her. Besides, Olivia would enjoy being home with Thea, and once Thea started first grade and was gone most of the day, Olivia could follow through with her renewed desire to earn her nursing degree. So she felt excitement as well as regret. Of course, all her plans hinged on winning the custody case.

That damned case.

It loomed over everything. Some days she still had trouble believing her in-laws were actually doing this to her.

Despite the worry it caused, she managed to put the custody suit out of her mind as the busy morning progressed, but it came hurtling back when she got a phone call from Austin over her lunch hour.

"The hearing has been scheduled for this coming Friday afternoon," he said without preamble. "Our instructions are to be at family court at two o'clock."

Olivia swallowed. "Will…will we know right away?"

"I don't know. Depends on the judge. I checked the docket, and Judge Lawrence will be hearing the case."

"Do you know him?"

"It's not a him. Her name is Althea Lawrence, and she's been a judge in family court for almost twenty years. I'm told she's very good. Very fair. Very family friendly. She has four kids of her own."

Olivia closed her eyes. Before, even though she'd known all of this was actually happening, it had somehow seemed surreal. Now it felt totally real. And frightening. In just four days, her entire future would be determined by some woman she'd never met, a woman who would hear so-called "evidence" against her and then rebuttal witnesses who would attest to her good character and fitness as a mother, not to mention the unknown recommendation of Joan Barwood, the caseworker who had visited her.

"And Thea will be questioned?" she asked faintly.

"Probably. We've been instructed to bring someone along who can stay with Thea during the hearing, because they won't allow a child as young as she is to be present during testimony. She'll be in a room nearby especially set up for young children, and someone will need to be with her until she's called."

"She'll actually be called into the hearing itself? Be questioned in front of all of us?"

"I'm not sure. She might be interviewed in the judge's chambers. Or maybe the judge will go into the children's room and talk to her there."

"And we won't know what's being said?"

"We may see the interview on closed circuit television. It's up to the judge."

"Everyone in the court room?"

"No. I think just you and me, your in-laws and Jackson Moyer."

Olivia fought back tears. "I hate this."

"I know you do. I hate it for you. And for Thea. But take heart, Olivia. We have a really good case, and I think we'll win. Just keep your chin up and let the truth speak for itself."

Yes. And she'd also pray. She'd pray like she'd never prayed before.

"What do you think I should tell Thea? I mean, surely she needs to be prepared."

"I've talked to a buddy of mine who's handled a couple of these types of cases, and he tells me it's best to be honest with her. Explain that her grandparents think it would be best for her to live with them, but you want her to stay with you, and that because you disagree, a judge has been instructed to find out how Thea feels."

"What if she asks questions about her grandmother? Questions I don't feel comfortable answering?" Olivia thought about how just the other day Thea had wanted to take the new kitten and go and visit "Mimi" and Olivia had to put her daughter off.

"I know it's hard, but be careful what you say," Austin said. "The judge will probably ask Thea what you've told her, and it's best you don't criticize either grandparent."

Olivia couldn't help thinking this was all kind of like a nasty divorce where a mother who loved her child had to make sure not to let that child know there were any bad feelings.

They talked for a while longer, and then Austin got another call and said if she had more questions, he'd be available that evening and not to hesitate to call him.

But as reassuring as Austin had been, Matt was the one Olivia really wanted to talk to.

She decided to call him right away, but his secretary told her he was in court and wouldn't be back for several hours. "Shall I have him call you?"

"No," Olivia said, "I'm at work. But tell him I called and will call him tonight."

Then she went back to her department and explained to Helena she'd have to have Friday off, and why.

For the rest of the day, even though Olivia did her job thoroughly, she had a hard time thinking of anything else but what was in store for her at the end of the week.

Olivia dressed carefully for the hearing at family court. With her mother's and Stella's approval, she put on a simple dark green dress with a round neckline and slightly flared skirt that ended just below her knees. Sensible two-inch heeled pumps, a single strand of pearls and tiny pearl earrings completed her ensemble. She carefully applied her makeup: just a bit of foundation and a touch of eye shadow and mascara. A rosy lip gloss completed the picture. She thought she looked like exactly what she was: a young mother from a small town.

"Perfect," her mother declared. She hugged Olivia, saying, "Honey, it's all going to be okay."

"I hope so," Olivia said, swallowing her fear. But no matter how many times she reassured herself, she couldn't make her heart stop its too-fast rhythm. Even deep breathing didn't help.

I can't lose Thea. I can't.

She was so grateful Matt would be there today, even though she knew his mother would be furious when she saw him, obviously giving Olivia his support. He'd also told both her and Austin he was available to testify on her behalf. Olivia hoped that wouldn't be necessary because no good would come of his openly challenging his mother like that. And yet, how could she tell Matt to stay away? Especially if, as he believed, the judge would be swayed by his presence?

Olivia had been instructed to be outside the courtroom by one forty-five that afternoon, ready to be called when the judge returned from lunch. She hoped the scheduling meant that her case would be concluded by the day's end and not be carried over till the following week.

Austin was meeting them there. Olivia, Thea, Norma and Stella arrived a little after one thirty. When they walked into the courthouse, Olivia saw Matt and Austin standing talking. She also saw her in-laws, accompanied by a very tall, imposing man—whom Olivia assumed was the famous Jackson Moyer—at the other end of the hallway. Vivienne looked in her direction only once, then abruptly turned away. As always, the woman looked impeccable in a dark blue ensemble.

"There's Mimi!" Thea said, a big smile lighting her face. "Can we go see her, Mommy?"

"Not now, sweetie. Later, maybe," Olivia said, trying to keep her voice normal even though her stomach was churning. Matt turned at the sound of their voices, and their eyes met. In his, she saw encouragement and support. Instantly, she felt better.

He smiled at her, walked over and drew her into a hug, whispering, "It's going to be okay."

"Matt, your parents can see you," she said, pulling away even though, at that moment, what she wanted most in the world—aside from winning today's case—was the comfort of his arms.

"I don't care," he said. Then, shocking her, he said loud enough for her family and Austin to hear, "I love you, and I don't care who knows it."

Olivia didn't know where to look…or what to say. She could feel herself blushing. It was one thing for her family to suspect how things stood between her and Matt, quite another to state it so publicly.

Her mother touched her arm and smiled at her reassuringly. "We all love you, honey. Everything's going to be fine."

Olivia's eyes finally met Austin's. In them she saw resignation. But she also saw Austin's integrity, strength and determination. He would do his best for her, no matter what. He gave her an encouraging smile, then echoed her mother's sentiment. "It really is going to be fine, Olivia. I promise you."

She took a deep shaky breath.

And prayed everyone was right.

Matt sat in the very back of the courtroom, even though he wished he had the right to sit beside Olivia, to hold her hand, to show the world how much he believed in her. His mother had given him a cold stare as she'd walked in; his father had evaded Matt's gaze.

Matt was glad he'd been able to persuade his sister to stay away. There was no sense in her getting embroiled in this lunacy. If he'd thought Madeleine's support for Olivia would make a difference, he might have advised her to come despite his mother, but he didn't think it would, so it had seemed more prudent for Madeleine to stay out of the fray.

A few minutes after all interested parties had settled into their places, the door leading to the judge's chambers opened and the bailiff called, "All rise!" as Judge Althea Lawrence entered.

Once the judge was seated, Matt studied her. He'd boned up on her background and knew she was fifty-three, a plus because sometimes older judges tended to be more conservative. She came from a fairly large blue-collar family and had put herself through college and law school with a mix of scholarships, loans and part-time jobs. That background was also a plus. Odds were she'd be much more inclined to identify with Olivia than with Vivienne. And the final plus—she was a mother herself.

The judge greeted the participants, then read the petition aloud. When she'd finished, she said, "Mr. Moyer, as counsel for the petitioner, let's hear your first witness."

The first witness turned out to be Janice Rosen, the ER nurse who had attended when Olivia brought Thea in after the incident in the backyard where her lip had been cut. Jackson Moyer adroitly questioned the nurse in a way that made her answers seem as if the accident had been Olivia's fault because she hadn't been watching Thea the way she should have.

When Moyer finished, Austin rose.

"Do you have any children, Mrs. Rosen?" he asked, smiling at her in a friendly way.

"I do."

"And how old are they?"

"Five and seven."

"Boys or girls?"

"Two boys."

"I'll bet they can be a handful."

The nurse grinned. "Two handfuls."

Austin chuckled. "And I'll bet they can get into things in a second. Even when you're in the room."

"You can say that again. I've gotta have eyes in the back of my head."

"Have you ever left them playing outside while you ran into the house to get something?"

"Of course. Who hasn't?"

Austin nodded. "That's right. Who hasn't?" He looked at the judge as if to say, *And I'll bet you have, too. Because a parent can't be with a child every second. And even if they are, accidents will still happen, won't they?*

"Have one of your boys ever had an accident at home?" Austin said, turning his attention back to the nurse.

"Objection, Your Honor," Jackson Moyer said. "We aren't here to investigate Ms. Rosen's parenting skills."

"Sustained," the judge said. "Move on, Mr. Crenshaw."

"One last question, Mrs. Rosen," Austin said. "Did the attending physician note anything unusual about the circumstances of Thea Britton's accident that day? Did he feel it was caused by neglect? Recommend that CPS be called?"

"No. Nothing like that."

"Thank you. Nothing further."

Matt relaxed a bit after that. Austin obviously knew what he was doing. He'd made the witness comfortable, been friendly, and hadn't tried to intimidate her with his questions.

The next witness was Phyllis Grimm, who lived next door to Olivia's mother. She testified about an incident that had taken place on Thea's third birthday when Thea had darted toward the street. "Her mother's whole family were standing right there and nobody was holding that child's hand! She could have been killed."

Jackson Moyer nodded sagely when she'd finished. "Thank you, Mrs. Grimm," he said. "We appreciate your taking the time to come here today and tell us about this truly frightening incident."

Austin greeted Phyllis Grimm respectfully as he approached and echoed Jackson Moyer's thanks for her appearance in court. Then he said, "Isn't it true, Mrs. Grimm, that in addition to her mother's family, both of Thea's Britton grandparents were also present during the stated incident?"

Phyllis Grimm visibly stiffened in her seat. "I don't know who all was there. I just know it was a noisy party they were having and I happened to be looking out the window when I saw the little girl run into the street."

"A noisy party? But it was held inside, wasn't it?" Austin consulted his notes. "And the party was actually over, I believe. Mr. and Mrs. Britton were leaving and the others had walked outside to say goodbye to them."

The Grimm woman, whose sour look hadn't changed, shrugged. "Whatever."

Matt knew the woman had an ax to grind with Norma Dubrovnik because of a broken fence that separated their property. She had demanded that Norma replace the fence. Norma had tried to reason with her because the fence was on the dividing line of the property, and each owner traditionally paid half when the fence was a common one. The dispute had gone on for months now.

"Did you also see that Thea was chasing a baby rabbit? And that before she reached the street her mother ran after her and caught her and that no harm came to her?"

"No, I didn't," the woman said angrily. "Do you think

I spend all day looking out my window? I just know the mother wasn't watching her child properly."

"Your Honor," Austin said, "we will be calling a rebuttal witness later who will verify that Thea's mother was, indeed, watching her child and that Thea was caught before she ever went into the street." He then turned to Phyllis Grimm, saying, "No more questions for this witness."

The next witness was a young woman who testified she'd seen Thea falling off a swing at the park because Olivia's mother's attention was elsewhere.

"She got very upset, too," the woman said.

"Thea?"

"No, the older woman, the grandmother. She was so shook up I had to take care of the little girl myself. Luckily she wasn't hurt badly. Just a knee scrape."

"So the child's grandmother wasn't able to manage a child as lively as Thea Britton," Moyer said.

"Objection, Your Honor," Austin said. "Leading the witness."

"Sustained."

"Withdrawn, Your Honor." Moyer turned to Austin. "Your witness, Counselor."

Austin did his best, but he was unable to shake the woman's staunch belief that Norma Dubrovnik hadn't been capable of the kind of vigilance and energy necessary to provide adequate child care.

"The grandmother told me she felt dizzy herself," the woman insisted. "And now I've learned she's a diabetic! My sister's a diabetic, and I know how careful she has to be to eat the right things at the right time. I'll bet that was the problem. She was probably having low blood sugar."

Matt grimaced. Austin quickly protested that Norma's

diabetes had no bearing on the issue at hand, and the judge concurred, so Matt relaxed. Still, personally, he hated hearing anything negative about Olivia's mother, because she was a wonderful person. The last witness before Vivienne herself would appear was Officer Tom Nicholls. Matt was surprised. He'd expected a bystander or two from the festival; what he hadn't expected was one of the police officers.

Officer Nicholls spoke unemotionally, just gave the facts of what had happened at the festival when Thea disappeared. Without accusation, he admitted that dozens of officers were involved in the subsequent search, as well as many others not involved in law enforcement.

Jackson Moyer cleverly continued questioning him about specifics of that day and managed to elicit the information that the reason Olivia and her family had been distracted and not realized Thea had wandered off was because her grandmother Dubrovnik had collapsed from a diabetic blood sugar low.

As the afternoon wore on, Matt could see that Norma's condition was going to play a big part in his parents' case against Olivia and her judgment as a mother. He could only imagine what his mother would have to say when she had her turn to testify. Poor Norma. She was going to be the scapegoat here, and if Olivia lost custody of Thea, Norma would always feel guilty.

"But isn't it true, Officer Nicholls," Austin asked when it was his turn to question the man, "that the petitioner, Vivienne Britton, was ultimately the person responsible for Thea's disappearance from the festival? That if she hadn't interfered, or had at least notified Thea's mother, that she had found the child, none of the hundreds of people involved in the search would have been necessary?"

"That's one interpretation of what happened," the officer said, "but it's my understanding that Mrs. Britton—the elder Mrs. Britton—found Thea Britton wandering alone and took her home with her for safety reasons."

Matt's jaw hardened. Obviously, his parents—his mother, more exactly—had been at work here and influenced the officer's thinking.

It was almost five o'clock before Nicholls had finished testifying. Judge Lawrence looked at the clock, then said, "It's too late for more testimony today. We will resume hearing this case Monday morning at nine o'clock. All parties should plan to be here for most of the day."

Jackson Moyer and Matt's parents immediately stood and, without looking in Olivia's direction, walked out of the courtroom. Neither parent acknowledged Matt as they passed by.

"I think things went well," Matt said when he joined Olivia's group. His eyes sought Olivia's and he could see how exhausted she was. The strain of the proceedings had already taken a toll.

"I agree," Austin said. "We refuted every claim they made, and Monday, when our witnesses testify, it's going to make an even bigger difference."

Olivia tried to smile, but Matt could see how hard the afternoon had been for her. He knew the testimony about her mother had been difficult to hear. He was thankful Norma hadn't been in the courtroom herself and was actually surprised Jackson Moyer hadn't somehow been able to get that information in. Then he realized the disclosure would probably come when his mother got her day in court.

"Olivia looks tired," he said in an aside to Stella. "Did she drive here today?"

"No, she and Thea rode with me and Mom."

"Why don't you let me take her home?"

Stella smiled in understanding. "That's fine with me. I'll take Mom to dinner somewhere before we go back."

Olivia didn't protest when Matt told her the plan. When the two of them went to collect Thea, they found she'd fallen asleep. Norma herself sat quietly crocheting. She rose when they entered the room.

Olivia explained and she and her mother kissed goodbye. Norma smiled at Matt and he bent down and kissed her cheek before she left to join Stella. "Don't worry," he said quietly. "It'll go much better on Monday." Then he picked up Thea and, accompanied by Olivia, left the room.

As they walked out of the courthouse together, Matt saw his parents standing on the sidewalk in front, talking to Jackson Moyer.

"Matt..." Olivia said faintly.

"Don't look at them," he said. "Hold your head up high and keep walking."

She only hesitated a moment, then did as he'd instructed. His heart felt full to bursting.

He had never been prouder of her.

Chapter Fourteen

"Would you mind getting the mail for me?" Olivia asked after Matt had brought Thea into the house. Because she'd missed her nap, she hadn't awakened on the drive home and was even now sleeping soundly on the daybed in the study.

Olivia wondered what Matt had thought when he'd deposited her there. Was he remembering the Monday night they'd made love on that very same bed? She knew she was. Every time she looked at that bed she remembered that night.

"Sure," he said.

While Matt went outside to the mailbox, Olivia walked back to the kitchen to figure out what she would feed Thea for supper. Maybe it was a grilled cheese and tomato soup kind of night. Or maybe she'd call for Chinese takeout. Thea loved the honey-glazed shrimp that was a specialty of their favorite restaurant.

"Here you go," Matt said, walking into the kitchen. He handed her the mail: a bill from the water department, an L.L. Bean catalog, two other pieces of junk mail and a large Priority Mail envelope.

Olivia looked at the envelope curiously. The return address was that of a law firm in Austin. "What in the world?" she said, pulling at the tape that would open the envelope.

She stared at the letter that had been inside. As she read, her mouth fell open. The law firm—Standish, Davis, and Standish—were pleased to inform her that she and her daughter, Dorothea Lynn Britton, were the main heirs to the estate of the late Jonathan Pierce Kendrick, who had died the previous week. The estate was worth an estimated twelve million dollars. Olivia or her lawyer were instructed to call their law office as soon as possible for more information and details on claiming the estate. Stunned, Olivia handed the letter to Matt.

He read it quickly, then looked at her. He looked as bewildered as she felt. "Who is this Jonathan Kendrick?" he asked.

"I have no idea."

"Twelve million dollars?" he said softly. "And you don't know who he is?"

"No. I've never heard of him." Olivia frowned. "Could this be some kind of hoax? A scam, maybe?"

"No, I don't think so. Standish, Davis, and Standish is a well-known and very reputable Austin law firm. In fact, I know the younger Standish. Kenny and I went to law school together."

"It says to call them." Olivia looked at the clock. It was almost six o'clock. "Do you think they'd still be there?"

"Let me try," Matt said. He pulled his cell out of his

pocket. A moment later he said, "Yes, may I speak to Ken Standish? Tell him it's Matt Britton." He smiled at Olivia, mouthing, "We're in luck. He's still there."

Olivia sat down at the kitchen table and motioned for Matt to do so, too. She listened as he began to talk to Ken Standish, explaining that he was her brother-in-law and had been with her when she'd received their letter about Jonathan Kendrick's estate.

"Of course. I understand," Matt said. "Here. I'll let you talk to her yourself." He handed her his phone.

"Hello?" she said.

"Hello, Mrs. Britton. This is Kenneth Standish. I'm guessing you're shocked by our letter."

"That's a good description. I can't really wrap my head around what you said. I mean, why would a perfect stranger leave me and my daughter so much money?"

"Yes, well, I can understand your confusion. Look, Mrs. Britton, I'd love to explain everything to you now, but I don't think it's a good idea to discuss this over the phone. Or in the presence of your brother-in-law."

"But...why not? I don't understand."

"I know you don't. But it would just be better if you and your attorney come to my office Monday morning. Wait. Is Matt your attorney?"

Olivia swallowed. Looked at Matt. He was frowning. "Um, no. Not really."

"Good. I think it's best your attorney is a neutral party."

A neutral party?

"Um, I actually do have an attorney. Austin Crenshaw."

"Really? I know Austin. For something like this, he's a great choice. I'll give him a call. Set up something for Monday."

"Monday won't work, Mr. Standish. I have to be in court in San Marcos on Monday. Which is actually why I have an attorney."

Ken Standish was silent for a moment. Then he said, "What about tomorrow? Would that work?"

Olivia wet her lips. "Yes. That would work."

"Okay, I'll call Austin and he'll call you and let you know what time. I'm looking forward to meeting you."

"M-me, too," Olivia said.

"Well?" Matt said when she disconnected the call.

"He…wouldn't tell me anything. He said I should bring my attorney and come to his office and then he'd explain. He…he said it would be best not to say anything over the phone."

Matt's frown intensified. "I don't understand this."

"I don't, either." *A neutral party.* What had Standish meant?

"I think I should go with you tomorrow."

"Um, Mr. Standish said just to bring Austin."

Now Matt's expression turned to bewilderment. "What? No one else can come? Not even me?"

Since Olivia couldn't say "particularly not you," she simply said, "He stressed that I should only bring my attorney."

"But Olivia, I don't—" He broke off whatever else he'd meant to say because at that moment, Thea walked into the room. She was rubbing her eyes and yawning.

"Hey, sweetheart," Matt said, smiling down at her. "Did you have a good nap?"

"I'm hungry, Mommy," Thea said.

Olivia knew, just from the tone of Thea's voice, that she was cranky and would remain out of sorts until Olivia managed to get her in bed for the night. "How about some tomato soup and grilled cheese?"

"I want a chocolate milk shake!" Her lower lip protruded.

A tantrum seemed imminent. "I can do chocolate milk. But I don't have any ice cream to make a milk shake," Olivia said in her most persuasive voice.

The look on Thea's face would have been comical if the atmosphere hadn't already been so tense. When thwarted, Thea could be impossible. "I want a milk shake!" she shouted. For good measure, she stamped her foot.

Olivia's eyes met Matt's. "Sorry," she said, preparing herself for the coming full-fledged thunderstorm.

"Why don't I run over to the store and pick up some Blue Bell?" Matt said. He gave Thea an even bigger smile. "Then you can have your milk shake."

Thea looked at him, her face a road map of her thoughts.

"Would you?" Olivia said gratefully. She knew she shouldn't give in to Thea, but she was too worn out to be the perfect parent tonight.

By the time Matt returned, Thea was settled into her booster chair and more or less happily eating a grilled cheese sandwich, accompanied by a big daub of ketchup—she'd passed on the tomato soup—and Olivia was tiredly drinking a glass of wine while trying not to think about the tense day in court or the shocking news she'd received less than an hour ago or who Jonathan Kendrick was or why Ken Standish had not wanted Matt to accompany her tomorrow.

"Thank you," she said to Matt, getting up and putting the ice cream in the freezer until Thea was finished with the sandwich. "Would you like a grilled cheese sandwich, too?"

"I'm not hungry," he said. His eyes were troubled. "When do you think she'll be ready for bed?"

He wants to continue our earlier discussion. "I think she's ready now, but getting her there will be a problem."

"How about if I help and after she's down we can talk?"

Olivia fought her exhaustion. None of the stress she felt was Matt's fault. She had to remember that. "Matt, please don't take this the wrong way, but I'm so tired. I just want to go to bed myself. And really, what is there to talk about?" She dropped her voice to almost a whisper, even though Thea didn't seem to be paying any attention to them. "I don't want to talk about the custody hearing and there's nothing more to say about that letter until after I meet with Mr. Standish tomorrow."

"So you want me to leave?"

He's hurt. "Please don't be mad. I promise I'll tell you everything after tomorrow's meeting."

His shoulders slumped. "I'm not mad. I'm disappointed."

"In *me*?"

"I guess I thought you'd take me to that meeting. That you'd want *me* to be your attorney."

For just a moment, Olivia considered an evasion. But if they couldn't be truthful with each other, how could there ever be real trust between them? Their relationship would be doomed regardless of the outcome of the custody suit. "Mr. Standish said it was better if my attorney was a neutral party."

Matt's face revealed his shock. "And he was referring to *me*? What does *that* mean?"

"I don't know, Matt. I'm just telling you what he said."

"But, Olivia, that doesn't make any sense. Don't *you* want me to be there?"

"Of course, I want you to be there, but—"

Thea chose that moment to bang on the table and demand her milk shake. "I've got to tend to Thea, Matt." Exhaustion caused her to sound impatient, but suddenly the stress of the past weeks just seemed to pile in on her. "Can we table this discussion until after my meeting tomorrow? Hopefully, that'll shed light on everything."

Matt wasn't happy; that much was obvious, but he didn't argue. Instead, he just dropped a light kiss on her mouth, said, "Let me know what time you're going tomorrow, and get a good night's sleep. And remember… I love you."

"I love you, too," she murmured.

"Mommy!" Thea yelled.

"One milk shake coming up," Olivia said, forcing herself to move, even though all she really wanted was to sink down into one of the kitchen chairs and bury her face in her arms. But she was a mother, first and foremost. So she sighed and opened the freezer door. As she took the ice cream out, she heard the front door open and shut.

Matt was gone.

And tomorrow couldn't come soon enough.

Austin and Olivia were ushered into Ken Standish's office at ten o'clock Saturday morning. Olivia felt better than she had the night before, although her stomach was still tied up in knots because she hated the way she and Matt had parted. On top of that, she still couldn't wrap her head around the fact that some man she'd never heard of before had left her and her daughter an estimated twelve million dollars. In fact, even though she and Austin were in Ken Standish's office, nothing about why they were there seemed real.

"I'll get right to the point," Standish said after inviting Olivia and Austin to be seated and offering them something to drink.

He was a pleasant-faced man with a warm smile. Olivia liked him immediately.

"I know you're wondering why Jonathan Pierce Kendrick named you and your daughter his heirs," he continued.

"Especially since I've never even heard of him," Olivia said.

"The reason for that is, while he was alive, he chose to keep his identity secret. But he always intended that after his death the truth would be revealed."

"What truth?" Austin asked.

Standish looked at Olivia. "Jonathan Kendrick was your late husband's birth father. And your daughter's grandfather."

"What! But—" She stared at the lawyer. How was this possible? Could it be true?

Standish nodded. "I know. It's hard to believe. But it's true. And it can easily be proven by testing your daughter's DNA. Mr. Kendrick had his DNA documented many years ago in anticipation of this day."

Olivia sat there, stunned. Had Vivienne known this? Did Hugh? Did *Matt*? Is that why Standish had suggested Matt might not be a neutral party?

"My God, Olivia," Austin said. "Do you know what this means? There's no way your in-laws will win the custody case now."

"Custody case?" Standish said, frowning.

"Yes. The elder Brittons are petitioning the court for custody of Thea, Olivia's daughter," Austin explained.

"On what grounds?"

"That Olivia is an unfit mother. The charges are ridiculous, of course, but the court won't just take our word for it now that an accusation has been made. CPS was notified and has conducted an investigation. We'll be hearing their recommendations on Monday."

Standish turned to Olivia. "I'm very sorry to hear this. If I can help in any way, I'll be happy to. Um…" He cleared his throat. "Mr. Kendrick had you thoroughly investigated, himself, both initially, when you married your husband, and periodically over the years. In that way, he always looked after your daughter. So Austin is right. You've got perfect leverage now. Not just the fact that Hugh Britton is not your daughter's grandfather, but everything documented in Jonathan Kendrick's files."

"But even if this is all true, maybe my father-in-law knows all about it," Olivia said.

"He doesn't," Standish said. "Mr. Kendrick's papers explain exactly why he kept his identity secret. It was to protect your mother-in-law. He wrote you a letter, Olivia. Why don't we give you some privacy and you can read it, and after you read it, we can talk more. In the meantime, I'll explain to Austin what steps will need to be taken for you to claim the estate."

Before he and Austin left his office for a nearby conference room, he handed Olivia an envelope. Olivia's hands were shaking when she opened it.

Dear Olivia,

You don't know me, but I know a lot about you. I've kept track of you for many years—you and your beautiful daughter, my granddaughter—my only grandchild, in fact. After Mark died, you and she were the two reasons my life still had meaning, because I have never been blessed with other children. I've often regretted my promise to Vivienne to keep my identity a secret, especially since Mark's death. I understood her reasons for silence and respected them. I loved her—we were once engaged, you see, before she met Hugh Britton and broke our engagement—and we reconnected, briefly, during a rough patch in their marriage. That's when Mark was conceived. Neither of us knew it until after she and Hugh had reconciled, and by then, she wasn't willing to leave him.

I kept my promise of silence for a long time. But now that I'm facing my own mortality, I think I made a mistake. All these years, you and I and Thea could have known one another, and I could have perhaps made your life easier. I'm sorry I didn't come forward sooner, but I hope that doing so now will make a positive difference in your life. If others are hurt by this disclosure, I'm sorry, but the truth needs to be told, for many reasons.

I admire you and respect you and think you are a wonderful mother. Please tell my granddaughter how much I love her and how proud I am to know I am responsible for some of her genes.

With much love,
Jonathan P. Kendrick

Olivia's eyes were moist when she finished reading the letter. He sounded like such a lovely man. How she wished she'd known about him sooner. And yet, she couldn't help feeling bad for Hugh. Did he have any idea Vivienne had been unfaithful to him? That Mark was not his son?

And Matt.

Did Matt know? Suspect? She didn't believe he did; he would have told her if he had. Especially since he'd freely admitted to her how much his mother had favored Mark. Even Mark had told her about Vivienne's favoritism and how uncomfortable it had made him, because Mark had loved and respected Matt. The brothers had been close, despite Vivienne's adulation of her youngest son.

And now Olivia knew why that adulation had existed. Vivienne must have still loved Jonathan Kendrick, even though she chose to stay in her marriage. Olivia could almost feel sorry for Vivienne. Almost. But nothing excused the unhappiness Vivienne had caused in other people's lives. It especially didn't excuse her recent behavior.

Still…no matter how or why Vivienne had become the person she now was, Olivia didn't want to be the one responsible for exposing her sins to the world. After all, she was *still* Thea's grandmother. Still Mark's mother. And still Matt's mother. And even if Olivia were willing to face off with Vivienne, the truth might destroy Hugh.

I can't do that to them.

Olivia was still thinking about the letter and its ramifications when Austin and Ken Standish came back into the office.

"I've made a decision," she said.

Both men looked at her.

"I don't want to use what we've learned today as a weapon against my mother-in-law."

"But, Olivia—" Austin said.

"No." Olivia shook her head. "I won't be persuaded otherwise. You said yourself we have a strong case. I don't want to expose her. I don't want to hurt Hugh… or the rest of the family."

"We do have a strong case, and actually, I received a phone call from the investigator I hired to look into all of Vivienne's so-called evidence while Ken and I were giving you privacy to read your letter, and he's turned up something potentially very good for our case. But you could still lose. There's no telling how the judge will rule. And once a ruling is made, it will be very difficult to change."

Olivia shook her head. "You can't use the information about Mark's paternity. I won't allow it." Making this public would ruin Vivienne. It would ruin Hugh. And it would completely ruin any chance of any kind of reconciliation with the family. "When Thea's older, she'll have to be told the truth, but not now. Not like this. No matter what she's done, I won't destroy Vivienne's reputation."

"Olivia, be sensible. They are trying to destroy *yours*. They're lying about you, using any means at their disposal to try to take your daughter away from you. You have to fight back."

"I will fight back, but not that way. I can't. Tell me what our investigator found."

Austin sighed. "Vivienne is the reason Thea wandered off during the festival. I know we all thought it was a kitten or some other animal that drew her attention, but it wasn't. Our investigator found out Vivienne did it on purpose, just to make you look bad."

"How could the investigator possibly know that?"

"Because she was seen doing it. He has a sworn eyewitness statement."

Olivia was stunned. Did Matt know his mother was behind Thea's disappearance? She remembered the way he'd called his family after finding out Thea was missing. How he told her he hoped the custody case could be settled without dragging all of them through the mud. He must have, at least, suspected.

And he'd never said anything.

But almost immediately after thinking all this, she was ashamed of herself. How could she doubt Matt, even for one second? He couldn't have known. Not Matt.

He would have told her.

Chapter Fifteen

Matt couldn't concentrate on anything Saturday morning. He went into the office to catch up on paperwork, but he accomplished very little. He kept waiting for his phone to ring, willing each call to be from Olivia. When, at one o'clock, she still hadn't called, he finally texted her.

Austin will call you, she texted back.

Austin? Why couldn't *she* call him? What the hell was going on?

Twenty minutes later, Austin called.

Matt listened without interrupting as Austin told him what they'd learned in Ken Standish's office and then what his investigator had turned up concerning Thea's disappearance from the Fall Festival.

"I'm frustrated, because Olivia has forbidden me to use the information about your brother's paternity, which, on top of what the investigator found, would ensure she'd keep custody of Thea."

Matt wasn't shocked by the information about his mother luring Thea from the festival—it was exactly the kind of thing she *would* do and he was surprised he hadn't suspected her.

Nor was he really shocked about Mark. He'd always known Mark was the favorite of his mother's children, and now he finally understood why. He'd also known about the problems in his parents' marriage. They'd been evident from the time he was old enough to understand. But he had always imagined his father might be the unfaithful one, not his mother. In some ways, knowing this made her seem more human.

"Look, Austin," he said, "Don't worry. I'll take care of this."

"How? Olivia said—"

"They're my parents, not Olivia's."

"She said she couldn't live with herself if she exposed your mother."

That was like Olivia. "Like I said, I'll take care of this."

As soon as the call ended, Matt packed up his briefcase and headed out. He drove straight to his parents' home.

"You have your nerve, coming here like this," his mother said when he walked into her sitting room.

"We have to talk."

"We have nothing to say to one another."

"Is Dad here?"

"Your father is golfing. Now please go."

Matt suddenly felt sorry for her. Her entire world, the one she'd built so carefully, was about to fall apart. But he hardened his heart. He couldn't afford sympathy. Not when so much was at stake. "I'm not leaving until we talk about Jonathan Kendrick."

Her face stiffened with shock.

"He died last week. Did you know that?"

"J-Jon died?"

Matt saw the way her hands trembled as she clutched them in her lap, but his resolve didn't waver. He explained the circumstances of Kendrick's death as Austin had explained them. And then he told her about the will and the letter Kendrick had written to Olivia.

"Austin Crenshaw wanted to present this information to the judge on Monday, but Olivia—the same woman you have done your best to smear—told him she couldn't be a party to something like that. I, however, have no such qualms. So if you don't want the world to know about you and about the circumstances of Mark's birth, you will go to court Monday morning and drop the custody suit. Because if you continue with this vendetta against Olivia, I will expose the truth."

By now, his mother had recovered her aplomb and the sorrow he'd glimpsed earlier had disappeared. She was once again the regal ice queen ruling her kingdom. "You wouldn't dare."

"Yes, Mother, I would."

"You'd be ruining your own life. No one will vote for you for dog catcher if you go ahead with this."

"I honestly don't care."

"You're bluffing."

"I'm dead serious."

She stared at him. "You mean it."

"I do."

"I won't forgive you for this."

Matt suddenly felt exhausted. "You only have yourself to blame. I'm just the messenger. And the son you always considered second best."

"That's not true."

"Which part? The blame? Or how you've always looked at me?"

When she didn't answer, he said wearily, "All of it *is* true, but you know what? It doesn't matter anymore. Because I know exactly how you can make it all up to me…and keep your reputation intact."

She didn't interrupt as Matt told her he loved Olivia and intended to marry her, if she'd have him. "And you will not do anything to oppose our marriage or to make her unhappy. We don't have to play happy families all the time, because we won't live in Crandall Lake. Since I'll be working there, and I know Olivia wants to go back to school, I plan to buy a house in San Marcos. But no matter what, you will, at all times, be civil and you will not say one word against my wife, to anyone, ever. Do you understand? Because if you do, I promise you, you will never see Thea again, and every bit of what I found out today will be made public."

In her eyes, he could see acknowledgment that she was beaten. "So I have your word that you will call Jackson Moyer today? And instruct him to drop the custody suit?"

"Yes," she said through gritted teeth.

"And you agree to the rest of my terms?"

She nodded curtly.

Matt felt as if the weight of the world had been lifted from his shoulders as he walked out the front door. He couldn't remember ever feeling happier, and he couldn't wait to tell Olivia she no longer had to worry about anything.

Olivia was overjoyed when Austin phoned to tell her Jackson Moyer had called him to say that the Brittons were dropping the custody suit.

"You're sure?" she said.

"Yes. Apparently, after I called him, Matt convinced

your mother-in-law dropping the suit was in her best interest."

Olivia had barely hung up from the call with Austin when her phone rang again and Matt's photo popped up on the screen.

"Hi, Matt," she said, answering.

"Hey. Did Austin call you?"

"Yes."

"Good. I just wanted to be sure you knew. Listen, I'm at my office. I have a couple of things I need to wrap up, then I'm coming over. Okay?"

Olivia looked at her watch. It was three o'clock. "Okay. I'm going to take Thea to my mom's. I'll be back by four."

"See you then."

Her mother hugged her fiercely when Olivia told her the good news. "Oh, honey, I'm so happy this nightmare is over. Do you know why the Brittons backed off so suddenly?"

"Little pitchers," Olivia said, glancing at Thea, who'd gone into her mom's living room and had already pulled out the toy box her mom kept for her visits. "I'll explain everything later, okay? Right now I need to go back home." In a lower voice, she said, "Matt is coming by. We need to settle some things."

"I understand," her mother said. Then she smiled. "Give him my love."

Olivia nodded, but inside, her stomach clenched. Vivienne may have dropped the suit, but she would still hate her. In fact, she probably hated Olivia more now than she ever had. And no matter what concessions Matt might have wrung from Vivienne, she would find ways to make Olivia's life even more miserable than she had in the past. There was no way she and Matt could marry. No way they'd ever be the kind of close, loving family Olivia craved. It exhausted Olivia even to think about years and years of drama and stress.

Wouldn't Olivia be a lot better off accepting Eve and Adam's offer and moving to California? Sure, she'd miss Matt terribly, but she'd get over losing him. After all, she'd gotten over losing Mark, hadn't she? Wouldn't they all be better off if she and Thea made a fresh start far away from the Brittons?

As she drove back home, that question hounded her.

She just hoped when she finally saw Matt face-to-face today, she would know the answer and be brave enough to accept it.

Matt put on his favorite Sirius station and sang along with the radio as he drove the fifteen-mile distance between San Marcos and Crandall Lake. He felt jubilant. Although he'd always believed there would be some way to allay Olivia's fears and force his mother to accept his choice of wife, he knew now he'd always had a small particle of fear lodged down deep.

But no more.

All fear was gone. His mother no longer had any power over him or Olivia. They were free to declare their love to the world. He grinned.

Free to be together.

Free to marry.

Free to have other children, sisters and brothers for Thea.

Happiness made him laugh out loud. He couldn't wait to see her.

Olivia got back home by three forty-five. Knowing Matt would probably be right on time, she hurriedly changed her flannel shirt for a bright red sweater, ran a comb through her hair and freshened her lip gloss. Even though things might not turn out happily for them today, she still wanted to look her best.

She heard his car turn into the driveway two minutes before the hour. Her heart immediately accelerated, and she swallowed. She took several deep breaths and by the time he rang the doorbell, she felt as ready as she'd ever be.

It hurt to see the happiness on his face. It hurt to know she'd doubted him, even for an instant, because she could see the truth in his eyes. He had never lied to her, not even by omission. He *did* love her. But was his love enough? That had always been the question.

The smile on his face faded as their gazes locked. "What's wrong?"

She shook her head. "Let's go into the living room and talk."

He sat on the sofa, and she purposely sat across from him in one of the side chairs. His frown deepened. "Has something else happened that I don't know about? I would have thought you'd be jumping for joy."

In that moment, everything seemed so clear to her. But how to begin? "I'm happy about the custody suit being dropped, of course. And I'm grateful for what you did to make that happen, because I couldn't have allowed Austin to expose your mother to the world. But I've been doing a lot of thinking in the past few days. And it all boils down to this—your mother is going to resent me even more now than she ever did before. I'm sorry, Matt, but I just don't see how there will ever be any future for us."

He shook his head. "My mother won't give us any more trouble. I can promise you that."

"Why? Because you blackmailed her? Threatened her? You must have. She would never have backed down otherwise. I—I don't see how we can have any kind of future together that's built on that kind of foundation." Olivia willed herself not to cry, even though she wanted to weep at the expression on his face. She knew she was hurting him terribly, yet how could things be any different?

"This is crazy talk," he said, jumping up. "You can't really intend to allow my mother to rule the rest of your life. To ruin what we have together." Coming over to where she sat, he took her hand and pulled her to her feet. Gathering her in his arms, he held her close.

She could feel his heart beating and she closed her eyes.

"Olivia, I love you and Thea more than life itself. Life won't be worth living if I can't live it with the two of you." He stopped for a moment. "The question is, do you love me? I feel you do, but I need to hear you say it as if you mean it."

"Yes," she whispered. "I do love you, Matt. So much."

His arms tightened around her. "Then that's all that's important. Everything else can be worked out."

"But—"

Ignoring her attempt to interrupt, he said, "Listen to me. We don't have to live in Crandall Lake. We can live in San Marcos. Or, if you feel it's best to get away from my parents, I'm willing to relocate anywhere you want. As long as I'm with you, nothing else matters."

"But your life is here. Your job…"

"Is just a job. I can work anywhere."

"How? You're licensed here in Texas."

"I can take the bar in another state. Hell, I can do something different if I want to. I've invested my inheritance from my granddad Britton. Plus, my intended is a wealthy woman, isn't she?" He laughed to show her he was teasing her. Then he became earnest again. "I know how much you want a close and loving family. I've always known that. I want that, too, Olivia. But think about it. We'll have each other. We'll have Thea, and we'll have more children, won't we? We have your mother, your sister, my sister, Eve and her family. If my parents want to be a part of this, they can be. And if they don't, that's their choice, isn't it?"

Yes, she thought, it *was* their choice. Matt was right. He was right! Blinking away her tears, she looked up. Oh, God, she loved him so. "And, if necessary, you'd really consent to move somewhere else? For me?"

"I'd do anything in the world for you. I've told you that before."

Their eyes held for a long moment.

And then, smiling, he dipped his head and kissed her.

She sighed into the kiss.

They stood together for a long time. And when kissing was no longer enough, he scooped her up and carried her into her little study. This time, when they made love on the daybed, they didn't have to worry about being quiet so as not to disturb Thea. And they didn't have to hurry.

As their lovemaking reached its peak and they came together in a joyous blend of bodies and hearts, Olivia knew she had finally found the home she'd wanted for so long. "I love you, Matt." Now that she'd said it without fear and doubt, she wanted to keep saying it over and over again.

"And I love you," he murmured, wrapping his arms around her. "Let's get married right away. We can get a license on Monday and be Mr. and Mrs. Britton by the end of the week."

"I'm already Mrs. Britton," Olivia said, laughing.

He chuckled and nuzzled her neck. "Smart aleck."

"You know, when Mark and I married, it was such a hurried affair because he was leaving for Afghanistan and your mother...well, you know how your mother was. Would you think I was silly if I told you that this time, I'd like to do it right? Even if your parents don't come, I'd still like a real wedding. I want a pretty dress and I want Thea to be a flower girl and Stella and Eve to be my attendants."

"Of course, I don't think that's silly. But I also don't want to wait a long time. We're not like other couples who can move in together. There's Thea to consider."

"I know."

"So how long?"

"Two or three weeks?"

He sighed and tightened his embrace. "If we can make love again now and then again later, maybe I can survive waiting a couple of weeks."

She sighed happily. "Slave driver."

"Quit wasting time talking."

* * * * *

Don't miss the other books in Patricia Kay's
THE CRANDALL LAKE CHRONICLES,
THE GIRL HE LEFT BEHIND
&
OH, BABY!

Norma Dubrovnik's Haluski (Noodles & Cabbage)

1 small head of cabbage
1 16-ounce package of flat noodles
2 medium-sized white or yellow onions (or more, if you like)
Olive oil (original recipe called for butter)
Salt and pepper

Peel and slice onions into thin slices. Slice cabbage into thin slices. Sauté onions and cabbage on low-to-medium heat in olive oil in large skillet until tender. This process can be speeded up by lowering heat even more and covering skillet. Be sure to turn often so vegetables don't burn. While vegetables are cooking, prepare noodles according to package directions. Drain well. Add cooked noodles to the frying pan with the cooked vegetables and toss well. Adding several tablespoons of butter to taste is optional. Add salt and pepper to taste. Can be served as a main dish or as a side dish.

Note from Patricia Kay: This recipe is one my mother made all the time when my sisters and I were growing up. It's still a family favorite.

Norma Dubrovnik's Kolache

Yield = 6 rolls
Start early, dough has to rise twice.

Dough:
6 cups sifted flour
½ cup sugar
1 ½ sticks margarine or butter (softened)
2 cups milk (let stand at room temperature)
1 package dry yeast
2 eggs (at room temperature)
1 ½ teaspoons vanilla

Mix first two ingredients together. Dissolve yeast in ½ cup warm water with 1 teaspoon sugar (let stand 10 minutes). In a separate bowl, mix eggs with lukewarm milk, add vanilla. Add yeast and egg mixture to flour mixture.

Knead dough until easy to work with.

Let dough rise for about 2 hours until double the size you started with.

Nut Filling:
1 pound pecans or walnuts = 3 rolls of kolache

Grind the nuts in a food grinder or process in food processor. Add ⅓ cup of warm milk and ⅔ cup sugar for each 2 cups of nuts. Mix well. Then beat one egg white until stiff, add a teaspoon of sugar, mix all ingredients together.

Apricot Filling:
Use homemade or store-bought prepared apricot cake or pastry filling.

To Bake:
Grease cookie sheets. Divide dough into balls. Roll into an oval shape on floured board. Spread filling evenly over the dough (not too thick). Roll lengthwise, like a jelly roll. Cover filled rolls with a clean dish towel and let rise for about 1 hour.

Before baking, brush tops and sides of rolls with milk. Bake at 350 degrees for 35–40 minutes. Cool thoroughly before slicing. Serve with butter. Makes a wonderful, special breakfast treat or dessert anytime. Can be frozen.

Note from Patricia Kay: My husband and I made this recipe only once before he passed away. We experimented, because the original recipe, told to me by my mother before she passed away, was for twelve rolls at a time. (She always gave some to family members). Some of the ingredient amounts had to be adjusted, but our experiment turned out to be delicious. I know my mom will be smiling down at anyone who tries her recipe. Enjoy!

MILLS & BOON®

EXCLUSIVE EXCERPT

When Dea Caracciolo agrees to attend a sporting event as tycoon Guido Rossano's date, sparks fly!

Read on for a sneak preview of
THE BILLIONAIRE'S PRIZE
the final instalment of Rebecca Winters' thrilling Cherish trilogy
THE MONTINARI MARRIAGES

The dark blue short-sleeved dress with small red poppies Dea was wearing hugged her figure, then flared from the waist to the knee. With every step the material danced around her beautiful legs, imitating the flounce of her hair she wore down the way he liked it. Talk about his heart failing him!

"Dea—"

Her searching gaze fused with his. "I hope it's all right." The slight tremor in her voice betrayed her fear that she wasn't welcome. If she only knew…

"You've had an open invitation since we met." Nodding his thanks to Mario, he put his arm around her shoulders and drew her inside the suite.

He slid his hands in her hair. "You're the most beautiful sight this man has ever seen." With uncontrolled hunger he lowered his mouth to hers and began to devour her. Over the announcer's voice and the roar of the crowd, he heard her little moans of pleasure as their bodies merged and they drank deeply.

When she swayed in his arms, he half carried her over to the couch where they could give in to their frenzied needs. She smelled heavenly. One kiss grew into another until she became his entire world. He'd never known a feeling like this and lost track of time and place.

"Do you know what you do to me?" he whispered against her lips with feverish intensity.

"I came for the same reason."

Her admission pulled him all the way under. Once in a while the roar of the crowd filled the room, but that didn't stop him from twining his legs with hers. He desired a closeness they couldn't achieve as long as their clothes separated them.

"I want you, *bellissima*. I want you all night long. Do you understand what I'm saying?"

Don't miss
THE BILLIONAIRE'S PRIZE
by Rebecca Winters

Available November 2016